HE WAS HER ENEMY, HER LOVE . . .

Merry forced herself to look into his eyes. "Please let me go. Please."

"Love, I can't." Devon brought his hand to tilt her face, his broad palm at the base of her throat; his lips were warm and dry on hers, and a few strands of her hair were caught as stinging silk in the kiss. The blood began to pound in her throat.

"You kiss," he said softly into her curls, "as though each time were your first." He lifted his hands to her shoulders, feeling their soft graceful swell beneath his palms. She turned her face away, her lips throbbing, not wanting him to see as she slipped her tongue over them, trying to soothe the unfamiliar sensations she felt there.

"You've had your revenge," she whispered. "Now let me go."

"No, my dear, no. Let us see if we can make your body turn traitor. Kiss me again, and you can tell me afterward if it was worse than dying."

THE
WINDFLOWER

Laura London

A DELL BOOK

Published by
Dell Publishing Co., Inc.
1 Dag Hammarskjold Plaza
New York, New York 10017

Dell ® TM 681510, Dell Publishing Co., Inc.

ISBN: 0-440-19534-9

Printed in the United States of America
First printing—June 1984

Dedicated fondly to
Vivien Lee Jennings

CHAPTER ONE

Fairfield, Virginia. August 1813.

Merry Patricia Wilding was sitting on a cobblestone wall, sketching three rutabagas and daydreaming about the unicorn. A spray of shade from the swelling branches of the walnut tree covered her and most of the kitchen garden, but even so, it was hotter here than it had been inside. A large taffy-colored dog with thick fur stole past the fence; she noticed it as a flicker of movement in the corner of her vision. Light dust floated in the air and settled on the helpless leaves. The breeze brought the scent of baking ground and sun-burnt greens.

There was no one about to disturb her solitary concentration, or to mark the intriguing contrast she made with the homey products of the earth that grew freely near her soft-shod feet. Her appearance suggested a fragile, pale icon: lace and frail blossoms rather than fallen leaves and parsley plants. She was a slender girl, with delicate cheekbones set high in an oval face, and dark-lashed eyes, lazy from the day. Early that morning she had put up her heavy hair in anticipation of the heat, but the ivory combs and brass hairpins were working loose and silky red-gold strands had begun to collapse on the back of her neck. It never occurred to her that some might find the effect charming; it merely made her feel hot, untidy, and vaguely guilty, as though she ought to return to her bedroom and wind her hair back up. She would have been so much more comfortable, she thought, if she dared sit as the housemaids did on the back stoop in the evening, with the hems of their skirts pulled up past their knees, laps open, bare heels dug into the cool dirt. A slight smile touched her lips as she imagined her aunt's reaction, should that lady discover her niece, Merry Patricia, in such a posture.

Setting down her pencil, Merry spread and flexed her fingers and watched as a tiny yellow butterfly skimmed her shoulder to light on the ground, its thin wings fluttering against the flushing bulge of a carrot. The beans were heavy with plump rods, and there would be good eating from the sturdy ruby stalks of the rhubarb. Merry looked back to her drawing and lifted her pencil.

The rutabagas weren't coming out right. The front one had a hairy, trailing root that jutted upward at an awkwardly foreshortened angle. Though she had corrected the drawing several times, the result remained an unhappy one. It would make a better exercise to continue reworking the picture until she had captured the very essence of the vegetable, in all its humble, mottled-purple symmetry. . . . Merry was disappointed to discover in herself a flagging interest in the rutabagas . . . discipline, discipline.

Discipline and a hot afternoon sun are the poorest allies, and while Merry forced her pencil back to its labor the dream invaded her mind once more.

Last night the unicorn had come again.

Ten years ago she had had the first unicorn dream, after seeing an impression of the creature fixed into the sealing wax of a letter to her aunt from England. Merry had been eight years old then, and as she slept the unicorn had come to her, like a tiny toy with great soft eyes, and she could pull it after her on a string. As she grew the dream had altered. She would dream of meeting with the unicorn in an enchanted wood, and they would run between the trees, a race which neither won, and afterward they would drink from a secret spring. She wasn't allowed to have pets; but her dream unicorn was satisfying, exclusively hers, and would always come again if she went to the edge of the woods and called. Her aunt would never find out about it because it lived in the wild and was only tame for her.

Then it left her dreams and hadn't returned for years—until last night. It had burst through the window in a frightening rush of energy, glass flying everywhere, and it had reared in the corner of the room, pawing and snorting, looking bigger than it had been before, its muscles white and glistening beneath its creamy hide, its chest broad and heaving, its horn poised and thick. She had cowered beneath the covers, but curiosity caused her to look in small peeps and then long gazes. Its eyes were different now, still big, but there was knowledge there, a frightening intelligence, and it tossed its head, beckoning to her.

He wants me to ride him, she had thought in her dream. *Am I too afraid?* She was going to leave her bed and go closer, but before she moved, it turned in a sudden dash and leaped through the window, hooves flashing in the moonlight.

The fantasy hoofbeats faded slowly from her daydream, slipping away into the dimly lit part of the mind where dreams lie in safekeeping. Merry came back to reality as the soft walking rhythm of a flesh-and-blood horse prosaically replaced her midnight creature.

She had been expecting no visitors, so she looked up quickly toward the sound, toward the narrow pebbled carriageway that split her aunt's two-story red-brick house from the old frame barn. From behind the potent green of a ridge of lilac bushes, she saw her only brother emerge and watched with unbelieving elation as he worked his sweaty animal over to the shaded wall beside her.

"Carl! Oh, Carl, hello! Hail! Salutations! *Guten Morgen!*"

Leaning forward in the saddle, her brother said, "I take that to mean I haven't arrived at an unwelcome moment? Who's been teaching you German?"

"Henry Cork—but that's all he knows, so it was a *short* lesson." Grinning her delight in a way she was sure must look foolish, Merry set down her sketch pad and extended her hand. Three months it had been since she had seen him, a comparatively short interval. Heroes, it seemed, didn't make the most attentive brothers. "How did you know to find me back here?"

"One of your abigails told me—Bess, I think. She's sitting around front, shelling peas and dickering with a trunk-peddler over a card of buttons," he said, taking her offered hand. "I imagine it will ruffle April's feathers that I didn't have myself announced."

It was clear from the unemotional tone of his observation that this was not a circumstance that would trouble him overmuch, but because her brother's casual dislike of their aunt made Merry uncomfortable, she sidestepped the ramifications of his remark and said, "Not at all, Carl. Family needn't stand on ceremony. How glad I am to see you. But I'm surprised! I thought you were in the capital with Father." Her expression changed. "Has something happened? Father—is he . . ."

"He's well. Same as always. Tough as a horseshoe, although Mrs. Madison says he doesn't get enough rest. I don't know. I didn't come to talk to you about him." He gave her hand a brief squeeze before he released it, and then removed his hat, brushed back his hair, which was red-gold like hers but not as thick, and put his hat back on. He was gray with road dust and had tired, fine lines on his lean face, around his eyes, unusual lines on one so young, mapping the intensity within. She could tell he'd ridden hard. He was wearing civilian clothes, riding clothes which flattered him less than his officer's uniform, making him look more like the young adult of twenty-one he was and less like a man used to drilling recruits.

He glanced around with shaded eyes. "Can we talk here?"

"Of course." She lifted her feet to the top of the wall and hugged her knees, looking up at him with a slight tilt to her lashes. "The only ears here are on the sweet corn."

"But the potatoes have eyes," he answered with a reluctant smile. "Is that what you've been doing, sketching vegetables?"

"Trying," she said. "There are riches in shape and shading under the leaves, but I've a poor hand this afternoon." She held up her sketch pad for him to see.

"Hmm. Amazing. Like life. I can't see what you find amiss with it."

Merry only smiled and closed the sketchbook. "Will you come in the house, Carl? It's almost teatime, and we've got cider cooling on ice chips."

"Later." He waved his hand impatiently, as though dismissing an inane courtesy. "I need you again, my girl."

Her heart quickened. "To draw, do you mean?"

It was the pride of her life that twice before she had been able to help him and the American cause. He had taken her once to a coaching inn and once to market day at Richmond, where he had quietly pointed out men suspected of collaborating with the British. She would make her best effort to watch them without seeming to and later had rendered the faces in detailed sketches. Carl saw to it that the drawings were reproduced and circulated, which neutralized the British agents as effectively as if they'd been captured or hanged.

It had been a small thing to do for her country, especially compared to the ultimate sacrifice American soldiers were prepared to make on the field of battle; the smallness of it had stirred within her embers of dissatisfaction with the useless gentility of her life. These yearnings would surely have wounded her staunchly pro-British Aunt April, so Merry kept them to herself and tried to find solace in painting watercolor portraits of heroines like the courageous Mrs. Penelope Barker, who, thirty years ago in the First War of Independence, had stopped the British from commandeering her carriage horses by pulling her absent husband's sword from the wall and slicing to ribbons the reins in the British officer's hands. Inevitably Merry had tried to daydream herself into Mrs. Barker's shoes, but even if she'd possessed a sword, Aunt April would never have allowed such a gruesome object to hang on the wall, and the only horse they had was poor old swaybacked, buck-kneed Jacob, whom no one would want to steal. Furthermore, if enemy troops came within a hundred miles, Aunt April would undoubtedly whisk Merry away to a place of safety.

Carl shoved his hat back over his sweat-lacquered curls. "If you'll do it. Want to work with me again?"

"I *dearly* want to draw for you again, Carl." She stretched out a hand to stroke the horse's soft, damp muzzle, smiling at her older brother. Motherless, they had been reared separately; he by their austere, unloving father, she by Aunt April, their mother's sister. If she had seen Carl twice a year as a child, that was often. His boyhood had seemed to her an entrancing miracle of kite string and fishhooks, Latin tutors and wooden boats that really sailed. Unaware that she herself had become anything more than the awkward, overprotected girl-child who knitted mittens in the winter and stitched samplers in the summer, she watched as Carl grew taller, more clever, more self-confident. He was not an affectionate man. He hadn't once remembered her on her birthday. He rarely offered himself as a confidant or a protector, and yet, through his patriotic activities he had brought into her life a rare and precious dimension.

Teasingly she told him, "You're my only chance to grab a little glory, you know. I suppose I'm not to tell Aunt April, again?"

"Not unless you want her to forbid you to go. Anyway, that's been taken care of. Father wrote a letter to cover us, saying that he'll be in Alexandria this Thursday on government business and wants you to meet him there for a visit." He jumped from the horse's sweating back. "Come with me while I walk the horse."

She slid from the stone wall and put her hand self-consciously to her hair. "I ought to fetch my bonnet, I suppose. I imagine I look all scraggly."

He looked surprised and irritated. "We're just going down the lane a bit. Does it matter so much?"

Instantly she shook her head and joined him in the bright, battering sunlight, embarrassed that she had been so petty. "Then Father knows about it," she said.

He glanced down at her as she caught up to him and tried to match his stride, her eyes blinking out the sun's stinging rays. "He knows you're going to draw for me again, Merry, but—" A bee, attracted by the sweating horse, buzzed around their heads, and he swatted at it. "But he doesn't know where. Truth is, I lied."

Shocked and honored at once by his confession, she said, "You lied to Father?" Her father had been forty-five when she was born, and now his wreath of white hair, long hooked nose, and still eagle vision made lying to him seem futile. He appeared to be looking for the lie in the face of every man he met. "Why?"

"Because it's not a place I should take you. I wouldn't either, if it wasn't such a rare opportunity. There's a man who is going to be there at nine o'clock Thursday who—no, I'll tell you about it later. But it's important. I would never take you to such a rough place if it wasn't important."

"A rough place? Do you mean a prize fight?"

He gave a rueful grin. "Is that the roughest place you can think of, Merry?"

The lane angled away from the kitchen garden, into a green meadow dappled with pink clover and birdsong. Merry had been holding her skirt carefully above the path's red dust, but at Carl's words she let it drop and snatched up the silver-seeded head of a thistle. She held it before her, flourished a hand over it, and said in an important voice, "This, my dear brother, is a crystal ball."

He had no particular taste for whimsy, but because she was young and female and his sister, he said indulgently, "Is it? Divine for me then, ma'am."

"Let me see!" A soft breath of air from her pink lips sent a powdery cloud of feathered seeds spinning off across the high June grass. Staring with comical intensity into the thistle globe, she said, "Yes, it's becoming clearer now! I see—a room. A rough place! There are men there, some of them unshaven, and they are—horrors, they're setting great flagons of ale upon a maple-wood table and leaving dreadful water rings! The high corners are dripping with spider webs, and the side tables beg to be dusted." She glanced at her brother. "How am I doing?"

"Shockingly well. A body would think you'd taken to tavern-haunting."

"The doors to Mr. Hardy's taproom were open as we walked home from prayer meeting last Thursday, and I took a good look inside." Taking in a deep breath, Merry turned the thistle in her hand and was about to blow into the remaining plump hemisphere when the breath choked short in her throat and she said in a startled voice, "Carl! Does that mean you really *do* intend to take me to a tavern?"

Frowning heavily, he said, "There. I've shocked you, have I? There's worse yet. The tavern's on the coast, and isolated, and we'll have to be there after dark. Furthermore, the place is frequented by some of the lowest rogues that . . . Look, here's the straight truth— the tavern's a smugglers' den."

When Glory smiled, she smiled with a vengeance. The thistle's dark-green stem slid from Merry's suddenly numb fingers and was crushed under the hind hoof of the ambling horse. Her first instinct was to ask Carl if he really meant it, but she stopped herself. Never had he looked more serious. With experimental bravado she said, "Then I'll be able to find a good price on some English cotton for Aunt April."

He was too much a soldier not to be pleased. "Well said! And things aren't quite as bad as they seem on the surface. We'll be in and out quickly—and things are likely to be more unpleasant than dangerous. Sal and Jason will be with us."

"Our Boston cousins?" They were Carl's friends much more than hers. "I haven't seen them in over four years! But I had thought from Father's latest letter to Aunt April that Jason would be at Sackets Harbor with General Wilkinson?"

"Making Jason an aide to Wilkinson was the worst idea somebody ever had. Jason's never bothered to be discreet about his belief that Wilkinson was wrongly acquitted at the Fredericktown court-martial, and within a bare twenty-four hours of his arrival in Sackets Harbor, Wilkinson arranged Jason's transfer down to Knoxville to fight Creeks with the Tennessee militia. He has to report to Jackson within the month, but he and Sal are eager as dying saints to run a paid agent of Britain to earth with us before Jason leaves."

The lane dipped to a narrow stony brook that bordered a field of Indian corn, and Carl loosed his gelding's reins and watched as the horse dropped his head into the gurgling water.

"And the war news?" she asked quietly.

"Is nothing you wouldn't have read in the newspaper. If we can get the Northern Army into Montreal before winter, we could have Britain out of North America by spring! We'll win this bloody war yet, Merry. Justice is with us." He scooped a round, glistening stone from the brook and lofted it hard into the corn, scaring out a large crow, which flapped tiredly away toward a far stand of trees.

"Farewell hope, then, Britannia," cried Merry, pulling a handkerchief from her sleeve and holding it up to wave in the hot breeze.

As he watched her his face changed, as though a new and uncomfortable thought was first entering his mind. He said suddenly, "We can't take you to the tavern looking like that."

"Why, of course not, Carl. I *told* you I should have returned to the house for a bonnet . . ."

"No, not a bonnet. An old hat, felt, I think; cheap felt. And I'll need a shabby dress."

She couldn't resist it. "Oh, are you going in disguise as well?"

He gave her a wisp of a smile. "Of course, I'll be in disguise, but not in skirts, Merry."

"What then?"

"You'll find out Thursday night."

The modest home that Merry shared with her aunt had been pretty once, with its brick patterns of Flemish bond and richly detailed interior woodwork, the latter mostly covered now with muting layers of olive house paint. The kitchen alone was large, but the other rooms were high with many windows broken into small square panes that charted the faded carpets in white sunlight.

Since Aunt April had had the care of it the house had grown homely, though it was meticulously kept. Here were neither the bleak look of poverty nor the irritating frothings of a trite taste, but rather a place made dreary by the bewilderment of a lady unable to decorate within the boundaries of a limited income. There was no money and very little access, therefore, to gilt porcelain, to chairs with graceful legs turned in the workshops of Sheraton, to fine tables with gold inlay, to paintings by men with great names, to fabrics so supple that they inhaled light and breathed it out again, made new and glowing. Gone forever were the exquisite, expensive things that Aunt April had touched and smiled at and draped on her body in the childhood spent across the Atlantic's bitter waters.

Only in Merry's room had April made an effort, with chintz hangings and animals cut from nursery prints set with care into colored heavy-paper frames. The rest of the house had been left alone and clean, its fixings growing old-fashioned and paler with each scrubbing.

That evening Merry sat as she always had with Aunt April in the "green drawing room," never quite realizing how laughably grandiose was the title for this tiny parlor with its faded chartreuse-and-vanilla-dotted wall covering and shabby mustard-colored wing chairs. The room was always too hot, in the winter from the oversized white stone fireplace and in the summer because Aunt April was too worried about flyspecks to leave the window open. The heat filtered into the horsehair stuffing in the chairs and drew from the fibers the scent of that long-ago sacrificed animal. But tonight the warm weather had rendered the perfume of the stables so strong that even Aunt April had reluctantly agreed that the window must be opened.

In the glowing twilight Merry could see families walking together on the village green, fathers pitching their little sons up to ride on broad shoulders and stooping to toss balls to their daughters. Sweethearts walked in pairs, sometimes laughing, sometimes earnest, and the parson was taking his nightly two turns for health, tipping his hat to the ladies as he went. To Merry it might have been another world,

because Aunt April had shunned the other villagers so completely
that all save the most thick-skinned had long since ceased to visit.
Twenty-five years ago Aunt April's father had packed up what was
left of his once illustrious fortune in a few cloth bags, bought his
family passage to the New World on a leaking, rat-infested hull of a
refitted slaver, and left England and an angry flock of creditors
shaking their fists from the wharf. The shock of being reduced in the
course of a day from irreproachable respectability to a position close
to that of the wretched poor had been the death of April's mother,
father, and older sister, and the same fate might have befallen April
and her younger sister, Annette, had not Annette had the good
fortune to have been knocked down by a horse being ridden by a
young civil servant, who, full of remorse, had decided he was in
love with Annette and married her, rescuing them from a state of
dire poverty.

Carl and Merry were the result of that union. Not five years after
Merry's birth Annette had died politely in her sleep from a weakness
of the heart. Aunt April went on to run her sister's motherless
household with such sterling competence that before he was out of
mourning gloves for his wife, Mr. James Wilding had decided to
remove himself from the house on the slim pretext that he didn't
want to trouble April with his maintenance. Taking his son, he set
up a small, comfortable home for himself along one of the rutted
lanes in the nation's brand-new capital and proceeded to make his
way up the ranks of the Treasury to his current exalted position.
Each month without fail he had sent to April a sum of money to
maintain herself and his daughter, Merry.

The arrangement suited him, for he had never been at ease in the
company of any woman, not excepting his highborn wife, and had
more than once told April that he didn't know what to say to little
girls anyway. If Merry had been a boy, well, then, that would have
been different. . . .

And so April had stayed, raising her dead sister's child, hating the
rawboned land that was to her a prison, flaunting her royalism to her
offended neighbors, and searching with desperate, secret restraint for
some way to return to England and her vanished life.

In her turn Merry had developed like a tree split by lightning, both
halves continuing to grow; one side an intense loyalty to her prim,

well-meaning aunt, and the other side an exciting patriotism, pride in this rough, wild, unmapped country. It seemed always that she must protect her aunt from how different the two sides really were. When Merry was little, the village children had shouted at her: "Tory, Tory, shoot the redcoat," so she had stopped playing outside their own garden and never told Aunt April why. The other children had to content themselves with sticking their tongues out at her in church when they could get away with it, until they grew old enough to tire of the game. Merry had grown up lonely and shy, and the village, not understanding, said what a shame it was that her beauty had gone to her head and made her a snob like her aunt.

Opening the polished marquetry cap of the sewing box, Merry pulled out the pillowcase hem she had been monogramming for Aunt April. It was tedious work after the quick, fluid pen strokes of drawing, and Merry glanced over to where April was sitting ramrod straight on the settee, the sensible lap desk balanced on her knees. She was a narrow woman, narrow everywhere—in the hips, the shoulders, the face, the hands; Carl would have added, in the mind. Her hair was light, fine, and had a tendency to wander, and her voice was marred by a tremor left from childhood measles. For as long as she could remember, Merry had felt only one emotion whenever she had looked at her aunt, and that was love.

With painstaking deliberation Aunt April was transcribing a letter to England, to a friend who had years ago ceased to care. Faithfully every month Merry's aunt wrote to more than a dozen ladies and received back, at the most, two letters a year. It seared Merry's heart to watch April's elation when letters came, but it hurt much worse to watch her aunt hide her disappointment on those days without number which came and went with a barren post. There was nothing Merry could do except ache with impotent pity and hate the callous British aristocrats who ignored her aunt and those letters filled with forlorn pleasantries.

Merry was about to thread her needle when April, with a sudden irritated gesture, jerked the quill from the paper and slid it into its holder, and stretched her neck like a turtle, sniffing the air.

"Segar!"

"Aunt?"

"I smell tobacco!" Her aunt set the lap desk with a clatter on the side table and went to the window, bending from the waist to peer out into the velvet-black evening, gesturing toward the dark lacy mound of the honeysuckle bush. "Henry Cork!" she called. "Are you smoking in those bushes?"

Henry was Aunt April's only male servant. He'd come under an indenture from Ireland, where, he was wont to tell the admiring maidservants, he'd not done a day's work in all his forty years. There was only one area in which he'd ever chosen to invest his energy, and that was in doing everything he possibly could to send Aunt April into a tizzy.

After a minute April called again, "You . . . Cork! Are you out there?"

She was answered by silence, and a palpable waft of tobacco smoke, which even reached to the corner where Merry sat.

"Shall I go out and talk with him, Aunt April?" she asked.

"No, no, it's not the least use. If he sees you coming, he's bound to run off, and who knows what mischief he'll get into. I suppose I should be grateful that I can smell where he is." She came away from the window to trim the wick of a sputtering candle. "Plague take that man! How many times must I read to him from the Virginia Charitable Fire Society pamphlet: 'May not the greater frequency of fires in the United States than in former years be ascribed in part to the more general use of segars by careless servants and children?' " April turned to her lap desk and pulled out the evening paper. "Why even tonight, in the *National Intelligencer* . . ." She gave Merry a look heavy with significance and carried the paper to the window, holding it so that the candlelight enabled her to read from it in an unnaturally loud voice. " 'There is good reason to believe a house was lately set on fire by a half-consumed segar, which a woman suddenly threw away to prevent being detected in the unhealthy and offensive practice of smoking.' " Her aunt paused and peered into the darkness again.

The honeysuckle bush began to shake with Henry Cork's half-suppressed laughter, a sly, roguish chuckle that filtered into the room and hung there as pungent and smoky as the spent tobacco. Aunt April blinked her eyes in exasperation and slid down the window with a certain force. The incident seemed to have put her out of the letter-writing mood. She went to the sewing box and drew from it the gaily colored alphabet sampler that she said she was designing for Merry's firstborn child. The project had astonished and amused her niece, who didn't know a single unrelated gentleman of marriageable age and could scarcely imagine herself talking to one, much less (very much less) creating a child with one.

Tightening her embroidery hoop, Aunt April said in a gloomy voice, "I can't think why your father would want to have you visit Thursday. Thursday! He's never been one for visits on Thursday that I can remember." She threaded pink silk on her needle in a single swift stab. "And I can't understand why your brother wouldn't stay for supper. Such a *sudden* boy." A swirl of her forefinger knotted the thread. "I know what it is. I offered him tea. He despises me for serving tea. Sometimes I think he despises all civilized things."

Merry was caught in a churning muddle of embarrassment and conflicting loyalties. "Oh, no, Aunt April, I'm quite sure that . . . that is, I know tea is your very favorite drink, and . . . if we are to be free in the United States, that means people are free to drink what they want, surely."

"That's not the point of view of Mrs. Patterson."

Merry set down her pillowcase. "From the Society of Patriotic Ladies?"

"Oh, yes indeed. She was here this afternoon, dispensing recipes for drinks that might be substituted for imported teas. Liberty tea, for instance, can be made by boiling loosestrife. Have we any in the cow field? And one can make do with strawberry leaves, raspberry leaves, or leaves from the currant plant."

Merry went to her aunt, taking her aunt's hand in her own. "I'm sorry, Aunt April. Did she . . . was she condescending?"

Her aunt smiled wryly at Merry. "Dreadfully." She stared at the black square of the window, and her smile faded. "A goose farmer's daughter, at that. She has nowhere from which to condescend. In England that woman wouldn't have been received into our home!" April's faded blue eyes were melancholy. "That was another life. England . . . cool mists; the grass as fragrant and sweet as wintergreen candies. Our home, with deep rooms scented of beeswax and fresh flowers, and filled with friends in bright silks. Oh, you'd laugh if you saw how we used to dress, with hairpieces piled in stacks on our heads, sometimes more than three feet high, stuffed with cotton

bunting and doused with white powder until we looked like a crowd
of grandmamas. Monstrous, the satirists called it, but that was the
fashion. My, we thought we looked like something—'prodigious
elegant' was what we used to say. I don't believe I had a single care
in the world.'' April returned Merry's handclasp. ''Oh, how I wish I
could have those things for you, not this savage land of heat and
mosquitoes, and fathers who visit only once a year. And brothers so
overcome with the heat that all they want to do is make a war.''
Aunt April shook her head, her lips tight, the skin on her cheeks
drawn. ''What could be important enough to make a man shoot at
another? For the United States to be warring with England—the idea
is absurd. We *are* English. We speak English, we eat English food,
the very gowns on our bodies are woven on English looms.''

Yes, indeed. That was certainly true. And it was a mark of shame
for Merry to walk through the streets wearing British cotton while
loyal Americans had switched proudly to coarse homespun. It was
useless to try to explain that kind of thing to her aunt. Instead Merry
said gently, ''Americans aren't only English, Aunt April. We're
Dutch, French, German, Spanish—''

''Criminals,'' said April, ''malcontents, and religious fanatics.''
She thrust her needle into the pink crossbar of her sampler's italic
letter *A*. ''There are times, Merry Patricia, when I feel I could give
my two arms if only I could take you with me and travel back to
England.''

CHAPTER TWO

"What did Henry Cork do then?" asked Jason, twisting around in the jouncing wagon's bench beside Carl and toward Merry's shadowed form in the wagon interior.

"Nothing that night," she said. "Aunt April shut the window and ignored him. The next morning he was up at sunrise, slipped out to the orchard, picked every last one of the apples on our trees, and passed them out to whoever walked past the fence. And do you know why he said he did it? Because he was tired of cider and apple pies."

Jason laughed just as the wagon passed over a rut and snapped the sound back into his throat. One of the marionettes that Carl used to cover his spying swung on the wagon ribs and knocked its pine legs into the back of Merry's head. Fending off puppet feet, she studied her cousin's rocking silhouette. He was touching twenty, and adolescence had finally ceased to ravage his complexion. The waves in his sandy hair were looser, his chin more square, his freckles as numerous, and his sarcastic tongue, so she had discovered, quite as sharp as it had ever been.

His sister, Sally, was two years his junior and just as sandy and freckled, but without the nervous energy that had made Jason such a difficult child. She was thin as a sapling, with wide-set gray eyes and a nose that Jason had broken by accident on her ninth birthday with an errant swing of his cricket bat. Only last month she had become engaged to a hell-for-leather young captain in the Navy.

Since Merry and Carl had met Jason and Sally at the coaching inn at Point Patience, they had been nice to Merry. Too nice. Jason was making a painfully obvious effort to rid his speech of swear words, and several times before the day's end she had noticed Sally staring at her with the friendly sympathy accorded someone who is young and easily shocked. Merry, at a loss to know what she did that engendered this kind of response, had been trying particularly hard to hide the worst of her shyness.

Through an open flap in the wagon's canvas roof Merry could see the stars and the high, moon-silvered clouds passing through, making them wink in sequence. The feeble blue starlight fell across Sally, who knelt beside her on the wagon floor, busily stuffing feathers and straw into a square of homespun.

"I think Cork is taking miserable advantage," said Sally. "Why doesn't your aunt give him the heave-ho?"

"She tries. Each time she's said 'That's it, get out,' he's developed back pains and taken to his bed. Aunt April says she doesn't doubt that if we and our maidservants got together to throw him out, he'd likely lie on our front walk moaning and railing until we half died of shame."

Carl said tartly, "Aunt April will never get rid of him, take my word on it. She's too addicted to having him around to complain about." He pulled the team around a corner and added over his shoulder, "How are you coming, Sal? We're nearing target."

"Done," she answered him. "I'm ready to pin it on. Don't turn around again, either of you. Right, Merry, up with your skirts."

"Are you absolutely sure that this is necessary?" said Merry doubtfully.

"My word as a gentleman on it," Jason said, staring carefully forward. "Trust us, there's a good girl."

The idea for the addition to Merry's costume had come within minutes of meeting Jason and Sally. Jason had looked Merry up and down in her disguise of sloppy black felt hat and faded calico and then said, "Carl, are you off your head? That's not good enough!"

Merry had sat alone on the bench seat of the unhitched wagon while her brother and cousins stood off in the coach yard and argued in low, intent voices. The upshot had been that they had decided, between them, to buy a piece of cheap bedding and reshape it to pillow Merry's stomach into an imaginary pregnancy. Merry had stilled the horrified protests that rose to her lips, afraid of being thought a prude, and more afraid yet that Jason's objection to her appearance might have stemmed from his thinking she looked too young.

There was another jolt that heaved the women against the side of the wagon. "Carl, slow down, will you?" called Sally, "or I'll turn Merry into a pincushion. Here, Merry—you hold the pin papers and hand them to me, head first, please."

"All right," said Merry, gamely resigned to her fate. "What size do you want first—minikins or middlings?"

Sally finished her work as the wagon made a last descent and skated around a fast curve onto the crisp gravel beach. To the east a flat tongue of land stretched into the black crashing sea, and at its base sat a battered tavern, reminding Merry of the biblical parable about the man who built his house upon the sand. The old frame building seemed to be participating in the party that was going on within it. From the gray look of it, it had joined in many such in the past. A square board sign saying The Musket and Muskrat, illustrated by crude sketches of same, clacked and squeaked in the wind on its rusted hinges, and a number of shingles, the livelier ones, clapped rhythmically to the skittering fingers of the breeze. As Merry watched, one of them let loose and slid from the roof to sail into the darkness like a bat. Through the dingy windows, which let squares of cheery yellow light escape, could be glimpsed a roiling scenario of flailing fiddles, stomping legs, flying skirts, and tilting flagons.

Carl jumped from the wagon to hitch his team in the crowded horse shed while Merry climbed with Sally out of the back.

Prodding the fake hump of stomach into place, Sally said teasingly, "Ugh! Is that realistic!"

Behind them Jason said tersely, "Let's hope that's the common attitude, shall we? Sally, you know what to do. Merry, keep your eyes cast down and cling timidly to my arm. If you catch anyone smiling at you, don't, for God's sake, smile back."

"And Merry, try to walk awkwardly," said Sally, mimicking her brother's tone as they started toward the door, "like a woman about to give birth. Yes, that will do perfectly." They both laughed— Merry hadn't changed her walk at all.

"Oh, lordy, Sal, don't make her laugh like that or we'll be in the soup," Jason said.

"Why?" asked Merry. "Aren't women allowed to laugh in taverns?"

"Not when they're as fetching as you are." Jason pinched her lightly on the cheek. "Shush now. And act cowed."

She looked startled and then felt like an idiot. The amazing novelty of a compliment brought the blood running high in her cheeks as she stepped over the threshold and saw her first of the smugglers' lair.

Earlier in the evening the floor sand had probably been swept in a fanciful pattern, and perhaps the smoke from the clay pipes of the patrons had made matching idle curlicues in the air. But now the sand had been spread into an anonymous covering by the shuffling of many feet, and the curling smoke had faded into a bone-colored haze that smarted the eyes.

Whatever order the crude tables and chairs had begun the evening in was well broken, as were some of the hapless pieces of furniture. The air was alive with the reek of sweat, fish, and roast corn, and a roar of conversation that nearly overwhelmed the music from the fiddles and squeeze box that enlivened the near corner of the room. There were a few, not many, women scattered among the rough-clothed men in the crowd, and from the look of the river peddlers, bullwhackers, and men of the sea that were sitting, standing, and chatting, one might guess that they would have been as comfortable pulling, pushing, lifting, shouting, and breaking and entering. A plank laid over two tobacco casks formed the bar, and behind it was a stair to the sleeping room with a sign above it that read: Five Only to a Bed. No Dogs Allowed Upstairs. Organ-grinders to Sleep in the Washhouse.

The host was a skinny, energetic Belgian immigrant with a grizzled red and brown beard and a bald pate. He joined them right away, clapping Carl on the arm and smiling genially at Jason. In thick accents he said, "Hey, you're the fellows that do the puppets, right? Glad to see you! Are you going to make me a show tonight? Good. Real good! You can put the stage by the fireplace, hey?" He winked. "When folks come over to watch, they get real hot and thirsty and soak up my good wine like sponges. They have plenty to drink, they put plenty in the hat when you collect! Good for me; good for you! Ha, ha! Easier for these fellows to make it home without that heavy money in their pockets, hey?''

Fascinated, Merry watched as her coconspirators played their parts with a brisk competence that stilled her own worries. How well they knew what they were doing, Jase and Carl in short jackets and flat-brimmed hats with frayed red and blue streamers, and Sally with her hair flattened under a triangle of paisley wool, frizzled ends lank with hair oil pulled forward to straggle over her gamin face.

Sally pulled Merry to sit with her at a heavy gray table near the fire and gave her a cozy grin, motioning toward Jason when he returned from the wagon with the unwieldy shadow-box puppet theater. Carl followed, holding two puppets aloft in salute. The fiddles stopped scraping, and the crowd gave a cheer of comfortable appreciation. The act was a popular attraction.

The puppets were nearly three feet in height. The first was an aristocrat with an exaggerated sneer painted on his lips and dressed in absurdly foppish clothes with glass jewelry; the other puppet was a revolutionary, outfitted in sansculotte rags, a cockade, and a wide, anarchistic grin. They were attached to long handles by very active springs and had rolling joints at the elbows and knees. Merry felt like laughing just looking at them.

Jason talked the part of the aristocrat, in a high comical lisp, and Carl made the sansculotte the essence of hearty vulgarity. It was a routine they had developed as schoolboys, with many refinements since, and like every good puppet show, it was a delight for any crowd, children and adults. The sansculotte would bellow a republican anthem, and the aristocrat would take a swipe at him, and then the aristocrat would try to sing "God Save the King" and the sansculotte's musical sensibilities would be violently offended. And at the end they were both yelling their respective anthems and trying to turn each other into splinters. The place was in an uproar, and when the play ended with the sansculotte shouting the aristocrat into a dead swoon, the applause was long and loud, and Carl and Jason were surrounded by backslappers.

For all their roughness Merry began to discover a certain charm to the company, which was raw and lively, like the salt winds that seeped through the rotted moldings on the windows. A fair number

sent a grin and a wink her way, but they were good-humored ones
mostly, and when they seemed too bold, she looked away from
them, into the fire.

It was midway through one of these retreats that she caught an
intent look on her brother's face. Carl glanced at her and hoisted his
glass suggestively toward the door.

The man had entered whom she had been brought here to observe
for later sketching. He was pale, loose-skinned, and bird-faced, his
chin a fallen pouch, his ears perked forward like the handles of one
of Aunt April's china pitchers. It was the face of a man distrusted
on sight. He picked his way across the room to a roly-poly bulldog of
a man sitting alone by a far window, and the two greeted each other
with such a show of hand pumping that you'd have thought one of
the pair had just been wed.

The entering man was a traitor, the bulldog-faced man the unknown who received his secrets, and the secrets were the departure
dates of American ships trying to slip through the British blockade to
trade with neutral ports in Europe. Carl had friends in the Navy who
thought it might be very useful to slip false information this way, as
soon as they could discover to whom the information was being
sold. Using Merry's sketches, Carl said, it wouldn't take long to
find out.

"Can you do them?" asked Carl, come to lean over her shoulder.

"Yes. It won't be hard. If you and Jason want to start packing the
theater . . ."

"You've had enough time already? Good girl! Will you look at
Jason? What a sharper! He's been around two times already with
that darn money box of his."

"Well, collect him, Carl, and let's go!" said Sally, casting a
glance of sisterly exasperation at her brother. "The sooner we're
gone, the better."

"I haven't forgotten that for a minute," Carl growled back.
"Start for the door. We'll meet you."

Following her cousin to the door, Merry paused to smile back into
the room and think, *That was easy, that really was easy,* and then
somewhere in the middle of the smile and the middle of the pride,
the tavern doors opened, front and back. Simultaneously two gigantic men stepped inside, surveying the crowd impassively before

blocking the doorways like sentries. The men were twinned, with shaven heads and bristling cavalry mustaches, and fat chests woven of muscles like the coiling bands of a constrictor snake. Belts of weapons alarmingly festooned their dingy white sleeveless shirts: two pistols, primed and cocked; three wicked curved knives; and each man unsheathed a short, hideously sharp sword and slapped it across his chest, sending a thrill of fear through the watching, suddenly quiet crowd.

Beside Merry, Sally absorbed a quick gulp of air and pushed her hand on Merry's shoulder, snapping "Sit down! Sit!" with as little respect as she might have given a jumping puppy, and Merry sank promptly and unresentfully into the nearest chair.

They were joined almost immediately by Carl, Jason, and the landlord, whose complexion had paled like chalk dust.

"Good girl, Sally," Carl said, sliding into a chair beside Merry. "We want to be as unobtrusive as . . . Merry, what happened to your hat?"

"Hat?" Merry's hand traveled involuntarily to her uncovered hair. "I . . . Oh. I must have left it by the fire. It was so hot that I took it off and—"

She stopped, caught in Jason's glare, and he said to her in a stony voice, "Well, don't as much as turn your head from here on out without permission, do y'hear? The last thing we want is to increase the chances that Carl and I will have to fight for your virtue, because, believe me, missy, we aren't likely to win."

"That you ain't," said the landlord nervously. "Those devils by the door are from the *Black Joke!*"

"Not Rand Morgan's ship?" asked Carl.

"The same." The landlord seemed to shudder. "It's said they never leave a place without taking a life with them. It was true last time they were here, let me tell you."

"Pirates?" Sally whispered, half to herself. "Oh, Jason—not pirates."

"Stay calm, will you? Sit still, don't move, and try to act like you don't see anything, just like everyone else is doing."

"Aye," said the landlord. "Don't do anything to draw attention. Let's pray they're not here looking for women."

Merry and Sally found each other's hands under the table. There

were footsteps outside, and the guardian of the hind doorway drew
aside a step or two.

Merry had heard of Rand Morgan, of course. Who had not? He
was a legendary figure of her childhood, and she had grown up
thinking that one day he would vanish with the pixies and the
wizards and the dragons, that one day an adult would admit to her,
"There's really no such thing as . . ." But like tornados and wild
fire, Morgan was a boogey that made the transition into her mature
life without losing his fearful qualities.

Rand Morgan. They say he wore an emerald slit from the belly of
a priest when that unfortunate divine had swallowed it to prevent its
theft. Ten years ago the *Queen Anne* had disappeared without a
trace, and whispers said that Morgan had seized a fortune in bullion
from her hold and then locked her captain and crew in the first
mate's cabin, setting the decks ablaze and leaving the men inside to
a flaming grave. And just last October the *Black Joke* had seized an
unarmed merchant ship and taken from it the governor of South
Carolina and his five-year-old son, holding them at cost of their lives
until the governor's distraught wife had gathered a ransom of fifteen
thousand dollars.

Merry watched as Rand Morgan, the stuff of myth and nightmare,
came walking through the tavern door.

He was tall enough to have to stoop slightly as he entered, and he
had black, heavy-lidded, deep-set eyes, which looked around the
room seeing no one, seeing everyone, intense and sleepy at the same
time. The face was impassive, as if carved in stone, with heavy
cheekbones and a broad brow; it was a face made to split the sea air
and crash the waves of fortune's hurricane. His long hair was
midnight black, thick and unruly on his brow, and of the same hue
as his silk shirt. There was an aura about him—an air of the
craftsman, one whose mastery of certain skills made him indifferent
to the judgments of the uninitiated. That is what frightened Merry
the most—his indifference. He didn't look evil, only as if he did not
care. If she had seen him on the street, she would have known he
was not like other men. She wondered if this magnetism had been
there and had forced him into a life of piracy, or if it had come to
him as a mantle of the reputation he had gained.

Morgan moved through the gaping crowd like visiting royalty, companioned by two men. The younger of the two was near to seventeen, an age that normally might have led him to be described as a "youth," and yet there was nothing of youth in his coldly Scandinavian face, with hard, milk-blue eyes and lips that looked as though they had never known a smile. His hair was dead straight, almost white from the burn of salt and sun, and so long that it touched his hips; it was pulled across his right shoulder to lie in an ivory fall over one side of his chest. His exposed ear was pierced and held a loop of black thread. As he moved into the room Merry saw pale stripes on the chestnut-tanned skin of his naked back that she shudderingly realized had been inflicted with a whip.

The exotic boy ranged tigerlike between the tables, oblivious to the tension around him—the indrawn breaths, the nearly exploding lungs. Finally he stopped; everyone breathed again except the unlucky patrons whose table he chose, who scurried away like lizards from fire. He gazed disgustedly at the mass of bottles, empty and full, at the table, and the unplayed hands of piquet and scattered coins which were strewn by each chair. Reaching out, he tipped the table, sending its contents clattering to the floor, followed by a single card, the jack of hearts, which flipped in the air twice and landed gently like a leaf on the floor.

The violent little scenario caused the third man to laugh and murmur some remark which caused the spirit of a smile to pass over Morgan's lips, so faint as to be only felt rather than seen; and the pirate's features held fleetingly the telltale softening of affection.

Bound by the pounding urge of fascination to see the man that Rand Morgan could care for, Merry's gaze left the long-haired boy and the pirate captain to center on their companion.

He was half-turned from her, his face toward Morgan, so her first impression was of a man of perhaps a little more than medium height, each inch of him hard, flowing muscles knit arousingly into a well-carried, sensuously slender frame.

A dark jacket of supple leather hung from his wide, relaxed shoulders; below were snug, faded denims and wine-colored boots cut high to the knee, which looked expensive, despite their scarred toes. It was hardly Merry's habit to study the male anatomy, and certainly not to admire it, and yet there was something in the shapely play of line and curve and sweetly made muscle that captured the eye, however modest.

With a graceful movement he bent to upend a chair, and his hair, as bright and glowing as a harvest moon, swung in a lively arc. He dropped into the chair facing Merry; all at once she could see his face.

The stranger had one of those rare, wonderful faces that truly deserve to be called arresting. It was so much more than handsome; this man was beautiful, in a way uniquely masculine, as arrogant and tender as a Renaissance archangel sitting in liquid, unattainable splendor, the half deity made mortal, with eyes that held light like faceted gemstones. It was an urbane face, stamped with humor and humanity, in marked contrast with the delicately erotic mouth, and as she stared at him Merry felt the hot embers of that same confusing blend of yearning and fear that had brushed into her soul when she had dreamed of the unicorn.

But this man was a pirate, a member of one of the most vicious and carnal orders of men that had ever plundered the earth's good few. Lucifer, it seemed, was too smart to appear always with his horns and tail.

CHAPTER THREE

Devon Charles Crandall sat back in his chair, raising the heel of his boot to rest it lightly against the trestle table before him. He picked up his sand-scoured glass and with a gentle movement of his wrist sent the pale wine into a slow whirl. After watching it a moment he raised his gaze to where his half brother sat, the great emerald winking evilly on his chest.

"Do you know," said Devon, turning an interested gaze back to the wine, "I think it's beginning to separate."

"The scum coming to the top," said the pale-haired boy next to the pirate captain. "I told you. American wine tastes like it was fresh from a pig's . . ."

A raucous burst of laughter from the next table covered the end of his sentence. Rand Morgan reached out to pluck the wineglass from the younger man's fingers and casually tossed the contents onto the tavern's dirt floor. Refilling the glass from his own bottle, he handed it back and said, "Try the rum instead."

"Oh? Is it better?"

"It's worse." The pirate captain smiled. "But it's quicker."

Devon returned the grin and lifted the glass. "To my speedy intoxification."

The rum *was* worse, as it happened. Devon mentally tipped the hat he wasn't wearing to his misspent youth, which had forged his iron palate.

The unease of the crowd had altered little since their arrival, save perhaps that the stares had become both more frequent and surreptitious. Devon was used to being stared at. His position in life had made it inevitable, and even in those remote places where he was unknown, his looks had made him far from inconspicuous. What he saw here was different. Here they were afraid. What a heady, corrupting power it was, to have men fear you, and his half brother had been years on this coast, flashing his emerald and nourishing his reputation for stone-hearted savagery. Morgan had come here to terrify, and before the night was over, he surely would. However different Devon's purpose, their interests were hardly incompatible. He looked back into Morgan's sleepy gaze.

"How do you like the natives?" asked the pirate captain, sending a slow survey around the room that made the other tavern patrons look as though they would have liked to crawl under their chairs.

Devon shrugged. "I've seen them before. In Cadiz, in Le Havre. The mongrel waterfront."

The boy looked up from his ale and said in the purring, even voice that was the closest he came to good humor, "We can't all of us be blue bloods. Listen, Dev, have you got the horn colic, or what?"

It was, all in all, the kind of remark one might expect from a boy who had lived his first twelve years in a Caribbean brothel. Devon took a pull of rum and smiled. "No more than usual, I don't think. Why? What am I doing?"

"You've looked four or five times at the copper-headed wench by the puppet box."

Amused, he said, "Four or five? Is that so many?"

"It is for you. Especially considering the size of her belly."

"Poor Cat," Morgan murmured. "Look at her again. She's a beauty."

The boy leaned his head back and shook his hair vigorously from his shoulders. "She is if you say she is. They all look alike to me."

As Devon watched, the girl looked at him, met his gaze, and turned quickly, fearfully away, as though in shame. She was drinking nothing, and her clasped hands lay on the table before her, the fingers fervently knit. He was too far away to see whether they trembled. He supposed she had heard by now of Morgan's identity and was wondering what it might mean to her. There was tension in the slightly averted profile, with its Venus-on-a-seashell oval frame, and soft rose-petal lips.

"If you want her, she's yours," said Morgan in a quiet, bored voice.

Once, long ago, there had been a man inside Devon that would have been shocked by the suggestion, though even then he would have had the poise to hide it. The sophisticated corruptions of his young manhood in the years before he met Morgan had been many and varied, but raping women in an advanced state of pregnancy had not been among them. Perhaps it was the rum, but he wondered what other things he had destroyed inside himself as he had slowly exorcised the part of his soul that would have flinched from Morgan's words.

Underneath the peerless face of an angel Devon's ice-encrusted spirit disdained the female sex. Every woman he had ever desired had been his for the asking, and the result on the inner workings of his mind had been unsavory in the extreme. Morgan could have told anyone interested that on the digits of a one-handed gypsy you could count Devon's positive relationships with women.

"I don't think so," said the man Devon had become. "Thank

you all the same. Tonight I don't find myself feeling sufficiently creative.''

"Why the devil not, Carl?'' Jason was saying in an urgent whisper. Each passing minute had made him look, to Merry, increasingly high-strung. He had certainly become increasingly profane. "We'll have to take the risk, to get the girls out of here. Even a damned-to-hell pirate knows that a woman in Merry's condition . . . Monk's buttocks, it doesn't make a spit of difference whether it's real or supposed, as long as they believe it's real! What can they think but that Sally's taking Merry out to use the convenience? The girls don't look, do they, as if they're able to up and ride off for the Army?''

Carl leaned forward on his elbows, lifting the fist that he had been lightly and nervously rapping against the table. "Maybe. Maybe. But what if it misfires, eh? And it ends up drawing more attention to them?''

"More attention? What in the devil does that mean?'' Jason hissed back. "You've seen the way that gorgeous blond son of a bitch has been looking at Merry.''

"The odds are, though,'' said Sally calmly, "that given Merry's state he won't do more than look.''

It was through clenched teeth that Jason said, "I'll bet with the odds every time, Sal, but not, damn it, when the stake is Merry's rosy pink— Here, what's this? Carl, take a gander over there.''

The rough fellow who had been sitting at the table with the man Merry had come to draw had gotten up and was walking toward Morgan's table with an agonizingly set grin on his bulldog face and a reluctant shuffle, as though he had little faith in the steadiness of his knees. He nodded eagerly to Morgan and boomed a few words of greeting. Morgan stared silently back, his eyes glittering in a strange way. With great casualness he pulled a knife from his belt and held it in front of him, examining it as one would a curiosity. And it was a curiosity—the blade was a long brass crescent, with small hungry slashes running backward on the edge like shark's teeth.

Shaking like spooned jelly, the ruffian spread his arms in an expansive, conciliatory gesture and began to say something in a rapid voice that collapsed into spasmodic coughing. The crowd watched in horrified fascination as Rand Morgan slipped his wicked

blade into the lamp chimney on the table. Blue flame licked at the
serrated edge, making it glow red.

"Carl, what's he doing?" Merry was unable to keep the apprehension from her voice. "What are they going to do?"

"I don't know," said Carl, suddenly won over to Jason's point of
view, "but whatever it is, I don't want you in here to watch." He
glanced at his cousin. "We'll do it your way, Jason. Sally, you and
Merry slip out the back door—it'll be less obtrusive. If there's any
talking to be done, you take care of it."

Sally whispered to Merry, "Lean against me and do your best to
look faint. Can you do that?"

Merry mustered the beginnings of a smile. "With dazzling
authenticity—I *am* about to faint! Carl, are you sure you and Jason
can't come with us?"

"They're likely to kill us just for trying," answered Jason. "Now
go, and quickly."

Merry felt Sally's arm slide around her waist. She let her head
droop to her cousin's shoulder, and they walked toward the door.
Many in the tavern watched them go, with eyes frightened and
curious, but no one in the tableau around the heating blade seemed
to take notice of them. The pirate who was guarding their intended
exit drew up and stepped in their path.

"Go on back to yer chairs and sit down," he growled, jerking his
head.

"Please—my sister is feeling unwell," answered Sally. "I want
to take her outside to lie in the wagon."

"Later." The word was a soft growl.

"Please let us go. She is not many weeks from her time and needs
rest. A shock could make the baby come early." Sally gazed at him
wide eyed, and in a voice that carried she added, "I beg of you. I'm
sure you had a mother once yourself."

The pirate's hard, impassive face seemed to flicker, betraying an
unfathomable emotion. He lifted the sword blade a bit, signaling to
Morgan's long-haired companion, who looked hard at them across the
room before nodding dismissively. Without another word the pirate
moved aside and let them pass, his face an unreadable slab once
more. The door closed softly behind them, a sound which occa-
sioned tremendous relief for them, and they stood and inhaled the

cool salty air. The moon, too bright almost to look at, was laying a
burning silver trail on the surf crashing on the coast; they could see
it far off over the black tree line. Sally and Merry glanced at each
other and fled down the steps with such dispatch that Merry tumbled
over the last two and landed hard on her knees, catching her
petticoats in a tight bunch beneath her. The dozen dainty brass pins
that held on her pillow were thrust hard into the soft flesh of her
stomach, and giving a sharp cry of pain, she jumped to her feet,
yanking her skirt away from her. Promptly she was answered by a
series of tiny metallic pings that sounded like an honor guard of
Lilliputian infantry firing a twenty-one-gun salute. With an audible
flump the bundle of straw and feathers collapsed out of her dress,
littering the damp, pebbled sand like dirty snow.

In startled dismay Merry cried, "Sally! My pins have popped off
their heads!"

"Damn, *damn,* damn! If men can invent a steam engine that goes
five miles an hour, *why* can't they think of a way to make pins in
one piece so they can't snap apart!" Sally glared at the bundle at
Merry's feet. "Stupid things! Thank the Lord it didn't happen
indoors! Merry, you stay here, gather your stuffings as best you can,
and I'll race to the wagon for more pinheads."

"Sally, please! I want to come with you. It won't matter, will
it?"

"Yes, it matters. They may well have someone watching the
wagons, and if they see you're not pregnant, we've lost our excuse
for being outside the tavern. If they think we've come out to fetch
the militia, we're as good as dead."

"But, Sally—"

"You'll be fine. Just stay here, and don't be afraid if it takes me a
little while. I've got to move cautiously. The yard may be alive with
Morgan's men, and I want to avoid as many of them as possible."

"What if somebody comes?" whispered Merry.

"Hide under the stairs." Sally's whisper was as hushed as the
darkness into which she disappeared, and Merry was alone in the
tavern's black shadow. Before her lay the night beach, echoing with
the boom of the midnight surf, stinking with the tidal litter of dying
seaweed and dead crabs. Massive boulders humped the shoreline,
like the backs of enormous turtles. Had one of them moved? No, no,

of course not. With a shiver that had nothing to do with the night breeze, Merry knelt on the gritty sand and began energetically to gather her shedded pile into her cotton bag. Her breath came tight and quick. Not a nuance of either the absurdity or the danger of the situation was lost on her.

As abrupt as a thunderclap on a still morning came the squeal of corroded hinges as the tavern door behind her opened, catching her in the middle of its lengthening rhomboid of light. Merry's spine injected a paralyzing terror serum through her body that turned her muscles to damp paper. The cotton bundle slid from her fingers and opened as it hit the ground, showering her with a geyser of feathers and dust.

The door slammed shut, and there were footsteps on the porch and steps. Merry raised her eyes, helpless, humiliated, frantic, and saw standing in the starlight before her Morgan's companions, the blond archangel of a man and the long-haired boy. Her galloping heart sped blood through her fragile veins until she was nearly deafened by its pounding rush, and with fear-dulled senses she saw dimly that the blond man was laughing.

In one flashing second the boy sank an iron grip into the curve of her shoulders and hauled her to her feet. He gave the fallen bundle a nudge with his moccasined foot.

"Congratulations, little mother," he said in a dangerous tone. "Is it a boy or a girl?"

Three lives besides Merry's own hung suspended in the balance. She croaked, "Don't kill us! Please! We weren't going to bring the militia."

"The devil you weren't," snarled the boy, his fingers pressing tighter into her aching shoulders.

Behind him she heard the blond man say, "Softly, Cat." Then with a laugh, "You had a mother once yourself."

"No, Devon," snapped the boy. "I was spawned." He took a handful of her bodice and shook her back and forth slowly, as easily as he might have a cloth doll. "Stupid, lying bitch. I ought to feed you to the sharks. Where's your friend?"

She would have died rather than expose Sally. "I don't know."

This time the shake was painful. "That isn't what I wanted to hear. Do you want to learn the hard way how little patience I've got?"

He put back his hand to strike her, but even as she recoiled shudderingly from him the man called Devon stopped the boy with a gesture. "Cat, no," he said. "I know it doesn't seem worth the trouble to you, but there really are better ways to do these things."

To her surprise the boy released her. She staggered on legs that had little strength to hold her, and Devon encircled her shoulders with a light protective arm. It had been a night of one shock after the next, and Merry's unaccustomed senses blazed as he caressed the tumbled curls from her taut cheeks.

"If you like, don't tell us where your friend is," he said. "Just tell me why she left you."

Merry's voice trembled. "She had to bring more pins, so that no one would see that I was really not—that I was not . . .''

The boy swore and said, "If we get militia, *yours* will be the first throat I'm going to cut."

Devon brought the back of his hand softly down the side of her face. "You think she's lying, Cat?"

"Oh, I suppose not," the boy said irritably. "It's ludicrous enough to be true. Look, if you don't want the wench mauled, then you'd better stay here and keep her out of sight when the crew comes. I'll go signal. And who knows?" He swept up a hunk of the filling from Merry's cotton sack and tossed it casually into the breeze. "Maybe this time you'll be the one who gets to stuff her."

He left them, running lightly down the silver beach, his white-blond hair catching the moonbeams, gleaming like a passing banshee.

Caught still under the drape of Devon's arm, her body stiff, Merry raised a hand despairingly to her forehead.

"Do you know," he asked her in an amiable way, "that you're white as a sail?"

Her palm fell to her cheek; the skin was clammy under her shivering fingers. She was ashamed of her cowardice, her crying, the whimper in her voice. There were probably a hundred spunky things that a woman of spirit would have thought of to say, and all she had managed to do was plead pitifully for her life. In a bitter epiphany she saw herself as she was, an inexperienced, awkward teenager, endowed with more imagination than poise.

Knowing she must confront this man, she turned to face him, but since the top of her head came no higher than his shoulder, she found herself looking straight at his chest and made the unsettling discovery that he had no shirt on under his jacket. Hastily she looked up at the gemstone eyes, which were tucked at the corners with a smile.

In all her upbringing there had been nothing that taught her how she ought to behave now, and the only thing she could think of was a line from a penny dreadful that one of the maidservants had once let her read. Somehow, though, looking at the clever face above her, she doubted that a proclamation of "Unhand me, sirrah" would achieve much more than a laugh. Reworking it into the vernacular, she said, "Let me go." It was the best voice she could produce, but it was a forceless one for all that, and it cracked embarrassingly on the last word, so she was hardly surprised when it produced no immediate results. "Please," she added.

He slid his hand under hers, where it lay cupped on her chest. His hand seemed warmer than her own, and drier, and the shock of the unfamiliar intimacy made her stumble backward into the rickety porch railing behind her. She spun and clutched at it to save herself from falling. The railing gave under the pressure of her hand, sending a stream of splinters flying to the ground. The self-reproach came, instantly and automatically.

"Oh," she said numbly. "I've broken it."

She heard his soft laughter behind her and wheeled in fear, the broken railing held tight across her bosom.

"Be careful, there might be nails," he said, and in a gentle imperative added, "Hand it to me. I'll fix it for you."

She put it in his hand and then thought, too late, *Merry Patricia Wilding, if you had half an ounce of courage, you'd have whacked him over the head with it.*

"You're very amusing, you know," he said conversationally as he was sliding the railing back into place, matching the holes with the nails.

For the first time since she'd left the tavern, she felt an emotion stirring within her that was not terror.

"I wasn't aware that I was being amusing," she said, a terse edge to her voice.

He finished the task and turned to look at her. "I never supposed you were aware of it. But don't you think you were being a little overly conscientious? Under the circumstances.''

It was much the kind of thing that Carl might have said, and it hit uncomfortably close to the truth. Before she could stop herself, Merry bit out, "I suppose *you* think nothing of knocking whole villages to the ground.''

"Nothing at all," he said cheerfully.

"And terrorizing innocent women!" she said, a tremble in her voice.

"Yes. Innocent ones," he said, running his palm along her flat stomach where the stuffing had lately been, "and not so innocent ones."

She nearly fainted under his touch. "Don't do that," she said, her voice cracking in good earnest.

"Very well," he said, removing his hand. He went back to lean against the porch, resting on the heels of his hands, his long finely muscled legs stretched before him, and gave her an easy smile. "Don't run away from me, little one. For the moment you're much safer here."

Something in her face made him laugh again. "I can see you don't believe it," he continued. "But stay with me nevertheless. If you run off, I'll have to chase you, and I don't think we want to scamper across the beach like a pair of puppies."

She wondered if that meant he wouldn't invest much energy in trying to catch her if she did try to run and if it might not be worth the risk.

Reading her thoughts with alarming precision, he asked good-humoredly, "Do you think you could outrun me?"

It was hardly likely. A man used to safely negotiating the rigging during a high wind would be quick enough to catch her before she could even think of moving, and strong enough to make her very sorry. Involuntarily her gaze dropped to his hard legs, with their smooth, rhythmical blend of healthy muscle.

"Like what you see?" he asked her.

Merry's gaze flew to his, and she blushed and swallowed painfully. In a ludicrously apologetic voice she managed, "I beg your pardon."

"That's quite all right." He reached out his hand and stroked beneath her chin. "Much too conscientious. Would it surprise you to know, my little friend, that having you stare at my legs is the most uplifting thing that's happened to me all day?"

It was not the kind of remark she had remotely conceived a man might make to a woman, but there was something in his matter-of-fact delivery that made her suspect that he had participated in a great many conversations in precisely this style. Wishing she could match the ease of his tone, she said, "It's a pity your days are so dull."

"Oh, yes," he said with a glimmer of amusement, "in between knocking down villages and making people walk the plank, pirates really have very little to do."

Merry wondered briefly how she could ever have been so foolish as to have actually *wished* for an adventure.

"I don't know how you can talk about it like that," she said weakly.

He smiled. "I take it you don't usually flirt with villains."

"I don't flirt with *anyone*," Merry said, getting angry.

"I believe you don't, darling."

For a second his kind, enticing gaze studied her face, and then he looked away to the south, where a tiny flicker began to weave through the rocks. Another star of light appeared, and another, dragon's breath in the night.

"My cohorts," he observed. Offering her a hand, Devon inclined his head toward the dark-blue shadows that crept along the tavern's north side. "Come with me. Cat is so often right about these things, and I'm sure you don't want them to see you."

"*More* pirates?" said Merry hoarsely, watching the lights.

"Six more. Seven, if Reade is sober."

She hesitated, not daring to trust him, her face turned to him with the unconscious appeal of a lost child.

"Come with me," he repeated patiently. "Look at it this way. Better one dreadful pirate than seven. Whatever you're afraid I'll do to you, I can only do it once. *They* can do it seven times. Besides, I'm unarmed. You can frisk me if you want." His arm came around her back, drawing her away from the tavern. Grinning down at her, he said, "As the matter of fact, I wish you would frisk me."

She went with him, her footsteps passive as a dreamer.

It seemed quite unnecessary to tell him. Nevertheless Merry said, "I've never met anyone like you in my life."

"Probably not," he said. "Would you like to sit in this wagon?"

His question was a baseless courtesy, because before she could answer him, before she was able to see a wagon, he had slid his arms under her knees and shoulders and tossed her effortlessly inside to land on a thick pad of dry straw and sawdust.

The wagon had high sides, but it was open to the sky like a tumbril, its air spiced with dish timber. Gray moonlight picked out neat stacks of wooden ware: nest boxes, dumb-bettys, washtubs, sets of plates and bowls made of white ash and wrapped in jute strings.

As he joined her Merry knelt and, bracing the heels of her hands on the high, jagged grain of the wagon's sides, peeked through an oval knothole. The light spots were closer now, on the beach, and in their acid-yellow flare Merry could see a line of heavily armed men, moving swiftly toward the tavern.

She turned to Devon, sitting at his ease against a wagon rib. His knees were drawn up and his wrists balanced there, the hands lightly clasped. If he had been sleeping, he could hardly have looked more relaxed. In a desperate voice Merry said, "My—my husband is still inside."

"Which was he, the freckled boy with the puppets? They won't hurt him or his partner."

Whether or not it was the truth, she had no choice but to accept his word. There was nothing now that she could do for Jason and Carl, and nothing she could do for Sally. Sick with anxiety, she watched the pirates closing on the tavern, faces blankly purposeful, some bare chested with muscles rippling, some bedecked in fine clothes that must be loot from some rich man's plundered vessel, the tailored velvet jackets slit at the seams to fit over heavy biceps, the inset lace ruffles stained and lifeless. Hardly a face was unscarred, and one stout, bare-skulled fellow was missing both his ears. They carried enough weapons for three times their number: a shining, clattering inventory of axes, daggers, and pistols hung thick on them like so many pans on a tinker's cart.

Without planning to she began to count the pirates as they went into the tavern, her lips moving like a schoolchild's.

Diverted, he watched her. "How many are there, then?"

Merry turned to his voice, to look with serious, credulous eyes at his stirring countenance. "Reade must be still in his cups."

"Quick, aren't you?" he observed. "I am being honest with you, sweetheart. Your friends are safe. Morgan's after a different man."

"The man who tried to talk to him?" Merry asked through a dry throat. "He—is he also a pirate?"

"Yes. He's been poaching in Morgan's territory. It was tolerable, until he started to fly Morgan's flag. Things like that make Morgan a little irritable. It may enhance his reputation for being everywhere at once, but it adds nothing to his pocketbook."

From inside the tavern came a terrible shriek, cut off abruptly in the middle.

Devon said calmly, "Morgan doesn't like screaming."

"What are they doing to him?" she whispered.

"They're only frightening him. He'll survive. Tell me, who are you?"

She had spent so much time in the last few months asking herself that question that it shocked her when he said it, as though a live recoil of her own thoughts had snapped back into her mind. He was the only being outside herself who had ever asked her who she was. Everyone else had always assumed. Who was she? It mattered little that she couldn't tell him the truth, because she had no answer that satisfied herself.

"I—am nobody." It had slipped out, before she could stop it.

He accepted it without a blink. "Is that your name or your avocation?"

"It's both," she said and looked away from him.

"I see." He settled back against the side of the wagon. "Have you always been nobody, or did you become nobody when you married Mr. Nobody? Do you like being nobody?"

She was alarmed to find herself beginning to smile and hoped he didn't see. "I only meant I wasn't *anyone*."

"Oh, well, you didn't have to tell me that. I knew the minute I saw you that you weren't just anyone. Did your husband send you outside because I was staring at you? I suppose he has quite a problem with that sort of thing. Is that why he makes you pin pillows under your skirt?"

Blushing violently, Merry said, "It wasn't a very good idea."

"Oh, no, I think it was a very good idea. Tell him from me, it worked while it lasted. You look cold. Would you like to get into my jacket?''

Rattled, and bewildered by his seeming non sequitur, she blurted out, ''Oh, no, if you take off your jacket, you'll have—''

''Nothing on underneath,'' he finished cheerfully. ''I'm afraid that was the idea. Does your husband sleep in a nightshirt?''

Merry accidentally conjured up an image of Jason, her pretend husband, in a nightshirt, the white linen flapping around his knees like a scarecrow. How in the world did people manage in marriage?

''Well, of course,'' she answered, too innocent to catch his drift. ''What else would he sleep in?''

He slanted a look at her and put his hand to her chin, stroking her bottom lip with his thumb. ''Are you sure,'' he said, ''that you're married?''

Merry looked into the lazy eyes and wondered what he would do if he knew that her brother and cousin inside the tavern were officers in the American military, there on what amounted to a mission of espionage, and what he would do if he knew that she could herself draw a sketch of him that would make him a marked man, perhaps even bring him to the gallows. Fear lent conviction to her answer.

''Yes, I'm quite sure.''

He traced a fingertip over her cheekbone. ''Happily?''

Another trap yawned at her feet. It was a dangerous game; she was a pitifully inept player, and a debilitating, strain-induced fatigue had well nigh nibbled away the last of her wits.

''Hap— I don't know. No, I mean yes. Yes, of course I am. Whenever you meet people, do you ask them so many questions?''

''Sometimes,'' he said softly. ''I'm rather an inquisitive person. Are you?''

He was so close, so very close to her, and she could feel his breath like a cool caress on her cheek, between the silky play of his fingers.

''I-I-I don't know'' was all she could produce.

He put his other hand to her other cheek, cradling her head. The stars above seemed to her to begin a slow whirl and to brighten and pulsate.

''Are you curious now?'' he whispered.

''N-no.'' It was a half truth.

"Why are you afraid?" he asked in a gentle way. "Does your husband hurt you?"

More than ever Merry was taken beyond her depth, for the things she knew about marital intimacy could have been written in long-hand on the head of a thimble. Improvisation and "I don't know"'s nearly exhausted, Merry said nothing and sat listening to the sound of her panicked heartbeat, as, gently, he laid his lips on hers, touching her with the sweetly probing eroticism of an experienced lover, and then drew away. He put his fingers to her lips, and under their subtle, clever pressure her lips parted slightly as his mouth returned to hers, stroking the soft openness. One long, slender finger played in the wisps of hair at the side of her head and traced the outline of her ear, pausing to toy with the sensitive earlobe, and then his broad hand lifted her hair from the back of her head, as if to encompass and steady the spinning sensations she was feeling there. Then he turned her head from side to side, dragging his lips across hers.

Merry had never known there could be such a thing as physical desire and was more than unprepared for the pounding sweetness of his kiss. It was a new world, velvet black and golden, every physical sensation she had previously experienced a pale ghost of this new overwhelming thing. When his lips touched her cheek, they left a trail of fever, and her skin seemed to melt under his fingers, as though they were entering her body.

She made a small, involuntary whimper, and he stroked her shoulder reassuringly, dropping his hand to her waist and pressing her close to him, her shivering small body warming against the satin of his bare skin. She began to sway under the powerful feelings he stirred in her, and he steadied her with his open hands, his arms around her, his palms flat on her back, and then his mouth came down again upon hers, insistent and urgent. He slipped his hands down until they were cupping her buttocks and lifted her to him with a firm pressure, and the cloth that separated her wanting skin from his could not impede the tingling flow of desire that caused her to move instinctively against him, the innocent wish to be crushed seamlessly against his body growing, blotting out all else, until she began to feel frightened by its powerful pull.

"Please. Oh, please," she gasped, her mouth moving against his.

"Yes?" he answered in a slow voice. "What would you like?"

It had been too much, all of it, for her previously unawakened body. Lifting trembling fingers to her swelling, burning lips, Merry forced herself to speak. "I'm not what you think. I don't know what you think I know."

The starlight lent sharp outline to the otherworldly beauty of his face, and yet, as clearly as she saw him, it was difficult to tell what he made of her words. After a minute he reached up a careful hand to stroke a drift of hair from her forehead, cupped her shaking fingers in his own, and tried to still them.

"You really are afraid, aren't you? Come here." He folded her tenderly in his arms and brought her head down to his shoulder.

Had she wished to push herself away from him, there would not have been the strength in her spent limbs. Her cheek lay against the heated, porous leather of his jacket, and through the calico gown that covered her breast, she felt his chest, moving only slightly as he breathed. Dear Lord, what if he should start to question her again? What if he guessed her lies?

From behind the wagon came the light sound of running footsteps, and then Sally called out, muted but urgent, "Merry? Merry! Are you here?"

Relief hit Merry like a blow because her need was desperate, but shame followed swiftly and hit more painfully. She should have felt nothing, *nothing* except distress to find Sally near her danger.

Sally, not seeing her immediately, began to cast about in a panic, and then to race for the tavern, as if to go back in. She had nearly reached the light when Devon vaulted lightly over the side of the wagon and stopped her, clamping his hand over her mouth and saying, "Hush! She's safe. But she won't be and neither will you if you run yelling into the tavern."

She fought his grasp and muttered something Merry couldn't distinguish through his muffling hand.

"After you promise not to scream," he said, "I'll let you go. Do you understand?"

Under his hand she jerked her head in a hard nod, and as soon as he had freed her mouth, Sally cried, "Where is she? Where is she? What have you done with her?"

Calling her cousin's name, Merry struggled to scale over the wagon's side, her legs twisting clumsily in her skirts. She might have fallen if Devon hadn't stepped to catch her around the waist and eased her way to the sand. For a moment Merry's legs shivered under her and nearly buckled, and then with a cry she ran into Sally's wide-flung arms. As from a distance she heard her own voice begging, "Help me, Sally."

Merry put back her head to look into her cousin's face and saw that Sally was glaring fiercely at the blond pirate.

"Don't!" Sally said to him in a savagely angry voice that sounded as if it was strangling in her throat. "You've got to let her go! She's so young. If anything happened—she'd never recover from it. In the name of pity . . ."

Devon had settled back against the wagon, long legs crossed, arms casually folded at his chest, and his shining golden hair caressed by a black breeze. He was watching Sally in an intent way without seeming to be listening to what she said.

He took his time before speaking, and when he did, his tone was dangerously mild. "I wonder if it would be worth my time to discover what two young women of obvious breeding are doing in a low-life tavern."

"The puppets," said Sally, too quickly.

"Ah. Itinerant puppeteers. The common folk." His beautiful mouth curved into a smile that quit before reaching his eyes. "And yet little Venus here has hands softer than an infant. She's never been within a furlong of a scrub bucket. As for yourself, Miss Sally, no matter what silly disguises you adopt, your speech and manners belong to a lady."

His tone robbed the words of any shade of a compliment, and there was a calm conviction in the indifferent voice that showed that it would be futile to argue. A threat rolled in the sea air, as thick and sizzling as hot oil over coal.

In a cool voice that made Merry pink with admiration, Sally said, "It's unwise to put too much stock in these superficial judgments, sir. *Your* speech, for example, marks you as a gentleman, while your manners suit . . ."

"The gutter?" he supplied, his smile widening a fraction. "And they get much worse than this. It's a good thing for you to think about."

It was too much, even for Sally. "The devil take you, sir. We don't know anything that would interest you!"

"How do you know what would interest me?" he asked her smoothly, inclining his head. "I'm willing to believe you haven't been foolish enough to tell Venus much. But you, Sally—it's what's in *your* mind that intrigues me."

Sally lifted her chin in brave defiance and snapped, "It'll take longer than you've got to beat it out of me."

"Without a doubt. I wouldn't waste my time beating you, dear, because you have already shown me a quicker course." Almost gently he said, "How much would you let me do to Venus before you started answering my questions?"

The shaft hit home with lethal accuracy. Over her head Merry heard Sally's horrified cry, and Merry felt her legs grow cold and seem to recede from her body.

More than a minute passed before he said, "You're a clever girl, Sally, but you're an amateur." He uncoiled from the wagon and slowly crossed to them. "Give me your hand."

As Merry watched, Sally obeyed him warily. From his own right hand Devon slid a heavy diamond signet and dropped the ring into Sally's palm, curling her fingers around it with his own.

"Give this to the man you'll find at the stables, watching the horses. Tell him to hitch your team."

In stunned thanksgiving Merry's eyelids drooped closed, and she heard Sally's awed whisper.

"You're letting us go?"

Devon's hand fell on the back of Merry's head, slid caressingly under her curls, and stroked slowly over the line of skin behind her ear.

"One has a certain reluctance to maim anything so lovely," he said. "I've a feeling, my brave Sally, that you wouldn't recover any better than she would. I wouldn't be so nice a second time. You know that, don't you? And if it had been another man . . ."

"Yes," said Sally quietly. "I know."

"If you value her so much, you won't risk her again next time." His fingers traced the satiny skin on Merry's neck.

"Go to the stables," he said, turning. "I'll send out your men." Like Lot's wife Merry watched in rigid silence as he moved toward the tavern, the faint light touching the smooth, sensual roll of his hips, the graceful shoulders, the moon-kissed hair. He entered the tavern and pulled the door closed behind him, leaving them safe among the sand and the surf and the stars.

Sally's legs slowly buckled, and she sank to sit on the wet grit, ducking her head down to her knees, and with bent wrists laid her palms on the back of her head. She laughed for a long time, half-hysterically, and when finally she stopped laughing, she said, "Dear God, what a man." She looked at Merry, her cheeks wet with the tears of her laughter, and said, in a calmer voice, "We're lucky to be alive, the way we botched that one. He kissed you, didn't he? I guessed it. You look that upset, no more."

In a voice that shook, Merry said, "If you had heard me, Sally . . . I was a whimpering ninny. I should have fought him."

Sally chuckled tensely. "Fought? Him? What would you want to do a thing like that for? Merry, when a man like that kisses you . . . Never mind, don't blame yourself."

Merry lowered herself to the sand and put an arm around her cousin's back. "Why do you think he let us go? Doesn't he suspect who we are?"

"I have no idea what he suspects, honey. But I think that he was afraid he would have to kill us if he found out. Who in the world could that man be?"

"I heard one of the pirates call him . . . Devon."

"Devon? Devon . . . Are you sure that's what it was? Devon! Heavenly days! You don't suppose—"

"What?"

Sally smiled. "Oh, never mind. It's impossible. A ridiculous thought. Come with me, and let's hurry before he changes his mind."

CHAPTER FOUR

August passed like a dancer, graceful and sweating. Frog song thrilled from the reed grass, raccoons hunted among the ripened cornstalks, and turtles slumbered away the afternoons on gray rocks comforted by the sun.

At Merry's home the cook boiled the rutabagas Merry had drawn, and served them in a lamb pie on the fourth Tuesday of the month. An owl with long downy ears took up residence in an old squirrel's nest inside the walnut tree that overlooked the garden, and Aunt April was pleased because it would keep the mole population down. Henry Cork went to the Quaker meeting house and preached violently and at length about the Holy Virgin and the Catholic saints until the Quakers were driven from their own building.

And the unicorn came often. Merry could feel it when she came to her room at night, waiting in the twilight behind the dark folds of the curtains.

The pictures from the tavern were to be the last that she would draw for Carl, who had said not so jokingly that it would be better to let a few British spies wreak havoc with the war effort than expose Merry to that much danger again. Merry was ashamed of the new secret woman inside her who questioned whether he cared for her so deeply or whether he was worried about how he'd explain things to their father if anything happened to her. Even under the blight of that cynical thought she missed him, and she wasn't likely to see him again, or Sally and Jason either, until Sally's wedding, which would be next June, war permitting.

Merry had worked and reworked the sketches Carl wanted, and the results had pleased him. She had been able to draw not only the traitor but the man he had been with—the pirate John Farley, whom Rand Morgan had come to the Musket and Muskrat "only to frighten," which, Carl had told her later, had included cutting off the little finger on each of his hands. She had drawn Morgan as well, and the boy called Cat, although not without a lingering, superstitious fear that the act might make them materialize before her. Carl had sent the sketches to the Secretary of the Navy, William Jones, for use at his discretion.

The only face she could not draw well was that of the blond man who had hidden her from the other pirates. Each sketch she made was wrong in one way or another. No matter how hard she tried to capture them, his tantalizing features remained memorable in their effect on her, elusive in their reproduction. It was difficult to draw such a beautiful face; her hand seemed to rebel against that unnatural perfection. Or perhaps some secret avenue of her mind had closed him off and shut away the sweet pain of remembered passion. It had all become less real to her with the waning of the month; the spying, the seacoast tavern, the pirates, and Devon. Hot and sticky September filtered in, bringing moments when she even asked herself if his kiss had been another fantasy like those her imagination had made for her in the past.

And as the days of September began to lessen and the night at the seacoast grew further away *it* became less real as well, gathering to itself the arabesque curlicues of legend. She would play the evening through in her mind like a playwright working on a script, and give it different endings and plot twists: She salvaged her pride with fierce resistance; she resourcefully captured the pirates single-handedly. Then there was the one ending she couldn't acknowledge. It had come to her in a dream of scruples abandoned and fear tossed away, a dream of submission and resultant joy, her senses reeling with the warm, sweet scent of his skin, his golden hair like silk under her fingertips. There was something in the power, the energy, the intelligence of this man that made him different, the way gold is from copper, and diamonds from glass chips. Anything he chose to do, he could have done well; why had he chosen to do it with Rand Morgan? Quick riches had been Carl's guess, for Devon wasn't a man who seemed likely to be content with little. But there, how quickly one could fill with speculation the vacuum of the pirate's background and identity. He was a man who would remain a mystery, and the secret would likely die with him on the blood-slicked deck of a burning ship.

Life had waxed more complex. Merry would sit by the duck pond in a clump of ferns watching the water beetles scud between the lily pads and think about the secret people she had discovered hiding inside her, the whimpering child who had appeared at her first taste of real terror, and the woman learning desire in the arms of a pirate. Surely she must exorcise them both.

Her home was safe and as rich in pretty domesticity as it was sterile in challenges to the soul; it was as though she were living in the clean, pink interior of a moon shell. The months passed in fluid order, filled with precious detail and suppressed longing. And Merry tried to let the pleasing minutiae of her days blot the gloss from her newly awakened senses.

Autumn was warm, wet, and golden; the mosquitoes were intolerable. To repel them, each night until the first frost Merry slept with brown sugar burning on coals in a chafing dish near her bed and woke daily to the sharp tang of charred sugar.

In October she husked corn with the housemaids. The project lasted a whole week because Aunt April despised as too plebeian the American custom of inviting the neighbors over to a husking bee. For days the fresh garden air was busy with the rustle of dry husks and the snap of cobs cracking and laughter as well, for Henry Cork did his best to claim the traditional kiss from any maiden who came across a red cob, and the housemaids pelted him with smut ears in lively battles.

November brought them chillier days. The itinerant woodchopper came in his coarse boots, carrying his broad ax and his canvas bundle. When he moved on again, there was an artfully balanced stack of wood by the horse barn for their winter fires.

Christmas! Mistletoe and red holly berries, ribbons and wax candles, chains cut from gaily colored paper and hung in swags around the drawing room, and Aunt April at the aging spinet playing "The Boar's Head Carol" and "When Christ Was Born of Mary Free." On Christmas morning Merry and April sat through services in the

unheated church in itchy woolen mittens and heavy caps under their
best bonnets and then walked home to the delectable meal April had
prepared of stuffed roast goose, brussels sprouts with almonds, roast
potatoes, apple yule logs, mince pie, and a plum pudding sprigged
with holly and glowing blue brandy flames. In the evening they sat
by the hearth nibbling on oysters cooked with lemon on toast that
her aunt called angels on horseback, and opened and exclaimed
happily over their gifts: light imported cologne to Merry from April,
a lilac gauze scarf to April from Merry, and to both of them a
generous length of pale-green mohair for new drawing-room window
curtains from Merry's father, and a three-volume set of *Mysteries of
Udolpho* from Sally. And that night as they walked arm in arm to
their bedchambers they both agreed that no Christmas together had
been happier.

In January Merry sewed the new drawing-room curtains with her
aunt and made twelve fine, large cheeses, and in late February,
when a traveling showman came to the village with a moose to
display, Merry snuck off in Henry Cork's company to see it. For
nine pence one purchased a ticket to see the beast and a handbill
praising its excellence. The handbill read: "The properties of this
fleet and tractable Animal are such as will give pleasure and satisfaction to every beholder." Fleet the Animal proved to be, but tractable
it was not. Through some mysterious expedient that Merry suspected
was related to Henry Cork's presence near its cage, the moose got
loose, bit the showman, and galloped off into the woods, providing
a great deal more pleasure and satisfaction to all beholders than its
hapless owner had anticipated.

Far away the war raged, and the town children ran under gray
skies shooting each other with stick rifles and hiding as scalping
parties behind the starkly winter-bared trees. The parson's youngest
son stole away to become a drummer for the 56th Virginia Militia,
and the Richmond *Enquirer* was thick with advertisements like the
one urging: "Gentlemen wishing uniforms embroidered in a prompt
and neat manner will please apply to No. 6 Babcock Alley."

The campaign against British Canada had failed miserably. At the
Châteauguay River a sizable chunk of the American Army got lost in
a swamp and shot each other up, while the main body fled in wild
retreat before a small British force when the British buglers sounded

a dramatically overconfident charge. Merry heard through her father that Carl had retired to winter quarters at French Mills with Upham's 21st Infantry, where the food and housing were abysmal and the sanitary conditions of such a nature that a gentleman could not relate them in a polite communication to his daughter.

And from Sally came the tidings that Jason was ill but improving from a Tower musket ball in the hip, taken in a skirmish against braves from Weatherford's Red Sticks near Fort Strother, on the southern frontier. In a flurry of concern Merry sent wool socks to Carl and one of the homemade cheeses to Jason and received back a friendly note from Carl and a very funny letter from Jason about the adventures that had befallen her cheese on its way to him, as deduced from its condition on arrival. They said little of what they must be suffering, and their courage awed and inspired Merry.

March arrived. Sap ran in the maple trees, and it was time for sugaring off. The *Almanack* advised its readers: "Make your own sugar, and send not to the Indies for it. Feast not on the toil, pain, and misery of the wretched." With that grim proverb in mind Merry threw herself energetically into the maple sugaring, and after a day spent hefting sap buckets she strolled happily into the hallway with the joyous fragrance of boiling maple syrup following her from the kitchens. Glancing toward the whatnot, she saw the Richmond paper. In a mood of innocent contentment she lifted it. The front page story heading jumped out at her from the sober news sheet. In the headline was Rand Morgan and his ship, the *Black Joke*.

The *Black Joke*, it seemed, had taken the American merchant ship *Morning Star*. Once aboard, the pirates had "made carnage of the hold, carrying off ruinous quantities of spirituous liquor, drunk as much as they could hold, and wastefully bathed themselves in the Surplus. The Captain's psalm book was villainously used for 'target practice,' and the trunk of a Boston merchant was invaded and costly clothing cast upon the deck for the guffawing wretches to make peacocks of themselves in. Further, the First Mate's spectacles were taken from him and put upon a pig. A cargo worth forty thousand dollars in gold was seized as well as a goodly amount of medicines. All the meanwhile the fifer from the *Morning Star* was forced to play a hornpipe until he dropped from exhaustion and was

carried aboard the pirates' ship to be conscripted into their own
crew. Also aboard were three women, and of their use at the hands
of the pirates this editor prefers to say nothing.''

Merry found Aunt April in the green drawing room, peering down
in a dazzled way at a sheet of superfine stationery. Another confusing bill from the mantua-maker, thought Merry. Without looking at
the letter she kissed her aunt on the cheek and said, ''Good evening,
Aunt April.''

April looked startled, as though she'd been woken from a catnap,
and folded the paper in her hand so hastily that Merry had a fleeting
impression of secrecy.

''Merry Patricia! My, but you can come quietly into a room. You
look tired, dear. I'll ring up the tea.''

The words were said in a flustered, rather disjointed voice that
made Merry think that perhaps the bill had been high because of the
blockade and her aunt was afraid she'd have to apply to Merry's
father for extra funds this quarter. Wondering why her aunt didn't
tell her about it, Merry said, ''No, thank you, Aunt April. I had a
cup of milk in the kitchen on the way in.''

''Did you? Well, I'm glad. You look tired to me. All this maple
sugar making—I don't think it's been good for you. You've never
been very strong.''

As long as Merry could remember, her aunt had been saying that
to her. She had always accepted it before. Now she asked, ''Why do
you say that I'm not strong?''

''Why, I mean merely that you're not *robust*. One can see looking
at you that your bones are delicate, and . . . Merry Patricia, what's
going on in that little head of yours? You don't look well to me, not
a bit well.''

Merry sat down. ''It's just that— Aunt April, have you read the
evening paper?''

''I've skimmed it, of course, but I haven't delved—oh. Ah, ha.
You saw that dreadful story, did you, about the pirates? Why they
find it necessary to put things like that in the public press so young
people can be exposed to that kind of degraded story is more than I
can imagine! No wonder you don't look well. I felt ill myself after
reading it. Horrible. Put the whole thing right out of your mind.''

But bright in Merry's mind was Morgan, black-eyed, the emerald glowing on his chest, and Cat with the long hair and cruel hands . . . and Devon. Had Devon taken one of the women and held her delicately, talking in a gentle, quiet voice as he had with Merry, hypnotizing her with his comforting, and then plundering her defenseless mouth with his lips? It was the kind of thing that an editor might prefer not to mention. Merry watched her aunt go to her lap desk and lock away the stationery sheet. When her aunt had turned back to her, Merry asked her, "Aunt April, why wouldn't the newspaper say what happened to the women?"

She could have sworn her aunt blushed. "I think they said too much as it was! I can't think that your father would want you to read things about pirates and women."

"Why not?" Seven months ago Merry would have hardly been able to frame the question to herself, much less ask it of her aunt. It was an unbearable thing, this being desperate to know. She looked everywhere in the room but at her aunt. "What do pirates do to women?"

As it happened, Aunt April was as embarrassed as Merry. She went to peer miserably out the window, as if she was afraid someone was hiding outside listening, and swallowed with difficulty, as though she had an infected throat. "One would suppose—that is—" Another swallow. "One imagines that the pirates had their way with them."

Before she lost her nerve, Merry asked, "Which way is that?"

"A perfectly normal question for a young lady at your stage in life," said Aunt April with the nervous certainty of one trying to remain calm in the face of all hell breaking loose. She made a great play of arranging the new window curtains, the color running high over her cheekbones.

A wayward and rather poignant thought occurred to Merry. "Don't *you* know either?"

"I was never married, Merry Patricia, and my mother died before she had ever an occasion to tell me. . . ."

It came to Merry suddenly where she had learned that meekly apologetic voice that had so amused the pirate. She felt her lips twitch upward into a grin. "But you must have gathered *some* idea."

"Some idea perhaps, but it's hardly anything that I'd care to . . ."

A giggle sprang from Merry's grin, and she shook an accusing finger. "If you think I'm to be put off with stalling, Aunt April, then . . ."

"Oh, very well. If you *will* hear it. I warn you, though, it's only the merest scrap that I chanced to overhear my mother telling my sister. I daresay this is going to sound quite peculiar but"—April stared fixedly at one of the low shrubs in front of the house—"it seems that a man—climbs on top of a woman—"

Surprise brought Merry to her feet. *"On top of?"*

"There! There, you see? I've made a poor job of it." The window curtains crumpled under Aunt April's fretting fingers. "You'd probably have been better off if I'd said nothing! That's all I know. First they like to kiss, and then climb on."

Merry sat down again and concentrated her gaze on the wall covering's vanilla dots. When she could control the quivering of her lips, she said, "It doesn't make sense."

"I quite agree with you, dearest. But how many of the things that men do make sense? Take fox hunting, or prizefights, or making war, for that matter." She added dismally, "Men have drives."

"Do women have them too?"

"I doubt that it could be the same. Can you imagine a group of women turning outlaw, attacking ships, and forcing their will on men? Do you know what I think? A lady would do best to marry a rich man who could afford to keep a mistress and so would have less energy left for his wife."

"Oh, Aunt!" Merry laughed, launching herself from her chair to take her aunt's hands from the curtains and plant a cheerful kiss on each one. "Then from this day forth I will take special care to encourage only my wealthy beaux." Striking a coquettish pose, Merry fluttered her lashes at an invisible gentleman, placed, if he had been there, where he must have been tripping backward over the tea table. "Dear Major Moneybags," she said grandly, sweeping a full court curtsy, "I shall agree to your obliging proposal on the one condition that you will keep yourself a woman and climb on her more often than you will on me!"

Aunt April smothered a smile. "Such nonsense. We aren't discussing this with the proper gravity, and I don't know what people would think if they were to hear us. Really, sometimes I fear that we get a little batty, living here like this, two women alone." A strange look came over her features. She went to her lap desk and thoughtfully stroked her hand in a wavy pattern across its highly polished surface. "We don't get out enough."

Through the ages women had been making the same kind of statement, but Merry had never, never expected to hear it from her aunt! Aunt April, who hated to travel, who detested American social life. With disbelieving senses Merry heard her aunt ask, "Merry Patricia, would you like to come with me on a trip to New York?"

CHAPTER FIVE

For more than two centuries New York City had been spreading across the rocky island that had once been nibbled by glaciers and later had served as the fertile hunting grounds of clever Indian trappers, before the Dutch had come, and the British with their guns and liquor and lust for empire. The city that Merry found was tame, dirty, and crowded. Pigs wandered at will, munching on garbage and street dirt which the citizens diligently piled in the alleys to be hauled away twice a week by the Department of Scavengers. Milch cows meandered between neat gabled houses, dining on the bark of the Lombardy poplars, planted with well-meaning innocence along the narrow walkways. Within a brisk walk of the carpeted homes of the rich were the Five Points slums, where more than thirteen families might share a single privy.

Everything here seemed remarkable to Merry: the vast markets that fed so many, the sobering bulk of the prison, the libraries, the almshouse, the botanical garden. There was not a street you could pass without seeing evidence of the city's awesome complexity, where misery rubbed shoulders with grandeur in no more wonder than the pauper and the banker have when they pass each other on the pavement.

Today New York was celebrating Evacuation Day, commemorating that proud memory in the First War of Independence when the British had been forced to take their scrambled leave from the city before General Washington's triumphal entry.

It was noon, and Merry's gaze caught the gleam from a church tower as its great bell began to dance. The voices of other bells joined in. From the Presbyterian Church, the Trinity, the Dutch Reformed, French Episcopal, and Baptist came brilliant thunder that laced the cool air between the hard claps of cannon salute.

In front of Merry the parade was retreating down the straight stretch of Broadway. A unit of dragoons had been the last of the military that would pass them. The workers came next, under bright printed banners that snapped in the shifting breeze. The hat makers, the pewterers—and the blacksmith trade with a wonderful float that carried a working anvil and red fire, where three men stood forging an anchor, even as six horses pulled them along.

What a day it was, what a parade! Merry glanced to her side, at Sir Michael Granville, wondering how the tall British man could remain unruffled in the face of a patriotic display that commemorated a humiliating defeat for his own nation. His expression was much as it might have been if he were watching the hunting dance of tribesmen in loin cloths and feathers—as if it were to him a colorful, primitive spectacle full of naïve and pretty drama and simple symbolism. He was too well-bred to have said anything to confirm her suspicions, but condescension has its own particular odor, detectable like a yard where goats have been, even if one walks through it with closed eyes and covered ears. She hoped that soon she would be able to look at him without feeling at all intrigued.

It was Sir Michael who had brought Aunt April to New York. Aunt April had never shown Merry the letter, but it happened that Sir Michael was a distant cousin to the Dowager Duchess of St. Cyr, one of the few of Aunt April's correspondents who wrote back more often than once a decade. On hearing that Sir Michael had obtained permission to visit the New World in the entourage of the British prisoner-of-war exchange agent, the duchess had encouraged him to convey her respects to Aunt April. It was a compliment to the duchess's influence that he had actually done so after his arrival in the United States. Merry could imagine the missive he had addressed to her aunt, full of polite clichés and a vaguely expressed desire that they should meet. It must have been an unlovely surprise for Sir Michael to find a letter from Aunt April in his return mail, promising to be in New York within the fortnight.

In the face of that it was hard to understand why he had received them with kindness. Instinct, based on no solid evidence, warned her that Sir Michael was not a man who routinely bothered himself with unrewarded kindnesses.

Passing them was a wide float that nested a press, the printers aboard working with quick economical movements to make broadsides. Two youthful apprentices leaned off the back, tossing the fresh inked pages into greedy outstretched hands in the crowd. Sir Michael caught one and handed it to Merry with a smile.

"A souvenir for you, Mistress Merry," he said.

Mistress Merry, quite contrary, how does your garden grow. . . . It had been a favorite tease of the village children. Merry could barely hear it without wincing. She might have told him not to keep calling her that if she hadn't been worried that the pain would be exposed in her voice.

Glancing at the paper, she saw that it was an ode about the Battle of Fort George in last May, between her nation and his. No matter that his purpose here was peaceful. He was still her enemy. It was incredible that they hadn't discussed it, not once, although she'd been in New York a week. Aunt April had always been there, fawning and frightened, until this morning, when she had stayed in her rooms, avoiding happily the noisy, shoving crowds. Mostly Aunt April had talked to him about England: gossip, much of it, and the rest politics, the arts, fashion, and the latest books. They had talked of New York too, which ironically he knew much better than Merry, because he had been here often before the war. He had many friends here, and she met them at dinner at the mansion of the Austrian trade commissioner, where Sir Michael was staying and where he had somehow gotten an invitation for Merry and her aunt to stay as well.

Folding the paper in half, Merry considered Sir Michael's face, where deep half-circle lids lay open over green irises with spokes of silver. His nose was a nice shape, even if the bridge was rather high, and the spare line of his mouth bent stiffly at the corners when he smiled, producing a pair of shallow and not unattractive dimples. Scissored brown hair barely slit with gray curled forward stylishly over his ears. Carl, of course, was going to be furious with Aunt April when he heard about all this.

"What is war," said Carl's sister abruptly, scraping tight the paper's crease between her gloved thumb and forefinger, "if we can stand together like this and watch a parade?"

The green-silver eyes glanced thoughtfully at the crowd around them. "*They* don't seem to mind if we stand here together," he said.

Obviously not. It was the kind of thing she had discovered he was likely to say: a slightly preposterous half gambit that shook her unsteady poise with aggravating efficiency.

Around them on the pavement the many gay, anonymous celebrants moved, swarming and shouting and turning in a crisp sigh of early spring garments, freshly brushed for the day, just-turned white collars on the little boys and flat new ribbons for the girls. Even if the restless crowd could have identified Sir Michael as British, the men and women of New York, intelligent patriots that they were, had a far greater hatred for their own Madisonian government, which had declared this costly, tiresome war that was destroying the economy of their city. Damn the British Navy, which had blockaded their port; but damn, *damn* those idiots in Washington who had struck Britannia on her stuffy cheek and brought this clumsy war down upon the hapless American merchants.

"My point stands," said Merry and was grateful it came out sounding less feeble than she knew it was.

Granville lifted his hand, where wide dark knuckles rode from the black, tight-fitting sleeve of his coat. He was, by far, the most elegantly dressed man Merry had ever met, certainly *not* excepting those in her family.

"Do you see that pedestal?" he asked her, pointing into the

bowling green before them, to where a wide slab of marble lay beside a marshal, whose job it was to chastise anyone who stepped on the grass here, or harassed the spindly, long-suffering trees. "There was a statue of King George III on it, torn down in 1776 and melted into shot. It might have been one of those pieces that killed my uncle, fighting here a year later. He left four children below the age of seven, one of them blind." There was a short silence while she looked away from him. Then he said, "Merry, it goes back and forth. Will it really help if we blame each other?"

Will it really help if we blame each other? As Merry stood wondering if there was something wrong with his logic or her own, Sir Michael looked down at her, his eyes still in complex, mature calm, and said, "Anyway, we'll have enough time to work it out, won't we, on the way to England?"

It was a ridiculous error. Merry stared up at him with a start. "I'm not going to England."

Correcting her with the censureless care one might use with a child who has spoken a faulty lesson, Granville said, "You are. The day after tomorrow on the *Guinevere,* with your aunt. It's all right. You can trust me. Your aunt and I have talked about it, and I understand why she doesn't want it to become known."

And then he smiled at her as though he had not with a single sentence blown the sane structure of her life into slithering fragments.

A few moments had passed, blank and ugly, before Merry could organize her blood-stripped muscles into activity and begin to walk backward from the well-mannered face with its features slowly realigning themselves into compassion and concern.

"Merry? Dear God. What have I said? Can it be—could it really be that you didn't know?"

As he began to come toward her she turned and fled from him, her velvet slippers striking hard on the coarse gravel path, her heart banging in her chest as she wove between grouping families and the dull-green stacks of shrubbery that squatted like trolls under the elms.

For once, her size helped. Quickly he was lost in the tall crowds, and when she came to a break in the line of spectators, she gripped the iron railing that lined the Battery and kicked her legs over, one at a time.

The political societies were passing in review, and Merry dove through a herd of Republicans, with their buck's tails dangling forward from their hats. Some laughed drunkenly and tried to reach for her as she passed frantically among them.

When her feet found the neat ocher bricks of the sidewalk, for the first time in her life she lifted her narrow white skirt and ran full out over the busy pavement toward the house five blocks up Pearl Street, where Aunt April would be waiting with, she prayed, a denial of Sir Michael's words.

The house of the Austrian trade commissioner was ruddy brick, tastefully decorated in bluestone with eyelet window curtains in the upper stories that lent the home a friendly and feminine look. It was not the place, surely, where one would hear grim news. Merry nearly collided with a cake vendor as she swung through the white picket gate into the small cobbled front yard, and the sweet odor of hot spiced gingerbread swirled around her as she stopped to lean dizzily against the cistern that caught soft water from the rain roof. Then she climbed the stoop, knocked, and was admitted almost immediately by a pretty Austrian maidservant, who looked curiously at Merry's pale cheeks and glittering eyes.

The rooms within were narrow rectangles with low ceilings, eerily quiet at this time of day while their elderly host and his wife napped, nicely insulated from the street noise. Everywhere beautiful imported furniture in the French taste gleamed sleepily in the hazed sunlight, and walking soft-footed through the corridors, it was hard to believe that not many days' journey away American settlers lived in rough cottages and feared Indian attacks.

Willing temperance to her breathing, Merry laid her hand on the door and entered quietly into the cream-and-copper suite that her aunt had enjoyed these last seven days.

Merry's aunt, protector, and guardian was on her knees laying tissue-wrapped nightgowns in a cedar chest. Her gaze flew like a startled pigeon to her niece. She couldn't have looked more guilty if she'd been hiding a corpse.

"Aunt April, it's not true. Is it?" asked Merry tightly.

Aunt April stood, her face raw with worry. Beseechingly she offered her hand. "Merry—forgive me, Merry."

They were like mother and daughter. Between them there was no need for accusation, for evasion, or for lies. Merry saw confirmation of Granville's words in her aunt's fearful eyes, in the set of her chin; no spoken words could have announced the truth more unmistakably. Anger, love, and pity met between them and remained unspoken also, clashing and mingling like great waves, which broke in lonely desolation into helpless undercurrents. Compassion fought the keen smart of betrayal within Merry; moving clumsily, like a machine that needed oil, she took her aunt's hand. And when she could force herself to speak, the words came out like a sigh.

"Aunt April, we can't do it. We simply can't do it."

"There are papers of transit—Sir Michael has arranged them."

"My father will never allow me to leave this country," Merry said faintly, still hardly able to believe that this was really happening.

Aunt April looked as though she were experiencing physical pain. "But it doesn't make any difference. Not formally. Because, you know, your father put you legally into my care." April paused, and then her words came out in a flood. "Merry, an old friend of mine has offered to cover our fares. In fact, she has commissioned Sir Michael—well, perhaps not commissioned, but asked him— Merry, he is to escort us back to England."

"No." Unimaginable that Merry should say that word to her aunt. "I won't go, Aunt April. I *can't* go. I'm an American."

"You're not; you're British. Half-British. And from one of the first families of the country."

As gently as she could, Merry said, "A name disgraced. The name of a family that had to flee the country in debt."

April's gray eyes snapped. "A name is a name. Our connections were of the highest!"

Connections who never answer your letters, Aunt, thought Merry. Why in the name of heaven had one of them decided to invite April back now?

"Aunt April, I don't *want* to go."

"Oh, Merry." April put her hands on Merry's shoulders and drew her close, her embrace intensely loving. "What have you here? We live like nuns in a cloister, in a farming village full of bigots. You should be mingling with people your own age, your own class—you should have beaux and dances and nosegays and rides in the park. How are you going to be married here? Do you think your father's ever going to trouble himself with the matter? Every time I've written to him about it, he's replied that it will sort itself out. But it won't, Merry. We'll both of us only get older, lonelier, and more eccentric. People aren't like us here, Merry. They're too interested in superficial change, and not interested enough in the things that last, and that have lasted.'' She drew Merry away from her and gazed into her eyes, her hands pressing into Merry's shoulders. "Don't expect Carl to find you a husband! There'll always be something that interests him above you. Now there's the war. Then there'll be the business of reconstructing the country after the war, and then he'll take a wife and he'll have a family of his own to think about. Do you want to live on the fringe all your life, Merry? I've never said this to you before . . . but you're a beautiful girl, far too special for this rough backwater of a country.''

Merry took her aunt's hands from her shoulders and held them in her own and repeated, "I'm not going to go, Aunt April. I don't *want* to go.''

April slid her hands from Merry's, and she crossed her arms in front of her and walked slowly to sit on the edge of the bed, her thin shoulders slumping. As the cloudy tears slid down the pale cheek Merry suddenly saw the crumpled figure in a new way. *Why, she's not old,* Merry thought. *She's only forty. I always thought she was old.*

"I shan't go either, then,'' said April softly. "I can't leave you here with the country at war. . . .'' One of the pins slipped from her tired bun, and the freckled bird-boned hands replaced it. April walked to the window, looking out with the same look that Merry had often seen when she observed her gazing out of the drawing-room window at home—but, she realized, the hope that had been in the gaze was replaced by desolation. "I'm sorry, Merry. I wanted just one time to see my home again.''

Merry went to stand behind her. "Go without me—please, Aunt April.''

April shook her head in a definite way, and Merry knew she would never talk her into that.

For one human being to cause a tragedy in the life of another is a responsibility that not many would choose to shoulder. Adult resolution, patriotism, fear, and even common sense were seared to ash by love. Two days ago, if someone had asked her, she might have said that there was very little she would not do for her aunt, but now she realized there was *nothing* she would not do for her.

CHAPTER SIX

Putting up a very good front to cover her hysteria, Merry stepped into the carriageway, securing the neck button of her tan wool redingote, her gloved fingers slipping nervously against the dark-brown embroidery on her silk collar. "Such a nice slim neck you have, Miss Wilding," the village dressmaker had said and added emphasis to her point by cutting Merry's dresses a size tighter at the neck than Merry would have liked. This evening the sensation that she was being slowly choked was more intense than ever.

Across the yard Henry Cork was making fast the trunks in the hired mule cart. The trunks had grown dusty (not that Aunt April would notice such a triviality on this day of all days) from sitting in the yard all afternoon waiting for Henry to rent a cart and load them. You had to give Henry Cork plenty of time to do a thing.

Merry wandered to the hired carriage that waited, shabby as a workhouse hearse, to convey her to the dock where she would board the British ship that would sail on the dawn tide for England. One of the carriage horses eyed her curiously. She raised her hand to gently stroke its friendly nose as Henry caught sight of her and hurried over with the wind lifting his untucked red flannel shirt like a flag to expose the spiky black hairs on his round, chalky belly. Drooped over his bowed legs were baggy pants of gray sailcloth cinched with a frayed rope, because he doggedly persisted in losing the leather belts Aunt April had generously bought him, one after the other. No doubt he sold them. On her first day here Merry had heard him telling one of the kitchen maids what a sad time he had of it, being indentured to a tight old witch who wouldna' even give him a belt to make himself decent. . . .

Joining Merry, he said crossly, "The auld vixen, she's as good as kidnapping you, ain't she?" A string of tobacco juice escaped one corner of his mouth and ran down his long, grizzled chin.

"Oh, no, Henry," Merry answered, looking over her shoulder to make sure her aunt hadn't been following her closely down the stairs. "That's not true. We'll be back next spring—Aunt April promised. This is something my aunt has wanted for years, Henry. If she likes, she can stay, and I will come back happy, knowing that I let her have the chance to live in the land of her choice once again. And besides, it might be a lot different than she remembers it."

"Paradise would be a disappointment to her, the way she talks about England," he said.

"Well, if that happens, she'll be more content to come back," Merry ventured.

"Aye, the old besom. Yer old man is likely to load up a dozen men-o'-war and come sailing after you as soon as he gets wind of this."

"With Achilles, a dozen Argonauts, and a wooden horse?" said Merry. "I'm not Helen of Troy. Father will understand if you give him my letter. You won't forget, will you?"

"Don't fret yerself about that now, Miss Merry. I'll see that he gets it. You'll have enough to do, keepin' on yer feet on the wide, wide sea." There was the sound of a door opening behind them, and Henry winked at her strangely. "Ah, there she is now. She'll get a going away surprise from me."

"Henry, what did you do?" Merry whispered, but he had left her already, walking toward her aunt, outstretching his arm in a theatrical gesture to show April where he had strapped the trunks, as if daring her to find fault with his method. It was too late to ask him. Merry turned to the steps that the groom was letting down for her, hoping that in her aunt's happy mood even Henry Cork's devil-

ment wouldn't be taken too much amiss. Behind her she heard
Henry tell her aunt, "The trunks are on, corded nice and tight like
you ordered, ma'am."

"Thank you, Henry," answered April. Her aspect was nearly
benign. "And I shall just have to remember at the docks to have
Merry's trunk taken to my room and hers to mine."

Merry had had a headache all morning, a going-to-England
headache. It was painful, like an open wound with lemon water
dripping on it in regular pulses, alternated with a feeling of numbness.
The numbness was fading, the pain returning, and she dimly heard
Henry's voice in the background as she mounted the steps.

"Now why would ye do that, ma'am?" he was saying.

"I don't know what business it is of yours, Henry Cork, but we
changed trunks before packing so Merry could fit the new folding
easel and paint pots into the larger trunk. Now, Henry, when you get
back to Fairfield—" And then April added a few more domestic
instructions to the long list she had been providing Henry with since
they had decided to leave; at last she turned and joined Merry in the
coach. The driver released the carriage brake with a solid clack, and
Merry leaned out the window, waving at Henry, forcing herself to
wear a smile which she hoped desperately would exude cheer and
confidence. She had expected Henry Cork to be upset about her
leaving for England with her aunt; never would she have predicted
as the carriage drew her away that Henry Cork would look appalled.

The journey to the docks came to Merry as a series of vivid details
splashed against the blunt backdrop of her headache. The jarring
crunch of the wheels in traffic, the jostling stop and start, the high
breeze, the shouting of frustrated, traffic-bedeviled grooms ground
into her ears. Disciplining herself, Merry made smiling responses to
her aunt's stream of excited conversation. Merry hid her tears and
her terror inside, like battered islands in the nucleus of a hurricane.

The harbor lay in bitter silence. Everywhere one could feel the
effects of the British blockade. The roads had fallen into disrepair,
rutted by erosion in some places and overgrown with weeds and
grass in others. The ghostly, creaking ships stood rotting in their
slips, and here and there neglect showed itself in a torn and drooping
canvas, a skinned rope that no one had bothered to replace, a board
warping in the weather and needing paint.

It was an odd sight in the dying light. Where so recently there had been the scurrying of sailors up the mast and the steady thud and bump of cargo being unloaded, there was only the scurrying of the rats and the lap, lap, lap of water, forlornly trying to tug the empty ships away from anchor out to sea.

The sun dropped as their carriage passed the rows of bare masts, spiking up like the trunks of a burnt forest, to the British frigate HMS *Guinevere*. One of the few inhabited ships in the harbor, she rode high at her mooring, stripped as she was of cannon and powder for the diplomatic purpose that had brought her with immunity to this enemy shore. Flags and special insignia marked her peaceful intent, but still a discreet guard of American soldiers was quartered about her—"for her own protection," as they say.

The *Guinevere* rose out of the dark vessels around her, her burning lamps like a festival of lights. All Merry was to remember later was the blur of the lights, the friendly officers—from the British Navy—handing her down from the carriage with her aunt and helping them to come safely onto the deck of the slip, men with features she could barely distinguish. Under her feet was a pleasant tug as the moored frigate sidled in the ship; and she said and did what she hoped were the right things in the last painful moments before she was left mercifully alone, with her trunk, in the small cabin that would be her home for the coming six weeks. The door closed, footsteps pattered away in the corridor outside, and there was a small moment of panic brought on by the realization that she was now properly on the boat. She rushed over to unbind and throw open her trunk on the vague thought that it might distract her to unpack. But even unpacking required more than a vague concentration, so when the trunk lid had snapped open and she had lain it back to fall heavily on its hinges, Merry turned from it and walked to the window.

She could see the outline of the city—black and simple geometric figures that rose and fell slowly with the swell of the sea. There were fog-softened patches of yellow light from the streetlamps, and a low murmur of traffic—now and then a shout and the whinny of a cart horse. At the end of the dock a circle of light from a lantern picked out the complacent features of Sir Michael, who stood with one boot resting on a coil of rope, indulging in some quietly derisive laughter with two British sailors. Near to his foot the wind found a trio of withered brown leaves and tossed them playfully into the air before dumping them carelessly on the swell like a spoiled child.

In a carefully covered sconce behind Merry burned a single small flame, its light flinching in shiny, trembling patterns on the window's rusting metal frame. She felt a sudden coldness, and the skin on her arms tingled as though a light, flimsy wire had skimmed the surface of the hair there. She knew as though someone had told her in words that she was not alone. Her skirt hissed as she spun, staring about her in the tiny room, a bare open cube that held no places that could have hidden another human. There was nothing but thin, cloudy candlelight and shadows. Trying to still the foolish tremors of her heart, she took two steps into the room, slowly letting the air slide from her lungs; and for no particular reason she could have named, her gaze fell on a thick, lozenge-shaped shadow that lay like a pile of cinders near the door. It took her a moment to realize the strangeness of the shadow—there was nothing there to cast it, and it was moving; and as it moved in its territory it moved within itself as well, heaving with life. Two thousand minutely glistening black and hard-shelled bodies were making their way in well-ordered insectual haste across Merry's cabin floor.

Afterward she was able to reflect with mild pleasure that she had had the presence of mind not to scream. She had simply walked from the cabin, sternly repressing a certain gritty distaste as her feet crackled accidentally on a score of stragglers. Sir Michael had been in the corridor, in conversation with one of the junior officers, who turned and smiled with lush enthusiasm when he saw Merry, his youthful features reddening when Merry told him politely that her cabin was full of ants.

There had been, quite naturally, a good deal of commotion and a good deal of embarrassment later when the ants were traced to a bowl of dusty comfits in Merry's trunk. In two words, spoken in a sinking voice, Aunt April had laid the matter bare: "Henry Cork."

Merry's cabin was unlivable after the liberal application of acrid astringent poisons, laid down to kill the ants. Aunt April's tiny cabin was only large enough for her and Betty, her aproned, aging maid;

when the truckle bed was pulled out, there was no room to walk.
There were no vacant sleeping arrangements available; and yet Aunt
April was nearly stampeded with officers begging to give up their
beds for Merry's comfort. Sir Michael's offer carried the day, if
only because his were the only quarters not already being shared
with another. Sir Michael handsomely agreed to make himself comfortable in a hammock mounted in the captain's quarters.

An hour later Merry shut her eyes for the last time that day,
wincing against the headache, in Sir Michael's bunk. The mattress
was rude and lumpy, the stark long-sleeved nightdress she had
borrowed from her aunt felt scratchy, the sheets smelled as though
the ship's launderer had too generous a hand with the bleach cup, and
the hot skimmed milk the first mate had kindly brought curdled in her
stomach. But the Atlantic Ocean rose and fell beneath the *Guinevere*
like a mother rocking a cradle, and Merry fell almost immediately
and blessedly to sleep, with headache intact, her dreams fitful.

She was awakened some time later that night by a noise; and sat
up and opened her eyes in a single movement, and found herself
staring, from inches away, into a rotund, unshaven, and evilly
grinning face. She never saw the blow that came from behind to end
once more her wakefulness, and this time there were no dreams.

CHAPTER SEVEN

Consciousness returned with the scent of fermented fruit. Merry
opened her eyes to a darkness relieved only by thin, glossy spears of
sunlight. It had to be day. Could so much time really have passed?
She tried to move, wearily, and found first with annoyance and then

with terror that she could not. A hasty catalogue of her limbs and joints revealed that her knees were tucked up under her chin and there was no room to stretch out her legs and relax the cramps that were twisting her calf muscles into corkscrews. From without came a rumble of wheels and the murmur of voices. When she tried to call out to them, a sticky, foul-tasting wad of fabric slid deeper into her mouth, choking her words into a rasp that was barely audible, even to her own ears.

Bound, gagged, and thrust like yesterday's garbage into an aged apple barrel, Merry was being hauled off in an unsprung wagon toward parts unknown.

A nerve path cleared suddenly in her brain, and her hearing focused on a man's voice, startlingly close to the barrel.

"The thing I don't like about it is the bloody thin air out here. It's too thin to get aholt of, like thin soup, and it's hard to get enough of in one breath."

"That's right." It was a different voice, also male. "Ya always did have such a way with words, Jack. It's like the air is unsatisfyin'. One longs fer a thick blast o' that good solid New York air, reekin' o' coal smoke and horse manure dust. Out here how can a fellow tell he's breathin' at all? And that ain't the only thing. Yer citizens out here are stoopid. Like that last one we stopped and asked when we was a little bit lost awhile back. Why, he could've passed for a scarecrow—that big bleedin' straw hat. Downright pictureskew."

"That's *picterex*. *Picterex* is the word. And I wasn't lost—you was lost, Biddles. I know right where we are."

"Yeah—we're on the mother planet." There was silence, and then: "I ain't heard her move yet back there. Think I killed her? She was a puny little thing."

"Nah. She ain't moving 'cause she's trussed tighter than a parson's gout. And she ain't puny everywhere. Saw when I tied her, and felt it when we dumped her in the barrel." Merry could hear seagulls crying, and a new sound which she knew to be the booming of surf, and a salt scent mixing with the apple smell in the barrel. "See those rocks yonder? What say you we stop and have us a little taste of that crisp little apple we got rolling around back in our barrel?"

With desperate common sense Merry forced herself not to cry. *If my nose fills up*, she thought, *I'll suffocate*.

"That's th' tenth time you've suggested that, Jack, and by God's whiskers I want to as bad as you, but we already said there might be soldiers chasin' us two miles back, or somebody lookin', or who knows what. I say let's wait until we— Watch for that pothole, Jack."

There was a lurch and a bump, and the apple barrel with Merry in it lifted and came down again woodenly. There was a moment of excruciating pain before Merry's nightmares vanished as before, into blackness.

A thick gray light burned against the whitened skin on Merry's face as she rolled once more back to consciousness. Someone had taken the lid off the barrel. There was a new voice above her, a youthful voice, with crisp, businesslike accents.

"Look, I don't have time for any of that. If you were interested in that, you should have done something about it earlier."

She recognized the answerer's voice from the wagon. "How could we, and all? With Federals maybe breathin' down our heels."

The barrel was suddenly pushed onto its side, and Merry found herself being tumbled onto a sandy beach. She felt her knees crack as she straightened them and gasped with relief under her gag. She was in the foggy open, and it was very early in the morning. She found it difficult to focus her eyes—the effort of trying to look directly at a thing made her dizzy and nauseated. It was too much like looking at two images that passed back and forth, one in front of the other, so she shut her eyes. She had seen the same round, bewhiskered face that greeted her on the ship. She wasn't sure if it was Jack or Biddles, but whoever it was picked her up from the beach.

The young, hard voice spoke again. "You're breaking my heart. If you were stupid enough to let someone take your trail, you'd better put space between yourselves and this place as quickly as you can. No, not over there. Put her in the skiff if you want your money."

Her conveyor halted, started again, halted, as if in indecision, and then turned with her. His hand under her rib cage made it difficult for her to breathe. She twisted her face and opened her eyes to look at her carrier. He was looking at someone else.

"Damn you for a cold-blooded puppy. I crave the wench. It won't take long." His voice had taken on a wheedling tone.

"Yes, I know it won't—about ten seconds by the look of you," said the younger man. "And having waited two hours already, I don't have ten seconds. You were late, and I'd given you plenty of time."

It was Biddles's turn to talk. "God's toenails, man. It was bleedin' hard sneakin' on that ship. It takes time to crack a ship as heavily guarded as that one was. And then to look for the papers, find the papers, and pack them up—and then this little baggage here that we didn't plan on. It was only our native ingenooity that got us out of that one. If I hadn't thought of the barrel, we wouldn't have got away at all."

"Put her in the skiff," the young voice ordered again, and this time he was obeyed.

There was saltwater in the bilge of the skiff, and a coil of salty rope in front of her face, and a small boom waving above her head. Jack's arms left her body with almost tender reluctance.

"Don't blame her on me," said the younger man. "You should have made sure she didn't see you."

"We couldn't help it," whined Biddles. "She was lookin' right at us. What could we do?"

"Slit her throat," said the younger voice coolly.

"We charge more for killin', and you hadn't paid us yet. You wouldn't want us doin' somethin' extra you'd have to pay us more for, would you?" said Jack.

"That weren't it at all, Jack," said Biddles. "It's you, always wanting a woman. Comes in the way when we have a job to do."

Coins jingled. "That's ample," said the boy's voice, "for the botch you've made of the job." Light footsteps approached the skiff, crunching on the sand.

Before she saw him, Merry knew who it was. Seven months ago in a smuggler's tavern she had become acquainted with that cold adolescent voice when its owner had grabbed her and hurt her and threatened her life. She looked up helplessly into the hard blue eyes of Rand Morgan's reprobate companion, Cat.

The boy scanned her without pity or recognition or even much interest while the fog played mother-of-pearl patterns on the stark

bend of his tall cheekbones. On one side of his face sparkled the
engraved hoop of a silver earring as big as a bangle, and his pale
hair ribboned neatly from chin to hip in a thick braid knotted with
leather. His buttonless black shirt fell open to the low-slung waist of
his trousers, exposing the bands of tanned maturing muscle that
corded his chest and below. The collar of his buff greatcoat moved
idly in the wind from the sea.

Without taking his eyes from her own frightened ones he said,
"She saw you, so she has to die. I agree." He bent and pushed the
skiff out from the beach. She felt it break free from the sand and slip
into the water; his legs moved slowly against the waves. "I'll take
care of it. I told you I would, and I will. But you two had better be
far away from here when they find the body."

There was a shout from the beach. "You're not just keeping her
for yourself, are you?" shouted Jack. "We want to hear her hit the
water."

The sail flapped as Cat took the sheets, and he swore under his
breath at the shouting and shouted back to them over his shoulder,
his braid streaming behind him. "You'll get your splash. Now get
the hell out of here."

The dirty cambric nightdress was no protection against the cold
wind that dug like nails into Merry's skin. Tremors began in her
chest and rolled violently into her limbs, where the stiff wires of the
jute ropes were methodically gnawing the living flesh from her
ankles and her wrists, and her hair became fouled by the sloshing
bilge water.

Indifferent as a stone, Cat was working the sail, and after a time
there was the rhythmic slap of the bow against the waves as the
small craft made the open water. Settling back, the boy looked at her
and said in an abrupt way, "I can't help it. You'll have to go in."

Her resolution not to cry was broken as she begged behind her
gag, tears running down her cheeks, choking her. A whimper tore
from her throat, savage in its desolation. Cat hesitated for the space
of a heartbeat and then said, "Relax. What's a little seawater?"

He let go the sheets, leaving the sails to luff under the punch of
the wind. Bracing the tiller with his knee, the pirate reached for her
arm.

Her brain flaring with terror, she fought him in a pathetic way, twisting and squirming like a trapped mink into the rocking bow. The boy watched her, allowing patiently her futile moment of resistance before drawing her out and into his arms. One strong and fluidly muscled arm curved tightly around her shoulders while the other caught her under the knees and spun her over the side with a splash.

The water was green and foamy and arctically cold. It rapidly discovered the raw spaces of her body: where she had been struck on the head, where the ropes had flayed open her skin, and where, in being moved and carried and packed, thoughtless hands had scraped her many times against wood and metal. Half fainting from pain, she thought how it was said the drowning could view their whole life, flashed before them like a poor man's panorama, but all she could see was her wet, stinging hair that lashed her eyes, and all she could think of was the horrible thing that Henry Cork had told her once— that drowning victims are found with their lips drawn back over their teeth in a silent scream, only the effect of water on the facial muscles. Drowning was supposedly a pleasant death really, once one ceased to struggle.

Something cold and living brushed her cheekbone, and in a torrent of hysterical sensation she recognized the taut sinews of Cat's arm. He had not released her. Perhaps she was to be held under the water in the unflinching compassion of his arms until he was quite sure that she was totally dead. The last scattered drops of her reason evaporated, and she began to thrash wildly, her legs arching against the water, her arms knocking low fountains of seawater into the wind.

"That," said Cat's voice close to her ear, "will draw sharks. And they might hear you on the beach. Feel this?" An arm, hooked under her arms, tightened. "I'm not going to let you go. Just cooperate."

By the time he pulled her back into the skiff, Merry was crying stormily. She was dumped without ceremony again onto the spongy dampness of the bilge.

"I wish you'd stop wiggling," he told her. "I don't want to spend what's left of the day pulling splinters out of you."

Peeling off his greatcoat, he joined her where she lay and wrapped it around her; although it was wet on the outside from the ocean spray, it was warm inside where it had been against his body. Somewhere in the coat he found a handkerchief and made her blow her nose on it, and then he lifted the heavy tangled wool of her hair and, dragging it between his hands, wrung from it most of the alkaline seawater. Perhaps in his profession he saw a lot of crying women; anyway he made no reference during his ministrations to the convulsive, effortful sobs that racked her, and finally he sat back and took the tiller again.

The sea slapped beneath the bow as the small craft sliced through the fog. The minutes flew at Merry too quickly for her to guess when one left off and the next began. They came to a place where the fog shimmered like a fine clear powder, and ahead of the skiff a heaving mountain reared from the ocean. On its back rode the great triple spires of the masts; far below the skiff passed, tiny and bouncing like a waterbug, under the gargoyle figurehead with its pointed ears, opaque goiterous eyes, and red tongue, thrust out and drooling condensed moisture. Merry tried to sit up, staring, but a long thin foot, bare of covering, met her chest and pushed her quickly back to the floor.

"Down!" he said. "Or can you swim with your hands tied? If we capsize, I'd never find you. The water's too dark."

Merry heard a hallooing from the watch, and an answering shout from Cat. A rope came spinning down, and Cat made it fast and began to uncleat the halyards at the base of the mast.

A youth of about eighteen years let himself quickly down the rope, hand over hand, staring with blossoming interest at Merry through sable eyes set in warm, sun-honeyed skin. His hair was long and very dark, pulled back under a large red bandanna knotted on one side of his head.

"Cat, are you crazy?" he said. "Or don't you notice she's a woman?"

"Little though you may credit it, I *can* tell the sexes apart," snapped the boy, catching the luffing sails as they fell.

"Morgan's gonna wring your neck, mon. There's not a pirate ship from Maine to Christi that'll take a woman on board. Even Blackbeard—"

"Plague rot it! Will you quit the Blackbeard lore? It's most of it a bunch of cock and bull. No women on board. *I* could tell you some stories . . .'' Cat glanced at the other boy's eager face and said sourly, "But I won't. Why don't you do something constructive like lifting in the rudder?''

Ignoring him, the boy with the red bandanna dropped to his knees beside Merry's shivering form and gently lifted a wet curl from her nose. "Mon, she's got pretty eyes—like blue glass in a church window. And her body?''

"Is covered with gooseflesh and bleeding saltwater from every pore," Cat said, flipping his braid irritably out of the way as he expertly coiled a rope.

"So? She looks half-dead. What's she been doing all morning, dancing a blanket hornpipe?''

"No. But almost. And not with me. Look, you lazy sucker. See that nothing of an apple barrel behind you? Very good. Put it where His Lordship can get a look at it, will you, and with care, please. If it falls in the water, it'll be *your* neck that gets wrung.''

The boy gave Cat a grin with a gold tooth in it. "If you're so worried about the barrel, you bring it. I'll take care of Blue Eyes.''

"Fine. And then you can be the one who explains her to Morgan. No? I *thought* that would change your mind. And one of the side stays is loose, if you've got time . . .''

Frigid and terrified, and unable, it seemed, to control the tears making ceaseless icy streaks down her cheeks, Merry discovered what a singularly painful exercise it is to be carried over a man's shoulder like a sack of meal. Establishing her there with no attention to her comfort, Cat climbed the rope ladder, and with each jarring step his hard-boned shoulder jammed into her midriff, forcing gasps of agony from her that vanished into the choking folds of her gag. Her vision spun as she looked straight down into the boiling sea, where it dashed against the side of the ship, and saw the skiff shrink as they climbed.

Her hair was too much snarled in her face for her to see anything once they reached the deck, but she could hear the vibration of footsteps, and voices. Heedless of them, the young pirate carried her toward the stern and then ducked and took her down a flight of steps, to halt before a doorway. He knocked once, pushed it open with his foot, and brought her inside.

She had never seen a room as exotically luxurious as this one, let alone a ship's cabin. On three sides massive windows of wavy, diamond-shaped glass let in scattered light, but no vision beyond a gray impression of the heaving, watery horizon. A Persian carpet of the Fereghan type spread over the floor, a massive flowing field of madder red, its delicate pattern etched in densely saturated yellow and blue: two hundred and fifty Persian knots to the square inch, if anyone cared to count. Beneath the far window a beautifully carved line of bench seats were heaped with pillows in rich brocades of red and black, twisted with embroidered gold flowers. Not the smallest scratch or smear marred the high shine of the Chinese lacquered tables, Ming dynasty, or the intricate pictorial marquetry of the Belgian writing desk. The chairs were draped in ebony lambskin, catching copper glints from tiny flame tongues that licked the air behind saffron globes of Bohemian glass.

Gleaming deeply on one wall were Russian icons, sucking room light into their amazingly brilliant colors, and underneath them a bed with a perimeter as big as a stone tool house was hidden under a blanket of Siberian crown sable.

Cat dropped her on the bed's blue-black fur, where she lay, rigid and weeping in her bonds. Taking a stiletto from his belt, and ignoring her horrified eyes, he brought the knife to her throat and paused before using it to rip down the fabric of her soaked nightdress, freeing it from her body; and she lay naked before him, shaking furiously.

His cold eyes traveled over her, but with indifference, not with the prurience of one to whom such things were a mystery, and then he reached behind him, grabbed a square of cloth, and rubbed her limbs vigorously, not touching her intimately but not taking pains to avoid doing so either; and then he brought a blanket and covered her with it, tucking it efficiently around her, his long braid falling against her cheek.

The door opened, and Rand Morgan entered, stooping as he came in. A dark olive and buttonless coat with gold facings that had some time ago belonged to one of Napoleon's *garde d'honneur* casually encased the pirate captain's wide shoulders, and the huge emerald flickered erratically from the soft inky curls on his chest. The deep black eyes looked at Cat questioningly, and then at her; the granite face was as frightening in its seeming omniscience as she had remem-

bered it from the tavern. He spoke, the tone spiced lightly with
pleasant sarcasm.

"Dear me. Shall I come back later?"

"Don't be funny," replied Cat irritably. "I'm drying her off."
He reached back into the lacquered chest bolted to the wall behind
him, brought out a towel, and used it to dry Merry's hair.

Morgan's imperturbable gaze followed the youth's quick movements. "Why is she wet? And if one is permitted to ask, who is she?
Or were you going to wait until Christmas and surprise me?"

The self-assured, accurate movements in her hair stilled as the boy
looked up at Morgan. "I knew you wouldn't like it."

Morgan's eyes wandered, more slowly than Cat's had done, over
her form as she shivered beneath the blanket, and he said dryly,
"That doesn't seem to have been much of a deterrent. But you were
about to tell me who she is, weren't you? Don't mind me. I'm going
to smoke."

Morgan lowered his long-shafted limbs into a lambskin chair.
Beside him was a vertical tower the length of a man's arm with
many bulb-shaped chambers made from silver and blown glass
painted with floral decorations. A small brasier glowed red in the
footed conical base, and into it Morgan dropped a dark-brown
substance that looked like an oily rock as Cat brought a handkerchief
to her pinkened nose.

"You're the wettest wench I ever saw," he said disgustedly. "If
you'd stop crying for a minute . . ."

Merry could see Morgan's lips quirk at the corners. From the base
of the chambered tower he uncoiled a woven tube tipped with a
steaming ivory mouthpiece, which he laid backhanded between his
lips. Inhaling, he stretched out his legs contentedly; as he slowly
exhaled, a dense and billowing smoke scattered around him. Its
odor was sharp, rich, and cloying, and faintly tinged with roses.
Merry was an American girl and knew tobacco in all its incarnations:
smoked and chewed, growing in fields and at harvest, hanging in
storage and sold in shops, and *this*—whatever else it was, it was not
tobacco. Morgan closed his eyes, the thick lashes drooping, and
smiled slowly.

" 'Divine in hookas, glorious in a pipe,' " he said. "Speak."

Cat left her, and she felt pressure near her feet as he sat on the foot of the bed. "You know those papers Devon wanted?"

At the mention of the name Merry's heart pounded in her chest and then slowed.

"You had hired someone, hadn't you, to steal them for him," drawled Morgan. "Don't take too long coming to the point, babe; I may fall asleep by the time you get there."

"Give me a chance." He leaned over and tucked the blanket around Merry's feet. "When they got to the *Guinevere*, Granville was on deck, so they thought it would be all right. They didn't realize until they got in there that he had left a woman in his bed."

Morgan leaned back, took another drag, and murmured, "Slovenly bastard."

"I thought so," said Cat. "You would think he'd have put her out by then, especially since the *Guinevere* was to sail in the morning. Idiotically they let her see them."

Morgan opened one eye. "Then why isn't she dead?"

"Fear of the hangman," said Cat, "and minds set on ruttery. They brought her to me gagged and bound in an apple barrel. Devon, incidentally, will get his papers."

"I'm delighted, of course," Morgan said and leaned back, dragging deeply on the pipe. The blue smoke swirled around his black curls, making fantastic red-tinged shapes in the light of the candles. "Cat, I really am getting tired of asking you this question. Why isn't she dead?"

There was a short unfriendly silence that Merry spent shaking like a fiddle string before Morgan said, "The tenderhearted boy-child hated to drown the stray kitten, so he brought it home and hid it under his bed? What do you intend to do when she starts to mew?"

This second silence was kinder. Then Cat said, "Once you told me that trouble was the only thing that made your life interesting."

"Did I? How rash of me." Morgan drew another long inhalation. When it was finished, he said, "You should take her gag off. She can barely breathe."

"If I do, she'll start complaining. You know," the boy said, "women have an excessive regard for their comfort."

"Nevertheless." Morgan got up slowly and walked to the bed and sat down beside her; she could feel his rock-hard thigh next to her shoulder.

Seawater had fussed the knots of her gag into a sticky mat. Morgan's fingers tried them, gave up, and again Merry had to endure a knife, mercifully quick.

"Let's have a look at you," he said, pulling free the filthy strip of sodden gauze that had bound her mouth, "miserable, bedraggled little bird that you are."

She was no closer to talking now than she had been, with her skinned and swollen tongue and paralyzed jaw, and Morgan, understanding it, rubbed her chapped face lightly, teasing back the blood into her starving veins. The sudden glut of air in her throat made swallowing almost a torture.

He watched her with black shining eyes that held neither pity nor malice, and she could tell to the second when he knew her. The pirate captain's lazy eyelids opened, just a trifle, and a slow grin spread over the sharp line of his mouth.

"Cat, bring me some wine." Lifting her head on the slope of his arm, Morgan put a blue wineglass to her lips and, when she had finished, cleaned the clumsy failed drops from her chin. "Well, well. I should have recognized you, if only from the hair. But then, it was damp."

If it needed one thing only to make her situation worse, it would be for them to connect her and her night at the tavern with certain highly detailed portraits on placards, advertising rewards for Morgan's capture, and Cat's. But even if they knew about the posters, they could never trace them to her, *could they?*

Cat took away the cup. "Don't tell me you know her?"

"Devon's little friend," said Morgan with simplicity.

"You don't say?" There was a barely perceptible note of interest in the boy's voice. "Which one of the multitude is she? You know I can't keep them apart. Except for the one in Nassau who gives the great—"

Morgan interrupted. "This one doesn't give anything. She miscarries five-pound bundles of joy and straw at your feet. You remember the night we hunted, at the Musket and Muskrat? August, I think?"

"Damn! I believe you're right!" Cat said, putting a palm to her cheek. "He let her go, didn't he? And was in the devil's own temper for three days after. How in God's peach-green grass do you think she got from there to New York and into you-know-who's bed? Unless . . .'' There was an exchange of glances for which Merry did not greatly care. "That changes things, doesn't it?"

"It changes things," said Morgan, "a lot. Put her in Devon's room."

"No!" The words struggled out through the inflamed fibers of Merry's mouth. "Don't do that!"

"Be quiet, my child, or I'll throttle you," Morgan said, cupping her throat with a blunt, calloused hand. As she lay still and vanquished his hand traveled down to part the blanket, and his black eyes conducted a quick dispassionate study of her wrists. "What a waste of good skin. Your friends were a little crude with the ropes, Cat. You ought to give them lessons."

"I'll retie her wrists with something less abrasive. Given time."

"No. Even you can't work miracles, and she's damaged enough as it is. She won't need ropes if we use the pipe on her." Morgan glanced at her face. "Silly chit. Don't start crying again. I'm not proposing to hit you over the head with it."

The pirate captain took something long and white from a drawer and handed it to Cat. "Put this on her when you move her. If any of the crew sees what she's got, we're likely to have a riot on our hands."

Merry heard her lips break open and spill out a futile and meaningless patter of pleas as Morgan rekindled the glass and silver instrument and carried it toward her.

In steady arms Cat lifted Merry from the bed and settled her against his chest with her cheek pressing the smooth quilt of his braid, his hand curled around her naked shoulder where the blanket had fallen. Merry's protests continued without a pause as she said everything she could think of to try to make them stop and let her go. Morgan looked at her from time to time as he worked the hookah's stem into an inlaid bowl; but he did not threaten her again, having assessed, perhaps, that she had passed beyond being able to control herself, and in a minute it would cease to matter. He brought the bowl down on her nose and mouth. She refused to inhale at first, but Morgan gave her an expertly controlled slap on the cheek and said, "Breathe it."

She breathed involuntarily from the sudden pain and got a sweet, heavy lungful that cut like rake teeth in the lining of her bronchia. Above her Cat said softly, "Give her time, Rand. You can see that she's unaccustomed."

After a moment Morgan took the bowl from her and let her breathe air and then brought it back, and she heard his voice, from far away, saying, "Don't fight it, nestling. When you stop pushing it away, I'll know you've had enough."

CHAPTER EIGHT

The room where Cat left her was Spartan and dustless. He had tucked her into a warm, sweet-smelling bed with many soft blankets and had given her some water and food she hardly knew she was eating and had advised her to, for God's sake, try to stop acting like a fool. He asked her if she thought she could get up, and when she tried and could not, he said "Good," retucked the blankets, and left the room. She had a very long time to look about her and to think pale, shifting thoughts that bunched through her mind like sand bottlenecked in an hourglass, to fall, sinking and glittering, around her. It was sweet luxury to have her wrists and ankles unbound. But if one person ever again brought a knife close to her, to remove a bond or a shred of clothing, or for any other benevolent purpose, she'd be sick on the floor. She giggled, but there was a sleeping part of her mind that knew it was the drug that made her see humor in the situation; her surroundings merited only tears. However, she was dry now, and empty and floating, and tears were something that had happened when—fifteen minutes ago, three hours ago?—whenever it was that she had felt pain.

She snuggled down into the lawn shirt she had been given. It smelled good, as though it had been rinsed in something pleasing, and she whistled to see if her dry lips could work that way. They could not.

Devon's room. Devon. If this was indeed his room, there was no stamp of his personality upon it. Or perhaps there was: precision, lack of clutter; evidence of an orderly mind, the ability to minimize distractions. She had never thought to see him again, and now it seemed as though she might. It was the last extraordinary, excruciating jolt to four extraordinary, excruciating days. What, in an upbringing of painting root vegetables in watercolors and tapping sugar maples, was there to prepare her for men with hookahs and hoop earrings? Again she giggled and helplessly began to think of Devon.

She remembered his arms, gathering her for the kiss, the kiss she had not wanted and had been so unprepared for, the kiss she had forced herself to forget. . . . If her father could see her now, he'd have a fit.

Suddenly she stopped giggling and began rather desperately to fight the opium-induced stupor. She didn't know the right thing to do; but then a wandering thread of her mind recalled something told to her by Betty, her aunt's maid, who liked to take brandy in the mornings. If you took too much, she said, it helped to think of something dreadful, really awful, to bring your mind into a more stable orbit. So Merry lay in the pirate's bed and thought of her mother's funeral.

The funeral had been at night, and they had arranged Merry's hair with huge black bows that reminded her of bat's wings. She vividly remembered the harsh feel of the stiff black dress she had worn, made by the hastily summoned dressmaker. And on her feet the tiny white kid slippers she had been so proud of, ruined with blacking. They had draped mirrors and pictures with black, even the one in her bedroom of the laughing-ladybird picnic; and placed scutcheons in every room, hung the front of the house with a hatchment, and tied the window shutters closed with dull black silk and left them that way all winter. Her father had given away mourning rings, mourning the price, and hers had been too big for her small finger and had flopped back and forth. She had pressed it tightly into her palm so she wouldn't lose it and displease her father. Carl had taught her painstakingly to read the ring's motto: Prepared be, to follow me. But the worst had come that night after the funeral—that tedious and confusing church service when they had tried to make her get into her bed, made neat as a thread box with black sheets.

Merry sat up suddenly, sweating and shaking, and the ship's room came into focus. She experienced a flash of eager relief, like some-one waking from a nightmare. They were right when they said that funerals were to help the living.

Setting her feet carefully on the floor, she stood up, experimen-tally testing the strength of her numb-feeling knees—knees that collapsed as soon as they bore her full weight, sending her to the floor, flat on her face. One did not so easily snap one's fingers at opium intoxication, it seemed. She tried again to stand, this time quickly, clinging hard to the brass handles of a long desk set into the wall. She was up and swaying victoriously, slowly regaining her equilibrium.

The door, as she found when she reached it, was locked. And what good would it have done anyway to go out there? They would only easily reimprison her. And then there would be more ropes.

Still, it would be better to do something desperate than to do nothing at all. But she couldn't even think of something desperate to do, until she realized that the thing on the wall she was staring at, an ancient t-shaped instrument made of worn wood and twisted leather, was a weapon. It took a very long time for her to get it down, and a longer time yet to figure out what she would have to do to fire it so that the arrow didn't shoot backward, or flop out sideways onto the floor. The barbed point of the arrow was huge; it couldn't have been covered with a large orange, and really, the whole thing was ridiculous, but what other choice had she? It shamed her to think how she had cried, "No, no, please," to Morgan, like a child having a tooth drawn. The next man who walked through the door and tried to lay hands on her was going to wear her arrow in his breastbone.

Fortune, they say, loves a challenge. The lock turned in the door, and Devon stepped inside carrying a lamp.

"This is wonderful," he said, his gaze resting lightly on the weapon aiming straight for his heart. "You must be feeling much better."

With interest he watched her fragile hands tighten on the crossbow. His eyes picked out details—the fall of red-gold hair in a thick tumble over her shoulder, the full breasts only partially hidden by the overlarge shirt, the shapely leg she had braced before her, the beautiful flush spreading in her cheeks, the finely arched auburn brows, and the murder in the lovely deep-blue eyes. Morgan evidently had pushed her too far. For a minute Devon speculated on the pirate captain's motives while he sent his trained gaze over the girl a second time to find those things that only intuition could see: the complex emotions that trembled like tiny stars under the shadowed surface of her face.

By far she was not the first woman who had waited for him in a bedchamber, or even—fair though she was—the most beautiful, but she surely was the only one to distinguish herself by facing him with an antique weapon, obsolete by three centuries. Someone long before him had, for a prank, bolted the thing in this small cabin. The men who sailed the *Black Joke* had grown, with time, so indifferent to its presence that no one had bothered to rip it down and burn it. Common sense could never have predicted that this weakly, flushing girl could have pried it from the wall and made it ready. Good Lord, it was designed to be bent and cocked by a chain-mailed soldier standing on the bow with feet on the stock and drawing up the cord with both arms and the back. Here clearly was a woman who bypassed common sense.

There were a hundred ways, possibly more, that he could have quickly taken the bow from her, but none that would not involve her in some way with either pain or violence, however transient. Morgan, he knew, would think he was crazy not to disarm her immediately. After all, a bolt from that bow could penetrate the bulwark of a warship. . . .

"Will it make you nervous if I set the lamp on the desk," he said, "or do you want me to stand here like Diogenes? I'll do it very slowly, and don't worry, I never throw lamps at young ladies holding crossbows. Not in cabins that lie over a powder magazine." He carefully put the lamp down and smiled at her reassuringly. "Before you tack me to the wall, do I get a last meal and twenty minutes with my confessor?"

"I'll have to think about it. That's more than *I* was offered." She hadn't forgotten his particular brand of extreme good looks, but only vaguely had she retained a memory of its effect on her. Every organ from her throat to her kneecaps started to buzz like a cricket.

"From what I've heard," he said, "it's been nasty. Why don't you surrender the military hardware and let me see what I can do to make amends?"

Who could have told him that it had been nasty? Rand Morgan? Cat? It was difficult, somehow, to imagine a conversation between them about her. Why had it taken him so long to come to her? Not that he had reason to be eager. Had he been on shore? Perhaps. He was not dressed in a sailor's garb. The pirate's clothing was American and discreetly prosperous. The bone-colored coat, the white shirt with front frill and cravat, the natural leather trousers—it was a costume that her brother might have worn, though no other man could have given it what Devon did—which was Devon's body. How amazing he was. The marvelous perfection of his features had not robbed them of intellect or made them less subtly expressive.

She hadn't been close to him before in good light. For the first time she saw that his eyes were hazel, a rare mosaic of shining sparks that appeared almost golden. They were delivering a message of sympathy tidily packed in sensual glamour. *If he's to be trusted*, she thought, *I'll eat Aunt April's swansdown muff*. Merry destroyed the tiny voice in her brain that dissented with a savage mental kick.

"If you take one step closer," she told him, "I'm going to kill you."

The golden eyes studied her kindly. "You look tired. You sit down; I'll sit down; and we'll talk about it."

After some suspicious thought she decided that it might be a good idea to have him sitting. She wouldn't dare do so herself because the chances favored her not being able to get up afterward. *Details, Merry Patricia, apply your mind to the details*.

"Where's the key to the door?" asked Merry Patricia, trying to straighten her shoulders.

"Do you want to lock us in here together? I'm game, if a little shocked."

The man was enjoying himself too much. She was forced to repeat, this time more crisply, "Where's the key?"

"Outside. I'll be happy to get it if you—"

"No! Wedge that chair under the door handle. And then sit on the desk. Slowly."

Looking amused, he obeyed her. "For the charming lady with the harpoon, anything." He poised himself, as ordered, on the edge of the desk. "Here I sit, ready on the second to be skewered like a bottle-fly on a hatpin. When you think of it, I'll be a pretty unappealing corpse." Easing his elbows onto the shelf behind him, Devon grinned. "Now that I'm your prisoner, what do you intend to do with me? Or, if you haven't figured that out yet, would you be open to suggestions?"

She *had* figured it out in the long, feverish wait when she had achingly mated bolt and crossbow. "I wish to leave alone and unmolested in the small boat that I was brought here in."

"Can you sail it?"

"Yes," she lied—not that it was any of his concern. She knew it wouldn't be easy just because Cat had make it look that way, but then, it hadn't been easy to prime the bow either. It was all academic, anyway, because she had no other choice. Her gaze dropped and accidentally fixed on his elegant hand resting loose in the small flower of lamplight, and as she watched, it seemed to recede from her and return; the opium reminding her that it was still active in her system.

"We've been bearing east under full sail for three hours," he said. "How are you at navigation in the open sea?"

The hostage hours had blurred into one another, anonymous as a line of smashed pumpkins. Reorienting her scrambled senses, Merry decided that yes, the ship could be moving; but was the beautiful man before her lying through his straight white teeth about the ship's direction and how long she'd been on course? Some time ago she'd had an impression of nightfall. If it was night, then one could use the stars for direction, couldn't one? Unless there was fog. And today, at least, there had been fog. And if the night was clear, what could she do? Distinguish, if she could, the North Star, turn left, and pray that she'd eventually run into the Atlantic seaboard. She began to think of sharks and giant squid and whales and sea serpents and giant whirlpools. You couldn't believe everything you heard; much of it was probably tall tales, though, of course, there really were sharks. And squid. And whales. And other pirates.

Through fading hope and clouding vision she said, "Then they'll have to turn this ship around and bring it back toward shore."

His amusement was a thing felt, not seen. "My dear child, if you want to ask Morgan to turn the ship around, then I'll happily hold open the door for you. But if you think he's going to do it, you're dreaming. I don't blame you for trying; I'd do the same myself. The effort was fine. It's just not going to work."

"The more I think about it," she said with flaming blue eyes, "the more convinced I am that I ought to shoot you."

"Aim carefully then. It wouldn't surprise me if that was the only crossbow arrow between here and Europe."

Her arms were beginning to shiver from the bow's tearing weight. The point sagged toward the floor and was swiftly righted. It was only a matter of time before her brawnless muscles failed altogether. She estimated that she had less than five minutes to convince him that she really would do it. "By the time anyone on board discovered your death, they might have missed me on the *Guinevere*. They might be following us right now, to rescue me!"

"Probably you aren't familiar with the *Mactervish Book About the Sea for Boys*. Lesson Roman numeral one: Ship at sail leaves no trail." He lifted his hands and resettled them, heels down and fingers bent, on the desk's oak edge. Whatever he was planning to do to her was hidden from Merry behind the sugared surface of his gaze and the little smile, so warm and subtle that you could have made comfits from it and fed every widow in St. Anne's parish.

"Mary—that *is* your name, isn't it? Mary, put it down. I don't want to hurt you."

It was clearly a threat, however courteously posed. The best she could do with it was to respond as though she hadn't understood and smother her surprise that he had captured her name and retained it through the months.

"You don't want to—? I don't believe it!" she said. "If it suited you, you'd crush me in a minute. I might be a—a codfish, for all you care."

"Now we're getting somewhere. A nautical metaphor! By next week Tuesday you'll probably have learned how to stay on your feet during a ground swell. There's one coming, my dear. One learns to feel these things."

For a moment she thought it was a trick to throw her off guard. There was a long creaking pause, the sense of being suspended, and then the floor dove suddenly to the right as the ship plunged, nimble and swooping, down the side of the wave into the trough.

The bow slipped from her hands and discharged the bolt, sending it humming across the room like a flushed pigeon, to end with a cracking explosion as it ripped through a five-inch beam of solid hardwood, the shaft whipping noisily to and fro before its motion died in a dull vibration.

No doubt the noise was heard from poop to fo'c'sle. Ears tuned to the murmurings of the ship would trace the sound to its source, and Devon had to grin a little thinking of the ribald speculation it would probably cause in the crew's quarters. It was the kindest way it could have happened, but he could hardly expect the girl to realize that. She was staring at him, infuriated and frightened. Without moving Devon said calmly, "It's just as well. If you had killed me, I'm afraid Morgan would have tossed you on deck for the crew, and after they were done with you, there wouldn't have been enough left to feed the fish."

Below her lacerated wrists, Merry's hands tightened into fists. "I don't care what you say! I have the right to defend my virtue."

"I don't think Morgan would think that was a very good excuse. An unaccountable difference in attitude. You may have noticed," he said dryly, "that Morgan isn't particularly enamoured with virtue. But I'm curious. Did you learn all these high-minded sentiments in Granville's arms?"

After everything, she had to repeat the name before she remembered. "Granville?" Things were coming too thick and fast for her half-sleeping brain.

"I hear you made an unwise choice in your sleeping arrangements last night," said Devon, letting himself slowly off the desk. "I'm sure Michael is crisp and cozy in bed, but who was looking after the puppets?"

Merry's white cheeks turned scarlet. "I wasn't in bed with Sir Michael. I was in Sir Michael's bed."

"I believe we could make a nursery rhyme out of that. It has a certain cadence. . . . I didn't mean to start a quibble."

A tremor of exhaustion shook her, and a lock of red-gold hair fell forward, gleaming across her cheek. "I've been beaten, drugged, thrown in the ocean, stripped at knife point, and trussed like a Thanksgiving goose. You had better think again if you think I'm going to stand here and listen to your litany of insults!"

"Poor child," he said. "Let's end it then. Go back to bed, and I'll get you something to eat. The rest can wait until tomorrow morning." It was unfortunate that she was too distraught to realize that the flash of compassion in his eyes was genuine.

"I haven't an arrow anymore," she said, "but if you touch me, I swear I'll scratch your eyes out."

He stood very still, gazing at her through the gemmed eyes. "What do you expect me to do, let you jump over the side? Not *yet*. I'm not finished with you."

"I'll die first!"

"You," said Devon, "must have execrable taste in literature. So we're back to your holy virtue, are we? I see. You think my hot blood can't support ten minutes alone with you. You're passing fair, my conceited love, but what makes you so certain I have the ambition to lie with every pretty wench I kiss when I'm drunk?" From one of Michael Granville's creatures it was what he would expect, the obligatory show of reluctance that would vanish later as she gave herself to him like a supplicant with all those hideously pretty body tricks that Michael's ladies were expert in. Michael Granville, with Satan sleeping behind the thoughtful gray eyes; Michael had sent him women before.

This one was different because she had been taken, not offered. There was something so touchingly real about the girl's resistance that it made him wonder if she was in love with Granville. If that was true, it would be vengeance in gilt to send her back raped. Even as he framed the thought his gaze fell on her, and as much as he hated the master, he wondered how much harm he would be willing to do through this poor frail vassal with the lily skin and hair richer than a sable pelt. Incredibly it seemed as though his last words had confused her more than they angered her, almost as though she hadn't understood his meaning. But then, she was young, and her resources had nearly reached their limit. Coming to her with a noiseless stride he was just in time to catch her in his arms as her knees buckled under a powerful wash of dizziness.

He caught her up, supporting her, and she leaned against him, her will suspended. She wasn't heavy for him, but she was solid, and as she leaned into him he was very much aware of her physicality; the feel of her shoulders and back, the heavy softness of her breasts against his chest, her thighs against his, the gently rounded belly against him, and the cloud of golden hair, which, as he held her, seemed to rise in his vision like a fragrant amber mist. He delicately took a handful of it and touched it to his lips.

Softly he said, "Scented of opium and roses and wintergreen."

"Wintergreen?"

"From Morgan's nightshirt, bless his foppish heart," he said. "I'm sorry they hurt you."

She forced herself to look into his eyes. "Please let me go. Please."

"Love, I can't." He brought his hand to tilt her face, his broad palm at the base of her throat; his lips were warm and dry on hers, and a few strands of her hair were caught as stinging silk in the kiss. His arm tightened her to his body, as, on her face, his thumb drifted lightly over her cheekbone, then moved to her lips and, with gentle pressure, urged them open. The blood began to pound in her throat under the exploration of his lips and fingers.

"You kiss," he said softly into her curls, "as though each time were your first." He lifted his hands to her shoulders, feeling their soft graceful swell beneath his palms. She turned her face away, her lips throbbing, not wanting him to see as she slipped her tongue over them, trying to soothe the unfamiliar sensations she felt there.

"You've had your revenge," she whispered. "Now let me go."

"No, my dear, no. Let us see if we can make your body turn traitor. Kiss me again, and you can tell me afterward if it was worse than dying."

She kept her face away and pressed her hands against his chest. He turned her head and forced his mouth onto hers; the pressure of his hand and the searching of his lips were too great for her to resist, and their lips clung together, contact breaking, meeting, breaking. Her lips, burning and aching, needed to be soothed by a respite, and soothed again by the smooth touching of their like. Her hands opened and closed on his shirt front; her blood moved thin and hot, a molten flow through her veins. Intently he concentrated, feeling the warmth of her under his mouth, leaving her lips to touch on her warm forehead, and to taste the tears that shimmered on her long lashes, and then to return, plunging once more to dominate her lips. "Let us see," he had said, "if we can make your body turn traitor."

But there are times when, even though sick and driven, the mind is stronger. Her will forced her hands into fists, and she pummeled his chest until with quiet laughter he caught both her wrists in the grip of one hand and brought her knuckles to his lips, biting them gently.

She gasped. "I wish the arrow had pierced your black heart instead of innocent timber. And I wish you'd leave me alone."

"Oh, Lord—these challenges. It's too late for games, sweet child. Give me your mouth." And he took it again under his own, one hand at the back of her head, holding her still; and let the other ride her slowly. His sensitive fingers discovered the warmth of her below the rich linen fabric where the hidden skin lay, as fresh and finely textured as if it were made with the felting of a thousand cherry petals. It was an exercise in good manners to control one's breathing while one could, and though that small discipline had been always automatic and detached for him, he noted that the silent passage of air through his lungs was less than regular. It was rare for that to happen so quickly. The postponed reckoning from that absurdly trifling encounter in the wood wagon seemed to have heightened the desire that had, in honesty, been strong from its birth.

His palm tested the contour of her waist, as tight and narrow as a boy's, and the climb of her delicately voluptuous hips. He spread his fingers, luxuriating in the feel of her where from blood and bone and muscle had been sculpted a softness so rich he could taste it through his finger pads.

Merry cried out when his palm slid to softly cup the underside of her breast. It was shocking and queerly embarrassing, and very low down, below the pit of her stomach, her organs began to tighten into a hard laced ball that seemed to want to writhe and grow until somehow he would know how to bring her to ease. Never would she have suspected it would be so deliriously pleasant to have a man's hand on that part of her body. His knowledgeable fingers moved, discovering the things that made the blood work harder through her

veins. By the series of sharp little intakes of her breath, he knew
when he found the right motion, but the combined pleasure and
horror of it gave her the strength to beat again at his chest and
protest.

"Dainty flower," he murmured. "You see—we don't have to
hurt each other." He gently showed her his intention, his palm
traveling in a slowly hot circle, letting the balm of it penetrate
deeply into her drugged tissues.

It was too powerful for her, much too powerful, and she ripped
herself from his arms like a cloth torn in two. She began to back
away, shaking her head and choking on the nerve-storming frustration of having nothing articulate to say in self-defense. How in
heaven's name did one talk a man out of these things? Her brain,
reeling with opium and too-new eroticism, seemed to be jumping up
and down inside her skull like a March hare; her eyes felt like a pair
of wet, enormous puddles that might at any minute choose to flow
out of her head. It had been bad enough to cry in front of Cat; she
would rather die of a rat's bite than shed a single tear for Devon,
though God knew she was the world's worst imbecile to have it
matter.

Passion sharpens the features of most men; it was not so with
Devon. The vivacious bones in his face had relaxed into something
tender and unhurried that had not a thing to do with the driving stab
of his appetite. Bright was his hair, and his eyes had a humanity that
a saint would have envied, but *Oh, Miss Wilding,* she told herself,
watch his hands. With each unsteady pop of her heartbeat she could
feel herself growing weaker. *"You've never been strong, Merry
Patricia . . . ."* This time Merry Patricia would struggle to the end.
*If there's some way you can help me, Lord, then please do it. I'm
nearly out of ideas.*

There was a crumble in the muscles that held up her knees, and
she had to have help standing. Searching behind, her hands found a
table edge, and she clung to it in the twining seconds before the ship
lurched, or maybe the drug did in her damming blood, and she flew
backward toward the table's dark-grained plane. His arms were
around her then, under her shoulders, cradling her head as he gently
laid her on the table, her hair cascading onto the surface like spilled
gold dust. Now there was no turning away from him; the tabletop

was hard below her—but there was the mitigating warmth of his hands, cushioning her. Slowly he brought one hand up and, with the backs of his fingers, brushed aside the shirt, gently tearing the buttons free, letting one fair milky breast fall free and untrammeled. There was a brush of moving air against her bare skin before his hand found her. She took in a spare breath as his palm rotated lightly as a feather over the umber and coral tip of one breast, and then he nested its softness, his fingers sweeping her with their masseur's caress. Her betraying blood rushed to meet his fingers, and her body seemed to be manufacturing unknown serums that were heating and steaming into its every cell. Her chest was becoming so full of them that she felt she could almost have smothered had he not pressed his lips down on hers in a hard exploring kiss, where they shared in a deep urgent communion each sweet liquid, each searing molecule of oxygen. It was like drinking fire; it was like being brushed by a star; it was like hurtling through air as soft and thick and fluid as heated nectar. His intoxicated lips, honeyed still from the moisture of her kiss, made a lazy journey to her breast, resting there to coax the exquisite peak with his tongue, his tender probing forcing her to gasp for air as though her lungs were starving, the rise of her breasts fitting them more snugly against the quest of his lips.

Minutes had passed since Devon had been able to think about anything more than his need to bury himself within this charming opiated creature, with her enamel-blue eyes and velvet skin. Delighting in a desire that had not been so vivid for many years, he was slow to realize that her bare shivering legs were doing their best to shove him away. He pressed a broad palm to her thigh, and while the feel of it was enough to make his head swim, he was able, with kindness, to still the pace of her foolish struggles.

"Remind me tomorrow," he told her, "to teach you the best place to kick a man."

Her open senses burned under the sting of his amusement. "I intend before then to find it myself!"

"Oh, Lord," he said thickly, laughing, pulling off her. "A riposte. Soon we'll probably be sounding like Kate and Petruchio." Against the swell of her mouth his smiling lips quoted, "For thou art pleasant, gamesome, passing courteous, but slow in speech, yet sweet as springtime flowers." And when she tried to pound against him with her fists, he caressed her with a whisper: "Come, come, you wasp; in faith, you are too angry."

She knew the play. In an unexpected moment of self-discovery Merry found it a point of pride to cap his quotation. She said, "If I be waspish, best beware my sting!"

She felt the twitch of his cheek as his mouth curved into a grin. "Not such execrable taste in literature after all. Not that I've ever particularly liked that play."

Like the graceful turn of a dancer's wrist that alters subtly the sense of a ballet, the pirate's kiss changed. What had been demanding became comforting, light touching rather than brutal tracing. A different woman might have read pity there, but for one moment, for the flash of a falcon's wingbeat, Merry's spirit, with its undiscovered complexities, fused, frightened and resistingly, with his. They were, ever so briefly, two intuitive people swept together in a desire that chagrined the one and shamed the other. Kissing her, he mused that really he ought to be better organized about this; a woman who memorizes Shakespeare shouldn't be taken against a table like a field whore in Spain. Merry caught the rough shadow of his thought and read there, though more innocently, his amusement, and his admiration, and his intention.

There was no point in trying to pray, no point in trying to struggle, because by now the mind-trails to her muscles had ceased to obey her will. All that was left for her was to lie, inert under the beguiling caress of his mouth and the warm floating movements of his skilled hands over her body. Her lips were parted, the tip of her breast was hard and aching under his curving fingers, and she felt so idiotic that it seemed instead of kissing her he ought to be boxing her ears.

The ship moved beneath them like a great groaning elephant. Lantern light sprayed through the room, transforming every color Merry saw into a shimmering scale of green or yellow. Suns with black burning centers and sharp yellow runners littered her vision. Earlier today there had been another dark sun, and a reedy voice that said, "I crave the wench," and Merry drug-dreamed Jack in her mind and smelt his dirty whiskers and saw the greasy string of spit on his chin and knew that she was going to be sick.

"Devon," she said. And she had repeated it twice before he said, "Yes, love?"

"Devon, please help me. I—I—"

"What?"

Need suffocated the embarrassment attendant on what was about to happen. "I'm sick," she managed. "I really am."

She was the only woman who had ever lain in his arms and told him such a thing. He said in a reassuringly sensible voice, "What kind of sick?"

"*Going* to be sick," said Merry, groaning like the ship.

Devon lifted his head and saw that it was true.

"That's what you get," he observed under his breath with an expression that she couldn't understand, "when you force yourself on a seasick woman splattered with bhang and bruises."

She protested as he made to move her, but he lifted her in spite of it and advised her tartly that whatever she might enjoy doing flat on her back, egesting the contents of her stomach couldn't be one of them. And he did the civilized things that he could for her with simple decency; when he saw it was too late, he brought the washbowl and gave her the support of his arms, having an errant memory of doing the same for his cousin, Steven, at his . . . what? sixth birthday? fifth? That her young body should remind him of his smallest cousin was an uncomfortable thought; he retained it, using it to force moderation on the high pump of his pulse, which was slow in recognizing the change in circumstances.

Her stomach didn't seem to realize it was useless; the drug had entered through her lungs and would not be thrown off with a simple purge; and as she lay exhausted in his arms, on the bed, she felt once his lips touch the back of her neck and heard him say, with a murmur of laughter, "I hope, my love, that you realize this is an incalculable blow to my self-esteem."

She fell asleep with his patient fingers stroking her cheek. God, who had a much better sense of humor than she had ever before suspected, had heard her prayers with a grin.

CHAPTER NINE

Green waves washed over Merry, in every shade from bile to Nile. She breathed saltwater, and foam burned the lining of her nose. Above she saw a matte black sky and the glimmering phosphorescence in the cresting waves as they caved in upon her. The wind was a lamprey shrieking her name through a hundred teeth and snarling her hair, and as she tried to kick and swim seaweed tangled her legs, scratchy and slimy like the long fingers of salt goblins. Try as she might to keep herself up, there was something pushing her down, pushing her under, a pressure on her shoulders that would not cease, and she began to scream, and the sound was lost in the gulping surf as bubbling water slowly replaced air in her lungs. . . .

Merry burst from the dream into a still room, throbbing from the echo of her cry. Sweat rolled in silver pellets from her pores, blankets entwined her legs thigh to ankle, but, thank heaven, she was in a bed and not drowning. Using a corner of the bed sheet to mop the hot tears from her eyelashes, she began a rattling sigh of relief that died as she saw where she was and remembered. Her eyes picked out like old enemies the table bound by lanyards and set neatly with three chairs; the unfaded place on the walnut paneling that had held the crossbow; the inset desk; the two sea chests bound in leather and lashed to eye-pins beneath a wall of drawers carved with Poseidon figures riding the peaks of wooden waves. While she slept someone had dug out and discarded the arrow and the crossbow, removed the washbowl, taken away the damp cloths Devon had used to wipe her face, and then had left her discreetly and tidily alone.

Merry Patricia Wilding sat up and said, right out loud to the wrinkled bedclothes that covered her knees, "Good morning to you, parts of my body. Miss Wilding is in a real pickle. Stick with me! We're in this together."

It was much worse today than yesterday. Yesterday everything was muted by exhaustion, terror, pain, concussion, and finally drugs. This morning she discovered she was unhappily recovered from the worst of that, and there was nothing to stand between her and a grim-visaged future. Yesterday had been terrible beyond conception; today would probably be worse. No one ever has a good time on a pirate ship; no one except the pirates.

There was time now to worry about poor Aunt April, who would be horrified by Merry's disappearance, and time to wonder, tearful and headachy, if she would ever see Aunt April again. Or her father, Carl, her cousins. What would they think? That she had been abducted by some terrible and mysterious agent? Would they search for her, frantic in their worry? It would hardly comfort them to learn the truth.

Merry climbed from the bed, disoriented by the sea that threw the floor up toward her face, and walked to the cupboard where she had seen Devon find the washbowl. Yes, it was there, spotless and cheerful in thick white ceramic, paired with a brass can of water. She stuck her hand in the water; room temperature. She splashed it into the washbowl, then onto her face, and it ran down her cheeks and trailed down her throat. There was no towel. Pirates, probably, liked to air dry.

Below was a clean chamber pot, furred with dust; a tiny spider was sitting in a buoyant web stretched across the top. What pirates did about their natural functions didn't bear conjecture. Devon, no doubt, didn't have any. Why should he? In every other department he seemed to have been blessed with irritating superiority. She, on the other hand . . .

Merry had never used a chamber pot. Never. Not in deepest winter. Not in the middle of the night. Not if she had a head cold. It had been the outside privy, or it had been nothing at all. Chamber pots were too revolting.

She was still sitting on the floor, glaring balefully at the chamber pot, when Cat came into the room, with a copper earring and one fat, neat braid down his chest to his trousers. He carried a glass, had a cloth that was green and pretty slung on one arm, and over his shoulder was a rope. Visions of new and more degrading tortures flooding into her mind, Merry jumped to her knees, swung the washbowl into the air and sent it flying at his head. Her shaking aim was not true, but it came very close.

Accustomed to the lethal shrapnel of sea battles, Cat didn't flinch under the hail of dripping splinters. Merely he fixed her with an unswerving stare as he picked a sharp white shard from his braid.

"Charming," he said, "as the increase of a pearl-bellied anole."

"Which are?" she snapped.

"Lizards. Was I supposed to put a white flag through the door first or— Oh. The rope. Is it the rope? It's not for you. It's one of the ratlines from the mizzen. Needs a splice. See?" He opened the door and threw the rope into the corridor. Pushing shut the door with the heel of one hand, he joined her on the floor and put the glass into her hand.

"You look like you have a headache," he said. "Drink this."

"What is it?"

"Chopped up fairy wings, the heart of a narwhal taken during a lunar eclipse, spit from a consumptive. . . . Christ. Just drink it, will you? It's lime juice, with honey. Great for scurvy, but it won't do a damn thing for your head. Drink it."

She was so thirsty that she did, and probably would have, even if it *had* been made of fairy wings and narwhal heart. It tasted incredibly good on her parched tongue. When it was done, she faced squarely into Cat's ice-blue stare and began, "I don't know how you can expect me to have any confidence in the safety of anything you give me to drink. You drugged me—"

"That was Morgan's idea."

"And left me here to be ravished," she finished.

Cat looked her up and down and absorbed with some intelligence everything from the torn shirt, which partially revealed her heaving breasts, to the feet, which were dirty and bare, to the disheveled red-gold hair.

"Were you?" he asked politely.

"No!"

Mildly he said, "Well, then, what's your complaint?"

"No thanks to you!" she snapped, as though he hadn't spoken.

"Did you hear me asking for thanks?" In a movement without a single break Cat took back the glass, uncurled his knees, and stood up near the table. "I haven't seen Devon yet this morning. They say you shot the crossbow at him. Honestly. What a circus. You shouldn't have been playing with that thing—you might have broken your arm."

"You, of course," she said sarcastically, "would have been desolated to hear of it."

"You're yipping up the wrong tree if you have the idea that what *I* think matters," said the boy, smoothly emphatic. "I don't suppose that it'll do any good to tell you this, because you don't seem to have the faintest sense of self-preservation, but what you ought to be worrying about is how to sweet-talk Devon. Now, do you want to get dressed, or would you rather sit there all day with your shirt open?"

Even by his scale of things it seemed a little unfair. Merry said, "I don't have anything to wear because yesterday—in case you've forgotten—you cut off my clothes. With dispatch."

"You'd have preferred to be stripped lingeringly? I'll remember that for next time."

"I'd have preferred not to be stripped at all! Do you know what? I wouldn't apply a letter opener to an envelope the way you put your knife to me. Pardon me for my state of undress. Jack and Biddles forgot to let me pack a night bag."

"What do you expect from the scum of the streets? I hired them as burglars, not ladies' maids." He lifted the green film of fabric from his arm and sent it floating down on the bed. "Here you are. Fresh from Paris. Count your blessings; Morgan was toying with the idea of dressing you like a boy. He said it might be interesting. I'll be back in a few minutes, so don't waste your time."

A somewhat nervous evaluation of the object on the bed revealed it to be a high-waisted satin day dress done in a shifting spectrum of mint. In the same material was the twisted belt that pressed up under the breasts and the row of chevron puffs that decorated the hem. The sleeves were designed to fit tight, and nothing at all had been done about filling in the space between collarbone and bust.

If necessity was the mother of invention, the prospect of naked-ness was its midwife. One could only flinch briefly at the prospect

of wearing stolen clothing and then slip it on. What good would it
do to dwell on its probable capture, during some mad rummage of a
wealthy woman's trunk (pray God that it hadn't been ripped from
her body—no, it couldn't have been without damage) while steel
clanged against steel and the air was filled with black powder smoke
and the cries of the dying. *In three days, Merry Patricia, you've
sunk pretty low.*

The dress had been made for a young, stylish, and highly sophisticated lady; in fact, it had once belonged to the twenty-year-old
mistress of a sixty-year-old Barbados banker. It fit Merry every
place except one. When Cat came back to the cabin, he found Merry
sitting rigidly postured on one of the chairs, wearing the green dress
and clutching Morgan's wrinkled shirt high under her neck.

"*Now* what's the matter?" said Cat.

There was a modest silence. Then, "It's too small."

Walking around to her back, he found she'd made a success of all
the hooks and eyes but two, and after he had fastened them, he
looked down at her and said, "It didn't look too small to me. It's
obvious that it— I forgot. You're endowed."

Nakedness had been the fact of life where Cat grew up, and in
spite of himself he still felt that small prick of shock when he
encountered shame.

"Christsake. Most women would jump for joy if they were made
like that," he said, looking at the pink smears on her white cheeks.
"You can't hide behind that shirt all day; for one thing, Morgan's
likely to want it back. Do you want a modesty bit? Come, I'll get
you a scarf."

Cat opened the door and stepped back, bidding her to precede him
with an exaggerated flowing wave of his hand. In the bare corridor
she could see sky and white canvas through the open hatch that
topped a steep stair to her left, and on the right was the paneled door
to Morgan's cabin. She stood quietly for a moment while Cat closed
the door behind them and, passing her, pressed open Morgan's door
and gestured her inside.

Daylight can be a prosaic fellow. What had seemed exotically evil
by fog and candle seemed only exotically lovely this morning.
Sunshine slanted gaily into the room through the sloping stern
windows, and beyond the smoky glass a turquoise horizon rose and

fell in a hundred broken segments. The opium pipe was gone, the brocade pillows on the window benches lay in friendly order, the priceless icons on the rosewood-paneled walls were sweeter, flatter, and less hauntingly foreign. And the gimbeled candlesticks had globes of clear glass. Had they been orange yesterday, or had her concussioned brain lied about the color?

Yesterday reflected light had disguised a long glazed bookcase as a window. Her acquaintance with Rand Morgan might be brief, but it neither surprised nor reassured her to learn that the legendary pirate was literate. There was an open log book on the desk, along with an unrolled sea chart and a jumble of navigational tools: a brass cartographer's square, a reflecting circle made of silver and blackened copper, a delicately crafted Lanflois graphometer, a dry compass with copper engraving, a Spanish sextant and artificial horizon. She knew their names but not their functions. Carl, as a boy, had owned a tin play set of them. Before her was what appeared by the light of day to be a den of reflection, not a den of iniquity.

Cat found a gold scarf of shot silk in a lacquered chest and tossed it to her. She reached out her arm as the fragile fabric skimmed lazily down to drape there. Facing toward the sea, Merry changed the scarf for Morgan's shirt quickly and had just realized that there was no way to make the scarf remain in its carefully concealing arrangement when Cat joined her, discreetly viewing her difficulties, and handed her a pin brooch.

Swallowing a sigh, Merry fastened the scarf with the pin, which would have bought her entire hometown of Fairfield.

He watched her and said, "I don't know what you're so worried about. It's only a little cleavage." She glared at him and thought seriously about attacking him with the expensive brooch. Catching the look and interpreting it correctly, the boy said, "Oh, all right. Never mind. Listen. Would you eat oatmeal?"

Merry, glad at last to find something she could refuse, snapped, "I loathe oatmeal."

"Salt fish?" he suggested doubtfully.

"I've never eaten it," she said. "But I know I wouldn't like it."

Manifesting no surprise, Cat said, "Is that so? How about hardtack?"

Merry moved a red brocade cushion and sat down on the window bench. Tersely she said, "I'm sick. Seasick. Don't keep talking about food to me. I don't want anything to eat. *Seasick!* Do you understand?"

"Of course I do—unless there is something wrong with my eyesight. You're greener than head lettuce. Half the problem is that you've hardly eaten anything since the day before yesterday. We won't have anything fresh on board until we meet the *Terrible* this afternoon, so you'd better resign yourself to oatmeal."

Staring at him, Merry said, "The terrible? The terrible what?"

"Would you stop being so sensitive? Even for me, it's a little unnerving to communicate with someone who's skittish as a gingered filly." He straightened an errant fold in the gold scarf over her shoulder with the flip of one finger. "It's like trying to talk to a windflower. The *Terrible* is another one of Morgan's ships. I'm going to fetch you something to eat. You can stay in here and wait for Devon. He wants to talk to you."

With an anxiety she would have preferred to hide, Merry said, "Is there any chance that he'll—let me go?"

"I've already told you once. This time pay attention," said the boy. "Will he let you go? It depends on how silver-tongued you are."

Doom, thought Merry. *Gloom.* "On my good days I can sometimes put together as many as three sentences in a paragraph without more than a bare half dozen breaks in logic."

"Well," he said grimly, "maybe a taste of Cook's oatmeal will inspire you. I'm going. Put your wrists up."

Watching him draw a length of cord from his pocket, Merry cried out, "No! Oh, no! Please don't tie me again!"

"I wouldn't have to if you weren't always throwing things at people, or shooting arrows off at them. Morgan's likely to get fed up with it and give you a taste of the back side of his hand." He started to reach for one of her arms, but before he could touch her, he looked into her face. What he saw there made him stop and change his mind. Tactful as a nurserymaid distracting a capricious toddler, the pirate boy put one of Morgan's silver hairbrushes into her hand and said, "Brush your hair. I'll come right back. Don't move. Don't get in trouble."

And she did not, for when he came back, she was sitting exactly as she had been, staring at the paneled bulkhead like a strange-eyed ghost in glowing green, stroking the brush unknowingly through her curls. So he gripped her by the arm and brought her to a chair at Morgan's table and put the oatmeal in front of her, and a spoon in her hand. When she wouldn't eat, he thought a moment, then said, "If you don't eat it, I'll take back the scarf." Observing that her nose was turning pink again, he added quickly, "And if you start to cry, I'll take back the dress."

This was not the first time by any means that Merry had eaten oatmeal, but the oatmeal she had eaten before had been kept in Aunt April's whistle-clean pantry, not stored for two months in the hold of a seagoing warship, by its nature damp and alive with the stench of gunpowder and unwashed bodies. Even well-run ships, and this one was the best of its kind, were infested with vermin. Seamen were used to finding in their flour evidence of the rats, maggots, and cockroaches that shared their food supply. But Merry, after a childhood of fresh cream, Aunt April's marmalade on white toast, and vegetables fresh from the garden served in clever sauces, was not. Even her two days' fast would not make this meal palatable. Cat had to repeat his threats, and several variants, before she would finish the bowl.

Devon entered the cabin with Morgan as she was choking down the last mouthful. With a negligent wave in Cat's direction Morgan, his mind on business, had pitched his hat to a chair and leaned, one-handed, on his desk, flicked over a page, and entered something in the log. But it was not to his dark figure that Merry's quickened senses homed.

Devon by lamplight was a thing of beauty: the clever angles; the play in skin tone and hair of lucent pastels; the muted and unselfconscious movements of a graceful body. Devon by daylight was another proposition entirely, though not a whit less attractive: The searching sunbeams revealed a man twenty times more dangerous. The force of his character caught Merry like a plank across the chest.

Sun-detailed, he was harder, leaner, his eyes, shed of their polite fictions, were callous as those of a lynx; the fathomless volumes of charity suggested by the sweet lines of his face were simply not there. Before Merry in Apollonian splendor stood a man who was

capable of vivisecting her soul, with creativity, and putting it on to
fry like a Punjabi locust. When he wanted to beguile, he certainly
could; he was not beyond a rare and skillful act of mercy; but his
tongue had more sharp edges on it than a sheep shears, and his wit
he could wield by choice as the hacksaw or the scalpel. Margaret
Nelson, who had for four turbulent months been his lover, was
widely quoted as having said that he could sever your head from
your body, and you wouldn't know you were dead until three weeks
later, when your carriage hit a bump and you found your head sitting
nose-down in your lap.

And here sat little Merry Wilding, whose most trying moments,
ever, had come from Aunt April tetchy with the headache. The
instant brain-burn of staring into the eyes of six feet, two inches of
virile hostility made Merry drop her gaze to her oatmeal bowl and
look too well at the slimy clods of cereal that were stiffening in the
bottom like—no, better *not* to think what it looked like. Any more
vomiting and they were apt to throw her over the side.

Presented with a view of the top of her head, Devon let his glance
wander from the neat line of her parted hair down the narrow arms
to the giveaway movements of her baby hands. Victim and captor,
close together and aware one of the other, were sharing, had they
known it, the same image: the quiver of her mouth last night under
his kiss, the sensation of his hands on the soft flesh of her breasts. It
was a toss-up whether man or young girl was trying harder to perish
the memory.

In a voice as pleasant and light as goose down Devon said, "God
love us all, the wench is eating! Good morning, Cat. Have you
managed to repair her internal arrangements? What's that? Oatmeal?
I hope you emptied into it the contents of every bottle of aphrodisiac
in the medicine closet."

Her chin flew up, her eyes widened, but it was clear from her face
that she didn't know the word. Her alarm was merely the unease of
someone who has just found herself the butt of a baffling and probably tasteless joke. Devon saw her gaze fly to Cat and saw the boy
first reject her with his eyes and then, surprisingly, reassure her with
a spare shake of the head that he had put no adulterants in her food.
Merry's chin thunked back down on her chest in relief. From the
look of her the girl had no idea what an extraordinary phenomenon

was Cat's kindness to her; Morgan had this morning sardonically professed himself still reeling from the shock of it. But then, this flowerlike creature had no basis for comparison. She had never seen Cat with other women.

She was the third-string mistress of the man Devon hated, and she was no longer guarded either by nausea or by the urgency of his damned inconvenient need to take her to bed. Primed for butchery, Devon lifted his hand and darned his fingers into her heavy hair and drew her head slowly back until her gaze had no escape from his.

"Dare you eat?" he asked her, blandly tender. "One meal in Hades and you're never allowed up. Persephone had only a few seeds of pomegranate . . ."

It was a successful way to intimidate someone and about thrice as effective as he would have needed. The final lump of cold oatmeal had been stuck like a sand tick to the back of Merry's tongue, and it decided suddenly to ignore the esophagus and slip daintily into her lung. She coughed and sputtered for thirty seconds before Cat came and whacked her on the back with a slap that dislodged the oatmeal and very nearly rib cage from spine bones as well.

When Merry was able to suck in enough air to speak, she faced Devon, who had been forced to relinquish his grip on her hair.

"At least," she said, "when the king of the underworld dragged Persephone to hell, he had marriage in mind."

Or so Merry had heard the myth reported. All she had asked from her response was that it be in his classical category and that it be critical. Any mention of marriage and its application to her situation vis-à-vis Devon had been an accident. Marriage. It was an off-key note to have struck. From the swiftly gathering malice on Devon's face Merry knew the depth of her error even as she saw Cat wince.

Before Devon could deliver an annihilating rebuff, Cat rescued his hapless protégée from the fruit of her naïve words.

"Devon, try to look hurt," said the boy. "She don't have faith in your intentions." Then seeing the moment could stand to cool longer, he added glumly, "I'm sorry about the crossbow—I never thought about it. She was higher than a jackdaw. Who would have thought she'd get into mischief?"

"It doesn't matter," said Devon and smiled at Merry. He drew a slow finger down the line of her cheek. "There's something relentlessly disarming about a woman who pukes in your washbowl. Do you know, my sea nymph—and there are honestly not many women I'd say this about—that you're more amusing defending your virtue than I wager you'd be surrendering it?''

Across the room Morgan had turned, the dark, unkindly surface of his gaze moving like a nightwalker among the three startling blond heads. Jesus. Entertainment. Against odds to the contrary the puny, dove-eyed chit possessed a soul. *So you made yourself sick, did you, on Devon?* Morgan thought. *That was well done of you, my babe. I didn't pump you too fast, too full of opium for nothing.* Grinning a little, he collected Devon's cool glance and said, ''Can we blame her for being ill? With you such an ill-favored fellow?''

''His smile,'' observed Cat, ''has been known to raise blisters at fifty feet. Even when he's slept in his shirt. What did you say her name was?''

''Mary,'' said Devon. ''As in the Virgin.''

''No!'' Merry said, delighted to be able to correct him, though she did it through clenched teeth. ''With an *e* and two *r*'s. As in merry-go-round.''

Equally delighted, Devon gave her one of those blistering smiles and said, ''Or as in making Merry?''

The only thing left for her was a feeble sort of gulp. ''I didn't give you permission to use my name,'' she said, and it sounded inappropriately grandiose even to her own ears.

Devon said, ''I'd be happy to call you Miss something, or Mrs. something, for that matter. What's your surname?''

She ought to have been anticipating it. If only her brain hadn't been as furred this morning as her tongue. Not understanding what he wanted with her, she couldn't take the risk of telling him her last name. Merry Patricia Wilding was not a famous name, but her brother was a widely known and romanticized figure, and anyone who read the newspapers would have heard of her father. You were never anonymous when your name was Wilding. Looking into Devon's eyes, with their brilliant centers of filigreed gold, she would have been surprised had he heard her last name and not suspected a connection at once.

He repeated his question, and since she didn't have a ready alias, she was left harboring a pause as revealing as last season's bear grease in a porch bucket.

"A woman of mystery," said Morgan, at the side table, pouring himself wine. "Cat, fetch the thumbscrew."

Cat snapped his fingers with apparent regret. "I can't remember where I put it. It's been a while since I've screwed any thumbs. Captain, sir, it's the iron maiden or nothing."

"If you say so, child." Morgan rested his long body on a chair arm. "Personally, I can see her lashed to the yardarm, bared to the waist. I'm all in favor of something really vile and modern. Shall we bring it to the crew for a vote?"

"They," said Devon pleasantly to Merry, "are teasing. Until I decide otherwise." He gently loosened the cereal spoon that had been still fastened, unheeded, in the clawlike grip of her fingers. Bowl and spoon he delivered to Cat and then hooked a chair and straddling it backward, faced her over the rail. "Never fear, darling. For the moment all I want is the right to grub around in your pia mater. Hullo! You're nervous this morning! I only meant your brain."

Merry gathered every scrap and particle of the coldness that was making itself at home in the linings of her digestive tract and wove that coldness into her voice as she said, "Browbeat me, then, if it suits your mood. I prefer that to your—"

"What? My passion? Ah, love, what makes you so sure we're done with that?"

She had a second's warning before his right hand found her and slid gently under her hair to the thin, neat flesh that spread, soft as a gosling, on the side of her neck. She hadn't learned yet the trick of mastering her respiration; as he touched her Devon heard the sharp intake of her breath. His thumb braced, without pressure, on her rapidly pulsing artery, and the tactile surfaces of his curved fingers were slow on her skin.

Wishing heartily that she hadn't been so stupid as to have antagonized him on this, of all subjects, Merry said, in a voice that was embarrassingly hoarse, "Is it too late to retract any part of my remark that caused you offense?"

"No, but that time is fast approaching." The pirate's clever fingers were discovering her nape.

His touch was scattering her thoughts like leaves in a wind eddy. Trying what was quite possibly the most serious risk she had knowingly taken in her life, Miss Merry Patricia Wilding ventured, "Are you sure—" His fingers smoothed over the tumble of her lower lip, so she had to swallow hard and begin a second time with closed eyes. "Are you sure this is what you want? How do you know I won't bore you, next time, with a surrender?"

It was the closest she had ever come to the sort of wordplay at which he was so skilled. It was a joke, only a joke, and if he misunderstood: disaster. Like the gazelle, sick faced, who offered leftover salad to the hunting lion, Merry meant to placate and to make him laugh. Astonishingly she succeeded in both.

"What do you want to know?" she asked resignedly into the soft folds of his laughter.

The long firm-boned hand gave her cheek an approving pat and withdrew. "You don't have to abandon hope, my dear," he said. "Despite appearances, you're really quite safe, if you cooperate. Now. When did you meet Michael Granville?"

Sooner or later, Merry had known, it would come back to this. From the myriad tidbits of information she had culled since being brought on the *Joke*, she gathered that Devon had paid to have Granville's room searched and certain papers—what papers?—stolen, which meant the pirate and the English gentleman had a connection, probably unfriendly, but what went into it exactly was anybody's guess.

Merry stepped gingerly into the thought that perhaps Sir Michael was an agent for the British government. At the very least he would bring to London a full report of his American visit, though one assumed, naturally, that he had been closely watched during his stay in her country. Strange, that he had had such freedom to wander the streets, but then, what did she know about things like that? If Sir Michael was a spy, what would that make Devon? Surely Washington did not hire pirates to gather information for them! Things were not always as they seemed, she was fast coming to learn. If Devon was an American, please God, her trouble would be over.

Merry matched his clear golden gaze. "Are you in the employ of President Madison?"

Morgan choked on his wine and then laughed himself into a

stupor. And when the *ha-ha*'s had died to *ho-ho*'s and then to faint sobs, Devon turned to him and said, "I wish that you hadn't. I would have loved to bite 'Yes' on that one and see where it led to." He glanced back to Merry's drawn face. "As you see, I'm not. You will answer my question, please."

Could he trace her through Michael Granville? It didn't matter, because it was becoming rapidly obvious that any association with Granville was a hazard to her future well-being.

"I met Sir Michael on the *Guinevere* the night she was to sail."

"All right," Devon said. "We'll suppose, for a minute, that's true. Then what were you doing in the Musket and Muskrat in August? Don't waste my time trying to convince me you were there only to help with a puppet show. I saw the woman and two men you were in company with. Having you along was an invitation to trouble; they wouldn't have brought you if it hadn't been important. Your presence was instrumental to something. I'd like to know what that was."

Overset by the knife-edged accuracy of his perception, she denied it too quickly, and too sharply, with an incoherent paragraph of stuttered denials. Cold-eyed, he heard her out as she impaled herself on her own incoherence.

"Your delivery seems to be getting a little garbled," Devon said, "so if you don't mind, I'll help you. You say you're the wife of a poor puppeteer. Very well. How much money does he earn in an average performance? So much? I'm impressed. Where were you born? The name of the county? How long have you been married? And you're how old? The year you were married in? What was the last city you lived in? How many shows would you estimate your husband has given since you've been married? Multiply it, sweetheart. That makes the man a millionaire."

He was right. Merry buried her face in the shaking cup of her palms. Devon's voice, as beautiful and merciless as the rest of him, came gently to her burning ears.

"Whatever you may think, I'm not enjoying this either. Are you ready to tell me who was with you at the Muskrat?"

If she began to weep now, the explosion of fluid would drain every cell in her body. Head spinning, Merry loosened her tangling fingers with effort, laid her hands in her lap, and straightened her curling shoulders. Somewhere she found the strength to look into the profligate golden eyes.

"At the tavern, with the puppets. That was my husband—"

"His name?" asked Devon.

Not Smith, she thought. "Jones."

"Ah. Bill Jones? Bob Jones? Ebenezer Jones?"

Merry passed her tongue tiredly over her lips and said the first thing that pranced into her brain. "Jeremiah Jones."

"That was going to be my next guess," Devon said. "Biblical *and* alliterative."

Lord help her, it *had* sounded even more ridiculous said aloud than in her mind. Behind Devon she could see Cat shake his head at her in a pained way and pass his finger over his throat, in a gesture forecasting doom.

Devon crossed his arm over the chair rail. "I'll say this for you, flower, you fail with flair. Listen, my child, I've been gentle with you so far, but don't make the mistake of thinking that will go on forever. When you leave the *Joke,* it will be one segment at a time if you don't either begin telling me the truth or begin bringing a little more panache to your lies. Satisfy me, and I'll put you in the longboat as soon as we come near shore and have you delivered, unharmed, to the nearest coaching inn with enough money in your pocket to take you wherever you wish." He paused, searched her face, and continued patiently. "At the Muskrat you were sitting with one of Granville's men—"

"No! No! What are you saying? Who can you mean?"

"The innkeeper. If it's a coincidence, you had better explain to me how it comes about, because that connects you twice with Granville and his minions. You have two alternatives, Merry. You can be innocent, and I'll let you go; you can be useful, and I'll let you go. My suggestion is that you commit yourself to one course or the other before my temper wears out."

With his words she saw and understood, for the first time, the magnitude of her predicament. Had she really thought, minutes ago, that Devon's feelings for Granville were "unfriendly"? What blindness! What infantile blindness! Devon was no ruffian with an excess of spleen, no overzealous Yankee patriot. With those she might have had a chance. What Devon was, it seemed, was a deliberate, highly intelligent, ruthless man, and a word like *unfriendly* might patch a single square inch of the cosmos of Devon's hatred for Michael Granville. Michael Granville. What was he besides a pair of opaque gray eyes and well-bred condescension that had made him Devon's enemy? And—*minions?* She had been ready for a little innocent adventure to help her country at the Musket and Muskrat, not to land in the cross fire between the sacred and the profane, although it was a pretty good guess that in this war both the parties were on the side of the profane. It wasn't merely important that she disassociate herself immediately from Granville, it was a matter of survival. And there was almost no way that she could do it.

Apparently having decided she'd had enough time to ponder her fate, Devon said softly, "So, Mrs. Jeremiah Jones. Does your husband mind when you sleep with Granville?"

Last night, she remembered, the same insinuation had made her angry. Anger would have been heaven to the unhealthy exhaustion she felt now. There was a sharp ache starting behind her eyebrows, and she put her finger pads on it and rubbed hard.

"Now, see here," she said, staring down into her scraped wrists. "I *know* I might have been in Granville's cabin, but he was never in it with me. Doesn't it mean anything that he wasn't in the room with me when I was kidnapped?"

"He wasn't with you because he was on deck—but he'd only been there for a matter of minutes. Before that—"

"He might have been in the captain's cabin!" Pride was less important now than convincing him. "Or the hold? Or—or the powder room!"

Morgan's gaze shifted from the window, focused, and began to sparkle. "The powder room?"

"She means," said Devon dryly, "the powder magazine."

"Well, for heaven's sake," she sputtered helplessly, "*I* don't know the names of places on ships. How do I know where he was? I hardly knew him! Doesn't it make sense if I don't know him I wouldn't know where he was? I was only a passenger on the same vessel."

It was a good point, she thought, and she had about a third of a second to be proud of it before he said, "Fine. You don't know

Michael Granville. Then where did you get permission to sail on the *Guinevere?* Who do you know in British Court circles? What, no answer? Where was your husband?''

Feebly: ''He—he planned to come later.''

''For a royal command performance? I didn't see the show, but I heard the content. Seditious and antimonarchical. The swell gentlemen in London and Washington are having a war, my sweet. Do you know how many peaceful ships there are going between the United States and England? Unless he meant to float through the blockade on a buoy.''

''Regardless of where my husband was,'' said Merry with desperation, ''and how I got permission to sail on the *Guinevere, I still* have no connection with Granville.''

Without lifting his hard gaze from Merry's, Devon unhooked himself slowly from the chair and, with his hands just above her elbows, pulled her up and against his chest. Fright had distended her pupils until the radiant blue irises were only a narrow halo; they were so close that he could feel each breath she drew, each stammering flex of her heart, each tightening fiber of her muscle as she strained from contact with his body.

''Tell me, my small quaking friend,'' he said in a voice that was light and final, ''if you have no connection with Granville, what were you doing in the man's bed? And if you don't intend to be candid, I'd advise you to confine your invention to something I can believe.''

''Would you believe it,'' she said faintly, ''if I told you that it was because there were ants in my cabin?''

''Not,'' said Devon, ''unless you are an entomologist.''

Meekly she said, ''Nevertheless—''

''Nevertheless nothing. If you had traded cabins, why was there no woman's clothing in the room where you were sleeping? Or had you left it for the ants to eat?''

''That's just it,'' Merry said. ''The ants weren't only in my room, they were in my luggage, and the *Guinevere*'s third mate put such a strong powder in to kill them that—''

Devon cut her off. ''Is it your habit to travel with ants in your luggage?''

''A servant put them in,'' she said in an increasingly strained voice, "because he thought the trunk belonged to my—er, m-my aunt."

"For that," said Devon grimly, "you are going to win the cash prize, two silver buckles, *and* a side of beef. You've done enough spinning, Merry-go-round. Cat? Take her to my cabin. Lock her in. And give the key into the keeping of the most dissipated wretch you can find."

"As your grace pleases," snapped the boy. "In five minutes I'll have the key back—in your pocket."

As Cat led her toward the threshold, Merry stopped, hesitated, then said falteringly, "It really is true—about the ants, I mean. But there's no way to explain it. You have to know Henry Cork."

Devon didn't, so to him it was one more piece of whimsical idiocy from a young girl who was both the most whimsical and the most idiotic who had ventured into his orbit. When the door closed behind the girl and Cat, Devon turned with an impatient shrug toward the window and stared at the bright broken pattern of the sea. He never saw Morgan's arrested gaze find and softly hold the vacant air where Merry had been. . . .

For Rand Morgan, man of myth and nightmare, knew who Henry Cork was. Morgan could have spoken the next English ship and bundled her off; but he was not a man who conducted his charities with sentiment. As it was, he spared a brief regret about the opium, paused to be glad he hadn't indulged his fleeting desire to take Merry into his own bed, and passed, prayerlike, an apology to a near and concerned spirit.

The black eyes, with their discreetly veiled benevolences, considered the golden sun-spangled head that hadn't moved since facing the window. Every impulse of humanity called for meticulous sleight-of-hand manipulation; common sense called for iron restraint. Common sense won without a struggle.

When finally he spoke, Morgan's voice was friendly and spruce. "The old there-were-ants-in-my-bed dodge. Good thing you're too swift to fall for that worn-out hat trick. But what in the world will she do with a side of beef?"

Devon had learned a long time ago that it merited a man nothing to snap like a trout at each careless sally of Morgan's. Ignoring it, watching the ivory swooping arrow of a gull, he said, "Cat seems to be entertaining some fears that I'm going to ask him to beat it out of her. Tell him for me that I won't delegate my atrocities."

"Ah" was all that Morgan said.

Devon swung around and faced his half brother with hard, glowing eyes. "What the devil is that supposed to mean? What's the virtue in muttering 'Ah' at me from between your gritted teeth and staring at me like a bloody sarcophagus? Do you want me to give her to the sea?"

Innocently, honestly, Morgan said, "No."

"Or put her ashore?"

"God, no." That was honest too. Morgan smiled. "Why do you ask? You'll do as you please anyway. Will you still go with the *Terrible* this evening?"

"I have to. They've committed me to meet a man next Tuesday." Devon walked to the center of the room and settled the chair Merry had occupied back under the table. "I'll leave her to Cat. That should please him. What is it about her, do you think, that makes it matter to him?"

Morgan's head rested against the lamb's wool. His eyes were closed. "The boy's a born manager. She appeals to his maternal instincts. Give him a week, and he'll be premasticating her dinners." The blind smile became nasty. "You needn't worry. Whatever maudlin thoughts he might entertain in that direction, his appetites are otherwise."

As Devon well knew, Cat's appetites and what should be done about them were not a subject on which he and Morgan were ever likely to agree. "Since we're being worldly," Devon said, "what do you think the chances are that she was coerced by Granville?"

"Nonexistent," said Morgan and drained his cup with the serene look of a man without a single scar on his conscience.

CHAPTER TEN

They say it's bad manners for a sailor to lock his sea chest and one that did was likely to find it nailed shut when he came off his watch. Devon, it appeared, was immune to etiquette. One by one Merry tried each lock in the cabin: the cabinets, the trunks, the windows, the door. Everything but the chamber pot was closed off tighter than a vain man's corset, and neat as a Dutch cupboard.

Cat, wanting no more trouble, had left her not so much as a candle, but there was daylight filtering gray-blue through three high windows, each one big enough to have admitted a pair of clinched hedgehogs. Moving like a stubborn wraith through the slow filmy light, Merry continued her search for more than half an hour after even her singing persistence admitted it was useless. She flopped dry-eyed on the bunk bed and decided with a quickly fading flash of humor that it was outside of enough for Devon, who was a tanned and tarred villain of a pirate, to have the *audacity* to think *she* was deficient in the department of morals. As for Henry Cork, Merry remembered distinctly telling him last March, when he'd left a water bucket on the doorjamb and soaked the delivery boy, that someday those practical jokes were going to do someone a serious mischief. Ne'er, at the time, had she suspected that that someone would be herself. If she was *really* moral, she supposed, she would have found some way to hang herself with the bed sheets. But as anyone will tell you who's tried to hang themselves with bed sheets, it takes a good deal more ingenuity than it might appear to at first. She indulged in a brief, futile fantasy that Carl might somehow find she was here and come and shoot Devon. The fantasy expired on the thought that if Carl did come, it was far more likely that Devon would shoot *him*.

Poor, poor Aunt April. She must be sick with distress.

Like a decked sturgeon flipping uselessly from side to side, Merry turned from anger, to fear, to despair, and back again to anger. And Devon, whether from design or indifference, gave her confusion plenty of time to wind down to a numbed misery as she listened to the whirr of anonymous ship's noises. The rattle below the floor might have been a strolling skeleton; the heavy flapping aloft, the wingbeats of a giant, primitive bird. Raucous voices rose and fell from the deck and from the corridor, and once she heard Cat talking to someone at the stair head, his voice sharp and sardonic. Was there any chance she would be left in here—for days? For weeks? Until she was weak and starving and finally submissive?

When Devon came, she was lying on the bunk with the dying afternoon sunbeams, wondering if it was true that fear drove people out of their minds, and retracing her life to discover what she could have done differently that would have saved her from ending her days on a pirate ship.

The man whose pitiless hands held the fragile threads of her life came into the room quietly and closed the door behind him without turning, his glance touching lightly the skylit contours of her profile. She turned her face to him without moving any other part of her body.

"Well," she said, "have you brought your thumbscrew? Or have you decided to boil me in walrus fat and lash me to the—to the—"

"Yardarm," Devon supplied, looking helpful.

Her head disappeared under the pillow in a shimmy of glinting copper curls. "Go away!" she said in an agonized voice. "Just go away! Don't you have to batten down the hatches or something?"

His words, silky and beguiling, reached her through one hundred thousand goose feathers. "We only do that in a storm. Are you anticipating one?"

"Probably." Her warm trapped breath whispered over her lips and into her nose. "There's going to be a hurricane, and waterspouts, and lobsters as big as horse barns off the starboard bow. You'd better secure the lanyards to the halyards and winch the grinch and bind the thingimmy-chrunkers to the nautical-blubber. I hope we get swallowed by a whale!''

It took him an uncomfortably long time to erase his unbidden smile and cudgel into stupor the startling tenderness that crept through his expert guard. Then: "Are we getting tired, my love," he said slowly, "of waiting?"

A shocked head emerged from the pillow and snapped at him, "Don't call me 'my love'! It's an obscenity."

In less than a second he was beside the bed, his hands softly massaging her shoulders. "My precious Merry. There's no such thing as an obscenity. It's all done by rearranging letters of the alphabet, none of which has the raw power of a bosun's ball whistle. You know what you have to do to get out of here. Make your choice. And then watch me while I make mine."

Cutting like a scythe through his words were the sweet movements of his hands, drifting in a faintly suggestive rhythm that spread his hot, fluid magic in one fiery burst. So many danger bells erupted in her head that the space between her ears sounded like the carriage house of the Virginia Charitable Fire Society. She threw herself upright, breaking his grip, and twisted into a decent posture, being careful not to dislodge the skirt from her legs. The points of her shoulder blades lay as close as they could to the hard paneled wood behind her, and the fabric over her breasts felt unpleasantly tight.

She was with him, and they were alone. Why must that circumstance always mean that her chest hurt like she'd squeezed it in a clothespress?

"Stop it!" Her clenched fist covered her mouth. "If there's a spark of human feeling in you, then stop it! I can't tell you a word more about the tavern or the *Guinevere* than I have already, and I can't bear to be threatened anymore. Do whatever you intend with me and have done! What will you do to hurt me? What?"

"You break easily, Merry." His voice, soft and detached, might have belonged to a naturalist dissecting a common tree toad for the ninety-ninth time. "Which makes me wonder how you were able to stomach Granville. If you're not his mistress, that casts doubt on the rest of it too. Cat has pointed out that he found you in a particularly unrevealing piece of nightgear, and while that might be some new fetish of Michael's, I have to admit you handle like a virgin. One assumes that you're an extremely talented lady, but since innocence would help your case along, would you be willing to let Cat examine you?''

It was a crude tactic, and he knew it, so he let her hit him once, because it seemed fair, before he seized the scraped wrists and held them, letting his fingers play hard on the damaged flesh. As he felt her attack subside he loosened his grip slightly, and loosened it further still when he saw that the lower lip she held between her teeth to keep from crying was beginning to bleed.

"Yes, my flower, I don't intend to be a pleasant bunkmate for you, so you'd better rethink your silence."

"I'm not going to tell you anything. What do you mean, bunkmate?"

"I can't afford to let you go traipsing back to Michael with the story of what you've seen and heard—the time isn't ripe yet to flush my pheasant. I'd take the risk if you were more honest with me. As we stand, I don't feel disposed to do you any favors. And this being the only cabin in the ship where you can sleep, this is where you will stay—unless you'd like to sleep with Morgan, which I don't recommend. You might find his habits distressing. There's a cubbyhole near the bilge they use sometimes for a cell, but it has four inches of water on the floor and rats. The crew, of course, would be happy to have you with them in the fo'c'sle; you'd have your choice of beds, but you wouldn't get very much rest, and I don't think there's enough of you to go around."

Her wrists were still caught in his hands. She flexed her fingers to keep the circulation going and said, with ashen-faced fury, "I'm not going to traipse back to Granville and tell him anything. Most likely I'll never see him again. And I'm not going to tell him anything about your connection with Morgan because I don't know anything about it." Her voice was beginning to simmer like boiling water. "I have no relationship with Sir Michael. No relationship! None! Do you hear me, you fiend? I'm nothing to Sir Michael, and he's nothing to me."

There was a short pause before Devon said, "Isn't *fiend* a thought strong?" and released her hands.

"*Why* won't you believe me?" she moaned, dropping to the

bunk, laying her head down disconsolately. For a moment she dutifully reconsidered the "fiend" and then amended it: "All right, then. Barbarian."

"Just remember, in this exchange of personalities, that *I* wasn't the one who laid wait in *your* bedroom brandishing archaic weaponry. Tell me what you were doing at the Musket and Muskrat and I'll swallow your story about the ants."

"It's none of your business," she answered, with a last flare of hauteur. "What were *you* doing at the Muskrat? Why did Cat hire men to search Sir Michael's room? How do *you* like being asked all these questions?"

"Ask me after you've spent a few nights in my arms. I might be more willing to talk."

She dropped her head into her hands and began to cry. "I want to go home. I want to sleep in my own bed, and I never want to see another ship as long as I live. I hate the sea—I really hate it. I don't see how the fish can stand it. I hate opium, and I hate pirates." She felt her nose filling with tears. "I hate having adventures. You can't make them stop when you want to. Why does this have to be me?"

It was a nearly irresistible performance, and its effect on Devon was powerful. Gentle methods having failed, he had expected fear to work. So much for that. Either she didn't have the imagination or the experience to understand what he could do to her, as Morgan suggested, or she had a hapless and rather touching sort of courage. She was not an easy subject to torment, and the results of his calculated efforts were not pretty. It took much of his available willpower to lean one hand against the bulkhead and say coldly, "Our route is somewhat circuitous, but eventually we head south, where someone with your assets will bring a good price from the right buyer. I shouldn't have to lecture an American girl on the horrors of slavery. Or course, I doubt whether you would actually have to pick cotton. I'd advise you to think seriously on the consequence of your reticence."

She didn't look up, because she couldn't, and after a few minutes knew by the matter-of-fact click of the closing door that he had left the room.

Cat arrived after a tactfully long interval with a nasty bowl of something swimming with olives that Merry gathered he expected her to eat. He said that Devon had left on the *Terrible*, and no, he wasn't sure when Devon would be back. Maybe weeks. Maybe not. And it was a good thing she'd decided to stop being so prissy about the chamber pot. For two days after that, when he came, Merry turned her face to the wall.

In the small rocking room she might almost have believed herself a Bedouin princess riding box-enclosed on a stately, swaying dromedary with a monotony of sand stretching like the sea to the horizon. It would have been preferable to where she was now. In her mind she began a memoir: *Voyage Aboard the Pyrate Ship* Black Joke *During the Second American War of Independence:*

THIRD DAY OF MY CAPTIVITY
Wednesday, 20th March 1814

Day commences with fresh gales, flying clouds, and cold oatmeal. The ship is noisy and never sleeps. I can make more of the sounds than I could at first. Feet run, ropes scuttle, the ship's timbers thump as if to protest being used as a battering ram against millions of tons of water, and the wind whines in the sails. On deck they talk, shout to each other, and sing; sometimes there's a fife playing, sometimes a violin. I'm beginning to recognize Cat's footsteps, being as they're especially quiet. Asked him if that was how he got his name, but he didn't answer, only looked sardonic, so I suppose that it's not.

FOURTH DAY
Thursday, 21st March 1814

Squally during last night, with rain and thunder. Seasick again this A.M. Cat gave me a preserve for it, with wormwood, rose petals, ginger, and lemon, which he doesn't appear to have much faith in as a remedy, but I think I am better because of it. Have finally figured out how the ship's bell sounds the hours. Eight bells is four o'clock, eight o'clock, midnight and noon, and the uneven numbers—one, three, five, and seven—mark the half hours.

Can't see from the windows today; half the time they are fogged inside, the other half outside. Drew some blunt outlines of horses on the windowpane, but they ran. Which is a rather good pun, and I'm sorry there is no one here to share it. I think Cat's earring is a diamond. Lots of sparkle.

Aunt April, have you given me up for dead? I worry often about you worrying about me, about how grieved you must be. I pray that you don't blame yourself for my disappearance, thinking it was your fault I am missing because you decided to bring me with you to England. It wasn't your fault. How could you have known about the *Black Joke?*

FIFTH DAY
Friday, 22nd March 1814

There is too much time to worry about what it would be like to be a slave in the Indies. Devon would probably be happy to know I am very fearful, if he has thought about me at all, which he probably has not.

Have become obsessed with food and dream of roast goose with currant pudding, fresh strawberries, and white bread with sweet butter. The food on the *Joke* comes in combinations of salt beef and stale peas, salt beef and stale beans, salt beef and pickled fish, and for dinner salt beef and salt beef. The ship's biscuit is called hardtack, which is apt. Fresh water is stored in metal-lined casks, so it reeks of tin sweat and damp wood and tastes like a foot bath for gout. Cat says I am too finicky, and I will lose weight. Maybe no one will want to buy me then.

SIXTH DAY
Saturday, 23rd March 1814

Light breezes and a clear sky. Misery! This morning I realized that I'm going to begin to menstruate. What will I do? Tell Cat, I suppose, but I would rather die. There were worms in the A.M. hardtack. Cat says, "Don't think of them as worms. Think of them as meat." When I said "But they are *worms!*" he offered to pick them out for me, as though that made it any better, which shows, if nothing else, that we don't look at things the same way. Am not afraid of him anymore. Which is extraordinary, when you think of it.

Where is Devon? Will Michael Granville guess who was behind the theft of his papers?

SEVENTH DAY
Sunday, 24th March 1814

Pleasant weather outside. Gloom within. Appetite nonexistent. Bored. Frightened. Can't seem to pretend anymore that I am neither. Started my courses. Had to tell. Cat very matter-of-fact about it and helpful. Much better than Aunt April. The hardtack is tough as a stone. Cat says soak it in coffee.

When Cat returned that night, the stars were twinkling through the window, haloed by mist, their image blurred by an occasional splash of spray. Merry sat at the table, her head pillowed on her folded arms. Diagonals of reedy light picked out golden pinpoints in her hair, lying over her face and shoulders like swirling crimson smoke.

The boy's hands were not pretty, being ridged with tendons and scars, but they moved with delicacy in her hair as he stirred it to expose her pale profile. She sat still as an idol, the blue almond line of her eyelids closed as though in sleep or death. Through parted, barely moving lips, she said, "I think I'm getting scurvy."

Morgan's antiscorbutics were the best in the Atlantic; scurvy was never seen on the *Black Joke*. And, for God's sake, she'd only been at sea for a week. Cat opened his mouth to enumerate the reasons why she couldn't have scurvy and then shut it again without a word. As much as she, the young pirate had noticed that their differing logic could pass cheek to cheek in the same current without stopping to tip hats.

"Why?" he said.

Silence from the head on the table. Then, "What're the symptoms?"

"Let me see," he said. "Have you got eruptions?"

"Eruptions!"

"I hadn't finished. Are there eruptions on your arms and legs that look like fleabites?"

Her head came up, and the shiny disturbed mass of her hair fell in a soft slither down her neck as she pushed back the tight sleeves and anxiously studied the white skin on her arms. With reluctance she admitted, "No. What else do you have with scurvy?"

"Loose teeth. Do yours wiggle?"

Damned if she didn't try them. Every blasted tooth in her head. And when they were all discovered in perfect health, she had the nerve to insist that there must be *other* signs.

"Dysentery and foul breath," snapped Cat, running out of patience.

"Well! Really!" Her very blue eyes filled with resentment. "I might be in the early stages."

"The *pre*-early stages," he said. With one hand he set down the water can he had brought to her. "You'll have to develop something more interesting than acute hypochondria to worry Devon enough to loose you on dry land. Good night."

He was out the door and had it half-closed behind him before he heard her voice calling him softly from the black room.

"Devon said I should go free if you could tell I was a virgin. What does that mean?"

It was news to him, but he was not surprised. Devon was a master of double-edged intimidation. On the surface it was insult enough; and that faded into a fill-in-the-blank threat flavored of the black side of things nasty. It should have been enough to make her talk, except that, being who she was, the more lurid implications had winged right through her wholesome spirit. Cat stepped back into the room.

"It means that he was baiting you," said the boy. "He doesn't believe that you're a virgin."

"Couldn't you tell him that I am?" she said in a frightened voice. Her small head was alertly held, the face shadowed, and her breath flickered in the silence like an uncovered candle.

"Try to understand," he said, the words tight with irritation and unfamiliar pity, "it wouldn't make any difference. The man was trying to scare you, and since it didn't work, that's that."

"It didn't work? Heavenly name! They can hear my knees knocking all the way to Paris."

"I should have said, it didn't work well enough."

Not willing to let it go, Merry said, "Couldn't you at least *try* what I asked? Please."

"No," Cat said, his voice severe, his temper thoroughly evaporated. "Devon isn't stupid. And Morgan can see clear inside my femurs. He'd know I was lying. Besides, Devon's bloody likely to double-check, just to give you a lesson you wouldn't forget. He's not a man to push. Do you understand what it means physically? I didn't think so. The man's out to buffet your guts around, Merry. Strain every-thing he says through a cheesecloth." He saw her irises, thick as buckets of blue water, begin to slowly lose their focus. "Damnation. Don't look at me like that. I can't help you. Don't expect me to. There are two ways you can make peace with Devon. Pleasure him, or tell him what he wants to know. You're perfectly capable of doing either. Or both."

She jumped to her feet so fast that her chair skittered on the uneven floorboards. "You and your smug calculations. Hasn't it occurred to you that the *truth* wouldn't save my skin? If Devon found out what I *was* doing at the Musket and Muskrat, he'd peel me to the gristle."

Shocked and angry, Cat abandoned the effort to keep his tone polite. "What lunacy possessed you to make an enemy like Devon?"

"Don't you think I know I'm in trouble?" she shouted back. "Do I look like someone who's made a practice of consorting with pirates? What am I supposed to do now?"

"Take him to bed, damn it."

"Understand this. Never." She was screaming, without knowing it. "It disgusts every feeling!"

"Christsakes, are we talking about the same man? When Devon walks down the streets of Bristol, half the population has neck strain from staring at him. We've got practically to hire eunuchs with scimitars to get him the rest of a chaste night."

They were faced off like weasels. The air between them hissed with their fury; with a movement of his shoulder Cat's unbound hair flared and caught hers, and held, crackling with static.

"Pardon me for asking you to help!" she hurled at him. "My mistake! I'm not accustomed to people whose range of emotion is limited to irritation."

A hush fell. As their lungs competed wrathfully for the same oxygen Cat began to slowly digest her final words. His eyes widened, as she had never seen them before, and ate light like a mirror.

"Who were you expecting? Young Lochinvar?" he asked in a half-paralyzed amazement. The raised muscles in his shoulders began to relax, the white lines around his lips to warm. With a gentle hand he meticulously parted the wanton intercourse of their hair and put her snapping curls behind her arm. In a very different tone he continued, "My emotions aren't limited to irritation. At times I'm annoyed as well."

Crazily, considering the situation, Merry felt the keen pressure of a grin on her lips and an escaping laugh. Her resentment sank like an iron slug. And the boy's astringent blue eyes answered her in a softening that was not a smile but something as humorous and more intimate. It was the first time Merry had taken pleasure in being angry and felt neither ill nor guilty in its aftermath. Cat, she had learned, was uniquely shed of threatening complexities.

"Look," he said, shrugging his own hair back, "do you want to take a bath?"

"What do you mean, a bath?" she repeated, startled.

"Sit in a tub. Rub soap on yourself. Rinse it off. That kind of thing. You know; a bath."

Merry could barely remember the last time she'd been clean, not being able to do much of a job with a can of water and the worry that who knows who might walk in the door at any minute. Merry itched in places that she didn't know the names of. Almost cheerfully she said, "Where could I take a bath?"

"Morgan's cabin. He's on deck, and no one's going to come in this late."

"Won't he mind?" she asked.

"Only if you leave damp towels in a heap on his Persian carpet," he said, his hand on the door handle. "Well? Yes or no?"

Shyly she came toward him, though the curve of her forehead was skeptical. "You wouldn't—watch me, would you?"

"Oh, for Christsake. No; I wouldn't. The way you talk, you'd think I'd never seen a woman stripped, before you."

Three months ago Merry wouldn't have called that much of a reassurance. The new Merry Wilding had spent a week on Rand Morgan's famous pirate ship, lying her scallops off about her identity, and learning the rudiments of how to argue and how to keep her poise in bare feet and a thin nightshirt. It was the new and itchy Merry Wilding who twitched her twisted skirts into place and went with the pirate boy to Morgan's cabin.

She washed herself and her hair in a baroque brass hip bath behind a mother-of-pearl screen from China.

"Are you getting into your dress or do you want a nightshirt?" Cat's voice called around the screen.

"Nothing would induce me to borrow another thing from Morgan," Merry said emphatically, drying between her toes. "Especially since you said he was mad about the torn buttons, which were *not* my fault."

"This one's mine. I never wear it." "It" flew over the top of the screen followed by, of all things, a cranberry-colored man's robe. She had to laugh as she put on the robe because the arms hung ten inches past her hands and the hem swept the floor. Smiling, she came around the screen dangling the long arms in front of her, and the boy stood up and began to roll the cuffs for her.

"Are you cold?"

"No. How come you know so much about everything?" she asked him curiously. "You couldn't be much older than I am."

"How come you know so little? Why do you think we're the same age? How old are you?"

"Eighteen. How old are you?"

"I don't know," he said. "Maybe eighteen. That's what Morgan thinks, anyway." He swept a cushion of crimson brocade from the window bench and tossed it on the floor. "Sit down. I'll brush your hair."

She was so tired, and indeed so naïve, that she sank onto the cushion without a second thought. Registering her trust without comment, the young pirate sat behind her and began to put the silver brush through her hair with soft strokes.

The ship rocked them like a great wooden cradle, and the moon smiled through the window, casting latticed shadows over them and mixing drifts of kindly moonbeams in her hair where it lay across his knee. Soon she had half fallen to sleep; her blameless cheek dropped against the inside of his leg. Like a warm hand on the shoulder, her movement woke Cat from his reverie in time to see Morgan come

through the door. Cat forced moderation on the muscles that had
irrationally tightened and held Morgan's gaze as the older man
crossed the room in his easy stride and let his hand fall, briefly,
through Cat's hair.

"Pretty children," Morgan observed. He smiled thoughtfully as
Merry sat up, knuckling her eyes, looking as though she'd forgotten
where she was.

Cat handed Morgan the hairbrush and said to Merry, "Come
on—you look ready for sleep now."

"Do you know, Cat, instead of selling her in Trinidad, why don't
we keep her?" said Morgan suddenly. "Every boy should have a
pet." He encountered a sharp look from Cat, who, except for Devon
at his age, was the smartest boy Morgan had ever known. As Cat
was putting an arm around Merry and bringing her to her feet to lead
her from the room he said, "You're dreaming, Captain, if you think
I can afford a mistress on what you pay me."

Morgan's soft laughter followed them from the room.

CHAPTER ELEVEN

Merry was not crying when Cat brought her breakfast the next
morning, but he saw as he entered that she stuffed a crumpled
handkerchief under her pillow. Damn Morgan and his bloody mania
for rebirth by fire.

"Morning." He set down her breakfast. "Well?"

She dragged herself from the bed, looking indifferently into her
bowl, and said, "What a surprise. Oatmeal. Take it and throw it
over the side. I'm not going to eat it."

"Now look," Cat said, "don't go back to moping."

"Who's moping? Why should I mope? Wouldn't you mope if someone were going to sell you from an auction block?"

"I *was* auctioned on the block. Guess who bought me? It's interesting to know what you're worth in monetary terms."

She stared at him. "And were you expensive?"

"Extremely. But I was worth it, being young and multifaceted. Of course, you—"

"Are as young but I don't have as many facets?" she said quickly, indignant on principle.

"Merry, Devon isn't going to sell you from an auction block."

Her eyes blazed as she snapped, "Do tell. How chivalrous of him. I suppose he means to strike a private deal and save the percent that would have gone to the auctioneer?" She sat down in the waves of her skirt and thrust her face into her hands. "I'd sooner stay on the *Joke* and be y-y-your—"

"Oh?" His voice was calm. "Why *m-m-mine* and not Devon's?"

"Because I hate Devon!" The words, filtering through her dainty fingers, were startlingly convincing.

It would serve no good purpose to heave her into another argument, so he only said evenly, "Does it matter if you hate him? If you're going to play Adam and Eve with someone you don't like, it might as well be Devon, who's a fair hand at it."

"If he were Adam and I were Eve," she said with dignity, "and if the future of humanity depended on us, I wouldn't let him touch me."

Amused in spite of himself, Cat rested his forearms on the table so that his face and hers were at a level, his orderly braid dangling like rope.

"Merry?"

Merry's fingers curled down to expose the smoky blue fret in her eyes.

"I can tell you in a word what I'm like in bed," he said. "Quick."

Her arched brows knit, and she said crossly, "Good. It can't be too quick for me!"

"For God's sake, Merry. Do you always have to be so bloody melodramatic? You're spending too much time down here immersed in self-pity."

"What choice do I have?" she said, outraged.

"About the self-pity, plenty. Eat your oatmeal. I'm going to talk to Morgan."

And Cat asked for and rather surprisingly received Morgan's permission to take Merry up on deck.

The girl herself was a good deal harder to convince. Devon, it seemed, had planted a seed or two to keep her from trying to escape. Things too terrible to describe would happen if Cat took her on deck and "threw her to the crew," she told him, her face hot with emotion. Devon had shrewdly left the details to her imagination. It took Cat the better part of an hour to clarify for her that there was a difference between being thrown to the crew and having the liberty to go aloft under Morgan's protection. There was no question that if she was presented as a plaything, she would have been used as one. However, as she was Devon's inviolate property, any sea dog who laid a finger on her would find himself eating barnacles off the keel. And anyway, if she thought men lost their heads over sniveling eighteen-year-olds, she was wrong. "Now, if you were twenty-seven and were really good with your—"

"My what?" she interrupted, glaring at him.

"With your ability to deal with the servants," he finished dryly, "there would be more cause for concern."

She stood pale and still as a birch as he wrapped her in a worn coat of blue-dyed velvet trimmed with fur and even let him put a wide-brimmed straw hat on her, but Cat had to forcefully steer her aloft.

The noise and the clutter of the busy deck, the cold slap of the wind, and the brilliant vast sky exploded into Merry's numb senses as she came, blinking, onto the open deck. Hard light shimmered from the ship's brass work, white flame danced in the waves, and tilting back her head, she saw beyond the wide square sails, a bright bank of cumulus clouds, luminous and scudding high in a race with the ship. Everywhere there was motion. The *Black Joke*'s great bow rocked and speared the sea. The horizon lifted and lowered as the potbellied sails strained in the heady wind.

The deck had just been scrubbed, and her feet in Cat's moccasins slipped a little on the drying planks. It was a good excuse to look down and mind her footing instead of the men above her on the crosstrees of the masts or active on the deck. There were winks, smiles that were predatory, exchanges that she was glad not to hear.

"Cat—" she said.

He cut her off. "Try to show some spirit. You're a curiosity, like the five-legged calf." Cat's voice roughened almost imperceptibly. "Sweetheart, you don't have to shake like that. I *told* you. They won't do anything."

Morgan was on the foredeck of the vessel, fresh-faced, romantically disheveled by the wind, and talking to a narrow-shouldered black man whose height topped even Morgan's by more than two inches. A sharp scar cut the man's right eyelid and sliced through his pointed brow. His lips were deep-seamed and narrow, his eyes strict and without frivolity. The taut red linen of his shirt was lively as a cardinal against the ship's timber and rigging. Cat delivered Merry there, his hand on her forearm. She had the sensation she was being carried by the scruff of the neck, like a fox cub, and her knees, as she stood there, were so disobliging as *actually* to quiver.

Morgan laughed when he saw her, and when he had finished speaking with the tall man, he turned and said, "This is Mr. Valentine, our quartermaster. Put your chin up, nestling, so he can have a look at you. Oh, dear. Will we have to teach you how to obey an order? Ah. That's better. I'm pleased to see that in spite of everything you have a functioning neck." A neat movement of Morgan's hand set the straw hat farther back on Merry's head. He turned to the quartermaster. "Well, Tom?"

Thomas Valentine's meager smile touched one side of his lips. "That damned boy . . . Devon walks into a town, and women comely as sea sirens creep at him through the wainscoting. This one, of course, is . . . I'm surprised he's let business keep him away this long. Some of the men aren't too happy about her. You know. Having a woman on board is—"

"What?" Morgan was grinning, but the effect was its opposite. "Bad luck? A Jonah? Kittle cargo?"

"A damned nuisance," Valentine said frankly.

"This one needn't be a nuisance to anyone but Cat." Morgan's flexible, placidly timbred voice carried across the deck to more than a dozen actively interested ears. "All anyone need manage around her is a little continence. And if any of the men complain about having a woman on board, I hope you'll send them to talk to me. I'll be fascinated to learn who sails in my crew and still has the superstitions of a lake fisherman.'' Every head within a twenty-yard radius turned quickly back to its task; men who for one reason or another were not standing high just now in Morgan's credit betrayed themselves with whistling that was too nonchalant and an excess of diligence at their work.

Tom Valentine's good eyebrow rose. "You won't find me making an objection if Cat wants to install one of Devon's convenients on deck. Just so he keeps her out of the way. And I hope she's not a troublemaker.''

"If she makes any trouble, then with my blessing you're welcome to—'' Morgan delivered one of his less benign smiles to Merry while he allowed the hesitation to develop artistically and then cut it off exactly right with "Request that she desist.''

Mr. Valentine had no reason to worry. The last thing Merry wanted to do was make trouble. But Trouble, which for eighteen years had avoided Merry, had other ideas. Trouble was in a whimsical humor that morning, for Merry's next introduction on the pirate ship was to fat Dennis.

Morgan and Valentine moved off, and Merry stood nervously with Cat on the quarterdeck. Holding her hat with one hand, she tipped her head to stare up the one-hundred-and-thirty-foot length of the mast when something pink, dripping, and furred was thrust like a poker into the folds of her gown and between her knees. Too jarred to scream, she fell against Cat, who caught her hard against his hip with an arm encircling her waist.

"Merry!'' Cat said. "Are you all right?'' Not to her (she hoped) he added, "Damn! You stupid pig. Snuff it, will you?''

At Merry's feet there stood a grunting, sniffling pig, its ears flapped forward like blinders, trotters clicking angrily on the deck.

"Away with ye, Dennis! If that's the way ye have with the ladies, it's as well ye are a pig,'' said an old sailor, who had been sewing, his back to the gunwale and nested in the ecru hills of a sail. He had found his feet easily and pushed the pig away from Merry with his bare toes. The man's chapped pink lips spread over bottle-shaped teeth that ran with char lines, and his skin was seamed like broken biscuit crust, but kindness twinkled in the pale spearpoints of his eyes. "Don't fear, lassie. No harm'll come to ye."

Cat lowered Merry to the deck and sent the old man a look that she couldn't interpret; then, dropping to his knees, he cracked his thumb and mid-finger once. With hoggish ecstasy the pig drove its pink snout under the boy's hand, shaking its screwy tail and squealing. Cat said, "Pet him, Merry, he won't bite." Her hand was taken in a firm grip and slid around the pig's ear. "No. He can't even feel that. Under his jaw. See?"

The old sailor smiled at Merry's expression and at her attempt to befriend the pig, and he said, "There now. He's liking ye already. Old Dennis here, he was just a mite jealous, at firstly, seeing ye with Mr. Cat, here. Fair worships the lad, does Dennis."

Under happier circumstances there might be any number of pleasant jollities one could make about someone who drew the affection of a pig. A single look at Cat's face would have informed the slowest wit that none of these were a very good idea. Merry cleared her throat. "Dennis?" she said.

The older man gave her an encouraging grin. "Aye. Aye. He came aboard as a wee ruddy porker, with a yaller ribbon 'round his neck. We mean to eat him sometime, but who can do it with him being such a pet and all?"

"Oh," Merry said. "But—Dennis?"

"If there's a pig on a ship, everyone calls it Dennis," said Cat. "Don't ask me why."

"It's the porcine moniker," agreed the old man. "We sailors are a dry-witted lot, save for the nippy young ones like Mr. Cat, here. It's pleased to meet ye, I am, missy. Sails, ye can call me. I make 'em, I mend 'em—have done for fifty years. Come sit with me by the ridin' bitts whilst I do my work. There's protection from the weather, a bit. Wind this morning strong enough to unhair a dog, eh?"

"Yes, sir," said Merry, whose hair was starting to creep from under the hat. She perched self-consciously in the spot Sails had indicated with his gnarled hand.

"There we are," Sails said. "Shipshape and Bristol fashion. Cat, ye can be off about your work. It'll cause talk, to have ye hovering there like a snake watching its only egg."

Far above the *Black Joke* the sun was a lonely stranger, a flat circle with sharp edges that were blue and phosphorescent. A breeze rich in sea spice ruffled foam from the slate-covered ocean waves and made the ship deck lively with furling shirts and pant legs, swinging lines, fresh cheeks. Under the uproar of the great wheaten staysails Merry watched bright, busy light skitter on the sailmaker as he mended. His knuckles were swollen and red, like candied cherries. His palm was so tough that he used it as a thimble, but there was elegance in each minute turn of his fingers. He looked up at her with a smile from time to time after Cat had vanished belowdecks. Catching her glancing apprehensively around her, the sailmaker said, "Scruff-lookin' lot, ain't they? The black sheep of everybody's family; but nae so bad as they're painted, only younger sons wi' nary a penny to 'prentice them in a trade, sailors who made mutinees under ship's masters who'd made belayin' pin hash of their men, escaped slaves like Tom Valentine. Crew wi' Morgan, ye can make more than fifty times the year's pay ye would in the Navy, and if ye're already on the shark side of the law . . . Could ye cast me that pricker, next to ye foot? Aye, that's it. The wee marlinespike. There's a fine, useful lass. Now tuck yer hands in 'tween yer knees there—it's cold as blue flugin—an' I'll tell ye about an auld witch lady I know what lives in Liverpool. She can foretell a sailor's death to the hour, jest by fixing her hand on his pulse."

Sitting by Sails, Merry saw for the first time the *Black Joke* take another ship. The *Joke* had luffed up close upon the wind at the lookout's call of "Sail ho" and made such a casual chase of the far vessel that Merry barely understood the import of it until a bow cannon on the lower gundeck erupted with an ear-blistering crack, which caused her to bite her tongue.

The shot had been a warning, and as it subsided in a frothy splash off the other vessel's stern the *Black Joke* ran up its frightening standard, Morgan's Jolly Roger, the grinning skeleton caressing an hourglass. Sails had barely paused in his story about a Cree wizard who sold winds by the pouch for a pound of tobacco. Merry watched the bright dart of the other ship's flag shimmy and drop with near comical haste as she struck her colors in surrender.

In the hours that passed, the longboats went back and forth, leaving empty from the *Joke* and returning with copper-bound casks

and bales wrapped in cerecloth and once a rickety crate of chickens
that poked out their heads like jack-in-the-boxes and cackled
disapprovingly at the pirates. The scrawny rooster wriggled through
a broken slat as the longboat neared the *Joke* and crowed victoriously from the starboard bow. Merry watched as a pirate wearing a
black and white striped shirt went at the bird in a flying dive and
came down headfirst in the water. The other pirates in the boat
guffawed mightily, and the youngest of them, whom Merry recognized as the dark-eyed boy with the soft West Indian accent who had
spoken to Cat on the day he had brought her aboard the *Joke*, began
with sweetly exaggerated solicitude to help his comrade back into
the boat, but when the sodden pirate was almost aboard, the dark-
eyed boy sent him sprawling back into the water with the gentle
shove of a shapely booted leg. Men on the *Joke* began to gather by
the gunwale, laughing and calling mock reproaches to the boy, and
behind Merry the sailmaker chuckled and said, "That laddie, Raven.
Always up to a bit of fun. Good lad. Every inch of him a man."

On the longboat Raven appeared to be making a long-winded
apology to the wet pirate who was treading water furiously, spouting
cold seawater like an orca. The model of contrition, Raven offered
his friend in the water the end of an oar, began to draw him toward
the boat, and let go at the very last minute to send the man toppling
backward into a curtaining fountain of sea splash. The pirates on
deck were doubled over with mirth as the poor sodden fellow gave
Raven a crude gesture and began swimming to the ship, followed by
the longboat, oars diligently breaking water and Raven laughing and
pelting him with eggs.

No sooner had Raven set foot back on the *Joke* than he was
collared by Thomas Valentine, cuffed backhand, and given a lecture
that appeared to do him no earthly good, judging from his happily
unrepentant face. In the end Valentine had mussed the boy's hair
and sent him, with a kick, to "pick oakum."

It was an alarming surprise for Merry when not ten minutes later
Raven appeared on the bow deck with a coil of old rope and a
canvas sack. With not so much as a molecule of proper inhibition,
he flopped fore-down on the cold deck beside her with his chin in
one square palm. As a point of pride Merry tried to match the dark
gaze, sweet as an infant's, that dripped over her like hot cocoa as the

wind tickled through the waves of his long midnight hair, his big silky black jacket, and the loose legs of trousers that carried a belt of steel links. He had an uncommonly attractive face, with eyes that were almost lovely, wind-bitten skin, a straight nose, an untroubled brow, and a firm, clever mouth pleated with pronounced smile lines. The bodies of sailors, Merry was beginning to find, were uniformly superb, and on that bleak thought she looked quickly away.

Hindered by the insensitivity of the unselfconscious, Raven had no idea what he'd done to offend her. Poor beauty, she was almost as spooked today as she had been when he'd first seen her, fetching, even with her nose running. Tragedy dwelt like a blue flame in her big eyes; the shallow pulsebeat in the golden hollow of her throat was luffing like a spanker on a vessel that was hauled too close to the wind. He had seen the look before on women about to be raped, and he found no charm in having it turned on him. More and more he had begun to understand why Cat, who had no scruples in the bedroom or out of it, still hated to see a woman taken violently. Astonishing that the captain had kept her aboard when she was bound to set everyone's appetite to roast. But she was safe, perfectly safe. Morgan had cheerfully announced that he would see any man emasculated who laid a greedy hand on her, and Rand Morgan was a man who kept his promises.

Sails clipped a thread with a scissors made of the jaws of a piranha. "Devon's lady friend, boy," he said, gently reproving.

Raven twisted to look at the sailmaker. "Doesn't every shellback on the *Joke* know it? I've got ears."

"That's it, laddie. It's interested in having ye keep all the parts of yer body, I am. I'm thinking yer memory is shorter than it might be."

"Don't worry about my memory, old man," Raven said. "Bless her heart, would I do her any harm? It looks to me like she's scared enough already. Devon don't beat her, does he? He don't seem the type. Sweet-tempered."

Merry had bruises over bruises on her arms that could witness to the sweetness of Devon's temper. If Raven's words told her anything, it was how far down she was on the scale of Devon's affections.

"Keep yer oar out of it, lad," said the sailmaker, the narrow eyes kind and practical. "She be having enough to sink her without every nose in the Western Ocean trying to sniff out a bit of scuttlebutt on her to share with his mates. Ye can do better.''

Rolling smoothly to his hip and swinging into a sitting position, Raven wondered what in the world would be better. His experience with women was extensive for his age, but it was limited to a class of females that he could pull on his knee, and slip his hand into their bodice, and they would giggle and coo, and he'd take them to a bare pallet stuffed with a donkey's breakfast. Then he'd be the one to giggle and coo. And there was nothing on God's earth better than that. Still. The sun would set rosier if he could bring a smile to that sad, lovely face. That night, before sunset, he had.

He had brought tea for her, hot in a mug, and worked on the oakum until she had asked him shyly and warily what he was doing.

"This? Why, it's oakum." His fluid brown eyes filled with astonished compassion at so vast and touching an innocence. "A weak old rope shedded. It's used to caulk the ship's seams and such. Swells when it's wet. Valentine sets me to it when I'm on his black list."

"For pushing that man into the water?" asked Merry.

"No." Again the astonishment. Then, grinning, "For wasting eggs."

Within minutes he had coaxed her into helping him. Her finished pile grew ludicrously slowly. His was mountainous beside it. But he gaily praised her effort and to Merry's horror brought his particular friends from the crew to admire it. Mon, there had never been such oakum. The gulls would be carryin' it away for nesting. Such a good job, she was doing, did it matter that the *Joke* would have chewed the old oakum and sunk to Davy Jones before Merry had made enough to fill a single knothole?

Merry was not used to teasing, or strangers, or for that matter, men, and these, surely, deserved no more than the frigid turn of her shoulder. Their morals were low, their manners rough, their trade despicable. It was bad enough to have commerce with Cat, on whom she was dependent.

It took them the full third of an hour filled with a splendidly vivacious assault on her defenses to drag a smile from her, and once they'd had that triumph, she knew she might as well give up.

After the tentative bond she had made with Cat, friendship with

Raven was like being force-fed beer bubbles. Life had toughened Raven's treacle-sweet disposition, but the harsh discipline of twelve tender years at sea had neither stemmed his floodtide effervescence or lessened a natural love for the human race, who, in his case, had done precious little to deserve it.

Picking oakum was just the beginning. The next morning he had her up at daybreak to see a school of jellyfish, the shiny, throbbing bodies abob in blue water as far as the lens of a telescope would encompass. After that Merry found herself settled near the scuttlebutt, the cask where the crew could draw water and gossip, while Raven taught her knots: a bowline knot, a common bend, a rolling hitch, a clove hitch; and the fancy ones: Matthew's roses and Turk's heads.

With Dennis trying to climb in her lap Merry learned to name each sail, in order; and what could be told about a ship from the shape of her hull and her running rigging. There were ropes to be coiled, rigging to be inspected and repaired, leads to be taken.

The *Black Joke* was quite a place for a young woman whose eighteen protected years had allowed small outlet for a powerful natural curiosity. There were some questions that brought her silences and evasions, but to ask about the sea or the ships that sailed there was to have an answer instantly; to admire a skill was to have it demonstrated as more and more the pirates came to accept the novelty of her presence. She was as alien to them as they were to her. Few of them had heard a woman speak with the intriguing aristocratic accent that Morgan and Devon used. The gentility of her manners was a thing experienced only at the theater in low satires of the upper classes, and her face and figure were like those of plaster saints bought for a sixpence and given to one's godmother on fair day.

The ship was a tight-knit if not loving community, and one learned swiftly here to be tolerant and live without privacy. It was a democracy that elected Rand Morgan as captain unanimously and Thomas Valentine as quartermaster by a comfortable majority. Their leadership brought with it a meticulously enforced routine, the minimum of bloodshed, and fat purses. A dirty ship meant disease, bad rigging death in a storm, sloppy sailing capture and hanging, and the men on the *Black Joke* wanted to live and get rich. Major decisions were put to the vote of the crew, and while Tom Valentine could punish lesser offenses at his discretion, any serious crime went to a trial. It was not a bad life for men born paupers, and if their hearts of steel didn't exactly melt to molasses at a glance from Merry, even Valentine had to admit they softened.

The days grew slowly warmer as they rode south, and it became harder to wear the jacket that she must to preserve her modesty in the thin gown of green silk that she was rapidly coming to hate. Cat discovered her one midday slumped dizzily against a barrel and carried her below, applied wet towels to her red face, and with powerful doubts about its efficacy, brought her some of his own clothes and talked her into putting them on. It was not easy, and he might not have succeeded if she hadn't been halfway into a case of heatstroke.

The move into boy's clothes, initially mortifying to Merry, was a delight to the crew. When she came on deck dressed in Cat's loose-bottomed denim trousers and a short jacket, they greeted the change with shouts of good-natured laughter and honored the new outfit by teaching her to run aloft (climb the rigging), to shoot the sun (take a meridian altitude), and to arm the lead (prepare to take a sounding). For a lark Raven showed her how to throw a knife; they laughed when she held the knife as though it were a goat's stomach, and laughed as well when, at her first try, the knife went end over end into the sea; all laughed, that is, except the owner of the knife, who said "Hey!" forlornly. Her pride at stake, Merry's second try had buried the knife cleanly if inaccurately in the mast, and the pirates with great hilarity had thrown themselves to their calloused knees, pleading for their lives.

On the poop deck Tom Valentine was heard by those standing closest to mutter something under his breath about Tom Cox's traverse, "two turns around the longboats and a pull at the scuttlebutt," which is a polite name for killing time. Cat, watching also, had buried his forehead into the arch of his palm and wondered how he was going to explain it all to Devon.

CHAPTER TWELVE

On the day Devon came back, they were teaching Merry to fire the cannon. The *Black Joke* had dropped her anchor in the green ooze that floored a forbidding cove on the coast of Spanish Florida. Gulls scavenged in the warm white sunlight, and from the *Joke* you could see an ocher strip of beach scattered with shabby tents made from aged sails. Naked children ran like young animals in the breaking swell or played under the glowing browns of the sea oats that dotted the far dunes. Women walked to and fro carrying water buckets, goats grazed on solitary patches of salt meadow grass, pirates lolled against broken casks, drinking and swapping gossip.

There were other ships here, riding under bare poles and grounding in their beef bones—they'd thrown garbage over the side till they were fair squatting on it, or so Raven had told Merry. And at night there was a bonfire on the beach, with a great carcass dripping yellow fat turning on a spit. Crew from the *Joke* not serving their trick at lookout made off like small shot for shore, swimming if they had to when the boats were full. Merry heard the echoes of their bawdy songs drifting across the water until early morning. Clean and sober they left, and drunk and dirty they returned, and after not so many shore leaves it was getting hard to tell who was C and S and who was D and D except for Cat, who never drank to excess, and Morgan, whose manners never altered for the better or the worse, however many intoxicants he consumed.

At four bells, Merry stood at the stern. The shirt she wore was white and full-sleeved with blue cuffs, a front panel trimmed in blue braid, and a blue collar. The breeze playfully lifted the long tails of her red neck scarf as she watched Cat, cross-legged at her feet, putting the final stitches in the flaring hem of her new white pantaloons.

Bright-eyed drunk and enthusiastic, Raven arrived back from shore and sought out Merry. The peaking afternoon sun moved with surprise over the black varnished brim of a wide antique hat as he doffed it elegantly for Merry. No one was sure where he had got it, but it had an ostrich plume on it dyed livid lilac, and that raised a lot of speculation. The hat was transferred in short order from Raven to Merry, the feather bent round to tickle the underside of her chin.

"Stuck a feather in her hat an' called it macaroni!" sang Raven, stepping on Cat. "Tack me, Cat, don't you think she looks like that swell painted picture in Mme. Teo's? You know, the picture that Morgan says is a dead poor copy of a—a—what's his name?"

"Rubens," Cat said. "Don't *you* think Merry's a little short of flesh for that? And as for that hat—"

"Blackbeard!" cried Raven happily. "That's it!"

"I look like Blackbeard?" Merry asked as Raven tossed her to sit near the taffrail, eyeing her like an artist.

"Wait a minute! Wait a minute! Eye patch, that's what you need. We'll use Cat's kerchief, here. C'mon, Cat, you don't need a black kerchief, mon. Damned foppish, and black don't suit you."

"I think it does," said Merry, getting her right eye covered. "Black is— Oh, no! Ouch! What do you mean, sticking that pistol down my waist? Take it back!"

Raven stood back, admiring his harried creation. "Absolutely not, m'lady. Ain't loaded. Jeez, know what you need? Braids and matches. Blackbeard dipped hemp cord in saltpeter and limewater and set them to burning under his hat in a fight. Scared the devil out of his enemies, eh? Tell you what, Merry—"

"Come within ten feet of her with saltpeter and hemp, and you go over the side, you lushy idiot," said Cat, who had been in a particularly bad temper since morning anyway. "You're likely to singe off her hair. Go below, would you, and sleep it off."

Raven took direction only moderately well when he was sober. Drunk, he was about as responsive as a toothache. Merry found her wrist seized in his firm, joyful fingers, and she was pulled at a run to the lower gundeck. They collected, on the way, Will Saunders, the runaway younger son of an Indigo planter, a swarthy, rawboned boy genius with copious sideburns, who at the tender age of twenty-two had risen through the ranks to become Morgan's sailing master, and who, by virtue of an exceptionally strong head, was a lot more inebriated than he looked to Merry.

Below, Merry found the lint-speckled sunlight bursting in blinding squares through the gunports. Moist heat hung in the narrow oak gallery as in a sauna, and the black shafts of the cannons spewed the air with the reek of hot metal, brass polish, and stale gunpowder. In past battles body-spice had run as sweat into the golden floorboards that gave back the trapped scent, wet-baked and pungent.

Raven and Saunders were an uproar in the dour quiet that drew Joe Griffith, master gunner, from his nap in the fo'c'sle. Beaming with healthy middle age, the tattooed crucifix that was a charm against shark death on his chunky forearms gleaming like a blurred beetle, the gunner loved the cannons from fire-spitting fore to aft as though they were his children and had wept for a day during a hurricane when Morgan had ordered a long nine- and two six-pounders thrown over to lose weight. If Raven wanted to fire one of the little darlings, well, sure, he could. Except, Merry learned with a mixture of trepidation and excitement, that Raven meant for her to shoot it. A three-gun salute to the United States of America. Was she a patriot or wasn't she? asked Raven, having no idea that he was playing a major chord.

Merry had hardly spent her life pining to fire artillery, but there aren't many people who'll turn down the kind of chance to do it just once without hurting anyone. And a salute to the United States . . .

"You space your shots like they do in the Navy, see, by counting," Griffith said.

"No!" said Saunders, whose short military career had been spent fomenting mutiny. "With a verse. Here's one: 'If I hadn't been born a bloody fool, I wouldn't have joined the Navy. Fire!' Try it. No, with rhythm. Now. Got a salt pinch in your pocket? No?" he exclaimed, affecting horror, without giving her time to answer. "Disaster! Raven, quickly teach her a hand sign for luck!"

Raven, who was propped loosely against the bulkhead, looking like he might slither to the deck with a little encouragement, said obediently, "Hand sign. Merry, stick the middle finger of your right hand into your mouth and—"

"I won't. It's dirty!" she said with spirit.

"All the better, lovey. Wipe it on your britches first, if you must. Then—"

"Devil take you," snapped Cat, radiating disapproval from where he sat on a shot locker. "What she doesn't need is to learn a lot of filthy habits."

"You wouldn't catch Cat with his middle finger in his mouth," Saunders said dreamily. He leaned across the big gun, his grin like a scythe. "Who knows where it's been?"

"I do," said Raven, "and you would too if you'd noticed him last night with the fair Louisa on his lap. Eager, she was, to unwrap his pretty braids." Seeing from the corner of his eye that Cat was starting to get up, he added hastily, laughing, "Oh, I've done, Cat. I've done. Don't make shrimp bait of poor little me." Hiccuping giggles, he collapsed gracefully to the floorboards.

"Drunk," Saunders said affectionately, "as a fish. Don't put your finger in your mouth then, Merry. Spit in your left palm instead."

Staring open-eyed at Raven, Merry said, "I'm not sure, Mr. Saunders, if I really. . . ."

"Merry, lamb, you can't be delicate with superstition. Spit!" Saunders with Griffith was loading the cannon. "Hey. You call that spit? I've seen more spray from a sneezing kitten. Now, make a right-handed fist and smack the left palm. There you go!"

She had shot off two rounds, and dusted with gunpowder, she was trying laughingly to lift a twenty-pound cannonball in scorched fingers when she caught Cat by accident in her gaze and saw that he was staring beyond her toward the door. Alarmed by something she saw in his expression, Merry froze, and then turned.

Devon, still and relaxed, framed like a portrait in the narrow rectangle of the open door, was holding her in his silken gaze. She might have cried out, she wasn't sure, but her fingers splayed thoughtlessly from the shock of it and sent the cannonball humming across the deck at Devon. If he hadn't sidestepped quickly, he would have gotten it over his toes.

She never heard the single, curt syllable he uttered or the fluent string of dialogue he addressed to the men with her as he walked slowly across the deck. Except for a softly pulsating crackle Merry was deaf.

Raven had told her what she must do to protect her hearing, but he had accompanied it with so many conflicting and jocularly intended orders that she hadn't taken the right one seriously. In mime she saw Saunders dousing the match in a sand bucket, his lips energetically shaping an explanation to Devon. Griffith was dissolving in apologies. Cat was grim. Raven—Merry looked over her shoulder—was sleeping against the bulkhead, curled like a puppy. Devon, finished for the meantime with the others, turned his straight-edged attention to Merry.

She wondered how her face must appear to him; dirty, certainly, frightened, and a bit bewildered; not reacting in the proper way to the things he was saying, which she was glad she could not hear. She was probably giving off other signs she wasn't aware of, but still, it was amazing how soon he guessed. Catching her jaw in the firm arc of his hand, he snapped his fingers once by her ear. Merry saw him speak to her again, his face more gentle; this time she was able to gather that he was reassuring her that her hearing would return. It hardly seemed to matter. Her heart was beating in bass, and her insides had tied themselves into a bowline knot, a common bend, a rolling hitch, and Matthew Walker's roses. This was the last grape seed, proof that the events of the last month had driven her out of her mind; she was deliriously happy to see Devon. Delirium. That was a good word for it. The paralysis of the eardrum was joined somehow with a paralysis of the brain. It was not the right reaction, not the right one at all, and in fact, it was so nearly the opposite of what her reaction ought to have been that she had to wonder if some of her brain cells were facing backward. Heartsick at the monstrous betrayal of her body, Merry generaled it back into dislike and frigidity, hoping none of the hectic, pained struggle was showing on her features.

Devon took his hand away and said something curtly to Cat, and relief from Devon's scrutiny and his touch was so immense that tears came, hot and pricking like straw near the base of her eyes. Cat, it appeared, was having a lot to say to Devon, and although the strict formality of their conversation gave no clue to its content, the glances she was getting from Saunders and Griffith indicated that her well-being was directly and unpleasantly involved. There was a muted pop, and a sizzle, and Merry's hearing came back just as

Devon, evidently in the middle of a sentence, was saying, ". . . common sense because as I recall I requested—"

"I know what your orders were," Cat said, "but you weren't here, and she wasn't eating."

There was a second pop, and a loud mechanical buzz overlaid her hearing for another minute and then subsided.

". . . so she left a note," Cat was saying, "on the table telling me and hid under the bedclothes weeping while I read it."

"And of course," said Devon coldly, "she needed a healthful regimen of fresh air and exercise to survive the rigors of menstruation?"

"Take it up with Morgan," said Cat. "First he sent Sails to her and then Raven. If I were you, I'd ask him why."

Devon's beautifully shaped eyes were glinting softly. "He's already told me—" Devon gave the smile that wasn't a smile—"that he wanted to make a man of her. Lucky girl. Did it occur to you that if you had put your compassion in the right place and let her break, I could have let her go?"

He had left then, or almost left. Cat's voice halted him by the door.

"She doesn't break, Devon," he said. "You'd have to kill her trying. She doesn't break. She just collapses like wet sugar cake."

Merry spent the rest of the afternoon avoiding Devon.

Sunset hung in pink fronds over the cove. Where Merry sat on the bow, the slow shadows found her, lying on her cheeks like hands shading milk in the sunlight. She had huddled beside Raven, who was groggily awake and playing solitaire with a limp deck of dog-eared cards. She helped him when he missed a play, and he thanked her, not speaking, with a desultory pat on her knee or sometimes, absently, the empty air. Across from them, beside Sails, Saunders was teasing a high, delicious melody from a tin whistle.

More than five minutes had passed since Merry had said a word. Five minutes ago Devon had come aloft, and he was standing to the fore of the mizzen talking with Thomas Valentine. As Merry watched them a large snowy gull sank in swooping circles toward the deck and hung mewing in the face of the breeze near the mizzen. Devon looked up and smiled, his light hair falling back, his eyes shining. Drifting like a dream sequence, the beautiful bird circled again and landed on Devon's quickly extended arm. The gull tucked its black-tipped wings, and the bright yellow bill dove into Devon's chest pocket and found a biscuit.

Stopping in the middle of a song, following the line of Merry's gaze, Saunders said, "Devon's gull. Even the dumb creatures love the man."

"If only," Merry said tartly, "we were all so privileged as to be male *and* gifted."

Her tone penetrated even the haze of Raven's hangover.

"Milady, with the wind in the right direction you can hear the pleasure-moans of Devon's ladies over two counties," he said, twisting around to look at Merry. His dark, dark eyes were troubled. "I've never met anyone before who didn't want to own a piece of him. How is it you're exempt?"

"Oh, I'd like to own pieces of him. As long as each was disconnected from the other," she said stiffly. "You can play on the ace of hearts. Sails, you remember, don't you, that you were going to tell me about the time you saw the mermaid."

"Oh? Oh, aye! The wee mermaid. T'was near the Rammerees, off the Horn, ye see," began Sails, always ready to rig his yarn tackle. And as he spoke Merry shut her eyes and missed, because of that, the hand Raven stretched comfortingly toward her, and Saunders, moving silently on the softly rocking deck, who caught Raven's wrists in angry fingers and shoved it away from Merry with a warning shake of his head. It was all very well to have the girl for a playmate, but her heartaches would have to belong only to herself. Raven had to learn. It would be cruel to them both to let them develop the illusion that Raven could help her. And Sails, in pity, put his best into the mermaid.

More than a quarter hour later Merry still hadn't opened her eyes.

"And so," he said, "before she slipped off into the water, she gave me this very pearl to keep."

Merry had to open her eyes to look at the pearl, and Sails dropped it, white and precious, into her palm, where it sat like a cloudy tear. "It's beautiful. I've never seen one before. Please, tell me more about what the mermaid looked like," said Merry, who had trouble believing that any story told so seriously was a simple piece of fiction.

"As to that," said Sails, "she was scales from the navel down, like a mackerel, and hair blacker'n Cap'n Morgan's eyes, wi' wee points in it like stars. Seaweed was draped o'er her graceful-like, and there was a fine net o' gold 'cross her chest.''

Raven looked up. "So? Last time, as I recall, her breasts were bare and pale, and there was a diamond in her navel and a ruby in her—''

Saunders grinned. "Shush, child. Don't you know we have a separate version for the lassies?''

Joining them quietly and with shattering suddenness, Devon said, "And a ruby in her hair. Her nose,'' he went on, imitating Sails's brogue, "was petite, mind ye, and pointed like a wee puir fishie. Valentine tells me he knows some lazy sons of bitches who are going to be picking oakum tomorrow.''

Within a minute Merry was alone with Devon.

Tall and flat-hipped, he stood with his back to the gunwale, the sun a crimson globe behind him, catching delicate bronze tones in his hair. The fine-boned elegance of his features needed no blazing pastel sundown to flatter them; it was difficult to ignore the constant sensual promise of that experienced mouth and subtly arousing gaze. For once his expression was not hard for Merry to interpret. He was looking at her like a gardener mulling over what to do about the mole problem. It would have been nice to be able to match his stare with a cool one of her own; nice, but impossible. The blood rose steam-heated to her cheeks. Nausea sat in her stomach.

Aft, on the port side, men were lowering one of the boats to leave for shore, and their voices mingled in the glowing air with water lap and the whirr of wind striking feathers as a plover flew over the ship in a swift black arrow. From the galley came food smells and the sounds of Cook shouting at his help; the friendly sounds of shipboard domesticity that somehow tonight had lost their power to reassure. And when the hovering tension became unbearable, Merry got awkwardly to her feet and started to leave.

"Running again?'' he inquired softly, with amusement.

She had forgotten, over the interval of their separation, how cleverly he could control her. How irritating it was to have one's most private drives analyzed, reduced to simple logic, and hung like a kissing bough over one's head. If her emotions hadn't been in such turmoil, she would have lost her temper. As it was, she turned with a snap and walked back to him.

"Or," he said, "were you going to fetch more ordnance?"

"If you are referring to the cannonball," Merry said, "that was an accident."

"Really? With the floor toward me sloping uphill? Do you know, I'm beginning to envy men whose debauchees content themselves with a slapped cheek. No one could criticize your attacks for lack of originality."

The tone was, overall, more friendly than she had expected. She said lamely, "Cat hadn't told me you were back. I was startled."

"Startled. Were you? There was a lot of that going around. I left you very properly cowering on your bed and return to find you very improperly capering around a cannon. And here I thought all you could do was be pathetic."

That stung, but she was not about to let him know how much. "Pardon me. A full fortnight with nary a soul threatening to torture me and here I am, forgetting my place. Good job you're back to put me into it again."

"Good Lord! And a swagger too." A smile traced on the erotic mouth. "From Merry with an *e* and two *r*'s to Anne Bonney, scourge of the Indies."

Anne Bonney was a celebrated female pirate of the last century who ended her cutthroat career not, as one might think, on the business end of a gibbet, but in unsanctioned pregnancy. If there was a lesson in that for Merry, she had no wish to figure out what it was.

"Piracy is a hateful trade," she said, with a belligerence she would rapidly come to regret, "and if you think that wearing britches makes me into one, then I'll take them off right now."

As blunders went, it ranked among her worst. Catching the inference on the last word, Merry tried to choke it back in; naturally it was too late. She turned hastily to spare herself the shame of having to watch him laugh.

Before long she felt his hands, warm on her shoulders. She was pulled backward and settled kindly against the firm support of his body, the contact neither forced nor cruelly suggestive. Instead, it had almost a matter-of-fact quality to it and a reluctant affection. His fingers searching comfortably in her hair, found and exposed her ear, and she could feel his breath there.

"Don't be afraid," he said. "We don't punish maladroit ladies here by making them unbritch publicly." His lips brushed her delicately, barely touching her skin. "You and I probably aren't ready for anything as audacious as polite communication, but should we see if we can manage a crude facsimile?"

Light-headed from his touch and from the effort not to show it, Merry nodded. He turned her in his hands to face him and then stepped back and released her.

"Subjective evidence to the contrary, my sweet captive, I don't make a habit of carrying off and maltreating very young women, be they ever so unwisely bed warmers for my enemies. You amuse me, and that's probably going to save your life, but at best your presence is damnably inconvenient. Why don't we get rid of one another? I'm willing to make you one final offer: For the answer to my question, only one, I'll give you your freedom, plus a payment in gold, the sum to be your choice, within reason. And I'll make sure that you'd never be traced as the information source."

The telltale blush was still staining her cheeks, brightly spread like cheap rouge. She ought to have told him to stop right there. She *would* have told him to stop right there if her jaw hadn't been paralyzed with wrath.

He said, "All I want, Merry, is the name of either of the two men who were with you that night at the Musket and Muskrat."

His searching gaze was thorough, and Merry, having more than a nodding acquaintance with the swift processes of his mind, worked quickly to damper the telltale indignation. There would be no saying "How dare you! Do you think that I'd sell out my brother and my cousin for your filthy money?"

"I won't do it," she said with dignity and received back a long, cool stare before he shrugged and answered her good-humoredly.

"It's your life, angel."

"And now," said Merry, her expression brittle and sparkling, "you'll turn me over to the crew?"

"Will I? It isn't likely to do me much good. They seem to have already turned themselves over to you. Baubles for the fairy queen; toadstool umbrellas for the pixies; you have your own sorcery, don't you?"

It was not easy to tell precisely what he meant, but it didn't imply a great deal of trust. "I suppose," she said, "that you're disappointed not to find me lying dismembered on the deck."

"Try to see things sometimes in shades of gray, Merry. I'm interested in a little sensible compromise; the less I hurt you along the way, the better. You might try taking some of the responsibility for finding an intelligent solution."

"But I thought we already had one," she responded quickly. "You were going to sell me into slavery—"

"Did I say that?" His vivid eyes twinkled appreciatively in mock surprise.

Furiously, "You know you did! Why are you smiling about it now? Did you mean it, or were you just trying to frighten me? It's as Cat told me, isn't it? That you're out to buffet my—my emotions." She could not bring herself to say the word *guts*.

Slight as it had been, he caught, understood, and grinned at the hesitation. "Merry—" The dying sunlight graced her, pinking the white porcelain cheeks, where the skin was as finely textured as a young child's. There were times when her eyes became so wide and susceptible that their expression, like that in a caricature, was almost silly, a structural trick of sumptuous facial bones. It was hardly the kind of thing he would have expected to find endearing, and he might not have, had it not been combined in her with a dazzling lack of awareness. Not once had he seen her use her looks as a weapon, which was amazing, because it was a remarkable one, and it was not as though she had many. He would've sworn she'd been raised in a mythological kingdom where there were no mirrors. "I'm no more immune to sorcery than the next man," he said softly, gazing down into her blue eyes, fixed on him with an infant's unwinking stare. "Hoodlum though I am, I'm not going to barter away your seductive little hide." Nor was he ready to take the chance of setting her free until he learned something about who and what she was; and while, for that reason, he had tried to scare the truth out of her, Cat, as usual, was correct. You cannot keep a young and obviously fragile person in a state of constant terror.

"Then you'll release me?" she said, almost sick with hope. "Please. You've admitted you don't want me."

"No. You'll leave when you talk, Merry."

It was having to make statements to her of just that kind of stagy vulgarity that was most offensive to an intellect that knew better. Melodrama, which he'd always hated, seemed to be an integral part of the abductor role. The corners of his lips teased upward into a smile. "And you misunderstand. I said you were inconvenient—but not that I didn't want you. I do want you. Or have you forgotten?"

His hands found her waist in a movement that was swift and graceful, and Merry was drawn into a firm embrace before she'd had time to begin the work of relaxing the hard knot in her throat. Inside her skin was a body that was reeling, a heart bouncing painfully into ribs that seemed not to fit any longer in her chest. His clothes and hers, under normal circumstances perfectly adequate, were suddenly a shockingly thin layer, a sparse weave of threads that allowed too clearly the caress of one body by another. Exploded was the happy fiction that it had all been Morgan's drugs, the first night with Devon in his cabin, that had made her dissolve like ice crystals in an oven. As little as she knew about intimacy, she was getting a very strong hint from that space in her body where the blood was starting to convene; it had certainly vacated her head. Everything neck up was cold and giddy, and everything neck down was hot and swimming. And everything from her waist down was boiling like spiced stew.

She tried desperately to strain her hips away from him, and all she got for her pains was the flat of his spread hand sliding down her back, and then, resting on a part of her body she never mentioned by name, he cupped her gently back to him.

"Don't," he said, and in his voice there was a smile. "That's the best part."

All she could do after that was to close her eyes and pretend she wasn't there. His hands, behind her, were moving idly, discovering as though for the first time the down-soft hollows and fertile curves. Aware of the stiffly held angle of her head, he lifted one hand, threaded under the heavy surface of her hair, and massaged the back of her neck until her cheek relaxed against his chest and her body rested from its resistance.

"Where are we now?" he murmured. "Are we admitting we like it, or are we still pretending we don't?"

Clinging hopelessly to some remnant of pride, Merry said, "Why do you think it's *pretending* I don't?"

"Well." His hands drifted downward again and lifted her lightly into him. "There's the faintest trace"—he moved her softly—"of a response." Bringing up her face, he smiled at her with eyes so rich in warmth they could have melted cold lead.

She was trying to find a good answer as he tilted her head back and laid careful kisses on her eyelids, with their delicate shadowing of blue-veined tracery. Her cheeks burned under the graze of his lips, and then he moved lower, pressing his mouth over hers and spreading the rounded fullness, probing slowly through the velvet flesh. Faint and pressureless, his fingers played in the dainty lines of her ear. The hand supporting her back rocked her back and forth with languid sensuality. Under the press of his body Merry ached in colors; the reds of the shore fires, the brilliant russets fading in the western sky, the white milk-mist from the distant stars; she tingled every hue in the prism. The world was a collection of sweet and vivid light beams, and she was one of them, and mindless, a spinning miscellany of liquid cells. When finally he lifted his head, his breathing sounded soft and even to her, while she could barely pull the air in and out of her sore lungs.

She said, "If you're done, just prop me there against the foremast."

His laughter was quiet and enticing. "Don't you think we should go below and explore this in more detail?" When she said no in a voice that was weak but desperately convincing, he gently put her against the mast and let go. They'd made enough of a spectacle already, and though the crew would certainly expect him to express his possession by handling her when he wanted, it was not a good idea to present her too rashly as a love object. There were any number of men on the *Joke* who couldn't be trusted alone with her. He read that back in his mind, grinned suddenly, and added himself to the list.

Merry's hair had tumbled forward, a silky spill over the rise and fall of her high breasts, a waving arcade to her exquisite features. Her eyes were deep wells of stabbing blue.

"All we do together is fight or—or kiss," she said. "I think I'm becoming deranged from it."

"Dear me. Is that a plea to expand our relationship or a revised way of suggesting you want to end it? What can you do, besides fight and kiss?"

"Pick oakum," she said wretchedly, "and cry. I can't imagine the first would interest you, and you've already seen the second, so couldn't we have a truce?''

A gleam of humor lit Devon's eyes. "That's audacious of you, considering that traditional activities during a truce include, but aren't limited to, tending the wounded, exchanging prisoners, and plotting like a demon what your moves will be when hostilities resume.''

"If that's true, you've got no reason *not* to want one," she retorted, encouraged and disoriented by the relatively mellow tenor of his mood. "The wounded are all on my side; unlike you, I've got no prisoners to exchange; and it's perfectly obvious that you could plot rings around me." He was still smiling a little, but he made no response, so she added unhappily, "I know it may not matter much to you, but I have a family who must be very worried about me.''

"Write them a letter and I'll post it.''

"I'm sure you would," Merry said bitterly. "After you'd read it.''

The accusation moved him not at all. "I'll be the first to admit that being the kidnapper has immense advantages over being the kidnappee. I wouldn't be in your shoes for all the mussels in Dublin.''

"They are *not* my shoes. They belong to Cat, as does the shirt, and the britches. The gunpowder under my fingernails is Morgan's. The bruises on my wrists are yours. All that's left of me is a bit of white ash and bone meal encased in skin.''

She turned then and made the escape her pride had withheld from her earlier and, plunging down the darkened staircase, ran flat into Cat, who was coming up. He was more than a head taller, but she was on the stair above him. Their faces were nearly level as he stood, a thin, pale-haired shadow before her. With unruffled practicality he advised her to use the handrail or she would break her neck on the steps.

As he passed her, going up, she said brightly, through choking tears, "You must be worn to a rug, you've been working so hard this afternoon avoiding me.''

He checked in mid-stride, with a reluctance she could almost taste.

"You really don't want anything to do with it," she whispered. "Do you, Cat?''

There was a short silence, and then he sat down on the stair, the new moonlight a frosty cap on his colorless hair, the hard bones of his face shaded.

"No." An extended pause followed before he asked, "You've been talking to Devon?"

"I wouldn't call it talking. He circles around me like a carnivore and bites when the urge takes him. There's no more mercy in the man than there is milk in a male tiger."

"Panic won't help."

"Thank you," she said. "I needed a slogan. Panic won't help. That's an apt one."

It was warm in the stairway. Musty air scented with dried varnish fought off breezes from the deck, and the hatch opened to a purple, star-spotted heaven. Merry could barely see his hand as Cat waved it over the empty space beside him in a silent invitation. She joined him gingerly; the step was narrow. They sat together, not touching, and he said, "What was he? Angry?"

"I haven't the faintest notion of the workings of the man's mind. See a brown spider spinning on a rock; as soon know what *it's* thinking. I was buried under an avalanche of finesse."

"If there's an avalanche of anything, it's metaphors," he said. "Do you think you can tell me what happened without crucifying the language?"

A pause came in which Merry did a lot of fidgeting. Finally, "He kissed me."

Three short words, and the tone in which she said them revealed more to him than she would have liked. Long habit kept emotion from his face, though she couldn't have seen it in the dim light anyway. None of this was as easy for the long-haired boy as it had been two weeks ago; not that it had been exactly painless then. He had already done his best for her with Devon; but Devon had experienced hypocrisy in every possible permutation, and it would likely take a deposition from God to make the man trust that Merry's sweet surface went bone-deep. Nor had Devon any reason to be either rational or lenient with respect to anything connected with Michael Granville. The set of scarred fingers that Cat had clasped loosely around his opposite wrist were tense and icy.

"You'll have to accept it," he said, the slow words following one another in chilly succession, "if you won't tell him what he wants to know. I've told you already, and nothing's changed. Damn it, Merry, you know—or you ought to know—that a man and a woman who desire each other and share a bedchamber will inevitably—"

She leaned right over and shoved her face to within inches of his, until he could feel the warmth of her soft, shapely nose. "Will inevitably what?"

"Will inevitably find something stupid to argue about," he snapped and, making a frustrated gesture, left her alone on the stairway.

Merry, entering the cabin a few minutes later, was struck with a fog of hot air that hung pitch black and sluggish in the small chamber. She knew now by experience that it would take a few hours to cool. A faint breeze wheezed through the high gray square of an open window and carried in the hiss of seafoam and waves slapping the hull. Outside there was also laughter, interrupted briefly by the splash of a longboat meeting water. Merry ran to the bunk and climbed up to look out the window on tiptoe, and by the small closed lantern attached to the boat's bow, she saw that one of the eight passengers was Devon; his gleaming hair made him stand out like a fresh gold coin amid old pennies. He was laughing in evident delight at something Cat, beside him, was saying. Resting her chin on the sill, Merry watched until she could see only a slight bobbing glow from the lantern as the boat broke through the surf and onto the shore, where the nightly fires were blazing high, spraying torpedoes of sparks toward the stars.

Pipe smoke drifted in the window from the watch, and on the still deck someone began to sing "Hosanna to the Son of David." She hummed along while she washed in the basin, changed into Cat's nightshirt, and used Cat's ivory comb on her hair. Sitting on the bunk, munching an apple, she heard Morgan go by on the way to his cabin. He knocked twice as he passed, and said, "Happy dreams, nestling."

"Good night, Captain Morgan," she called and struggled under the blankets, the apple cupped like a doll by her cheek. This was the time of day she devoted to trying to think of some way to escape the *Joke*, and motivation had increased a thousandfold since morning. Tonight the exercise of planning an escape was more intensely therapeutic than usual because with it she could erase Devon from her thoughts for whole minutes.

The guard on deck was thick, since they were at anchor; rival pirates, evidently, didn't trust one another, and the consequence to Merry was that she could never have slipped unnoticed from the ship. The apple rolled from her relaxing fingers, and Merry drifted into a dream-active sleep with the moist flesh of the fruit plying its sugared acids against her lips.

She woke in the wee hours to rough footsteps and shouting on the deck above her, and the scrape of a longboat being secured. Will Saunders's baritone soared in song, and Merry could just make out the line, "He who once a good name gets may piss in bed and say he sweats." Hastily she rolled onto her stomach and pulled a pillow over her head.

In a few moments there was a firm tread outside, and her door came whacking open. The pillow was torn from her head and tossed on the floor.

"God. There's a wench in my bed," said Devon, standing over her.

She retreated full under the blanket and had it ripped off her too.

"Wake up, Anne Bonney," he said. "Your friends are aloft, waiting for you. Don't you want to be a lady pirate? There's Saunders and Erik Shay—hear them singing? No, now they've stopped. They want me to send you up to them, clad like a mermaid. Shame on them, they're drunk as friars. Or if you don't want to go up, shall I invite them down?"

"No! Devon, please—"

"Wonderful, Merry pet. Could you turn on your back and repeat that?" She felt the mattress shift slightly as he sat by her. "It's damned appealing. Again and more throatily . . ."

Merry reared to her knees in a riffle of white hollands, her hair flying over her sloping shoulders. "*They're* drunk, are they? And I suppose you're not?"

He twisted around to smile at her. The lamp he had brought in with him sat in its niche on the small desk, and an arc of rosy light reached into his glowing hair, discovering the moisture dewed there from the sticky sea mist. His supple skin appeared golden, his teeth neat and white, and his eyes made of moonlight. Fragrances from him caressed her; the tang of driftwood smoke and mineral-rich beach sand, the fresh breath of the wind, the bouquet of sweet wine.

"I am but 'lightlie merrie,' my bunkmate," he said, "and not transmuted into Attila the Barbarian. Wait. I'd forgotten. I was that already, wasn't I? Help me with my boots?"

"Boots? Are you taking them off?" she gasped in a voice anything but throaty.

"Of course I am. I don't usually sleep knee-down in leather."

One boot hit the floor, and she jerked with alarm at the thud.

"Now, Devon—" she began nervously, watching him work on the other boot. "Devon, I—I . . . Devon, please leave me alone. Go away. Go to bed. I want to go back to sleep."

"You're welcome to sleep, and I *am* going to bed. Dear child, this is my bed, gracefully occupied though it may be."

"You can't really mean to sleep in here," she said desperately.

"You can't really be so naïve as to think I won't."

Merry, forgetting that her new motto was panic won't help, said, "No! Devon, no!"

"Don't tell me," Devon said, starting to shuck his jacket, "that we've already degenerated to incoherent protests? I've been looking forward to a moving and articulate appeal to my submerged sense of decency. Please, if you won't be throaty, be eloquent. You haven't soured on a truce, have you? Think. It will be biblical; we shall beat our swords to plowshares, and the lion will lie down with the lamb."

"Not if the lamb has any say in the matter!"

"They don't, as a rule," he said. "One shears them seasonally, bleating or not."

The pirate's shirt was soft-textured and clean. His expression was tidy and his words hardly slurred. It didn't seem fair when she, unblamably asleep, should be handicapped once waked by a soggily semialert brain, eyes that itched under raw lids, and a tongue as flaccid as dry wool. If he wanted bleating, he was going to get it.

"I shall scream!" she said.

"As you like. Mind you, I feel compelled to mention that there are any number of otherwise civil individuals on board who are working their way into pleasantly intoxicated sleep. If you're noisy, someone's likely to come in here and stick a sock in your mouth."

Over the past few days Merry had had enough opportunity to observe men under the influence of alcohol to decide that it was probably true. His shirt, opening over tough, lovely muscle, made

Merry's throat contract involuntarily in a gulp. Grabbing the two sides of his collar, she drew it fiercely together and snapped, "There's not enough shame in you to wash a flea's foot! Do you mean to sit there before me and bare yourself?"

He swallowed a laugh, though his eyes brimmed with humor as they devoured her in fascination. "Ah, darling. Now I remember. No wonder I'm shocking you. Your husband slept in a nightshirt."

Caught off guard, Merry drew a blank, and it showed in her face.

"That freckled paragon, Jeremiah Jones," he said in a gently encouraging tone. "Your husband. Sleeps in a nightshirt. Recall telling me that?"

There was something unnerving about a man who could grin and "forget" a threat he'd made two weeks earlier; and then turn around and throw in your face an insignificant scrap of conversation eight months old. It wouldn't have surprised her if she'd been deliberately maneuvered into her present indignity of holding his shirt closed. She saw herself in five minutes trying to hold up his britches and shuddered. How he would love that! Before she had figured what to do, he said affably, "I don't want to throw you out of the bunk, you know; just share it. If that's worrying you."

"Don't work so hard to be funny," said Merry, who'd learned the phrase from Cat. She let go his shirt with a sharp gesture and put her bare feet on the cool floorboards and stood with her back to him. "If you're getting into this bed, then I'm getting out of it."

"You're safer than you think" came Devon's voice behind her. "Cat swept me off to the mainland and smothered me in drink and female hospitality. He didn't say so, but I gather the charitable zeal was on your behalf."

For so brief a statement it had a remarkable number of half messages. Miserably the one that penetrated to Merry most clearly was the image of Devon with a woman. She was disturbed and more than a little embarrassed by the discomfort it caused her.

"I won't hurt you, Merry," he said, his tone kind, warmly sensual, full of humor; the spider in a ladybug's shell. "Come to bed with me."

"No. I'm going to sleep on the floor."

After a short hesitation he said a very cheerful "Better you than me," and in an irritatingly short time the even pace of his breathing revealed that he'd fallen asleep.

There was nothing for Merry to do but dim the lamp and sit in the corner staring morosely into the dark, listening to Devon inhaling and exhaling quietly with intense (and undeserved) peacefulness. Perhaps she should wake him up and try to make him go, but there was no guarantee she'd have any more success than she'd had already, and there was no telling what he might do if she forced the issue. Better you than me, indeed.

On his boots Devon had brought in wet sand and water; Merry's resentment increased as rivulets of gritty water found her and began to creep stealthily to her skin through the nightshirt. It was fortunate that the air curling through the window was warm and soft. After a long time the ocean's roll lulled Merry gently to sleep despite her troubles. The tense column of her neck, which had so long held her head stiffly upright, went suddenly lax, and her head fell hard against the wall, painfully waking her.

Devon was awakened as well; Merry saw his light head rise from the pillow. He kicked off the blanket and came to her, dropping to one knee by her crossed legs.

"You hit your head?" he said.

"No," she said grouchily. "The *wall* hit my head."

"My, we're in a nasty mood. Was it my idea that you sit on the floor?" His fingers felt for and found the low bump on the side of her head. "You've got quite a knock. I had better get—"

"Don't get anything! It's just a little lump," she said, and her tone was so sullen he had to hold back laughter.

As he dropped his hand it touched the hem of her skirt. "You're all wet. What happened?"

"You forgot to use the mud mat."

"Did I? I'm sorry. Well. You can't sit in a puddle." Gently insistent, he made her stand up. "Be reasonable. You can't keep this going all night. Let me take this wet thing off you and put you in bed."

Merry retreated, a white cotton streak, to the other side of the table. Thrusting a forehead that was beginning to ache into his palm, Devon let the helpless laughter overwhelm him.

"Merry, I've got enough liquor in me to—God knows what, float a bugle corps or something. If you think I'm going to play chase around the table with you like an aging roué and buxom Bess the chambermaid . . . If I found you a hammock, would you sleep in it?''

It was a respectable compromise, and a way to preserve pride. Inside Merry snatched gratefully at the offer, but all she showed Devon was a nod. She was a little less grateful in a moment or two, when Devon returned with the hammock and strung it across the cabin for her. Merry had never slept in a hammock. As she stared doubtfully at the swaying band of cotton mesh Devon said, ''It's simple to use. But for the first time, you had better let me help you get in.''

''No!'' snapped Merry, in no humor to be patronized. ''I've slept in hammocks before. Will you go into the corridor, please? I'd like to change my nightshirt.''

''Why should I? You didn't while I was undressing. I'm going to bed. Put out the lantern if you want to be modest.''

After a moment's indecision she killed the lantern, then gracefully let the wet shirt fall and drew a clean one over her head and shook it down around her. She sighed with relief as the dry cloth warmed her skin, and with fading gooseflesh she tossed the old shirt over a chair.

From the bed Devon said innocently, ''I probably ought to have mentioned that I have excellent night vision.''

It would have been nice to strangle him with the hammock and have the bunk to herself, but Merry was too tired to spend time in that happy fantasy. The sagging line of the hammock smiled expectantly at her in the dark. She felt for and tried to smooth a place to lie in the tangled webbing. When she thought she had one, she turned quickly and jumped backward onto it. The hammock jumped too and dumped Merry facedown on the floor.

The hammock was obviously a creature to be approached with caution. She was so mad at it, swinging to the ocean beat above her, that a moment went by before she thought of Devon on the bed. She knew he wasn't asleep, even if he was preserving a discreet silence. Very likely the man was mute from ecstasy.

''It's been a while since I've slept in a hammock,'' she said from the floor.

"You might try giving it a sugar lump."

"Thank you," she said coldly. "If you have any other advice to offer—"

"Lie on the diagonal. I'm still perfectly willing to help you."

If he hadn't made the jibe about the lump of sugar, she might have softened. As it was, she'd rather break her neck than give him the satisfaction of putting her in the hammock. Raw determination got her into the hammock, on the diagonal, her arms and legs splayed for balance, and she lay like a capital X, rocking with the swell until the *Joke* dipped. Bucking enthusiastically, the hammock twirled a pirouette and slung Merry into Devon's hastily prepared grip.

"I make that Hammock–two, Merry–zero," Devon said, though he didn't have much breath left from laughing. "Before you've catapulted off every surface in the room—" He set her on the bunk. "Good night, Merry friend. I'll take the hammock."

Merry woke to a morning sparkling with sharp reflected light. Devon and the hammock were gone.

Moving stiffly, she dressed in the boy's clothes that no longer seemed to embarrass her: coarse gray leggings, knee breeches of a darker gray with a red patch, and a red and gray striped shirt with a square missing that matched the patch. Patch over patch, and a patch over all, they said of a sailor's wardrobe. Considering that, it was surprising how generous other men on the ship had been in offering to lend her their clothes; Raven said several times that he wished she was as eager to get into his britches as she was to get into Cat's.

When she went on deck, she found the *Joke* under full sail and Devon nowhere in sight. The land where they had been anchored was a smudge on the horizon. Angled off the stern, the sun shone unbearably white, spraying chipped light on the water and dry streamers on sails that strained voluptuously before the weight of a sumptuous wind.

Cat was busy. He sat on the gundeck casings, his braid down his back, a diamond stud bigger than a bean on his earlobe, and Dennis the pig trotters-up against his leg, the pig's head resting and drooling on his knee. Cat was cleaning his cutlass. A raucous group was dicing near his feet. Merry would have liked to go to him and pour out her troubles and uncertainties, but the boy pirate had never looked more unapproachable. He stared coldly through the urgent appeal in each glance she gave him. What he had done to help her yesterday and what he might do for her in the future were clearly not things he planned to discuss with her, and if he felt as angry and helpless as she did, it was not his way to share that with her.

Pride would not let her stand in front of him, showing she was lonely. She left quickly for the galley, waving at Sails as she went. It was the one place she could be quite certain not to run into Devon.

Beside Cat and Raven, Cook was the only person on the *Black Joke* under the age of twenty, and if he had any name other than "Cook," Merry was not able to discover it, which fate was better in some ways than that of his assistant, an ill-natured middle-aged man who was universally known as "You!" and sometimes as "Hey, You!" Cook had grown up in a pirate settlement like the one Merry had seen on the Florida coast. He was grandsired, so they said, by Sails, and Cook had the same sparkling gray eyes, the same soft lips that loved to talk. His hair was brown and curling, his cheeks scattered with freckles, and his nose nicely tilted. It made a cherubic picture if you were able to discount the nude female figure tattooed on his arm (which wasn't likely, given the rather startling posture of her legs). The nude was lovingly titled "Annie," which happened not by coincidence to be the name of Cook's wife, who worked as a housekeeper for Morgan on one of his island properties.

Cook had sailed with a small vessel that carried cotton from Haiti to Europe until Sails discovered the lad in a Port-au-Prince tavern, slumped on a straw pile, deathly ill with a heavy addiction to narcotic snuff. Once he was hauled back to the *Joke*, they had tried in a kind way to cure the killer habit, and when nothing worked, Morgan had said he'd shoot the boy if he touched another opiate. The boy had, and Morgan drew a pistol and shot him in the foot. This time the cure lasted, and now, two years later, Sails's grandson was fourteen years old.

The kitchen was squat and greasy. Fascinating clutter ran from corner to corner: tea chests and strings of garlic; tin jars of raw sassafras, sweet basil, cloves, and aniseed. There were ordinary items made strange by their enormous quantity: beef soaking in forty-gallon casks, eight gallons of mustard in a ceramic tub, oatmeal by the bushel; and a brass still to reoxygenate stale water from the storage casks that Cook called the Doomsday Machine. He said you were likely to disappear if you sat too close. Racks of boilers and pots clattered without cease from the ocean's roll, and simmering liquids sloshed on the stove, until steam and char smoke blanketed the galley.

Cook and his help, in faded britches, aprons, and nothing else, were chewing tobacco, sharing a rum bottle, cleaving onions on a scarred chopping board, weeping, and arguing about who was the last to use the lost whetstone. Looking up, seeing Merry, Cook said, "Hey, Merry. Hullo, sweetie." Over his shoulder to his assistant: "Hey, You! Don't blow your hooked nose on your apron! Use that rag. Jeez-us. Do I want to stare at your snot all day?" Spit tobacco, swig rum, toss another slice of shark meat on to fry. To Merry, "Sweetie, you hungry for breakfast? Jeez, but you look under the brine this morning." He pinched her chin. "Give us a smile, hey? What's the matter? Is Cat eatin' you about something? Know what I'll do? I'll kill that damned pig of his if he makes you cry."

"I promise I'm not crying. It's only the onions. Thank you for offering to kill Cat's pig for me, but I'm afraid it wouldn't be the least use, and I like Dennis very much and would hate to see him dead. Cat hasn't been unkind, and there's nothing you can do, except— I believe my nose is going to run. Have you— Oh, dear," she said, as he handed her the same rag his helper had just made hearty use of.

Raven, coming off his watch, wandered in a cloud through the galley door and almost put his foot in a bucket of hot grease.

"Stupid bastard," said Cook. Not caring that Raven was more than a foot taller, Cook dragged him ruthlessly backward and gave him a stinging clout that left a flour streak on the side of Raven's green bandanna. "Watch where you're going, hey? Want your arse basted? Idiot! Now, don't go fussing over him, Merry. Hittin' don't hurt him none, big dumb ox like that. Barely feels it. Did I black his eye? Slap a hunk of shark on it."

"No, thank you," Raven said hastily, smiling good-naturedly at Merry and making a quick, crude hand sign to Cook. "Hate the stuff."

"Do you think it smells like whale-brain fritters?" Merry eyed her prospective lunch without enthusiasm. "Cook does."

"Daresay it does, which is likely why I hate it."

Raven pulled himself up on a small table, the steel links in his belt rattling. "Since I was a kiddy I sailed on a whaler. Happiest day of my life, the day Morgan made a prize of her."

"Prize she weren't," sneered Cook's assistant.

"*That's* true enough," said Cook. "You never saw such a roll-along, blow-along, blubber-hunting tub.She was carrying so much sail that she had a wake on her like a dog wetting in the snow, and her hull sagged, bow and stern both. Stank so loathsome that the lads drew lots to see who'd board her, and sent the losers. Wouldn't have stopped her to begin with if'n we hadn't needed that extra longboat."

Raven's eyes closed in joyous remembrance. "Join! they told me, or die."

"Jeez-us." Cook threw a handful of onions into a copper pan. "Look at you, with that lie in your mouth; blushing like a blue dog."

Eyes still closed, still smiling, Raven clarified for Merry. "That is to say, not at all." His dark pretty eyes opened, and the smile focused on Merry. "The truth is, they didn't want me. I had to beg."

"Beg? I'd call it grovel," said Cook, laughing and slapping farina onto the piece of shark meat. "You shoulda seen him, sweetie. Jumped offa that crate of a whaler, swum all the way to the *Joke*, and pounced on Morgan, shedding water from his duck feathers all over the cap'n. Kissed Morgan's hand too, each inch of it from pinkie to wrist, hey, slobbering like a heifer."

"They weren't either, mon. Nice neat kisses. Morgan said so himself," said Raven to Merry. "Then he says to Saunders, 'Will, put this child in a blanket and return him to his ship. We can't corrupt anything so tender.' "

"What about"—Merry ducked to avoid the fresh sack of meal that the kitchen assistant tossed to Cook—"Cat and Cook? They're young too!"

"Aye," Cook said, catching the sack, "but we was *already* corrupted. There ain't no boy ready to sail on the main chance—"

"With pirates," Raven supplied, sotto voce.

"Unless," Cook continued, ripping open the sack with a foot-long dagger, "he knows fifty terms in slang for the private parts of a woman. So we asked Raven, and the only word he knew was— Ah, sweetie, don't cover your little ears, I won't say it. Anyway, there was old Raven trying hard to show how bad he was, and since he didn't know but one word, he started in to makin' them up. Jeez, what an imagination. Had the crew laughing so hard that they let the whaler scramble off like a sand crab, so in the end we had to keep him. Boxed his ears, of course, and meant to put him out at the next stopping place. Don't know why we never did.''

"Because I grew on you all," Raven grinned, picking up a mop, wielding it virtuously over a grease spot in the corner.

Cook grinned back. "Like a wart, you grew on us."

"Raven," Merry said carefully, "the whale boat—it was an *honest* way to earn a living."

"You wouldn't say that if you'd ever darted a bad-placed harpoon into a mother bowhead and seen her take an hour to die and her calf left to starve. Any day I'd rather rob a fat merchant ship. Insured to the gills, most of them. Ever see a whale that carried insurance? Whaling ships. Know what you get for supper? Black liquor and biscuits oiled in blubber.''

"You young bucks," growled Cook's assistant disgustedly. "Always got something to bilge about. A man ought not to be complainin' as long's he's got biscuit. Wait once till you're becalmed! Oncet I was on a little sloop that got caught in the horse latitudes with no wind for more than three months. Aye, we'd've gived our hands for biscuit, oncet all that was left of ourn was powder 'n' the grubs eatin' *that*. Water was yellow as mare's teeth, and stinkin', and we didn't get more than a cup, rationed, in a day. We ate the sawdust, and the oxhides from the main yard, and rats was going for half a crown each, if'n the selfish bastards what caught 'em didn't keep 'em to 'emselves.''

Catching the revulsion on Merry's face, he added slyly, "Aye, there's rats all right on the ships that sail at sea. Got 'em on the *Joke* too, same as any other. Don't see 'em in the day, but at night they creep out, when yer asleepin', and stare at you with'n their teeny red eyes, and then they come creee-ping"—he stretched out the word—"up and nibble on the dead flesh o' yer feet.''

Merry's white cheeks turned whiter.

"Nah, Merry, don't listen to him. Rats'll only bother you if you take sick and are too weak to—'' Seeing that this line of logic was not having a particularly salutary effect on Merry's blanched countenance, Raven abandoned it with careless finality and, insistently cheerful, switched to, "You've been down here long enough breathing smoke. You ought to go aloft and—"

"She won't go," said Cook. The boy had been standing over his assistant, frowning at the job the older man was making of rubbing clean the floorboards with a piece of canvas. "Hey, strike a light, You! Is that clean or is there enough grease left there to lubrify a harem? You're lazy as Ludlam's dog that leaned against the wall to bark. Put some spark in your soap, hey?" He tossed a handful of lye into his assistant's bucket. "That'll do it."

"Aye, and take the skin off me too," grumbled his assistant. "And turn my fingernails brown and buckled to barn shingles."

"So, who are you—Beau Brummell? When I set you to scrubbing, it's the only time yer hands get a good cleaning." The boy steered his attention back to Raven. "Of course she don't want to go up, loblolly. Scared of Devon. And you know what a foul humor Cat's in—not that *that* departs none from the customary."

Raven stared in an appalled way at Merry's bright eyes and burning cheeks. "Poor little soul! I wish—"

"Don't wish!" Cook snapped. "Or you'll *wish* you hadn't. She belongs to Devon, and it's his business the use he wants to put her to, and there's an end to it." But the gray eyes, resting on Merry, were so much kinder than the voice. "Tell you what, though; who says she can't stay down here long as she wants?" And over his shoulder, "Hey, You! Finished wiping the sideboard yet? Shake a leg, eh? And then go run up the chow rag to let the crew know what's coming and bring down the biggest wooden kid from the storeroom."

In a heavy sea, as many times as not, tall waves shook the ship, and food on its way from the galley to the aftercastle was dashed to the decks and fed through the scuppers to the angry ocean. Today, with light breezes and fair skies, Cook and his assistant could carry off the meal with safe footing. They were barely out of the door before Raven tossed down his mop, lit the small bowl of his pipe, and established himself comfortably on the table, feet up and against the counter. Merry began to laugh at the pantomime of sly indolence. An incautious movement of her hand set a copper pan spinning on its peg, upending an earthenware bowl that showered Merry with sugar.

Cook heard her soft cry and the crack of shattering clay. He flew back into the galley to find Raven standing over her, looking full of alarm and trying to gently brush sugar grit from her heavy eyelashes. Crystals caught and sparkled in the curve of her throat and cuddled thirstily down the line of her young breasts. It was not the kind of thing Cook was likely to look away from quickly, but when he did raise his eyes, he met Raven's polite but overstimulated brown gaze.

"Well," he said slowly. "Heaven help us. The girl's tried to make herself into dessert."

Descending belowdecks, the brightness and human clatter of the afternoon muffled behind him, Devon paused, his eyes adjusting to the dimmer light. The hallway air was thick with warm wood musk. Ship's smells. They delighted him, like the scents of rich coffee and forest humus at dawn after a thunderstorm. It was one of the amazing quirks of Morgan's character that the man could give to his pirate vessel the atmosphere of a home.

Last week Devon had learned of Napoleon's victories at Craonne and Reims. Again he felt anger at the well-meaning interference that had banned him from Europe, where he wanted to be, and driven him across an ocean to report on a war he opposed to high-placed men in England who had good reason to ignore his recommendations. Britain's war with the United States was a fiasco. The majority of Britain's great resources were being poured into the death struggle with Napoleon; this stupid secondary conflict with her former colonies wasted men and money.

As for the United States, it had been a piece of bloody-minded arrogance for the war hawks of President Madison's administration to declare a war when they didn't have the money to pay for it and, what's more, had indebtment outstanding from the Revolutionary War. With customs revenues down due to the tightening blockade the national income last year had been less than ten million dollars; and yet, he wouldn't be surprised if the United States had run up a debt of more than a hundred million dollars before the war was over. Yankee politicians were more likely to plunge their country into beggary than they were to raise taxes, accountable as they were at the next polling to a frugal electorate. It was one of the hazards of democracy. America was borrowing like a bride's little brother, and it would be interesting to find out who was going to have the verve to pull them from the brink of bankruptcy. Devon doubted that it would be the Madisonian war hawks.

The conflict between Devon's country and the fledgling United States was a string of petty incompetencies, and he was not a man who found it easy to tolerate incompetence, particularly in a war. It was the thing that had first drawn him to Morgan. Rand Morgan did things well and with flair.

There *were* reasons for Devon to be here, doing a job that was beneath his talents and not to his taste. It gave him a chance to spend time with Morgan and Cat, a boy well worth being made into somebody's project, especially considering who he was. Not, thought Devon with a grin, that Cat was any more amenable to being made into somebody's project than Devon ever had been. If you show promise too young, there are too many well-wishers eager to force you to realize it. Little though Cat's well-wishers might know it, the boy couldn't be in better hands than Rand Morgan's. Morgan never forced potential to perform; he just gave it the opportunity to grow.

What else had brought Devon here? There was an autocratic old woman who would be pleased to have him in England; and Devon had no desire to please her. And finally, it gave him the chance to pursue his private war against Michael Granville. In the same theft that had netted Merry, Cat had brought back a set of letters that linked Granville to felony insurance fraud. In his heart Devon briefly felt the tug of a faint and familiar agony. One day Michael Granville would pay with utter ruin for the murder he had committed. The penalty for fraud wasn't even close to adequate punishment for a man-monster, but it was more than Devon had dared hope for. Cleverly handled, it might be enough to bring him down. But it would be months before he could return to London and begin to use the incriminating papers, so he deferred his interest in the matter as neatly and purposefully as he had filed the papers in the locked cabin desk.

What he had not discovered on the mainland was the identity of the lamblike creature who had chastely shared his bedroom last night. Merry, sweet Merry with the haunting blue eyes; Merry, with the patrician features and the self-assurance of a birch leaf in a wind storm, who, Cat swore up, down, and sideways, was an untried girl. The Windflower, he called her. This morning Devon had left her in the blue light of dawn. Helplessly asleep, she must have thrown off her blankets; they had lain in a warm hill at the bed foot. She had been on her side, the nightshirt twisted tautly over the slope of her hip and riding high enough to expose her slim legs and soft arched feet, the toes small buds, back-curled toward the sole. He had laid the back of his hand against her palm. The skin was slightly cool, so he had drawn the blankets over her gently, without touching her again, and left.

Now, returning to the cabin in midafternoon, it was with the picture of the sleeping girl in his mind that Devon pushed open the door. He had assumed, without really having any reason to do so, that the room would be vacant.

Instead, he found Merry standing by the water can in leggings and knee breeches and naked to the waist. Her black shoes stood together by the bed, her shirt was rolled and thrown in a corner. Tiny angled chips—salt? sugar?—glittered on the flesh of her throat, and below her throat, where her loose hair curved inward, sicklelike over her ribs. Garlanded demurely by curls, dusted with crystals, her high lovely breasts were made of the most magical shades of pink. He could see that Merry was frowning down at herself in a critical way that her beauty little deserved. She held a rectangle of damp cotton that she had just used to wipe across her midriff. Her nose had a soot smear on the tip. *Merry at Bath.* Titian wouldn't have painted it, but, oh, my, he should have.

Merry looked up quickly, saw Devon, and started, dropping the cloth.

"Merry, dear," he said, picking up the cloth. "Do you need help?" His initial rush of feeling had been that rare unwanted warmth he felt sometimes with her. Desire came immediately after, so powerfully that he added, "Or—wait. I think I'm the one who'll need help."

Openmouthed with dismay, she crossed her arms over her chest. When she was able to tear her pained gaze away from him, she looked down at the placement of her slender forearms; as if angered by the inadequate coverage, she rearranged them, and when *that* exposed even more, she tried, in a frenzy of enflamed modesty, to hide her breasts with her cupped palms. Her motives were the highest; glancing back to Devon's face, she was disconcerted to find that her movements had achieved the opposite of her intended effect. Devon propped his left shoulder against the doorframe, as though he needed the support, and he was only half joking.

"Merry . . ." he said. "Merry. My poor girl. Don't tell me— were you trying to dampen my ardor? It's at your most lunatic moments that I can resist you least."

She could listen to his words, but his voice she felt. Its bright tenor entered through her skin, passed like a caress through flesh and nerves, and penetrated her spine, as luscious as a milk bath. She knew the voice. Even better, she knew the effect it had on her will.

"Go. Please," she said, trying so hard to put conviction into the words that they were spoken with the faulty tone of an overpumped pipe organ. "Please."

He shut the door with one hand. Softly: "Not on your sweet life."

She made a dash for her shirt in the corner and held it in front of her just before she was caught and gently encircled in his arms. Her fists and the shirt they clutched were trapped between her body and his. Under her rounded palms Merry could feel the fresh skin and tightly curving muscle of his chest and the steady heart rhythm mated with his languorous breathing. Inside herself Merry's less discreet organs were slowly escalating their tempo. Little staccato gasps marred the action of her lungs, and blood slapped in hot gushes through her heart, even as his hand molded her to his long body.

One of his hands burned over her back before it moved lower, tracing a hard, flat-palmed arc over her buttocks, and then, sloping under, drew her gently up on her toes. Their hips met, the hardness and detail of him caressing her belly, and she began to ache with unexplored need. Everywhere that a part of him touched her was stirred and soothed, as though by deep sunlight in spring.

His blond head bent, and she could feel his lips seeking her face, his breath warm on her mouth and chin.

"Truce," she whispered. "Truce."

"No, darling. Peace talks. A parley. Exploratory diplomacy."

His lips moved with hushed lightness over her cheek. His eyes closed, and when his mouth halted its slow search of her trembling lips, his open kiss was spare and subtle. He lowered his head a little, and his kiss moved to her throat before it traveled hotly along her jaw, to her ear, to her forehead, and came back to her lips. The pressure on her mouth deepened as he delicately teased her into parting her lips and entered her, dragging her into his kiss. His hands still pressing her to him, his lips on hers, he murmured, "Peace talks. And I surrender. Complete conquest. You win. Why are you always so shy with your tongue?"

Merry's arms might have been made from putty for all the strength there was in them as she tried to push away from him. The best she could do was turn her face. "No—this is terrible— My tongue? I never know what you're talking about. What do you mean about my tongue?"

His fingers, firmly placed on her chin, forced her resisting lips back. Before his mouth took her again, he said in a low tone, "Let me show you." After a moment he whispered, "Do you like that, Merry?"

If he hadn't been holding her, she would have dropped to the floor. She answered him thickly, her head swimming. "I think you're . . . There's something wrong with you! Aren't you embarrassed at all?"

"We can't be embarrassed yet," he told her in a voice made tender with sympathetic amusement. Lowering her feet to the floor without haste, his hand moved in a caressing circle that followed the contour of the soft flesh of her buttocks. "How could we be embarrassed already? We have to save something for the rest of it. What do you do further on? Go purple in your skin like ripe fruit?"

Merry, having never been further on, decided that it was probable. "More than likely," she sighed. His fingers quit her chin, and as they began to play erotic patterns on her naked shoulders, her cheek came to rest weakly against the warm skin of his throat, exposed by his open collar. "I'm beginning to *feel* like a ripe fruit."

His thumb stroked her ear, found the inner folds, and in another moment his mouth and his tongue explored there also. "Which?" he asked.

"Which what?"

"Which fruit? An apple? A cherry? Something tropical and exotic?"

"Something juicy." Her tone was so lugubrious that it made him laugh.

"Merry . . . sweet child . . . Merry sweet. Is this so bad, then? Is it?" He continued the rich movements of his hands, and his lower lip made a sensuous path down the rim of her ear. With great gentleness he let out a breath that fluttered the short silk-curls at her cheekbones. Touching her skin through golden wisps of her hair, his mouth wandered back to hers and began to slowly drink her heat-flavored kisses.

"We barbarians call it desire." He said it huskily, coaxing her body to a response. "We call it . . . Oh, yes . . . darling, yes. That's right. Did I say *right?* Such a forceless word." The kiss was long, hard, and rapturous, and at sometime during the length of it he whispered against her lips, "Here. Move with me, love. No. Don't be afraid. I'm not taking you to bed. Just the chair. All right?"

But she hadn't been able to answer him because she was falling, sinking through fathoms of thick blue water, warm with exotic fish and trailing, clinging seaweed. Scented fluids were moving into and out from her lungs and rainbow colors filled her eyes. When next she was aware of herself, she was on his lap, nestled against his chest, her body pressing sinuously into him. Her head was thrown back, dependent on the support of his arm, firmly placed behind her neck over the heavy cushion of her hair. With hot cheeks, through moist and swollen lips, she whispered, "Devon?"

His face nuzzled the bend of her cheek and then lifted, until his eyes, heavy with pleasure, could study her features.

"What am I doing?" she said. "How do you do this to me?"

"Ah. This?" One accurate finger was softly following her hairline. "This is magic. It's done with mirrors. Secret pockets. Sleight of hand. The coin disappears from one palm and reappears in the other. Everything depends on a willing and distracted subject."

"I'm not willing. I'm not. I'm just . . ."

"Distracted?" he suggested gently, running his thumb over the sensitized rise of her lips, and feeling her tongue touching in shy curiosity against his skin, he rewarded her quickly with an exquisitely probing kiss.

Opening her eyes afterward with the side of her face comfortably

nestled in the hollow of his shoulder, Merry said helplessly, "I
thought you told me— Do you remember that first night before I
was sick? You were going to teach me the best place to kick a man.
I wish you had. I don't know how to make this stop."

The innocence of the blunt confession was not lost on Devon,
though nothing of that showed in the love-hazed smile that she saw
form on his lips.

"Devon, what do you mean to do?"

Cradling her in his arms, his mouth on the hollow below her
ear, he said, "Fill you with honey, love."

His hair brushed her parted lips, cool and smooth as satin, as he
pulled away slightly. Holding her that way, finding her mouth again,
he whispered, "Merry, lift your arms. Put your hands on my
shoulders. We don't need this shirt, do we? Let me take it . . .
Better . . . and better."

In the warm space that separated their bodies, her unrestrained
breasts made scant contact with the fabric of his shirt. The slightest
of her movements made her skin rub against him, the soft press of
fiber washing her with emotions so tantalizing that a shudder passed
through her like a current. He felt it; and his mouth at the base of her
throat stopped its fluid quest to murmur a reassurance while one of
his hands left its courtship of her hip, paused tenderly on the lustrous
bare skin on the side of her body, and then gently covered her
breast. Moaning and frightened, she tried to pull away, but with
strong, gracious fingers he held her in his embrace, feeding pleasure
to her shrinking flesh until resistance gave way to bewildered rapture.
Devon's lips moved lower, making a discovery.

"Sugar . . ." he said. "Everywhere, you're incredibly sweet.
What were you trying to do, turn into a marzipan?"

She tried to answer him, but her tongue was thick in her throat.
"Dev— Let me go." It was a very faint whisper.

"Hush, little flower. Bloom under me. Bloom for me, Merry.
How did you ever grow to be so sweet? Would you like me to lick
you clean? I know where I'd like to begin. . . ."

His words made her arms cling to him as she found herself
straining weakly toward his seeking mouth as it found her breast.
Fever spread through her, delicious and fruity: sweet cherry juice,
apple wine, rosehips, and honey. She could see nothing through her

swirling vision, feel nothing but his warm hands and closeness and
the clean delight of his touch. He lifted her hair in one hand, letting
it fall in a tangled mass over her shoulders, and caressed the back of
her neck. Moving his hands down to cup her shoulders, he brought
his mouth to hers once again.

"Some for you," he whispered, and she tasted the transferred
nectar of her own sugar, a sensuous offering from his lips. Somehow
her hands had begun to stroke the firm, supple muscles on his back
and shoulders; and his pulse beats ran like surf under the unsure
motion of her innocent fingers.

"Magic," he said, his voice a husky erotic whisper. "Sleight of
hand. See how easy it is? You have it, too, little flower . . . you
have it too. No, Merry. Don't stop. Here. Let me help you. Like
this. Yes. Slowly. Merry. Merry. Kiss me."

Carried beyond herself, she touched him with her lips, moving
whisper soft, uncaring whether it was his mouth she kissed, or his
hair, his cheek, the smooth line of his brow. Pressing forward
against his hands and body, whimpering distractedly, she whispered,
"Please. Go away . . . I want to go home. I think I'm going to be
sick. I feel faint. Let me go."

"You have strange love talk, Merry-gold. Marigold, that's another."

"Another what?"

"Merry name. Merry-go-round, marigold, God rest ye Merry . . .
How good you taste, love," he said, his lips to her throat.

Her hand sloppily found his cheek and lay there, a tremulous
supplicant. "Devon, I can't. What words can I say that will . . .
cause you not to force me?"

His face came hazily into focus before her, the soft eyes shining.
He kissed her once on her lips and then drew back, looking down at
her.

"Do you know . . ." he said, gazing at the soot marks transferred
from her discarded shirt and spread by his fingertips over her
flushing skin. "Do you know that we look like coupling leopards?
Do you really want me to let you go? I don't know if I can. Why do
you want to stop?"

She couldn't answer him, only shook her head as though the
blood pounding hard in her brain had driven away all the good
reasons for chastity.

Given her physical response, another man might have laughed at her use of the word *force* and dismissed her protests as a routine and harmless hypocrisy. Devon knew better. He was an artist at making people do as he wanted, and if ruthless seduction could wring acquiescence from her unwilling body—what of it? He could have taken the girl in screaming resistance, and there was not a soul on the *Joke* who would have stopped him. Poor blue-eyed creature, she was his for the taking. And it was hardly the bit of whimsy he would have cared to cultivate in his character that now, when he wanted her most, was the moment he least wanted to take her against her will. All her fragility and sweetness were flowing into him, and whatever his more familiar inclinations were demanding, there was kindness there as well. The part of him that desired her was the part that also didn't want to force her. Whatever she wanted physically, and he was sure he wasn't mistaken about it, she wasn't prepared emotionally, and God knew what kind of wreckage there would be in the aftermath. Soot still powdered her foolish little nose, and he wasn't sure why that should decide him, but somehow it did. Holding her for a moment, stroking her shining hair, he heard with gratitude Cat's fluent footsteps in the corridor.

"Cat?" he called.

Cat pushed open the door with the heel of his hand, walked in, and froze like a pillar, the skin stretching tight over his sharp cheekbones.

"I beg your pardon," Devon said. "Your wench is attacking me."

Not making any attempt to repudiate his ownership of Merry, Cat replied, none too warmly, "You wanted an audience?"

"No. I want you to pry her off me. I don't think she knows what's happening." Finally, impatiently, "*Take* her, will you? Or you can rest assured that I will."

CHAPTER THIRTEEN

Under the hazy sunlight of an overcast heaven Merry stood in Morgan's spacious cabin the next afternoon watching Raven sitting in the open doorway rubbing sun-proofing ointment into Dennis the pig.

"It's nice for me to realize," she said cheerfully, "how much Cat thinks of me. Do you know that Cat uses what must be the same—yes, I'm *sure* it's the same cream on my face. Can pigs really sunburn?"

"Ah, well, sure they can, bless their small horny trotters. On land they've mud to protect them." He finished, wiped his fingers, and stood up, glancing toward the door as though he were about to leave.

"Well, that'll do it for the time being, unless," he said, grinning, "you need some stroked into your back too?"

"No, thank you. Besides, it's too cloudy for ointment."

"Days like this are the worst. Reflection or something, y'know. Saunders could explain it to you." Turning to look at her, lifting one shapely black eyebrow, he said, "You're solemn, lovey."

Merry couldn't help the faint color that began to stain her cheeks. Since yesterday in the afternoon, when Cat wrapped her in his own shirt and removed her bodily from Devon's arms, she had not seen Devon. Where had he slept last night? From certain tentatively tactful glances she had received from Raven, it was obvious that he knew, and why it should be just as embarrassing for her when Devon was known *not* to sleep with her as when he was known *to* sleep with her was a vexing question that she didn't bother to unravel. Possibly it was because she had the strong idea that Raven thought she and Devon had been fighting, and since the opposite of that was true . . .

Yesterday had shown Devon to her in a startling new light. She had spent the night trying to reconstruct the shattered picture of his character and to search through the debris for some kind of familiar consistency.

Not moving, she said to Raven, "Could you stay for a moment or two?"

"Surely, milady," he said gently. He waited for her to speak, and when she did not, he went to the table, sat in one of the heavily ornate chairs, and pulling the card deck from his pocket, began to play solitaire. He was concentrating discreetly on the game before Merry said, "I've been told often enough not to ask too many questions about Devon, but . . . Raven, do you think you might give me a little information?"

Looking up, he said, "Lovey, I'd give you the star belt from Orion. But information you're better getting from Cat."

"Cat's a clam."

"Ah. And Devon?"

"I can't ask him questions. I don't know him well enough to know what would be safe to ask. Raven, I've got to know more about him, or my life's going to evaporate. Does it look to you as though I'm in trouble?"

"Yes," he said seriously, not removing his gaze from hers.

"It's worse than you think. Much worse. Raven, please—who is Devon? Why can he come and go as he pleases?"

Stretching his legs before him, playing another card, he thought it over carefully before he said, "Devon is Morgan's half brother."

Inhaling quickly in surprise, Merry put a hand behind her and lowered herself onto the window bench, barely noticing as Dennis shuffled over her bare toes and laid his damp snout on her foot. At length she said, "They don't look anything alike."

"It happens that way sometimes. They say *my* father was a Dutch Jew and blond. Devon and Morgan were both got by the same father. Of course, Devon was born in England with a silver spoon in his mouth more than fourteen years after Morgan slipped into the

world with a silver cutlass in his. Born in Saint-Dominique, Morgan
was, on the wrong side of the blanket. His mother was the daughter
of a plantation owner. Twenty years old and had never been with a
man, so they say, but she gave herself to Devon's father like a wild
thing on a forest floor and was too proud to tell him before he sailed
back to England that he'd got her with child. She died when Morgan
was ten, and her family cast Morgan off, because all he'd ever been
was a shame to them. And the father never knew about the first
son . . .''

Her eyes were held so open and still that the lids began to ache.
She closed them slowly. ''And this silver spoon of Devon's?''

'' 'Nough of one to choke a man who didn't know how to use it.
He must be *someone* because every man on the *Joke* has a pardon
from the British crown, and we carry an English letter of marque. In
a way, see, we're legal. Privateers, not pirates.''

The puzzle pieces locked with a jolt. Fine hairs began to prickle
on the back of Merry's neck, and in a voice that didn't sound right,
she said, ''Devon works for the British government.''

''He works for the British government,'' Raven agreed. ''Mind
you, when we're in open water and Devon's not aboard, Morgan
sometimes has a lapse or two of memory. Hence the British sloop
you saw us take last week.'' Brushing a soft black curl from his
forehead, Raven redealt his deck. ''Devon, in his turn, ignores
Morgan's lapses and gets the cabin which he pays for, the right to
privacy in it, and the right to be put ashore when it's convenient,
and sometimes when it ain't convenient. He also has the right to
keep a prisoner, no questions asked. I guess this time around, that's
you, lovey. I'm sorry if this ain't good news for you, milady. You
don't look so great.''

Consciously she loosened the hands that she had tightly clasped at
her stomach. ''No. It's just that— You see, last night Devon was—
well, he did me an act of kindness that led me to believe that I
should perhaps tell him the truth about . . . But that's impossible.
Quite impossible if he's British—and a . . . a spy. No, don't get up.
Please. I'm all right. I'm glad you told me. You don't know how
glad. You may have saved my life. But—Raven, what would they
do to you if they knew you'd told me?''

"Nothing. Nothing much, anyway. It's not so serious as it would be if I tried to help you escape."

"Would you do that?" she asked, with a rearranged heart rhythm.

He smiled suddenly. "Y'know, darlin', I might. If I thought I could get away with it."

The words had barely left him when angry footsteps rang on the stairs. Cook came into the room with Will Saunders, and in a furious undertone the younger boy snarled at Raven, "For God's sweet sake, you poor-witted nizy. Will and I were on the deck above with Shay, and we heard every word you said like it was rung from a clapper, though Shay pretended not to catch it, bless him! What if it had been Reade with us, eh? Every stupid syllable would have gone straight to Morgan. At least sport oak"—Cook slammed the door behind him—"if you're up to talking like a simpleton."

Turning in his chair, Raven said, "I can't be down here in a closed room with her. Y'know Cat wouldn't like it. Sorry if I scared you."

"Sorry if I scared you!" Cook mimicked and, digging his hands into the red cotton front of Raven's shirt, dragged him violently from his seat. The chair toppled with a crack, the cards flew from the table, and Merry flew from the bench, causing Dennis to squeal indignantly. Inserting herself quickly against Raven's chest, crying out "No!" she barely missed taking the fist Cook had aimed at Raven's chin.

Twisting his fingers around Merry's arms, Saunders pulled her away from Raven. "Who are you—Pocahontas?" he said tartly.

Merry slapped his hand off her arm, glaring into Saunders's shrewd gaze. "Did I say you could grab me?"

He was out of temper with her, but even so, he felt a grin nag at his mouth. She was getting damned saucy for such a pygmy. He remembered, seeing her like this, that she had once fired a crossbow at Devon. Killing the grin, he said, "Listen to me, Miss Merry. None of us want to see you suffer, but if you talk Raven into helping you sneak off, he's going to wind up on the looped end of a line hanging from a yardarm. He's going to get scragged. Hanged. Do you understand?"

"Absolutely!" Merry said. "The next time I jump into the ocean and swim for the mainland, you have my word on it that I won't so much as ask Raven to point which way."

"Fishes go to Glory!" Cook said. "You can barely recognize it, Will, but do you think the girl's trying to be sarcastic?"

"Good for her! What with you jackals yipping into the room. Like to give old Dennis an apoplexy." Raven favored Cook with a happy-go-lucky smile. "Mind, you can grab me again any time you choose. The lady here has a way of throwing herself on me that I could get used to quick."

Cook shoved Raven's chest. "Like a rope dancer's pole, ain't ya? Lead at both ends. I've seen veal calves with more in their brain box than you! Think again if you think they won't hang you because you're a favorite. This ain't a whale boat, boy. It's a son-of-a-bitchin' pirate ship. Pirates. You know—*p-y-r*— Ah, never mind." Turning to Merry, he said grimly, "As for you, missy—"

"Wait!" said Saunders, going quickly to the door. "There's someone coming! All they need is to find us down here fighting, and ask why."

Moving rapidly, Raven righted the chair and sat in it, and Cook sped into the seat beside him. Merry found herself put back onto the window bench by Saunders's left hand as he scooped up Dennis with the other.

"Now, listen, you," he said to her in a tense whisper. "This time we'll keep your guilty secret, but don't try leading Raven astray again here, or I'll go to Devon and tell him you've been scheming to make sail on the sly. You'll end your days on this ship locked up so tight you won't be able to make your eyelashes flutter."

Saunders had meant to frighten her. Subjecting his effect on her to a quick study, he saw that he had been too effective. She was trying to appear defiant, but her lips were drawn and beginning to lose their color. Was it the threat to her or the threat to Raven that he had made too strong? He could have as easily said the same thing more gently from the looks of it, and now there was no time to correct the damage. Later he would seek her out and explain to her with more patience why it would be foolish for her to think about escaping the *Joke*. Or had the worried eyes and the white lips been there when he had come into the cabin? Raven could have said something to her—Raven, who was too well-meaning and honest to understand that sometimes keeping your mouth shut would help everybody prosper. Trying to soften the effect of his lecture, Saunders smiled at Merry, but the soft expression was too inconsistent with the cruelty of his earlier words. She gave him a glance full of blue needles and stared at the floor as Devon pushed open the door and strolled into the room.

At the table Raven and Cook were trying against all nautical odds to build a card house with a verve and jubilation that couldn't have been bettered by a work crew on the Taj Mahal. The glances they turned on Devon were blisteringly innocent, and Raven was overplaying it so badly that it was little wonder that Devon walked over to him and smilingly lifted the jagged tear Cook had just made in Raven's shirt.

Merry tried not to cower on the window bench as Devon glanced her way, assessed her idly, and said, "Children, children . . . Have you been fighting?"

"Devil a bit," Cook said. "Raven and I had words over a hand of cards. 'Twasn't nothing. You've played cards with me; you know how I get when I ain't winning. But you see how peaceable we are now. Building a—a—" He doubtfully regarded the tottering structures on the table.

"Card palace," beamed Raven.

"The pair of them," Saunders said, "are trying to impress little Merry with the magnificence of their erections."

Saunders thought he detected the trace of a smile at the corner of Devon's lips, though the arrogant blond man's stare was not encouraging. Will Saunders was as intimidated by Devon as any other man on the *Joke*, but he had promised Merry that he wouldn't give her away, so he tried again. "Care to try your luck too, then?"

"No, thank you," Devon said. "The competition is too—"

"Stiff?" suggested Cook with wicked glee.

"Possibly, but I was going to say—too numerous. Will, Tom wants you on deck. I'm going to board the American schooner and see if I can learn anything of interest. Good-bye. And take your"— Devon skillfully readjusted Dennis's wriggling pig body in Will Saunders's arms—"swine with you."

The speed with which Raven and Cook quitted the room behind Saunders laid a faint suggestion that they might include themselves in Devon's last category. Merry was still deciding whether she was also one of the swine who ought to get out when Devon shut the door and came to stand in front of her.

"Would you care to tell me what that was about?" he asked her. "The four of you weren't throwing around heavy furniture for no reason."

So he had heard the chair fall. "People have no privacy on a ship," she said. "I don't know why anyone wants to stay on them."

"Look at me!" he said.

It was best to convince him, if she could, that nothing of consequence had occurred. Merry tilted her chin up, willing herself to fully contact his gaze. If his tone had been demanding, his eyes held a caress. There was a fine-edged friendliness about him today that she had barely glimpsed once before, the night at the tavern when she had seen him first. The sweet novelty of it cut like tin scissors through the resistance she had spent the night building toward him, but however attractive the man was, and whatever the graces of his character, this man, this British *spy*, would never be for her.

Last night she had heard him whisper love words to her in long unearthly dreams, and in some empty place in her spirit she had prayed that the seeds of his inclination for her might grow into something more splendid and substantial. But daybreak is a saner time, and at dawn's first narrow light Merry had tucked away her absurd fairy-tale hopes. Whatever the kindness of his gaze this morning, there was nothing in it so noble as love or even so ignoble as lust; it was as though he had simply decided to dispense with an unsatisfied ardor. He had made a barrier, not because it would protect either him or her, but because it was common sense. In his glowing eyes, in the sensual line of his lips, there was no sign it might be a struggle for him to deny the joyous enchantment of yesterday's kisses and transform the gentle, playful lover into a temperate companion. Oh, no, Devon was not trembling on the heart-thrilling verge of denouncing piracy and taking up cobbling in her noble honor. It was hopeless, and she had known it even before she learned about his British military connections. Hopeless.

Drawing his thoughtful scrutiny of her to an end, Devon said, "If I had to guess—and it seems I do—I'd guess that Cook wouldn't lay hands on Raven because Raven was trying to corrupt you, so I'll have to assume it was the other way around. What would you try to talk Raven into that Cook didn't like?''

When it came to guessing, there was no one better at it than Devon. Merry concentrated on showing nothing, and his regard remained steady and quizzical. She had no idea whether or not she was successful. His outstretched hand came to rest on her shoulder, his touch molding lightly to the curving surface. She felt the stroke of his fingers, and his warmth penetrated slowly through her nerve-chilled and unwilling flesh. It was a clear demonstration that he could touch her and still not take her in his arms and do more. When he spoke again, it was to say lightly, ''Never mind. Just don't do anything foolish, Merry friend. If you aren't who you say you aren't—and I'm beginning to believe you—you have nothing to fear from me. You see, my mind is changing. I'm checking on one piece of your story, and if the item clears you—then we'll see.''

''What item?'' she said too rapidly.

''Don't worry,'' he said. ''I suspect you'll pass.''

No, I won't, she thought, *especially if it has anything to do with certain pictures I drew of you for the American government. Could you find that out? I don't want to be here if you do.*

It cost her a fiery and humiliating blush, but she said, ''About yesterday . . .''

Attractive creases softly bracketed his smile. ''It would take a savant with a micrometer to detect my conscience, Windflower, but you activate it better than most can.''

''Why?''

''I think''—his hand left her shoulder—''it has something to do with the way you fall out of a hammock.''

His words, though friendly, were dismissive; Merry got to her feet and started to walk toward the door. She stopped halfway.

''Devon?'' She turned back toward him where he stood, a dusky silhouette against the window's lurid flare. ''What American schooner?''

''You listen closely, don't you? There's a two-masted schooner, the *Good Shepherd*, lying off the lee bow. We've been playing cat and mouse with each other for hours now, and they've finally signaled that they're ready to talk.''

"What kind of American schooner would want to talk to pirates?" she said.

"She's a privateer, probably from Massachusetts, if Morgan's information is correct."

It was not safe to ask so many questions; still, surely he couldn't wonder at her curiosity? "If that's an American privateer, why hasn't she tried to blow us out of the water? The bounty on the *Black Joke* must be—"

"In the tens of thousands." Calmly, "Yes. The *Joke* went through a metamorphosis before we came within range of the *Good Shepherd*. The black caterpillar crystallized into a white moth. The figurehead that was a gorgon has been replaced by a genie in a turban, and the signature of the bow reads *Arab,* which is by no coincidence a letter-of-marque trader with a Baltimore certificate of registry, Commission number six sixty-eight."

"Then it's a trick," she said bitterly. "What happened to the real *Arab?*"

"Captured in the Rappahannock River and sent to Halifax. It's not common knowledge yet." Watching her face, he said, "Does this shock you? Your country does it too." When she would not answer him, he said, this time with amusement, "Ah, yes. I comprehend from your eloquently contemptuous eyes. You're raptly condemning the hateful trade of piracy. It's good for you to spare me a lecture. You had better leave the room before your discipline collapses. Good day."

Merry's sole consolation was that he hadn't been able to tell her to take her swine with her. Morgan's cabin door was too heavy to slam, but it made a satisfying loud thwack as she pulled it closed behind her.

An hour later she watched from her cabin window as Devon, looking beautiful and distinguished as an American privateer captain, got into a ship's boat with a small crew.

The weather was worse. A thin drizzle spanked the dark, roiling sea, and the restless air was kneaded by sticky-fingered fog. Cold reached out to her from the thick window glass.

Merry was about to give up her watch when she noticed a second small boat, moving like a shadow between the waves. As the boat approached she was able to identify its occupant as Joe Griffith, the

Joke's master gunner. Evidently he had taken advantage of the *Joke*'s halt to fish. The poor weather must have discouraged him though, for he rowed back to the ship, secured the small boat to a cleat, and agilely climbed a rope to the deck. For more than an hour Merry returned time and again to the window. The boat was still there. It amazed her that they hadn't hauled it up, with a storm threatening. Joe Griffith must have forgotten it; he had a tendency to lose interest quickly in things that weren't connected with the ship's cannons. If the boat took the storm damaged, Tom Valentine would probably have Griffith punished. Burdened with an overactive conscience, Merry went toward the door to remind Mr. Griffith about the neglected boat. She stopped, her hand on the door handle, a new and overwhelming idea sizzling like frying shark meat in her brain.

Her chest roasting, her hands cold as granite, Merry spun the idea through her mind, as if she couldn't believe that she'd come up with the thought by herself. Pulling a brown wool jacket over her suddenly chilly arms, straining to keep her voice low, Merry repeated the slowly emerging plan to the stalwart table, to Devon's desk, to a maddeningly noncommittal face she drew in the window mist. In the little fishing craft bobbing below she was going to row to the *Good Shepherd*. With a kernel of a smile she decided that if that name didn't betoken succor and divine benevolence for her plan, nothing ever would. She wondered if Devon would remember later that the last thing he'd said to her was: *You had better leave the room before your discipline collapses. Good day.* Perhaps, just perhaps it was going to be a better day for Merry Wilding than the man suspected. And somehow, in time, she would learn to live with the knowledge that she would never see Devon again. And Cat and Raven. No. None of that. No second thoughts. She couldn't afford to care. Aunt April was going to see her missing niece again. . . .

She waited until the bells told her that it was time for dinner before running lightly up the stairs to flatten herself against the boards and watch the rain-spattered deck. The mess pennant flew over the fo'c'sle, and in another minute Cook came with his helper, carrying covered kids of victuals toward the crew's quarters. They made three trips, with rain beating the wooden covers over the hot food and rising again as silver vapor.

Cook and his man would eat with the crew, and for more than twenty crucial minutes the ship's kitchen would be deserted. Breathing quickly, she forced herself to count to three hundred in case Cook had forgotten something and then pulled the jacket over her hair and stepped into the open. Around her the deck rang with water song. Thick rain clots drummed against billowing canvas, polished boards, and gun metal. Streams gurgled in the scuppers. The watch, in their steaming oilskins, were hardly in a mood to stop her for a chat, though Erik Shay—the fleshy giant who, long ago at the Musket and Muskrat, had let Merry and Sally leave the tavern— waved from the upper deck.

Once in the galley Merry rapidly located and stole a small paring knife, a discarded apron covered with grease, some coals, and a tinderbox.

She wrapped the tinderbox, the coals, and the knife in the apron, and buttoned her jacket and stuffed the wadded apron underneath. Running from the galley with her head down like a mole, she slammed into Tom Valentine's chest.

"Oh, my! Oh, dear heavens!" she cried out, disengaging instantly from him, to leave a wet spot on his immaculate flannel shirt.

"Anyone would assume," Valentine said, "that by now *somebody* would have taught you to curse. Don't wring your hands at me, you little fool. I'm not going to debauch you. You look guilty. What have you been up to?"

"Nothing! Nothing at all! I was only startled to see you. I went into the galley to get a—a biscuit. Because of the storm. I was hungry, and I thought in this bad weather it might take Cat a long time to get around to bringing a tray for me."

"It's only a rain," he said, "not a typhoon. Cat can bring you something to eat right away if you're hungry. I'll talk to him."

"*No!* That is, thank you, but—I'm not as hungry as I was when I—" It was awkward to lie stupidly to Thomas Valentine; it would be disastrous to try to lie to Cat. "The damp . . . the heaving of the ship . . . have made me a little sick. I should go lie down, I think, and sleep. If you see Cat, I wish you would tell him please *not* to bring food."

Back in her cabin Merry whipped the door shut behind her and leaned onto it with pounding relief. It was a good thing that Valentine's life experience had convinced him that white women were imbeciles, or he would hardly have let his suspicions pass. But what if he repeated the story of their encounter in the hearing of Saunders or Cook, who knew that she might try to escape? Perhaps her where-abouts were of such little interest to Valentine that he would forget the whole thing immediately—or perhaps not.

She made a short, unsatisfactory attempt at prayer, and then a feverish review of her plan, which reminded her to be methodical. So, methodically she checked to be sure the windows were closed, and with ears tuned for footsteps in the passage she pried open Devon's locked desk. Inside she found letters, neatly bundled; note-books filled with coded entries in an educated masculine hand; a packet of maps, some beautifully detailed, some less so; and desk supplies: a walnut sandbox, pencils with a cast brass sharpener, a green glass ink bottle, a whalebone letter opener, a penknife, and a tin tray of pens.

Overcoming an instinctive repugnance for stealing, she drew the damp apron bundle from her sodden jacket and replaced it with the letters; the notebooks were too big to take, the maps too bulky. There was no time to read the letters and discover their mysteries. It was enough to know they belonged to Devon, and that he possessed them meant that they must be somehow useful to his country's cause, which also meant the converse, that if *her* country had them, it would help the United States and hurt Britain, at least in the hazy realms of theory. If, on the other hand, all that she was getting away with was last year's bills to Devon from his linen draper, then Devon was going to have the last laugh when he found them missing. Any thought that it would be preferable to have Devon laughing when he found out her theft rather than in a murderous rage Merry quakingly dismissed as fainthearted and unpatriotic. Of course the worst would be if she were still here, on the *Joke*, when he learned what she was trying to do. This had better work. Or else.

Her frightened clumsy fingers spilled the water from the water can into the chamber pot and stuffed the water can with the coals and one of the better maps from Devon's drawer. And although the contents of the tinderbox were clean and dry, it took Merry five gut-wrenching minutes to draw a spark. The map flared, a soft licking flame that left black curled paper ash as it went out. It took another five minutes of unpleasant experiments before she created a fire that gave dark smoke without flame. Thick heat singed her face as she wrapped her hands in her jacket and thrust the can between its supports near the shaped splashboard, to prevent a fiery spill that might start a *real* blaze. She waited as long as she could in the storm of smoke and dead flying cinders. When finally her eyes ran and her skin cooked, she threw open a window, flung wide the door, and stumbled, choking, into the passage. Racing to the upper deck, croaking "Fire! Fire!" to Erik Shay, she didn't need to be an actress; black billows from the lower passage contrasted splendidly with the cherry color of her eye whites and the white tear tracks on her cherry cheeks.

It worked better than her best hopes. If fire was feared on land, it had a hundredfold the terrors at sea. On many ships it was a capital offense to smoke an uncovered pipe belowdecks, or in hours of darkness. Merry stood forgotten near the gunwale as the alarm spread and men rushed across the rain-slicked decks with sand buckets and water tubs. Dennis, the pink pig, skidding across the deck on wet trotters, bumping men and upsetting sand buckets, was the only one who saw Merry slip overboard.

In the detachment of undiluted panic she felt the turmoil on deck fade, and what she could hear best was the thunder of her breathing as she found the free-swinging rope ladder leading to the small boat and took the weight of her body on her arms. The rough jute burned her palms, and the sting of instant welts distracted her, when she ought to be remembering to brace her feet against the ship. The next wave trench that rocked the great vessel smashed her face-first into damp timber. Pain blinded her. She clung, swaying on the rope, while air curdled sickeningly in her lungs. Slowly she began to move again, lowering herself in inept movements that cut shoulder blades into cringing muscles.

Below, in the bottom of the boat, there were two inches of seawater, gray-green and frigid. As she set her feet in it the chill sucked through her moccasins and bit her flesh like an iron trap. Icy drizzle fell on her, and her hair whipped in wide circles as she opened the knot that held the boat to its cleat. She shoved off through the leaping sea as waves threw her boat against the massive pirate ship with a power that threatened to disintegrate her tiny craft

to splinters. The boat capered and swirled with giddy violence until
it and she were caught in a friendly undertow and hurled into the
empty ocean and fresh breezes.

It's one thing to watch someone row; it's quite another to try it
oneself in heavy seas, and this was a bad moment to begin wondering if the American privateers on the *Good Shepherd* would be
certain to help her and if there was any chance that Devon might
have lied about the *Shepherd*'s identity.

Around her the water shone dully, a desert of wet stucco pocked
with black rain blisters. The sea spit streaks of spray at her and into
her eyes. She shut her lids and sliced the slapping waves with the
oars. Again. Again. She was wet everywhere. The air was dense
with the cold steam of rain volleys and lacy wind-borne foam. Narcotic
cold began to seep into her tearing muscles, and she could row
faster. Misery mingled with half-crazed exhilaration.

In the pressing gloom she didn't know that the water in the boat
rinsed the hem of her breeches. The ocean had come midway up her
calves before she admitted there was more water in the boat with her
than could be accounted for by rain and sea spray. Too late she
understood why Joe Griffith had brought the boat back so quickly to
the *Joke*. It hadn't been because the weather was bad. It had been
because the boat was leaking.

Twisting her head, she looked through the driving shower toward
the *Shepherd*, a toneless oblong riding distant wave heads. It was
too far. The *Joke*, great and gleaming behind her, was also too far.
Not that it mattered. That bridge was well burnt behind her.

Her desperation mounted as she tried to find the leak and stop it
with her foot. Seawater rolled in around her, a frothy jelly soured
with rotting kelp and marine slag. Below, the sea beasts waited,
eager-jawed, cold as clay, and hungry. Every one of her inhibitions
evaporated at once. Merry snatched off her flaccid moccasin and
began to bail furiously, but soon water sluiced over the sides, and
the boat fell away gently beneath her, and she was kicking water
while the sea gripped her legs and tried to suck her head under.

She knew, remotely, that it was ridiculous, but her hands kept
bailing with the dissolving ruin of her moccasin, and her feet kept
moving heavily through the water, treading to keep her afloat. Her
back was toward the *Shepherd*, and she didn't see the longboat's

swift approach. In all her hasty thoughts it had never occurred to her that Devon, on the *Good Shepherd*, would see the smoke billowing from her cabin window and, because of it, return quickly to the *Joke*.

From the bow of the longboat Devon watched her trying to beat back the sea with her sieve of a moccasin. He was not the kind of man who did things like rolling his eyes skyward, but that gesture would have come close to capturing the flavor of his emotions. Behind him, working hard at an oar, he heard Max Reade guffaw.

"Lil gamecock, ain't she?" Reade called forward. "Look at 'er. Pluck to the backbone, eh? Damme, she's got bottom."

"To hell," said Devon, "with her bottom." It didn't make things substantially worse, though it hardly improved his temper that by the time they reached her, she was under the water and he had to go into the sea to save her.

The arm that came from nowhere to drag Merry toward the surface was obviously that of a giant squid, and she clawed at it, screaming seawater into her lungs until she was turned and could see as in a crazed time jump in a dream that it was Devon who held her. With chilled arms and quivering flesh she shot into his arms, clinging to him like a baby spider monkey.

Above wind and sea and rain she heard him say, "Well. You're all affectionate now. This is a dandy time for that."

His hand tangled into her hair, and when the grip was good enough, he took a second hold on the seat of her trousers and heaved her up and into the longboat.

Once before Merry had found herself drenched and frightened on the deck of a longboat, but this time there was no Cat here to wrap her in a greatcoat, blow her nose, and wring the sea from her hair. Now the raindrops were stinging arrows on her back as she sat doubled on her knees, shaking, coughing, and spitting up seawater into her cupped hands. Aside from Reade, who was cruel enough to laugh at her, pirate faces watched her impassively. Merry squeezed her eyelids shut.

She opened them again on Devon as he came into the boat beside her, wet hair in his face, the bright gold made dark and streaming. His eyes were amber jewels, dappled and self-luminous. He reached for her, and she was too tired to fight him; her limbs too much like

brittle sticks as he sank his fingers into her upper arms and shook her
hard. There was no strength in her jaw, and her small chattering
teeth bit into her tongue. Blood mixed on her chin with dribbled
seawater, and suddenly, below her chest, Merry felt the sudden
movement of a forgotten bundle. Her shirt slid from its tuck in her
trousers, and the stolen letters slipped out and landed in a sodden
clump at Devon's feet.

Back aboard the *Black Joke* Cat had been the first to understand
why there was a simulated fire in Merry's cabin and had spied
through a telescope the distant frenzied figure in the waves. But
Saunders across the deck had come to the same conclusion two
seconds later and caught Cat going over the side. As gently as he
could, Saunders put Cat to sleep with a belaying pin. Lowering the
narrow body carefully to the deck, Saunders shouted over his shoulder to one of the hands nearby, "Get a pair of chains up here and
keep 'em on Cat until that girl's either rescued or dead. And don't
give me that look. She's too far from us. Just too damned far."

Saunders picked up the telescope Cat had let go and watched
Merry's flounderings with guilt and anxiety and tried to estimate
whether the longboat moving out from the *Shepherd* would reach
her in time. The visibility was poor, and he couldn't tell who was in
the longboat, but Devon must be there, and Devon, with his superior
competence, would do everything that could be done to save her.

If Saunders's heart was an apple, no woman had ever had a bite of
it. Habit worked to erase the emotions Merry's struggles had raised
in him. She was nothing to him; a random female victim, oddly
adopted by the ship's crew from boredom just as the pig had been,
although Cat had implied once that the captain might have played a
role in that. Impossible. Morgan would never interest himself in a
casual ride-under of Devon's, and an unreliable one at that, judging
from the frequent nights Devon slept away from his bed.

Saunders raised the glass again, fighting the picture of a slender
girl in boy's clothes and a huge preposterous hat, awkwardly clutching a cannonball, her eyes as colorful as bluebells, laughing at some
silly joke of Raven's. Raven. The name entered his mind like a
scream. Will Saunders twisted quickly and raced with a jumping
heartbeat across the heaving, rain-soaked deck, over barrels, around

rope coils. He reached the after deck in the midst of shouting and saw Tom Valentine try to grab Raven, to be brought up short by a glittering blade in Raven's brown fist. In the flash of a second Raven had dived over the side.

Calm-handed and cursing, Saunders ordered the third ship's boat put in the water and went after Raven with Shay, Cook, and two others. Raven was such a strong swimmer that they had trouble catching up to him. They yelled to him that Merry was safe, that Devon had gotten to her, but either the boy couldn't hear them over the roaring sea, or worry had sapped his reason. In the end they had to haul him into the boat by force and beat him senseless to keep him from going back into the ocean.

When Devon carried Merry aboard the *Joke* and tossed her, dripping, on the deck, they were still trying to revive Raven. With a light stride Devon crossed to where Raven lay in a cocoon of wet canvas and blankets. The teenager's long lashes were curling dark fibers that dipped childishly against young cheeks grayed by the sea's cold touch. Behind him Devon heard Morgan answer the question in his mind.

"He won't die. Little Raven was just trying to swallow the sea so Merry could fall safely on a dry ocean bed. You should have been here. I haven't seen so many people jump off a ship since oyster season." Rand Morgan glanced around, and his cool gaze fell on his sailing master. "Ah. There you are, Saunders. Wasn't it your order that put Cat in chains?" The pirate captain's gaze shifted to Cat in his iron bondage. Morgan smiled slowly. "Not that I disapprove. It has a certain allure. But nevertheless I want him released. See to it, please. He's needed."

Kneeling to join his half brother at Raven's side, Morgan watched Devon lay two fingers on the unconscious boy's neck to find a pulse and silently count it. When Devon withdrew his hand, Morgan said, "I might as well tell you; we've had a surfeit of gallantry. It ran fore to aft, thrashing like a rabid weasel. I'm afraid Raven forgot himself with Thomas Valentine."

Devon looked up quickly. "What happened?"

"The boy drew steel."

Devon swore quietly. He looked down at Raven and then returned his gaze to Morgan's. "Will Tom let me take his punishment?"

"No. Don't make a fool of yourself by asking." Morgan paused.
And then, "About the girl—"

"Yes," Devon said. "About the girl." He stood slowly and
walked back to Merry. She sat as he had left her, huddled into the
gunwale.

Lowering himself in a smooth movement, he sat close to her in
the pouring rain, and with lazy deliberation he cradled her head
between his hands. Her hair was sticky and tangled with seaweed
and gave up water like a sponge under the pressure of his spread
fingers and gushed tearlike rivulets down his wrist and arms. Shock
was the only expression he could see in her face. Her eyes were
bruised and distended, with jelling salt forming caustic pearls on her
eyelashes; her fine-textured skin was icy to his touch; her blue lips
were parted and still.

"So help me God," he murmured, and in his voice Merry
heard all the acid violence of a tightly checked temper. "If you
try to escape from me again, I'll strap you to the bow cannon and flay
every inch of baby skin from your immature little backbone."

Working with patient hands, Cat carried Merry below, dried her,
fed her, put her to bed, and leaving Dennis the pig with her for
company, he locked her cabin door and delivered the key to Devon,
where he sat in the fo'c'sle spooning brandied chicken broth into
Raven. Cat did what he could for Raven, who was conscious and,
typically, had the unmitigated gall to complain about being coddled.
Leaving the fo'c'sle, Cat located Thomas Valentine near the bitts
giving orders to Sails and watching Saunders arm the lead. It had
taken a good quarter hour to talk Valentine into waiting until the next
morning for his retribution. All that was left then was to make a
curt apology to Will Saunders for the foully discolored black eye
that Saunders had got from him as soon as he'd got his hands out of
the chains.

Below, coming without knocking into Morgan's cabin, he found
the captain comfortably established in a lambskin chair and reading,
of all things, *A Woman Killed with Kindness;* and reading it with an
air of bloody-minded insouciance.

Cat noiselessly did his evening chores and then stood in the
lemon candlelight and casually stripped off every piece of wet
clothing. Naked, he put on a silk robe, and with rum and a

hairbrush he dropped into a chair across from Morgan. He unwound his braid slowly and began to put the brush through his hair with irritated strokes, tugging cruelly in a way he would never have done with Merry. The braid had set waves into his hair like a woman's, and when he shook it out, its length fell to the floor, a flood of ivory silk, and slid over the boar bristles of the discarded hairbrush.

Morgan, Cat saw, had continued to read. In a pleasant, graceful gesture Cat ran his hand under his hair and wound its shining flow around his wrist.

"I think," he said, "that I'll cut it. It's too much damned trouble to take care of."

Silence. Morgan looked up from the book, his eyes black and innocent. "As you like." Then, "It would make someone a pretty wig." For that he got back a cold blue stare. So he returned to his book and said, without looking up, "How did you expect him to act? He had almost to watch her die." Morgan read another page and closed the book, facing the unwavering stare. "So? You might as well say it, babe. A Cossack doing the mazurka couldn't stomp across the room with more drama than your pubescent disapproval."

Cat opened his hand and let the hair fall. "She didn't cry."

"When?"

"When I put her to bed. She didn't cry. She couldn't. I think she's forgetting how."

"Is that all, for God's sakes?" Morgan tossed the book on a small table. "Get up and bring her to me. I'll have her bawling so hard the dolphins will gather at the bowsprit and pelt us with old shoes."

In a steady voice Cat said, "I know about the boat. I asked Griffith who told him to leave it there. He told me that you did. She could see that boat from her cabin, and you knew it."

This time the silence was lengthy. The rain was a pretty hiss on the window. The wind purred. Finally Morgan said, "Aha."

"Which means?"

"*Aha* is an ejaculation, babe. It doesn't *mean* anything. You looked as though you were expecting some kind of an ejaculation, and so I"—that smile—"seem to have ejaculated prematurely. Pardon me." Another frigid silence from Cat. At last, relenting, Morgan said blandly, "Young people have got to try new things."

"Yes," Cat said. "But if one of the new things they try is drowning, it puts an end to any more experiments."

"The girl has been on the *Joke* long enough to have inspired someone to pull her out of the water when she falls in. Do you think I wasn't watching? If Devon hadn't left the *Shepherd* when he did, I would have sent a boat. Anyway, I thought you, in particular, would be pleased. You were so concerned about her virtue. Well? That's likely to stay intact now."

"You know that Devon's letters—*Granville*'s letters—were destroyed?"

"So I hear," Morgan said. "It's a pity she didn't choose to take the maps instead, but one can't have everything. I rather admired the desk break-in. It showed initiative."

"Oh? Was that part of it too?" Cat asked, low tones of anger filtering into his voice. "An opportunity for her to display untapped abilities? He'll never forgive her. For everything else, perhaps. But not for the letters."

With a disquieting grin Morgan said, "My dear! What a naïve thing to have said! How refreshing of you." Studying the blond youth, he added in a moment, "Don't take it all to heart. She'll do. I promise. One must suffer a little adversity if one wants to be interesting."

"Hurray"—Cat lifted his glass in a toast—"for adversity. There must be someone we can petition to bring back the Inquisition, the Black Plague, the Roman persecutions. Damn it, Rand. Does she *have* to be interesting?"

"Why not? I like interesting people."

Cat had been expecting exactly that response. He tipped back his head and drained the rum. Crow-black and shining, lamb's wool framed the Nordic purity of his features as he leaned into the chair and closed his eyes. "How far are you going to let this go? When will you put an end to it?"

Delicate surprise augmented the sparkle in Morgan's black eyes. "Why would I want to, when it's doing both of them so much good?"

"Absolutely," Cat said dryly. "Merry and Devon. They're as happy as a couple of toads croaking in a quagmire. You bastard. I suppose you think this is doing me good too. What if she *does* try to escape again? Would you let him flog her?"

"But of course. Naturally." Morgan laughed suddenly. "I'd love to see him lay a single strip on her white back. It would be the most potent lesson either of them ever got. The sheer heat of the self-discovery would burn the topgallant right off the mainmast. Why? Are you worried Devon will kill her in a fit of pique?"

"No. Devon wouldn't." Cat's eyes opened, and he turned them on Morgan and gave him an even look. "Is she your daughter?"

Surprise flashed in Morgan's eyes and was quickly concealed. There was a short laugh; a lifted eyebrow. "Shrewd. Oh, very shrewd, considering how little you've had to go on. My daughter. That would make her—what?—Devon's niece. My theology is a little scanty, but that would make any relationship between them incestuous, wouldn't it? Why, in particular, my daughter?"

"Because in the two weeks that Devon was gone, she was sleeping one door away from you, and you didn't—" Cat used the crudest word he knew for it.

"Interesting," Morgan said in a civil way. "You think I don't embrace incest for myself but promote it between my daughter and young legitimate brother? Don't work so hard, babe. Merry's not my daughter." He smiled at the window. "We have no relationship. Except that once, long ago, I loved her mother." In a long easy movement he stood, crossed to Cat, and removed the empty glass from the boy's lax fingers. His smile was lazy and potent. "Go to bed. Your new conscience is hotter than a fresh-laid goose yolk. We wouldn't want to wear it out."

CHAPTER FOURTEEN

The ship's drying sails breathed scent into the morning air, a sharp fragrance, distinct as geranium. Gull odor, in wet plucked feathers and smeared droppings, was everywhere, and the damp jute stank.

Merry woke to pungent smells and pungent memories. Dennis was gone, and cold biscuits were on the table with a clean, folded towel that had a note in it from Cat. Climbing back into the eternally rocking bunk, Merry read the note aloud to the cabin. It began without preamble: "You've slept late because I drugged you last night. Call me Borgia. I did it for your own *etc*. Interesting young women need long slumbers after a day of initiative and adversity."

Her hands dropped to the coverlet with the paper in them. Raising a fist covered with angry rust-colored scratches, she rubbed her heavy eyes and wondered if the last sentence was a quote that she was supposed to recognize. The prose style didn't seem like Cat's; an obscure literary reference? A common literary reference unknown to her and betokening some embarrassing inadequacy in her education? Probably the latter. Giving it up, she lifted the paper and began again to read.

"Wear your hair up. We're going to execute you at noon. (I jest.) I can't come down for a while. They're putting Raven on trial, and I have to be there. Explanations later. I've seen Devon in better moods. Be careful. Yours, Cat. D.T.C."

Which also was a jest. It meant Destroy This Communication and had become a national joke this year, ever since an enterprising newspaper editor in New England had discovered it imprinted on a pitifully innocuous dispatch from the secretary of war to Andrew Jackson.

Bracing herself, she stood up on the bunk amid a crackle of stiff joints. It hurt to bring up her arm enough to put her hand out the window with the paper in it. Her fingers relaxed, and she watched the paper flutter away in the wind, a bold white streak in the sunlight that rode a slanting air current into the ocean.

Then she washed, took clothing from the sea chest, soaked her hardtack, and worried. She had seen them last night working on Raven, but all Cat would tell her about it was that Raven had tried to swim after her, and that the cold water had made him ill. He would be fine by morning. Why were they putting him on trial? *Why?* Explanations later.

Taking a bite of hardtack, she pulled up her white pantaloons, their flared hem sliding over her ankles as she held the waist with one hand and nervously tucked in her white shirttail with the other. With shaking hands she pinned up her hair for Cat.

When it was all done, the washing, the dressing, the eating, the straightening of the bunk, then there was nothing left but the worry, which had gnawed itself into something more malevolent. What trial? *What trial?*

More than an hour passed. At last, unable to bear the tension, convinced that things were so bad already that she couldn't make them worse, Merry took up the tin biscuit plate and began to bang it against the door. Someone above must have been able to hear her, but she was ignored. She could imagine them listening, saying, "Let the wench bang. It'll keep her out of trouble. Soon enough she'll tire of it."

And that was true, and she had tired soon, but she kept at it, a stubborn staccato rhythm irregularly interrupted while she rested her hands. This time her will would outlast theirs. To be a pest is only tiring, but to be pestered brings the monkey up in anyone. Merry hammered until she heard Sails yell to her through the door.

"Merry! Merry, lass! Will ye stop that now?"

"I will if you'll open the door!"

"Lass, I canna'. I haven't the key." The reproach in the old sailmaker's voice was a gentle one. "Why are ye wearying yerself with that vexing ratcheting?"

"Where's Raven? What are they doing with him? Why is there a trial? What kind of a trial?"

"Och, don't fret on it so. There's naught ye can be doing. The lad's got himself into a mite of a fratch, and they're up above deciding what's to be done wi' him, so that he'll be rememberin' on the next occasion that he ought to be mindin' his elders."

"What kind of a—a fratch? Do you mean that he's to be punished because last night he tried to help me? No! I won't have it! Sails, do you hear me? I demand to see Morgan! Tell them to open this door!"

"Lass, no . . . Ye must be seein' sense now . . ."

But she could hardly hear the last words because she had the plate up and was slamming it against the door again and again. She wouldn't stop, nor would she listen to him as he went on trying in a kindly way to convince her that she must discontinue this foolishness.

When her situation changed, it changed quickly. She had barely time to assimilate the swift footsteps on the stair, the rapped-out order, the key turning in the lock. All she had was the broken part of a second to leap backward to keep from getting the thrust-open door in her face.

"My love, did you summon me?"

Devon stood on the threshold, the smile on him so sweet and barbed that he might have breathed attar of roses and brimstone. Hips down, he was encased in denim trousers that revealed more of his lean musculature than Merry knew was good for her to see. Hips up, he was bare, discounting an open leather vest, which Merry was trying hard not to do. They were pirate's clothes. He was a British spy in pirate's clothing, a wolf in wolf's clothing, and yet somehow his appearance was as neat and decorative as an enameled thimble.

Merry was all in favor of being belligerent toward him, even though she'd known it would be a little difficult to put that brave policy into practice. Face to face with him *a little difficult* was turning into *next to impossible*. Resisting an impulse to retreat behind the table, Merry said, "Certainly not. I want to talk to Rand Morgan."

"Do you? I'm sorry to disappoint you—his arrival isn't imminent. Tell me, did you sleep well last night, dear?"

"No," she said, paling another shade. "But I'll bet you've been up for hours, sharpening your fangs. What do you want first, an arm or a leg? Or are you going to go right for the throat?''

"Are we a willing victim, then, this morning?"

Her sigh was quick and frightened. "You know I'm not good at waiting, Devon. Do and have done."

"Bare your throat then, my love," he said. "I've come to invite you to see Raven flogged."

She had been expecting an attack, but nothing as indirect or as cruel as this. Her first thought was not to believe him, and she said jerkily, "Your sense of humor is a little wanting today."

"I agree. I suggest you keep that in mind. Last night when Tom Valentine ordered Raven not to jump into the sea after you, Raven pulled a knife on him."

Belief came slowly to Merry. She shook her head in abstract denial. "Last night he was injured. Surely after that they would not . . ."

"Yes, they would. Particularly since Raven announced chattily at his trial that he stands behind his actions last night and he'd do the same again if the need arose. If the child weren't so popular, he'd be dead. Come on deck with me. You can tell your grandchildren that once you saw a boy whipped on a pirate ship."

She recoiled from him, pride forgotten, hardly aware of her body's motion. "Devon, don't let them do it! Don't!"

"Merry . . . Little Windflower—" His voice was soft and textured. "You know so much. You must know that I don't have a vote here. Why else would you have stolen my letters?"

She would remember in her nightmares his expression in the boat when the letter bundle parted company with her shirt. She had taken those letters without having any idea what they contained. Now she never wanted to know. She heard herself say, "How dare you judge me for that? Or— Of course. You hire gutter trash to do your stealing for you. Everything I've learned about vice has been from you."

Quietly he said, "Merry, I offered you friendship."

Sick. She was going to be sick. "You offered me captivity."

"Which I promised to end."

"If," she said, "I met your demands."

"Oh, my dear girl," he said softly, "and you wouldn't have met them, would you? You should have told me the truth. Before yesterday afternoon do you think I could have hurt you?'' He came to her, his stride fluid and predatory, his gaze holding hers. He lifted his hand and turned it to brush the back of his curved fingers slowly down the tight slope of her cheek. ''What would you have done with the letters, Windflower? Sold them to the highest bidder?''

Merry grabbed his unresisting wrist in shaking fingers and held it stiffly, away from her face. She started to speak, to say something that would stop his words, but the chaos of her thoughts couldn't seem to make speech.

He waited for a reply, and when it did not come, he said, ''What happened, Merry? Weren't the things I offered you enough? What price buys entrance to your pretty body?'' And then, ''Would Raven's reprieve be enough?''

She was too anguished to examine his intent. There was strength only to unclutch her fingers from his wrist and to take a backward step that brought her legs up against the writing desk's sharp wooden edge. His hands encircled her waist, and she could feel the sweet heat from his uncovered chest as he drew her toward him. A pained whimper escaped her as his experienced fingers tilted her chin and his mouth sought her. The kiss was spark-hot and scarring, deeply arousing. When finally he had carried its message to the limit and dragged his lips from her, Merry was so angry at him and so filled with bitter sorrow that her power of speech returned, full colored.

''Very well!'' she flashed out. ''If you need payment in blood for a small act of charity.''

He released her completely, and with a deadly smile he said, ''Well, well. I believe you actually would. How noble you are. But I don't think I could stomach a sacrificial lamb, and besides, my pretty one, even though your charms have their moments, my interest in them is low just now. And none of it matters in the end because there's nothing I can do to help Raven. By all means though,'' he said, going back to the door and holding it invitingly open, ''go out. Look around. If you make the same suggestion to enough men, in time you might be able to find someone who wants to play.''

That last insulting reference made it especially difficult, but in spite of it she brushed past him and left the room.

Merry found Morgan in his cabin stretched out on his goliath bed eating allspice berries. He heard her out in silence, the pleas, the frayed threads of logic she wove to show why it was *she*, if anyone, that ought to be punished, and not Raven. When she was finished, he studied her for a minute, showing no expression, and answered calmly, without a trace of sympathy, "I can't have my men flashing steel every time they get excited about something. He'll be wiser in the future if we blood him a little now. Don't worry. We won't kill him."

In desperation she went to Valentine, her voice raised more than it should have been. He listened to her with wary annoyance and then said, "Cat! Where the blazes is he? Cat! Get over here and take her below."

She fought Cat furiously as he strong-armed her to her cabin, and even there she lashed out wildly and struck at him with her fists. The young pirate knew many ways to silence a hysterical victim. None was a method he cared to use on Merry, but when she would not let him quiet her, he pushed her to the floor and stilled her frantic struggles with his body.

"Merry, listen to me. Listen to me!" In one hand he caught her flailing wrists, the other covered her mouth. The deeply blue eyes glaring up at him were nearly delirious with anger, but to his relief they held no fear. "Damnation, Merry. Listen. You've stretched this as far as you can. Tempers are short. One more scream and you're likely to end the morning with your back bared by Raven's side."

"I don't care!" she said, the words muffled under his strong fingers.

"So what?" he snapped. "I do. If you won't clap a stopper on your tongue, I'll do it for you. Open your mouth again, and I'll drug it shut. I mean it. I'd rather humiliate you than hurt you. My choice."

Through his fingers she said, "Why *yours?*"

She was breathing in short gasps, but her eyes were calmer. He loosened his hold on her mouth.

"Because," he said, "haven't you noticed? I'm the one on top."

She was imprisoned in her cabin, and it was two days before she saw Raven. Cat unlocked the door the second evening and allowed Raven to enter before him. Standing quickly, coming toward him, she saw with unclad anxiety that the cloudless friendliness in his eyes was as bright as ever, although the firm facial skin was still gray from suffering. His easy sailor's grace had become stiff and awkward, and when she saw it, she ran into his arms with a cry.

"Merry! Here now, none of that," Raven said softly, flattered and a little embarrassed. "Don't take on so. I'm the same—sound of body, soft of brain. Ouch! Here, dear, don't hug me, please."

"I'm sorry!" she said, carefully and quickly redirecting her hands. "Raven, if I had known—"

"M'lady, it had nothing to do with you. I don't mind a thrashing now 'n' again, if it's in a good cause. I'd be right as a red currant by now if it hadn't been for Sails. Mind you, his intentions were the best, but to keep me company on the first night after, he took to reading from a sermon book. Forty pages, he read, and the print on them smaller than flea tracks, and titled 'The Divinity of Christ, by One Who Had Been for Thirty Years an Atheist.' Lord, by the time it was over, you pretty well felt like putting your fist in the nose of the man who converted him."

Raven's lips, smiling at her with kindness, were dry and set with pain twists. She stood tensely before him, her hand resting against the loose weave of his cider-colored shirt. She said, "Will Saunders calls himself your best friend. I can't understand how he could stand by and watch them beat you."

"If you want the truth," said Raven with amusement, "it didn't exactly break his heart to see them lay stripes on my back. Madder than an empty duck with his quaker stuck shut, Will was. You should hear him quoting Père Ardier on the subject of Caribbean males."

"I heard," Cat said and quoted, " 'While they are generally intelligent and well made—' "

"Thank you," Raven said.

" '—they are also unreliable, lazy, capricious, and ready at any time to commit suicide,' " Cat finished.

Grinning at Cat, Raven retorted, "And have you heard, mayhap, what the good father said about Swedes? 'Quarrelsome, insolent, arrogant, and prone to wantonness.' "

"That," said Cat dryly, "was quick. Why don't you sit down and quit trying to be jolly? Look at her face. She knows you're acting."

It was agonizing for Merry to watch Raven lower himself clumsily into the chair that Cat had turned backward for him. Again she said, "I can't understand how they could do that to you."

"Merry, it was a light sentence—" Raven began.

"Light!"

"In the Navy—any navy—I would have been hanged for it," Raven said cheerfully. "As it was, Valentine should have held me to a trial by combat, but you see, Valentine is the best swordsman on the ship, while I—"

"Would be hard put to slash your way out of a barberry hedge," Cat said. "I've told you, Merry, Tom Valentine couldn't let Raven go unpunished without looking like a weakling, and no one wants a weakling for a quartermaster."

Not convinced, not consoled, Merry angrily said, "And this is why, I suppose, they say, 'No man would go to sea on a ship who could contrive to get himself into jail'?" She turned away furiously, facing the window where the high rectangles showed a sky of deep slate, and a few stars made lonely, splendid pinpoints in the fading twilight. The room was hot, the surfaces sticky and pleasantly spiced with the warm raisins Cat had brought to her earlier. Their notions of justice were alien to her and seemed appallingly stupid. She could scarcely comprehend the logic that required someone to see a friend whipped to preserve some useless standard of consistency that was too harsh to begin with. And yet, what good would it do to harangue Raven about it when she'd already had the same argument through the door with Sails on two occasions, with Cook once, and with Cat every time he'd set a foot inside the threshold?

Behind her she heard Raven say, "Have you talked to Devon, then?"

Devon. The most alien and appalling of all difficult males.

In an abrupt way Cat said, "You know she hasn't seen him in two days. Gossip around here is thicker than Scotch thistles."

"Don't Cat say that good?" Raven marveled. "Hardly spits at all. Mind you, I didn't know that we *had* Scotch thistles thick around here, but then it's been a few days, think again, since I've been inside the hold."

The lilting tones, the tenderness in his voice were irresistible. Merry turned toward him, her hands back at her waist and resting on the bunk. She made herself smile and, working hard at keeping her tone lighthearted, said, "Cat is correct, as usual. I haven't seen Devon. He probably waits until I'm asleep to slip in and change his underclothes. I have a strong suspicion that he means to make me walk the plank."

Like her Raven hid distress under a smile. "Impossible. Pirates don't do that, you know. The newspapers made it up."

"Did they? Well. There's another myth about pirates laid to rest," she said.

"Yes, indeed. We never make people walk the plank. Too ghoulish. We simply"—Raven made a nimble diving motion with one hand—"throw them over the side."

She wasn't sure why that should make her laugh, except perhaps that Raven's expression was so droll. Looking highly encouraged, he put out a hand to her. "Come over by me," he said. "I can't fetch you. Give me your hand." When she did, he carried it to his lips.

Cat watched them a moment. Then he said, "Saunders is right. You're too involved with her."

There was a brief pause as Raven's winsome gaze found Merry's and then transferred slowly to Cat. "I may be," Raven said, "but so, my friend, are you."

Raven let a few days go by and then went with Will Saunders to try to buy her from Devon. And though Will never went near Merry when she was alone, because he said bluntly that he didn't trust himself, their motives were pure.

They found Devon in the captain's cabin, with Morgan and Valentine, drinking cici, which was corn gin from Chile made from maize chewed by toothless old women and fermented in water. There wasn't another palate on the *Joke* besides those three that could keep it down.

The transfer of women by purchase was a common enough thing. Devon heard their request calmly, and without smiling asked, "Why?" It was obvious that he was going to say no, as they'd already half anticipated, but they had to answer the man's question anyway. That was the rub. Raven wasn't sure how it could be, but while it wouldn't have been even slightly embarrassing to admit that their purposes were unabashedly carnal, it was ticklish beyond description to announce that they just wanted to let her go. As they spoke, facing into Devon's golden, autocratic gaze, there was the unavoidable if unspoken implication of reproach to Devon for the way he was treating her, which was a heavy breach of pirate etiquette. Even that aside, Saunders's explanation, tactfully phrased as it was, couldn't help having such a ring of romanticism and sanctimony to it that Morgan hardly waited for Saunders's finish and Devon's refusal before laughing himself hoarse. Thomas Valentine sighed and, fixing Saunders with a blighting gaze, said tartly, "If you don't all stop being so *damned* amusing about that wretched wench, Morgan will happily keep her around for the next twenty years."

The man had a point.

CHAPTER FIFTEEN

The sleek, heavy keel of the *Black Joke* slipped southward through the warm Gulf Stream, displacing thousands of tons of green water. Below, tiny sea creatures without number waged fierce microscopic battles, as indifferent to the human presence passing above as it was to them.

A brown floating wand of sargasso weed hid a herring no bigger than a child's finger. Grazing nearby was a bluefish that caught and ate the herring just before the bluefish itself became a meal for a passing squid. Satiated and gloating, the squid hurled through the water, gaining momentum until it had enough thrust to launch its tapered length upward, bursting through the surface into sky and sunlight. The squid soared like a flying fish, thirty yards, perhaps more, before it began to lose altitude and, dropping sharply, prepared itself for the thrilling splash that would come when it fell back into the sea. But the splash never came. The squid dropped instead into the bottom of the skiff from which Raven was fishing. Thus the above-water and underwater worlds came together.

Laughing with delight, Raven picked up the squid and put it in a bucket for Merry to see.

He brought it to her in her cabin after he had gotten the key from Cat. She was too happy to see him, too pathetically lonely. In the week since she'd been confined again in her cabin, he had come to see her as often as he could, and others had also—Sails had been in, he knew, as well as Saunders, Cook, Griffith, and some others—but they had to be discreet about it and quick, because though Devon hadn't prevented them from visiting her, he wasn't likely to be overly enamored of the idea. The man was still sleeping elsewhere. Cat, who ought to know, said that the highborn were the same in every way as common folk, but whenever Raven gazed into Merry's blue eyes or watched her smile, he wondered how Devon could possibly want to sleep anywhere else.

The squid was fascinating and frightening for Merry, and she envied the nonchalance with which Raven picked it up and let it wrap a sticky tentacle about his bare wrist. She was braving herself to do it, trying her best to ignore the sea creature's glowering gaze as she put out her hand, when they were interrupted by Max Reade on deck shouting, "Raven? Devil take the lad, where's he got to? If he ain't gonna take that boat out to fish, I sure as hell am. Damme if he don't say he's a gonna take that skiff night fishin', and here's the skiff back before the hour's out. Saunders! Where's Mischief got to hisself to? Maybe if he don't show up in about one second here, I'm gonna take my turn with the boat!"

The squid went back into the bucket, and Raven left Merry quickly with a regretful smile and a tossed kiss. For a minute or two Merry listened to the lively argument on deck, smiled when Raven won it, and putting her arm out the window, waved at him as he set off again in the skiff. Turning back toward the cabin, Merry realized suddenly that Raven had forgotten the squid. And, typically, he had forgotten to lock the door.

She was so closely watched that Raven's slip could do her no good, and she expected Cat to discover it when he brought her evening meal. But the ship's carpenter had cut his hand open on a ravehook while cleaning out some old caulking on the fo'c'sle, and Cat stayed aloft to attend him. Cook came instead, straight from the kneading trough, his tattoo powdered with flour. He set her wooden bowl of spiced cabbage soup and a tin plate of apple cake on the table and had glanced critically at the door, as though he were going to ask her why it wasn't locked, when he noticed the squid. Instantly diverted, he tried to talk Merry into surrendering the squid to him for squid soup.

She was so angry at the very suggestion that by the time he left empty-handed, he had forgotten about the unlocked door.

Merry spent the evening peering into the bucket while the squid turned desultorily in its ration of seawater, fixing her with a glassy stare and occasionally letting a tentacle slither sulkily out toward her.

Cat knocked on the door later, after she had gone to bed.

"Merry?"

"Cat, I'm in bed."

"Fine. Merry, have you got a squid in there?"

"Yes."

"Oh, for God's sake."

"It's just a little one."

"Merry . . . You don't want to go to sleep with that in with you. You'd better let me dump it out."

"No!"

"It'll die and stink."

"No, it won't. I've put it in my washbowl. It has plenty of water."

A pause. And then with resignation, "Oh, all right. Can I get you anything?"

"No. Thank you. I'm almost asleep."

"All right. Does Cook have the key?"

"Yes. Good night, Cat."

"Good night."

She wasn't sure later what had made her lie to him about the key. She didn't intend certainly to make another doomed bid for escape with its attendant horrors and promised punishment; so she might as well have told Cat. Perhaps it was her revulsion for being locked in that kept her from it. Or perhaps she was too tired for a lengthy explanation. And anyway, it was a clear example of her overly conscientious attitude that she should worry about whether or not her captors had arranged to have her securely enough imprisoned.

She awoke much later to blackness and the sharp sounds of activity on deck. The *Joke* was making sail. Merry tried to relax again into slumber. Instead, she found herself awake, listening alertly in the shapeless night and interpreting the vigorous noises above her.

Jim Selkirk on the foretop had sighted a sail to the windward, south by west, and distant by more than five leagues. The bucking motion of the *Black Joke*, as it began to breast the waves, told her that they were giving chase to the sighted sail, running close to the wind. They tacked ship to the westward, and later to the southeast. Merry heard the order to load the cannons. She wasn't particularly alarmed; she had heard the order given before and knew it often led to nothing more than a warning shot. What concerned her was what the squid would eat. She thought about it as she sat cross-legged on her bunk and closed her mouth so she wouldn't bite her tongue and held her hands over her ears to prepare for the percussive explosion.

The explosion came, howling like a banshee, and in a second's horror she realized that it had been no single warning shot but a broadside. The cabin tilted violently, hung suspended, and righted itself. Her dinner plate and cup went flying; her shoes skidded across the floor, and she had to grapple for the edge of the bunk to keep from following them.

Running to and fro, clutching up and stowing fallen objects, wedging her washbowl of squid into a cupboard for safety, she heard the air crackle as the other ship returned the fire. Spray rose, hissing against the *Joke* as a ball rent the water nearby.

The *Joke* was going into battle.

With wild heartbeats she listened to the repeated scream of cannon fire, the high whiz of musketeers firing from the rigging. Racing footsteps pounded the deck above her head until every timber around her began to vibrate. Shouts tore from hoarse throats. A piercing shriek from the deck above her mingled with the thudding crash of the ordnance, and she stifled a cry as she realized that one of the sailors she had befriended was dying in agony above her.

She flung open the cabin door, and the acrid reek of powder

smoke burned her face and lungs. The black grid of the hatchway framed the horror above. Through smoke-hazed lantern light she saw pirates moving quickly, their faces powder-blackened and altered over the glint of cutlass and grappling hook. Far above, boarding nets strung in the rigging made a weird webbed pattern against the stars.

A thunderous, shuddering crash threw Merry painfully against the frame of Morgan's door as the great hull of the *Joke* collided with the enemy vessel. Hell shone in vignette through the hatchway—the swarm of cursing, panting men resisting the fury of a boarding party, clanging steel blades becoming red, spitting scarlet in a spray as they flashed.

Cowering below the insanity, she could feel the cold tremors in her limbs, the sweat of fear damping her shirt, growing sticky on her face, trickling into her mouth.

Suddenly a body fell heavily from the sky, blocking the hatch in a grotesque sprawl. It was Jim Selkirk, shot from the crow's nest, and she stared upward, horrified, into his blank eyes. The dead fingers went lax, and his pistol broke free to drop to the deck before her and skitter toward her feet. She grabbed it up in a haze of instinctive reaction.

Again the *Joke* rolled. The floor tipped sickeningly away, and the backwash tossed her like a toy against Morgan's red oak door. She grabbed at the bronze latch for support as her feet slid across the dropping floor. The latch gave, and the heavy door swung open, throwing her into the room.

Inside, holding a swaying lantern candle by its black tin loop, was Cook's assistant, the man she knew only as Hey, You! He was hunched over Morgan's wide Belgian desk, the yellow candlelight falling in a long oval on the somberly gleaming surface and bouncing back to illuminate the man's face in carmine shadows. Wispy hair jutted stiffly out from the base of his russet stocking cap. His greasy leather gaiters were askew, and his brown plaid shirt twisted at his stout waist, as though it had been donned in haste. He turned, saw Merry, and began to come angrily toward her. She raised a hand instinctively to protect herself. Her hand still held the half-cocked pistol, and seeing it, he magically fell back, adopting a sly, wary grin.

"What are you doing?" she asked him.

"And who might you be to be askin' me that, eh? I may well be askin' you the same! Last I heard, the likes of you was supposed to be under lock and key. What would Devon say if he saw you with that barker in your hand? I've half a mind to call him. What would you say to that?"

The threat didn't exactly make her break out in a cold sweat. Devon had more pressing matters on his hands. And what *was* this man doing here? In theory the *Joke* was a democracy. The captain's quarters belonged to the crew as much as they did the captain. But Rand Morgan was still Rand Morgan, and in practice before anyone entered Morgan's cabin, they knocked, and all except Cat and Devon waited for an invitation to do that. Why would a kitchen assistant come here surreptitiously in the midst of the fray and why was he gripping a bulging canvas purse?

Not lowering the gun barrel, Merry said, "If Devon comes, will you show him that bag of money in your hand?"

"It's my share!" He clutched it all the harder. "It's what I got coming to me."

Merry knew well that none of Morgan's men helped themselves to spoils. Thomas Valentine divided the loot, in full view of the crew. Also the man before her seemed to have deserted his position in battle, and the punishment for that was fearsome—marooning on a barren island with enough water and food to last for one week. Suddenly she realized what this man's presence here must mean. She said, "You're planning to desert!"

"Well, ain't you just as quick as a berry! I ain't got time to stand here clappin' my jaws about it wi' ye, so let me be. We'll go our own ways and no one the wiser. This is no affair of your'n that I can see."

The tiniest bit of admiration mixed with the doubt in her voice as she asked, "How do you mean to get away?"

He was impatient to be off, and after a moment he appeared to decide that it would be faster to humor her with an answer than to argue. "There's a jolly boat half-lowered to the port that was meant, I suppose, to take you out of here if we was to be gettin' the worst of the fight. Old Tuck Simmons was to have the watchin' of it, but he's long since been blown into the sea. So while them bloody fools are killin' themselves to starboard, I'm meanin' to shamble off to the port."

"Are we near land?" she asked.

"Near 'nough. Now, see here. I've got to be movin' along, so—"

There was no time to think it over. Merry took a single slow breath and said, "I want to come with you."

A man of a different kidney might have been flattered, but Cook's middle-aged assistant was a realist and a well-developed coward. Every man aboard knew she'd tried to escape once before. He said sourly, "Well, you can't. I've got enough trouble without having His Powerful Highness Devon hot after my carcass." He started for the door.

Not for nothing had Merry Wilding spent a month of her life on the most notorious ship that furled sail on the Gulf Stream. Stationing her legs apart carefully for balance and effect, Merry put two hands on the pistol's walnut grip and aimed the bronze barrel straight at the man's retreating back.

"You!" she said. "Take one more step without me and—and, Saint Anne as my witness, I'll blow your ears off."

It was a solid improvement over her try with Devon and the crossbow. Morgan, if he could have seen her, would have been as happy as a King Charles spaniel.

CHAPTER SIXTEEN

The battling ships had a strange beauty from four hundred yards away. Against the night sky of transparent black the ship's lanterns breathed sheer golden light that caught as glistening streamers on the ocean waves. From the *Joke*'s stern lanterns twin haloes glowed like the eyes of a great sea monster. The battle raged in miniature; the slowly shrinking scene seemed a microcosm of madness, with flames licking the rigging of the other ship, sooty clouds of smoke rolling upward, and the shouting and shooting and clanging echoing and faint. It looked like an accident in an alchemist's laboratory. And Merry was leaving it behind as if it were a Punch and Judy show bypassed on a street corner.

Wearing denim breeches, a white shirt, and a kelly green bandanna over her hair, Merry sat in the jolly boat's bow with her pistol trained on the kitchen assistant, whose name, she had ascertained, was Michael Meadows. Meadows rowed, and Merry watched the battle through the oars as they rose and dipped, rose and dipped. They had gone more than a league's distance before Merry realized that she was looking at three sets of masts.

She exclaimed, "There's a third ship!"

"Eh? Oh, aye. A Portuguese schooner, sailing out of the Brazils, more 'n likely. Wouldn't be surprised if it was coffee she was hauling. Dumpy little rascal, ain't she? Them sails is patched like a whaleman's shirt. She's prize to that pirate bark that's putting up Satan's own fight against the *Joke*."

So Morgan was fighting another pirate ship!

"A pirate bark?"

"Aye." Meadows glanced over his shoulder at the ships. "That be Malachi Head. See his colors there, by the aft lantern? His flag's got the bloody dagger 'pon it. He's the devil's spawn, old Malachi. When he takes a ship, he sticks the men through with boarding pikes, and if'n there's women aboard, he lets his crew take their sport with 'em and then throws the lot of 'em into the hold. Then he bombards the ship, for target practice, see, till she goes down ablazin'. Him and Morgan usually gives each other a wide berth, but this time the lookout spied a woman on the captured schooner, and her with a babe in her arms and two little ones clingin' to her skirts. So Morgan brings it up for a vote: How many want to take Malachi Head's ship and steal his prize? Well, quicker 'n a trout's tongue every man jack on the *Joke* is finding some reason or other we oughta take the ship. Saunders says because there might be silver aboard the Portuguese, Valentine says we oughta be replacing the skiff you sank, even Shay, that son of a bitch, suddenly remembers some old grudge he's got against Malachi Head's bosun. Humpf! You know the real reason they wanna fight that Malachi Head? To save the young 'uns! I ask you!"

Dawn glimmered, a lilac fuzz on the horizon. Smiling into the trade wind's light breath, Merry said, "I think it's wonderful."

"Oh, you do, eh? For my money, being a hero is fine, but suicide is something else again. I can't see giving up yer life for a babe. They all die anyway," he said gloomily, coasting on his oars. "Twenty years ago, back in Dover, my wife had three babes in three years, and not one of them lived more 'n a day or two. And with the last one my wife dies too. Childbed fever they call it. I call it bad doctorin'." Meadows spit over the side. "She weren't no more than seventeen."

Merry was quickly and deeply affected. "I'm sorry," she said.

Meadows shrugged, grinning slyly through charred, stumpy teeth. "She was a shrill one anyway and never gived me a moment's peace, though I was sorry about the little ones, and that's a fact." He let one oar hang in the water and reached between his legs for the rum bottle. He took a long swig, and as he lowered the bottle his gaze fell on the bucket Merry had placed by her feet. "There it goes—he done it again! Put one of them arms out and wiggled it around."

Merry glanced uncertainly at the malefactor in the bucket. "He can't help it," she said, on the defensive. "The bucket's too small, and he *is* a squid, after all."

"Well, I don't hold with squids, nor octopussies neither. Ain't natural, a critter havin' all them arms. Fair gives a body the creeps. Dump him out."

"I'm going to," Merry said, "as soon as we're far enough from the ship."

"If that don't beat kissin'! Think a cannonball's gonna fall on him? Out he goes—or I don't oar another stroke."

It was not a threat Meadows was likely to carry out, with the eastern sky paling to slate and the rising light adding to their danger of detection and capture. But the squid must be half-starved by now. Decency demanded that she set it free. Merry put the pistol down in her lap, picked up the bucket, and leaned over the side until the bucket's wooden mouth was under an inch of water. Gently tipping the bucket sideways, she watched with a lump in her throat as the squid slid out and away into the glossily black ocean. It was one more link to Raven gone. Cat. Devon. The hand that she had braced against the side slipped as she drew in the heavy bucket, and her shifting weight sent the boat rocking like a tree cradle in the wind.

"Hey! Watch it! You'll tip us. And I could have had the gun off you too," he added morosely. "Don't you forget, if Devon should happen to catch us, it was all against my will—you had the pistol on me the whole time."

"I'll tell him anything you like, but he *won't* find us if you'd put a little Norwegian steam into your rowing."

"Humph." Meadows picked up the oar, and the boat began to move forward again. "Darn female. Likes to see a man work himself to death. And only a fancy-thinking fellow like Devon would have a woman that'd insist on running away with a squid in a bucket. There's the aristocracy for you."

There were times when it was particularly trying to listen to one of the men on the *Joke* place Devon on an exaggeratedly high pedestal. Ready to argue with Michael Meadows, ready to do anything but think about the insanely desperate thing she was doing, Merry said, "Aristocracy?" She tried, as an experiment, to sneer. "He's well-favored, educated, and bossy. That doesn't make him an aristocrat."

"Lot you know about it. He's got bloody aristocratic ways about him, and anyway, Sails says he is, and Sail's been with Morgan since he got his first ship."

Sails and the mermaid. Sails and the wind-seller. Sails and the ghost ship off Nova Scotia. Wonderful stories Sails told, but not true ones. "I'm sure titled British gentlemen frequently sail with pirates?"

"Beats walkin'." Meadows gave a short guffaw. "Course, not by much. Didn't know, did ya, that Morgan and Devon are half brothers?"

"Yes, I did," she said. "And that Devon is legitimate, and Morgan is not. I find it hard to believe that if Devon's family was as influential as you are implying, they would have allowed Devon to meet Rand Morgan."

"Well, a course they wouldn't," he said contemptuously. "Morgan met his fine little brother by accident."

There was a certain look in Meadows's eyes that warned Merry the tale was hardly likely to uplift her. Arguing with Meadows, it seemed, might be more taxing than she had bargained for. She had an intense and active curiosity about everything connected with Devon, but hard experience had taught her that there were things to be learned about Devon that one had better be in a well-rested state to hear. And she was tired, frightened, and in no mood to be teased—which was clearly what Michael Meadows had in mind. Turning her head, Merry stared at the fresh, paling horizon with a laboriously manufactured expression of indifference. She could feel Meadows's rheumy gaze study her. Then he said, "You in love with the fellow?"

A long pause. Finally, with a sigh, "What fellow?"

"Devon. You in love with him or what?"

"What," she answered emphatically.

"Yep. You love him. I can tell. Heh, heh."

"Mr. Meadows," she said, "if you want to think that, I'm not going to quarrel with you about it. I'm only going to say this once: I'm *not* in love with Devon."

As though she hadn't spoken, he said, "Yep. I can tell. Know what it takes to make a man like that fall in love with you?"

A miracle. "Obviously I don't, because he's not in love with me."

"Heh, heh. Know how to keep a man like that?" Meadows tipped his head down until he could tap with one finger on the part of his temple exposed by his russet stocking cap. "To keep a man like that takes brains."

As advice went, it was a little too general to be of any use. Anyway, some of the things you don't do if you want a man like that to fall in love with you are to run away, steal his letters, and refuse to tell him the facts he needs to acquit you of any connection with his worst enemy. That aside, Merry hoped, and feared, that she would never have to see the man again. Lifting with some difficulty the arm that had been bruised by Morgan's door, Merry began to rub the aching stiffness at the back of her neck.

"That Devon," Meadows went on. "The boy was a proper hellion in his teens, so they say. To give themselves a rest, his people sent him to look over some property in the Indies, and happens he was on a three master that Morgan took. Prettiest boy you ever saw, they say. The crew was dicing over who was to have their way with him, and Morgan, they tell, saved the lad from a fate worse than death."

"Pray don't continue!" Merry exclaimed, going rigid.

Highly encouraged, Meadows went on gleefully, "O' course, depending on who's telling the story, Morgan was after keeping Devon for himself. Hey!" Meadows protested, finding that he was gazing down the barrel of Merry's sea service pistol. Hastily, "Take your finger off that trigger there, missy. I was funnin'. Here, now, if you shoot me, you'll be rowin' the measure of the way yerself."

"I'd *rather* row than listen to any more disgusting nonsense. How far are we from where you intend to land us?"

"Oh, that be quite a distance yet, quite a distance. We can't stop too close, or they'll find us sure as supper. Not, mind you, that supper tonight is so sure. Heh, heh." Meadows watched her lower the gun discouragedly. "What's the matter now? Wishin' you hadn't run off so hasty-like?" He chuckled. "Morgan catches me, and it's a quick swing from the yardarm, but you—ho! Devon threatened to beat you if you tried to pull up anchor on him again, didn't he? Everyone heard him say it too, so he'd have to go through with it or lose face. Never been whipped, have you? Ask your friend Raven about it. Ask Cat. Brung up in a bawdy house, he was, on Ile de la Tortue. He come to Morgan with so many stripes on his back that

Morgan should've got a discount on the price.'' Meadows observed warily that the gun barrel had righted itself again. "Watch it, there! That thing's cocked!"

"I know it is,'' Merry said grimly, "and you're making me very nervous. When I grow nervous, my fingers twitch uncontrollably.''

This time he could see she meant it. Staring at the loaded pistol, he asked uneasily, "What could I do to make you less nervous?"

"Row,'' she said. And this time Meadows put his back into it. Neither spoke, and the only sounds were the rhythmically splashing oars and the sucking lap of the ocean as it moved beneath them. The battle sounds had faded to silence. The first searching tendrils of sun warmth fell softly on Merry's cheeks, the breeze made a gentle massage on her weary shoulders, and the sea whispered a rich melody to the new day. Shifting the bucket to her lap, Merry tucked the pistol between her knees, crossed her arms on the bucket, and rested her cheek on her forearm. She meant only to close her eyes for a moment. In that moment she fell deeply asleep.

Merry woke with a sick knot in her stomach and powerful light stinging her scratchy eyelids. Her muscles burned as though someone had stitched nettles in them, and her face, nestled against the bucket's rough unfinished surface, felt as though it had been rubbed down with sand. The stench of rum, pine, and sour sweat howled into her dry throat. Fabric covered her head. Overwhelmed by the feeling that she was about to suffocate, Merry grabbed wildly at it and emerged into blank white sunshine.

"Threw one of me shirts over you,'' she heard Meadows say. Blinking against the heavy light, she couldn't see him at first. "Shoulda been one of yourn,'' he said, "but as you didn't see fit to bring nothing wi' you 'cept a no-good nothing of a squid— Here, have some of this.''

A horn cup was pressed into her hands. The water inside was hot and metallic to the taste. Merry drank three cupfuls of it before saying, "Thank you. I've had enough.'' Shading her eyes and squinting, she was able to stand the light.

Meadows had raised the sail and lay comfortably stretched by the tiller. He had rolled his sleeves down to protect his arms from the sun and replaced the stocking cap with a dark, broad-brimmed hat that moths had long ago gotten the best of.

Moist waves of moving heat danced on the slow water around them, the swiftly evaporating slough of the mid-world sea. To the north was a high atoll of barren rock with calling seabirds landing on ridges above the tearing surf. The *Black Joke* as nowhere in sight. And that should have made her very happy.

Mechanically she lifted her hands and began to feed her fallen curls back into hot brass hairpins that were lodged, burning, against her scalp. To Meadows she said, "Thank you for covering me. It was kind of you."

"Who's kind?" Meadows said. "Not me. I just happen to know that you'll be needing your pretty looks where we're going. You ain't got nothing else to be bargaining with. Mind, there's some that likes the feel of a woman's skin fevered from the sunburn, but your head was alayin' sideways, and there ain't no one cares to see a face half red and half white like a harlequin."

The import of his words sank in slowly. "Are we not going to land on the American coast?"

"Silly wench," he said indulgently, readjusting his hat a step backward on his sweat-smeared brow. "Too far away for that. We'll land us on an island and find a better transport to the mainland."

It sounded like an unpleasant middle step. "Who lives on these islands?"

"Here? Slaves escaped from their lawful masters mostly, and renegade white cutthroats. Witch doctors. Lunatics what's run off from insane asylums. The scum of the earth, and worse."

Merry dropped her forehead into her open palm.

Pleased with his effect, Meadows said, "Where we're off to, see, is called the Devil's Kettle. Smugglers come 'n go from it, and I'm going to bribe me a passage to New Orleans. What you're going to do is yer business and not mine."

Merry said tightly, "I shall go to the—the authorities."

Meadows gave a crack of laughter. "There ain't no authorities in a hundred miles of here."

"There must be someone. Missionaries—or—or priests."

"Missionaries! That's a good one. Kind of missionaries we got around here, why, they'll be ready to teach you all kinds of things you can do on your knees, missy, but you can bet one of 'em won't be prayin'. Heh, heh. Maybe you'll run away into a swamp and get

eaten by an old granddaddy alligator.'' He made a chomping motion
with his jaw. "Gulp!" Meadows chuckled at her expression. "And
they got big old snakes longer than a mizzenmast that'll drop down
on you from the trees and squeeze you till you can't breathe no more
and then swallow you whole. And you make a lump in their middle
that don't go away for six months."

All in all, Merry had had better afternoons. There was worse to
come. From time to time Meadows took a yellowed sheet of paper
from his breast pocket. He shook it open, studied it, shrugged,
folded it up, and put it back in his pocket.

"What is that?" Merry asked, after the fourth such occurrence.

"This here's a map drawn by the hand of Mr. Benjamin Treadwell
himself. Yep. You've heard of Benjamin Treadwell."

"No."

"Sure you have," he insisted.

"No, I haven't. Is he a cartographer?"

"Course not. Ain't no kind of an ographer. Never met an ographer
in my life. Ben Treadwell's a gentleman and a smuggler, and used
to sail with Jean Laffite. And you know where Ben is now? Struck
out on his own and made it to the top of the smuggling racket. Why,
in New Orleans he's got him a house that any man of business
would be proud to own, with fancy lady friends, and the gov'nor
howdy-dos Ben on the street. A friend of mine, is Ben Treadwell.
Good friend. Old Ben, he used to work these islands. Knew this area
like the hairs on his own belly."

Merry craned her neck a bit to glimpse the map as he shaded it
with his hand to fend off the harsh, bleaching sun. After she had
looked it over, she said, "You've got the map upside down."

"Eh? No, I don't."

"You do. Look at the compass that's drawn on the bottom of the
page. The *N*—meaning north—is pointing downward."

Meadows squinted fiercely at the *N*. "That ain't no *N*. That's a
W. Look at it. One line down, one line up, one down, one up. *W*."

"It's not," Merry said. "That first line down is a wrinkle."

"*Wrinkle?* Ain't no wrinkle. I know a wrinkle when I sees a
wrinkle, and that ain't no wrinkle."

"Now, look," Merry said, borrowing her manner from Cat.
"That is an *N!* Smooth it out on your knee so that you can see it

correctly." With bad grace he did as she asked, and she tapped the
controversial letter with the barrel of her pistol. "See?" Firmly,
"An *N*. And directly across the compass from the *N* is an . . . an *E*.
Wait a minute! This compass has north opposing east and south
opposing west! Oh, this is a fine map indeed."

"It *is* a fine map! The compass that's drawn on a map don't mean
nothing anyway; it's the outline of the land mass that counts. What's
a female know about maps? Nothin'. Let me tell you something,
missy. I was reading maps before you was born. And watch that
pistol! I've no fancy to be shot in my manhood. This map is one
hundred per cent reliable. I trust it like I would the milk from my
mammy's paps."

Merry was not about to be dragged into a debate. "Oh, well,"
she said warily, "I hope you're right. I can't tell one of these islands
from another."

Satisfied with that, Meadows said, "That's because yer a woman,
and women just don't got a sense of direction the way men do. With
men it's born in 'em; females is just plain made different."

"Hallelujah for that," Merry said, and it was *not* a compliment to
the male sex.

"You oughta be damned glad it's so confusin' around here,"
Meadows said in a testy fashion. "Because it's so confusin' around
here that the *Joke* won't be able to trace us. Probably they'll look
around on the near shore and leave it at that. Take them forty years
to look through all these here islands and archipelagos and such."

As the day wore on, the likelihood that they were not going to be
found by the *Joke* began to seem less and less of a virtue, though
Merry would never have admitted it to herself.

They passed more than a dozen islands, weaving between them as
the land grew in narrowing perspective and then shrank slowly into
bright abandoned smears of color, dappling a seascape of pristine,
simple beauty. There was no sign on land or sea that a human
presence had ever touched this wild place. About them were only the
marks of happy nature, where creatures moved on their innocent
quests unconstrained by the greedy predations of man. Schools of
tiny fish sparkled beneath clean, colorless water; and sometimes a
shark passed below in silence, a swift, dark shadow amid the sunken
canyons. Kingfishers hunted in the warm sunlit shallows, and flocks

of killdeer plovers wheeled in screaming flight under giant castles of opalescent clouds.

The sun had dropped and became a brilliant orange ball on the horizon before they found Ben Treadwell's island. Merry surveyed the place over a sunburnt nose and for the second time that day dropped her aching forehead into her palm. If Ben Treadwell's island was a tropical paradise, it was designed for Lacor, the king of the trolls, and his seven bad fairies.

From the sea before them the vast cone of an ancient volcano, extinct, it was to be hoped, rose from the ocean depths, its steep slopes roughcast by a somber tropical forest. As they neared the mangrove trees growing straight out of the sea at the island's edge, Merry could smell the foul miasma that crept from their fetid bases, where brown water oozed between the tangle of their narrow arched roots. The shoreline was strewn with the jagged boulders torn from the limestone cliff above. Rain had pocked the cliff surface, and the residue of ancient embedded minerals ran as brandy-colored streaks from cracks that nested clumps of spotted orchids and dwarf shrubs with yellow blossoms. High above them turkey vultures drifted in a slow oval, black, mocking dots against the fading sky.

"Yep. Tropical heaven," said Meadows as he landed them on a shallow spur of beach. "The Devil's Kettle. See them loose spots there on the beach? That there's the sign wild pigs been diggin' here. Good island for game, this. That old Ben Treadwell. He's a knowin' one. About half an hour's walk up that mountain there is a trading post run by an old pirate by the name o' Jameson. Got him a woman there they call Fat Molly. She's something, she is. Short-heeled wench. Short-heeled. See the joke? Means she goes over easy on her back. Heh, heh . . . Well, Jeez, all I ever get out o' you is them sarcastic looks. No sense o' humor. So, get ye out o' the boat, or are we going to sit here till the Second Coming?"

Merry got out. But in three steps she'd crumpled to her knees. No one had warned her that after a period of time on a ship your body makes an adjustment to the sea's heaving motion, and the readjustment to a stable land surface doesn't happen instantly. Wheezy guffaws racked Meadows's sweaty body as Merry sat in damp sand with her brain aslosh; and a small crab ran up on its back legs, its pinchers held over its head, and inspected her with a pair of eyes that sat on wobbling stalks.

"Mr. Meadows," Merry said, "if you say heh, heh, heh to me one more time, I won't be responsible for the consequences."

Before long they left the beach, the silver light of the rising moon finding a narrow path for them through the boulders. A lone hawk, sitting hunched on a stone pillar, watched them as they disappeared into the jungle.

Patches of light and shadow fell through the leathery foliage onto Meadows's swaying back as he strode on confidently in front of Merry, waxing eloquent on the soon-to-be-sampled charms of Fat Molly. The air was almost unbearable, a thick syrup of insect hum and chattering birds. Wings flapped overhead, reptiles skittered in the dry mulch of dead leaves, and wisps of spider threads fell like spirit fingers on Merry's cheeks. She touched the butt end of the pistol wedged carefully into her belt.

Finally she said, "How long do you think we've been walking? It must have been at least an hour."

Meadows hesitated. "Well now, old Ben Treadwell, he liked his rum. And when he was a drinkin', he lost track o' time. So the tradin' post might be a wee bit more 'n an hour, think again. It'll be just a mite farther along here."

Farther along there was no trading post. With some misery Merry was about to conclude that the trading post was a fiction of Ben Treadwell's imagination when they reached a clearing. The jungle opened on the left to a broad view of the moon-silvered sea, and on a small rise above stood a shack. Meadows gave an excited "Ha!" and ran toward it, but stopped in his tracks ten feet from the entrance.

It was not a dwelling, Merry saw as she stood at his side, but a structure of stone and ironwork. An altar. And on the altar were china plates smeared with the residue of charred herbs. Between the plates lay sun-faded artificial flowers, dusty, unopened wine bottles, vials of perfume, candle stubs.

"Voodoo," Meadows whispered. "Makes your stomach turn, some of them stories they have about these here little devils they call baka that live under bridges and such and'll sneakity-weakity out in the night to eat of the flesh of them that walks nearby. They got these here cigouaves too, and they's a wolf with a man's head, and

they'll come up on a fellow and rip away that what a man's got that
a woman ain't. Mighty gruelsome. And them voodoos don't like
outsiders." He looked about uneasily. "Don't see any signs that
they've been here lately. Probably long since deserted the island.
I'm athinkin', though, that we'd best push on anyway. We're kinda out
in the open here " Suddenly, close by them, a white owl screamed
as it slaughtered a young wood dove. Merry and Michael Meadows
moved so fast that he lost his hat and she three hairpins. They didn't
stop until the path died at the edge of a brackish pool, where they
dropped, puffing and sweating, under the sweeping head of a giant
chestnut tree. When she could speak, Merry said, "The trading
post?"

With a ludicrously crestfallen air Meadows said, "Looks like it
ain't here."

Frogs chorused in the treetops, and from far off Merry could hear
the trickle of water over mossy rock.

"Old Ben," said Meadows uncertainly, "he could be quite a
joker, he could. I recollect one time when we was sleepin' on a
beach—I disremember where—he sewed up me blankets and stuffed
a live coal in there with me, and I had to jump into the bay to put it
out. Damned near burned to death and drowned all at once."

"I don't want to *hear* the name Ben Treadwell again as long as I
live," Merry said dangerously. But that was not to be. As she sat
resting with Meadows in the waving moonlight he began to recollect more and more incidents that reflected poorly on the absent Mr.
Treadwell, until finally Meadows had worked himself into such a
state that old Ben had changed into that damned rapscallion Treadwell.
Meadows finished with, "We'll just have to bed down here and find
our way back to the boat come morning."

The last month had done much to condition Merry to disaster. She
was, therefore, not going to cry. All she'd had to eat since yesterday
was Meadows's pilfered hardtack biscuits and a few wrinkled apples;
the grass she'd have to sleep on was damp, pebbly, and probably
full of spiders; and she was stranded on an island rife with snakes
and strange altars to the supernatural. Gazing at a tiny star through
the feathered leaves above her, Merry thought, *Devon, Devon, why
did I let you panic me into this?* She was too tired to fight off the
memory of his face, or of the lingering warmth that had come

whenever he touched her. And his golden eyes. It was so hot for her sometimes, looking into them, as though they held sun fragments. It might be a rather stupid thought, but for all Devon's faults he would never have gotten her lost in a place with voodoos and no supper. Tomorrow looked grim.

Meadows stood up and stretched. Announcing with satisfaction that *he* at least wasn't going to sit around under trees and moan like a girl, he hacked with his dirk at the base of the chestnut tree until he had enough of its flammable gum to kindle a small fire and a torch. He stood among the reeds with the torch, letting the rosy firelight dribble over the water. Almost at once a tiny dark head, like a coal scrap, poked up through a tangle of duckweed. Meadows plunged into the shallow water after it, and the hot night air was filled with *ah*'s and *heh heh's* and curses until he emerged a few minutes later, dripping mud slime, triumphantly holding a snapping turtle and sucking a bitten and bleeding finger. He set down the turtle on its back, and Merry quickly turned away her head as Meadows drew his knife.

When she looked back again, there was turtle meat roasting over the fire on a makeshift spit.

"Want some?" he asked her. "Tastes good. Mighty good." When she shook her head, he smacked his lips, taunting her with his appreciation. His spirits, at least, were improving.

"No, sir," he said. "Nothing like a full belly to make a body into an optimisht. Smell that fat crackin'! Say! Why're you lookin' so doleful? Come morning, we'll take to our boat. I'll lay odds that trading post is on the next island."

"Yes," Merry said glumly. "We can just follow the map."

He sidled over to her, carrying a spear of burnt turtle meat. "Come now. Eat a little," he said, offering her the spear. "It'll perk you right up. Nothing to be gained by starving yourself."

She looked at it dispiritedly and took a bite because the meat was hovering right under her nose and she didn't have the energy to reject it. The meat's odor was revolting, the flavor greasy. It was a meal only for the acutely hungry. Merry swallowed and took another bite.

"Yes, sirrah. That's turtle meat," Meadows said, grinning and watching her eat. "Some say it's poison."

Merry spit it quickly into her hand.

"But it ain't!" he finished and ducked, chuckling, as she threw the half-chewed piece of meat at him. She began to chuckle too and received into her open mouth the handful of sticky weeds that Meadows had tossed back at her in retaliation. Enough was enough. Tired she might be, but she was not going to take that sitting down. Merry snatched a long stick that was crooked at the end and flew at Meadows, advancing on him like a fencer.

"En garde!" cried Meadows, brandishing his meat spear.

Neither party had strength enough for a prolonged battle, so the match was short, zesty, and sparked with laughter. Excited sand fleas, kicked up in the dust, hopped around them, nipping. The exhausted combatants settled back under the chestnut tree, slapping insects off their arms and listening with weary pleasure to the night's song. How varied was the symphony of an evening at peace. The buzzes, hums, whistles, and the high bird calls soothed the senses like sleep. The luminous moon hung above them, close and gigantic. . . .

Merry woke, dazed and stiff, to the dawn's first breath. Meadows slept on, and on, and at last she came to her knees beside his dusty body and tried, rather playfully, to rouse him.

But Michael Meadows was dead. Prickly instinct warned her before she was able to roll him gently to his back, feeling the helpless droop of the muscle tone, the utter stillness of a body where function had ceased. His eyes were closed, the lids bloodless, his jaw hanging slightly open. This was not sleep. Sometime during the night the aging pirate's heart had stopped.

She sat on her heels for a long time, gazing with hollow sadness into the irrevocability of death.

Then she realized that she was alone.

She was not to realize how totally alone until she struggled on her own to the beach, following the siren scent of the sea, to find that her boat had vanished in the prankish crawl of a high tide.

Now she found a flat stone and began to dig a resting place for her companion in the soft sand. But crocodiles came from the depths of the pool to claim him before she could finish, and she fled for her life into a citrus tree and remained there, trembling in a fever bath of misery, trying to close her ears to the horrible sounds below.

She did not cry then, nor when she found the boat was lost, nor even as her accidental footstep discovered the one remnant of Meadows, his head. Instead she was mercilessly ill, and then she stood up to begin doing what her days on the *Joke* had schooled her to do—survive.

In the two weeks that followed, she learned the full meaning of being alone. As though she were the last soul on earth, she became her own companion in the grim desolation of long nights filled with milky starlight and heavy dew; of days thick with the rustling voice of the forest. Hours passed when she heard no sound but the palm fronds rattling in the scorching breeze like dry finger bones. The heat was deadly, a withering stench that left her clothing clammy with perspiration moments after she had washed and dried it on the speared fingers of a poinsettia bush. Minute insects, steel blue pinpoints with wings, swirled around her in a humming mist. Pink welts marked her body from their venom. She rose each morning shaking wood ants, brushing speckles of grit and leaf rot from her skin, and grieving for her family, who would never know what had become of her.

Unfamiliar vegetation was lush around her. She had no way to know which of it was edible and which was not, and her experiments did unspeakable things to her digestion. It became hard to recall just why running away from the *Joke* had seemed like such a good idea. As she tried one more piece of bitter exotic fruit and wondered whether it was cassava or manioc or the Lord knew what, she remembered the times on the *Joke* when she had eaten on deck with Will Saunders making double entendres about her lips and what her fingers were doing that were so wicked Merry had never figured out even one, though everyone within hearing had collapsed in gales of laughter. At the time she had never guessed that a day would come when she would regard those moments with longing.

CHAPTER SEVENTEEN

It happened that Devon was the one who found her. He saw her first from the far end of a sun-dappled meadow where fading day filtered in hazy spikes through the forest canopy. She lay innocently curled in clean elfin nudity under the drooping fronds of an orchid clump. Her back was toward him, the sweet misty flesh strewn with the curling ribbons of her damp hair. The curving line of her cheek and brow were barely visible under the drying gilded fluff that edged her face.

He said her name once, and then, acutely conscious of the wealth of emotion he had invested in the single word, he disciplined himself into less revealing silence as he ran lightly, rapidly toward her.

Merry had bathed. That finished, she had been about to put her ragged clothing to another cleaning when a headache had struck with sudden savagery. She had lain down for what was meant to be only a moment and had lapsed into the stupor that for her was replacing sleep. Then, though she had begun to believe that she might never hear it again, someone had spoken her name. Her startled senses knew suddenly that she was no longer alone. She turned and saw him.

Finding her alive and evidently unharmed tapped every feeling within him that he had spent the past days trying to contain. His relief was white-hot, searing, a blaze that was too bright to look into.

"There must be some kind of archive where we can have you registered. Two escapes from a pirate ship on the high seas is likely to be a record."

His presence penetrated slowly to her consciousness, and she heard not his words but his voice, the tone fresh and light, charmingly low, alive with intelligence, and not so shorn of feeling as he might have wished.

Her inhalation was a jarring series of broken gasps. Standing would have taken more strength than she possessed at the moment, so she stretched out her arms to embrace the part of him she could reach, which happened to be his leg.

"Devon!" she whispered softly. Her voice was unquavering, a tribute to her hard-won self-possession. The problem was that she couldn't stop saying it. And when she had said it many times, she changed it to, "Is it really you?" Over and over she murmured the words in a broken whisper.

Of all her possible reactions this was one he hadn't anticipated. He looked down at her small oval head, adjusting to her closeness. Against his leg he could feel the warm touch of her very soft breasts, the quick rise and fall of her shallow breathing, the fast beating of her heart. Her hair swirled around his calf and washed like a golden net over his boots as she pressed her lips into the side of his knee. Within the warm hive of her curls the shallow slope of her nose rubbed sniffing against his knee, and he could barely discern that the tip wasn't exactly dry.

This, after days of raw anger, after days of searching for her, forcing himself to accept the state in which he might find her. . . . Hideous visions of what she might have endured, briefly banished on finding her alone, were returning in force. He knew too well the nightmare that life could become for an unprotected woman in these waters. After a long hesitation he lowered himself to her side, and laying his left hand on her head, he stroked lightly over her shimmering honey curls.

She was well-bred and shy about her body. Yet she seemed unconscious of her nudity, her utterly lovely, compelling nudity, and beneath his concern he could feel the thrilling drive of his own desire.

She said his name again, in a voice that sounded shaky, and as if she had tears and hair in her mouth. His fingers searched and pulled clinging hair strands from her barely moistened lips, and as his fingertips brushed her mouth he felt the contact burn in hot channels through his body. Stupid, to kneel here nourishing it. He felt light-headed, odd, unable to recognize himself in the welter of tender emotions that were a torrent inside him.

Merry, however, saw nothing new in the clean-lined composure of his face. She watched through a nerve-wrenching mixture of revived fear and thanksgiving as he discovered her clothing beneath a citrus tree and handed it curtly to her.

"Try to cover a majority of everything irresistible," he said.

Lithe, dangerous, and familiar, he went to stand against a fallen cedar that supported a straggling growth of prickly pear in its dry roots. Then, hardly giving her time to react to his command, he snapped, "Dress, Merry. Quickly."

The words had been spoken harshly, though in a soft tone. Still, he saw they had startled her. Her nerves were a volatile, as shocked as his, and he watched her unsteady attempt to stand, watched her dropping clothing through her numb fingers and realized with something like despair that she needed help. It showed in her eyes; in the unnatural stiffness of her muscles. Exhaustion; poor nourishment; exposure. She was in no state to receive his questions or the attentions of his body. Yet even as he was making the decision to moderate his immediate need he felt the denial within, realized he was crossing toward her, pulling her close.

It was an act of instinct, of aching hunger that drove his fingers deeper into her curls to bring her face close to his. His mouth hovered just above hers, heating her lips, caressing them with his breath before he brought them softly, softly together. He coaxed against her still lips until they parted in confusion, permitting him access to the wild honey taste of her mouth. His lips stroked over, against hers, drinking her desperation, feeding her his, dragging her tighter, breathing in the heat and wet orchid scent of her body.

The panic of the preceding days disappeared under his warmly ravaging kiss like a mist burned off by sun rays. Her breathing deepened in quick and steady arousal, her mouth moving frantically under his, her blood pounding as his hands trailed lower, exploring the shallow cleft of her spine before returning to give sensitive guidance to the yearning of her mouth.

In a dreamer's sensuality she twisted into his body, absorbing the hard structure of his hips, her heart turning over and over as he brushed his mouth rapidly across her moist and pliant lips. His experienced touch brought back her head, opening her throat to receive his kiss, and then his finger, running lightly up and down her neck, sent shuddering thrills through her pleasure-flushed veins.

"Have you been hurt, Merry? Tell me, Windflower . . ." His voice sounded strange to himself, as though it were coming from an unknown part of his being.

"Hurt?" Dazzled, her tired mind absorbed the word and the path of his hands, cupping her face with poignant tenderness. But there was nothing poignant about the memories that were beginning to intrude. The idiocy again. Here she was, receiving comfort from a source that by custom dispensed anything but. After all that had happened, she had pushed back the knowledge that this man was less than a friend to her. Every living cell in her body burned for him, and against that, reality was a pale supplicant. But he had uncovered her anger, and it became suddenly a titan. "Hurt." The soft word was treacled in sarcasm. "I suppose you mean did Michael Meadows try to force himself on me? Oh, no. No one does that but you."

Emotion came to him in an uncomfortable flood at her show of tired defiance. How typically she could endow raw melodrama with the most prosaic gloss. Posturing around her became a useless exercise in self-delusion. He was still far from being able to fathom the depth of his relief at finding her safe. It was soaring, joylike.

She had pulled away, staggering slightly, thrusting her arms into her shirt like a trooper dressing under a barrage of unexpected artillery fire, fumbling with the drawstring of her trousers. She was breathing rapidly, the sound husky and abrupt, as though it came from an angry child. Yet the bright eyes that burned upward into his held thoughts that were fully adult.

"It might be reassuring," she said, "if you could let me know whether you're rescuing me or simply capturing me again."

They were so close that the slight gust of his laughter stirred the sweat-dewed hair clinging to the curve of her jaw. "This passion for detail. Don't ask too many questions. The answer might not reassure you after all." Was there some way to make himself immune, at least for this moment, to the thick curling quilt of her hair that invited his touch, to the tension in the delicate shadowed face, to the fresh and urgent memory of Merry canopied in orchids? And there was, he remembered, a boatload of hardened cutthroats turning themselves inside out worrying about her. He had seen enough of the extremity of their concern to last him a lifetime. "We could leave. Unless you've developed a great fondness for this little haven?"

One thing Devon did expertly was protect the privacy of his mind. She could almost watch him disappearing back behind his breathtakingly beautiful exterior, as though the process were a physical metamorphosis. Devon was a man, and not a collection of well-composed gears and pulleys connected with leather belts, but as she tried to match his pace toward the lee of the island where the *Joke* was anchored she wondered how that perfect body could function so well without a heart. Pride kept her from being the one to broach the subject of whether or not he understood why she had run away from the *Joke* and whether or not he intended to punish her.

It would have surprised her to learn that he wasn't thinking about punishments at all. For the first time in a life of clear-thinking certainty Devon was learning doubt. And he was finding the lesson a singularly painful one. His motives, his feelings, even the logic of his imprisonment of her were being called up and explored. His conclusions, tentative as they were, were affording him no comfort.

Purple twilight surrounded them as they reached the starlit jumble of limestone boulders and low, spiky vegetation that edged the beach.

Raven found them first, at an odd ticklish instant when Devon had turned to her and hauled her close, inexplicably, startlingly, without speaking, whispering her name. He drew back when he saw Raven, releasing her to the boy pirate's gentle consolations. A single shot from Devon's pistol brought the others, who had been searching too; they joined them like shadows, to see Merry and scold, or tease, or sympathize, as their natures dictated.

It was Raven whose bare, slim arms encircled her lovingly and held her as though she were something precious while they sailed the jolly boat toward the *Joke*. Another time he would have avoided that kind of contact with her because it would have put too many of the wrong sort of ideas in his head, but that worry seemed a little petty just now. Her earlier tide of defiance had faded into a vaporous tiredness, and her hands, clinging to Raven's shoulders, felt to him cold as a polar sea. Gently he separated their bodies and began to rub the chilled flesh of her palms and fingers.

"Hear me, lovey. You've got to start being more careful about your getaways," he said softly. "I'd like to know what possessed you, making sail on the sly with that rascally galley help of Cook's— what's his name?"

"Michael Meadows." She curved herself back into the comfort of his strength.

"It's not like I was the prized plum from the Garden of Prudence myself, but—Michael Meadows! I couldn't believe it. The man don't know his arse from an ax handle," he said, the tartness and worry in his voice softened by his voluptuously slurred vowels. "And where in sweet heaven is he anyway, leaving you on your own like that?"

Even in the dim light he could see the change in her face. With sensible kindness he suggested to her, "Dead, is he?"

Devon had been watching the interchange in a manner that Raven had privately noted fell far short of enthusiasm, so Raven was surprised when the blond man remarked dispassionately, "Dead and eaten. I found an interesting fragment."

Getting interested, Raven said, "Don't tell me! What et him?"

"A crocodile," Merry whispered, her wide-open eyes fixed in remembered horror at the elkhorn corals reaching in pointing fingers upward through the eerie green curl of the surf.

Raven's arms tightened around her and held on like armor until they came to the *Joke* and he disengaged his indignantly protesting body from her to deliver her into Cat's ascetic grip. But much later that night, after she had been put to bed, Raven was frank with Will Saunders.

"If that don't beat everything," he said. "That Meadows. There wasn't a piece of responsibility in the whole of him. Just like him to up and get himself eaten and the bits strewn for anyone to come upon, and Merry left to fend for herself. You want my opinion? Eating was too good for him."

In the morning Merry woke in the sturdy bunk of the cabin on the *Black Joke* she had come to think of as her own. Fuzzy sunlight poured through the open windows above, and the ship bucked and straightened in the leaping motion she had learned meant they were at sea with all drawing sails set.

Cat was sitting on the bunk, and he looked as though he had been there for some time. His weight slightly constricted the cotton sheeting over her feet. He was stretched back at an angle, supporting himself on his elbows, his shirt opened to the waist, his hair draping in loose swags over his cheeks and dropping behind the prominent ridge of his shoulders. The light softened him, giving a white glow to his body and the illusion of a flush to his cheekbones with their gaunt sensuality. His eyes, blue-snow colored, were assessing her in a hard way that seemed able to extract silent information from her mind. He waited courteously for her to speak first, and she would have if she could have thought of something clever. Finally he shrugged upright and handed her a glass from the table. Watching him over the rim, she drank down the contents and made a face.

"Ugh! What was that?" she said.

"Don't ask. I see you're thinner. I would have thought by this time you'd know enough to keep eating no matter what. If you'd roll over on your stomach, I could do something about those weals on the backs of your legs. Thank you."

She felt him draw up her nightshirt to uncover her legs. Her smile curved against the pillow as he treated the scattered bite marks, the cool sting of alcohol tingling pleasantly against her skin, his touch light, efficient.

"They should do something about the insect problem on these islands," she said presently. "It would encourage industry."

"I don't know that industry needs to be encouraged. You've been industrious enough already."

When he finished, he came around to the side of the bunk and pushed her onto her back and sat looking down at her with his palms resting on either side of her waist. His unbound hair was so fine and clean that each silklike fiber moved independently of the rest and streamed in a flaxen spill down his arm and over her stomach and thighs. His expression would have terrified the Merry Wilding of four months ago.

"I wish you'd stop doing crazy things," he said.

Pressing her head backward into the pillow, she gave him what tried to be a placating smile. No effect. So she made a copy of one of Raven's rude hand signs.

"That," he said dryly, "wasn't even the right finger."

She could feel her placating smile becoming a little sheepish. "Aren't you even going to say how glad you are to see me?"

"No." An incidental movement of his head sent his hair over her like a caress. "I was hoping that you had made it to New Orleans. With Michael Meadows, of course, that wasn't likely. Did Devon tell you how we were able to locate you?" After she shook her head from side to side in a negative, he continued. "A couple of months ago Meadows happened to show Will Saunders that miserable scrap of paper Meadows had the audacity to call a map. Thank God Saunders is bright. He only saw the map for a few seconds, but he was able to draw it from memory. The reason it took us so long to get to you was that we spent days searching the Devil's Kettle and terrorizing the occupants before Rand thought to turn the map upside down. And that led us straight to you. Incidentally, Raven and Saunders have been trying to circulate the story that Meadows broke into your room and forced you to go with him."

Her eyes widened involuntarily. "Does Devon pretend to believe it?"

"Michael Meadows was the last man on the ship with the gumption to carry off any woman of Devon's. Besides, there's a small matter of a squid that everyone knew Raven left in with you and which vanished when you did. Meadows might have kidnapped you—but he was hardly likely to make off with your damned mollusk."

Hope died. There was no way to sit up without knocking flat into Cat's body. Merry wriggled upright against the wall, and his tumbling hair brushed over her lower body and then lay, tickling, on her knees and bare ankles. "What's the crew thinking?"

In a facile movement the boy pirate swung his head back slightly. The gesture pulled his hair from her legs and settled it behind him.

"We've spent almost two weeks looking for you," he said. "That was two weeks without a prize—without even looking for one. The decision to search for you was fairly popular, given that you didn't leave in the steadiest company—but no one likes to have commerce interrupted. And there are some missing gold pieces, which one assumes Meadows took; but can you prove it was him and not you?"

"Well." She smiled too brightly. Every nerve was alive and jumping. "I guess it's the bow cannon and a cat-o-nine-tails for me!"

"Is it?" he said dryly. "From what Raven told me in confidence, last night you put up a little insurance against that with Devon."

From brightly smiling to brightly angry. "If Raven told you that was why—"

He interrupted. "Raven didn't tell me anything of the sort because, innocent that he is, it's never occurred to him that you and Devon don't ride together. It's part of your protection that the men think you belong in every way to Devon, and no one other than Morgan and I and possibly Sails knows any different." Moving away from her, he lifted the empty glass of herbal tea he had given her and held it in a loose clasp. "Last night, if it wasn't insurance with Devon, what was it?" Then, absorbing the look she was giving him, he snapped, "Listen, I don't want to discuss this either. But there's no one else to tell you, so I'd better. I turn, take a breath, and whenever I look back in your direction, you're in deeper. About last night?"

"If a dog had arrived last night and pulled me off that island by the trousers seat, I would have kissed the dog," she said defiantly. Why, of all people, had Raven chosen to confide how he had found her with Devon to *Cat?* Cat, who had several times pointed out that for a woman who professed to hate Devon, she was to be found in his arms with unaccountable frequency. Cat saw things too clearly. Eventually desperation might force her to confide to Cat the humiliating and overwhelming things she felt for Devon. Today she still needed to feign indifference, even though the young blond pirate was probably seeing right through it. She slid out of bed and stood up in her bare feet, facing him. "Go on. Tell me. How has kissing Devon made this disaster worse?"

Cat set the glass down on a tin tray without breaking his contact with her eyes. "Sweetheart, first I have to teach you the word for ladies who seem like they will when they won't."

"Whatever the word is, I'll bet it was invented by a man," she snapped. "There's a bad name for you if you will and a bad name for you if you won't."

"Did I say it was fair? I only wish you'd pick something out and stick to it. For your sake."

He had opened the door and almost closed it behind him when she said quietly, "Cat, did you grow up on Ile de la Tortue?"

He returned silently. After examining her face he said, "Someone's given you an earful about me? Was it Meadows?"

She had the urge to drop her eyes but refrained, with effort, and nodded.

With an expression that coldly disguised any trace of feeling, he asked, "Curious?"

"No. I just wanted to tell you that if it's true—"

"What?"

She took a breath. "If it's true, I'm sorry."

The relaxation of his facial muscles was so gradual and subtle that she couldn't perceive it until he came a step closer to her and stroked his hand once through her sleep-ruffled curls, very gently. "You poor, extraordinary girl," he said. "Merry, you don't have to be sorry. . . ."

By eight bells, when she heard the watch change, yesterday's headache had come back in force. By three bells that afternoon it had become so painful she could barely think. Room light hurt, and the incessant scrape of men walking and working above hurt. The steadily rolling dip of the vessel became agonizing. Earlier she had been sure that it must be her unexamined fear about what Devon was going to do to her that had created the demon throbbing under her scalp, but as the pain went on and grew worse she began to think perhaps it was the heat, which was as bitter here as the North American winter was cold. The air around her steamed, and she had begun to sweat like a mare, and the prickle of perspiration on her temples hurt too. She wet a towel in the water can, and without thinking to wring it out she sat at the table, burying her face in wet fabric as it splattered on the table and dripped over her forearms.

The room seemed like a furnace, and the pain in her head was like a swelling sun before she began to call weakly for Cat. Making her way to the door, whispering his name, she put her hand on the latch for balance, and surprisingly it gave. Why hadn't they locked her in? She found the stairway and wobbled on deck, where a hurricane hit her of bouncing sunlight, and noise, and familiar faces she could hardly identify.

On the bow with Tom Valentine and Sails, Merry saw Devon, standing like a young Apollo with the shameless breezes molding and displacing the clothing around his body. His golden eyes discovered her quickly, and he broke off his conversation to come toward her with his fluid, springing step, holding out a hand to her.

"Merry!"

Sunbeams backlit him in a dazzling aura. To her tumultuous senses his approach and his gesture were a threat. She recoiled against a mast as she said, "Don't touch me."

He stopped a few feet away, his expression becoming wary. "Is there something wrong, Windflower?"

That unthinking use of his pet name for her was unsettling. God in heaven, he had his nerve asking her in that artless fashion if something was the matter. Why didn't he look as warm as she was? Leaning her blood-hot head against the mast, she said, "I want you to let me go."

There was a moment's silence, and then he said, "No."

"Yes!" she came back, almost screaming the word.

The brilliant eyes hardened. "You've been damned troublesome, do you know that? Give me one reason why I should accommodate you."

"Common decency." Merry bit off the words sharply.

"It's rather late, isn't it, to bring the virtues into this? Unless you think we'll be able to make up for lost time."

The swelling mound of the great canvas sail above her head slapped in the wind, attracting her unsteady fancy. When she looked back at Devon, her mind had frighteningly destroyed every memory of what they had been talking about, except that it had been hostile. For some reason it seemed fiercely important to disguise the lapse from him.

"Could that be a reference to what happened between us yesterday?" she said, because some nearly defunct sense was telling her that the remark was somehow relevant.

"No," he said, cold-eyed. "However, don't let that stop you if you think it's something we ought to be fighting about."

Cat had warned her about this, but his advice had been so obliquely delivered that she couldn't remember what it was. Something about being consistent, she thought. Cat. She needed Cat. And here was Devon, waiting for an answer.

"I'm not going to stay here to become your mistress," she said desperately.

His response came quick as a slap. "That tune is getting monotonous. Do you think you could learn some new notes?"

"Perhaps. If you'd first master the prelude." Her head and body burned until she could taste ashes. "Am I a mechanical music toy to be wound up and run down at your pleasure?"

"*Damn*. I wish just once that you'd stay wound up." There was a fine-drawn temper in his voice; his hedonist's mouth smiled without humor. "God forbid that you and I should do anything the simple way, Merry mine, but it would probably save time and help us right to dead center of the argument if you'd tell me what's igniting it."

A pause followed. They stared at each other, she angrily, he coolly, until a tongue of wind fumbled through her shirt buttons and lapped at the moisture on her burning skin. Violent tremors seized her, rattling her muscles. Hot waves crawled over her flesh like the breath of an open oven. It must have lasted only seconds, though to Merry it seemed to go on and on. During the course of it she saw Devon come toward her in a colorful blur of movement.

"Merry?" The tone he used this time was new to her. She felt his hands find and hold her shoulders, trapping her before him. Panicked by the contact, she dragged herself out of his grip and wobbled back, her dry, fevered hands fluttering defensively in front of her.

"I'm not a pet. I don't want to be handled," she said.

He made no further move toward her, though anyone watching him except Merry could have seen the discipline of that was not easy for him. His eyes held a deep frown. When he spoke again, his voice was soft and deliberate.

"Love, I know you're not a pet. No one will touch you if you don't want them to, but you must go below and—"

"And what? Go below and wait to be assaulted?" Shivers coursed through her voice. "Or go below until you're ready to whip me? *Or* are you going to find some way to combine the two? Oh, how well I know how ingenious you can be."

Through a sight field that was filling up with shimmering red stars, Merry saw a black-haired boy approach her from the direction of the mizzenmast. He was running, with compassion and worry etched well into his comely teenage features. For less than a second she knew it was Raven, and then that name was lost. He looked at Devon and then at her and came toward her. Between the heat and the pain the idea came to her that Devon had sent him to whip her, and she cowered from him, moving backward blindly on the sliding deck, her flowing hair snarling in the rough lines of the rigging. Devon held the boy back from her with a sharp command.

"Please, mon, let me help her," the boy said. "You can see she's—"

"I know. But she might hurt herself if she's forced. Get Cat."

A gull screeched, and Merry retreated once more, her fists cupped over her ears. The cool caress of the wind grew stronger as she neared the gunwale, and she stood, swaying, with ocean water spotting her clothes at the ship's edge. Strong arms caught and pulled her back to safety, but as she opened her eyes the firm grip on her waist was too tight and terrifying. Twisting a neck that had no flexibility left in it, she saw that Devon held her and tore out of his hands. Her ill-functioning mind willfully misinterpreted his action, and she clung to the heavy lines strung to the foremast, weaving precariously over the edge as the tall ship rolled. Over rushing water and timbers that creaked, she heard her own voice babbling about torture and pain. With difficulty she realized that she was saying, "You don't have to drag me. What else do you think I expect from you but mindless barbarities? Flog me, then. . . . Where do you want me to go? The bow cannon, didn't you say? Where is it? I want to be everyone's ideal of a brave woman."

An older man with sharp gray eyes and the tools of a sailmaker hanging from his belt was talking to Devon, and when he finished, she heard Devon say to the man, "You're right. But I can't do it."

The sailmaker answered, "Aye, laddie. Better 'tis another in any case." Then, "Willy, be a good boy. See what ye can do. Easy does it."

Insulated by the scorpion pain inside her skull, Merry couldn't see the tanned young man approach her, and she hardly heard one word in three that he spoke to her. She leaned back tiredly against the lines, feeling the vibrant blast of the gray sea under her neck. The young man's slowly enunciated words began to come to her.

"Merry. Listen to me, sweeting. It's Will Saunders. You remember—big brother Will. You want to walk to the bow cannon, don't you? If you take my hand. No. All right. But come with me, won't you? You don't want us to . . . to have to be rough with you."

Eventually she felt herself begin to respond to the patient commands, and when she reached the nine-pounder in the bow and fell against it, she gasped, "How do you like your victims? Should I drape myself across it, like laundry spread to dry?"

"No, Merry." This time the voice belonged to Devon. "Sit by it, rest your head on the chase, and wait."

Merry dropped to her knees, looping her arms over the cannon, hugging it like a flood victim in rampaging waters, dropping her face against the sweating metal. Sobs began to hiccup from her aching throat. Superheated tears traced quick rivulets over her skin. After a while she remembered to look up, but her field of vision had become a mosaic of pretty, abstract shapes and colors, like a pattern on cloth, their meanings only loosely symbolic. The colors faded into a soft gray, and then she realized Cat had come and that he was talking to Devon.

As Cat came down beside her the sleek rope of his braid slid over Merry's hand, and she caught it and carried it foolishly to her burning cheek and saturated the pale hair with her tears. His hands were sweetly cool where they touched her with a calm and sexless assessment. Even so she whimpered, "Don't hurt me."

"Never, sweetheart," he said. "Let your head fall back against my arm. That's it. . . . Merry, tell me where you're having pain."

She had tried to listen to him, but each word slipped away separately from her as soon as she heard it. Sounds around her were hauntingly muted. She stared distractedly at the rolling tears that were landing in fat oily bubbles on her hand. A cold cloth, laid against her neck, her ears, her cheeks, brought her gently back.

"Merry, where's the pain?"

Trying sluggishly to concentrate, she evaluated her unfriendly body. The headache was gone. It took her a long time, following false and benumbed nerve routes, to learn that the pain had spread downward.

"C-Cat—I've been whipped. . . . I th-think I've been whipped."

Devon said something, a sharp exclamation, and over her head Merry heard Cat say, "Don't start that, for God's sakes. It's the fever talking." His voice had grown less calm than his hands. "Raven?"

"On the other island, the one Will and I searched"—the soft Caribbean vowels were slurring heavily—"they had buried two men. They had a fever—"

Cat said urgently, "Did it begin with back pain?"

"No. A rash."

Merry was lowered to the deck with dizzying speed, and Cat tore open her shirt. Groggily angered by the indignity, momentarily recalled to sanity by the uncomfortably hard surface striking her shoulder blades, she said in a cranky voice, "Don't treat me like a blighted corn ear. I can hear you talking about me. And I don't want fifty people looking at my rash."

"You don't have a rash, Merry, peach. That's one possibility eliminated." Devon's voice came from close to her. "Can you slide your arms around my neck? Including every and all circumstances, there hasn't been a time when I've wanted more to take you to bed. . . ."

She returned to awareness in Morgan's cabin. Wet cloths covered her aching limbs, and the diamond cut windows dropped light on her eyelids. The sun, which had been bright when she opened her eyes, smeared to dun, and when she looked again, the room was dark and the windowpanes were thick with stars. A quiet voice—Devon's?—was saying, "She's much cooler now."

"I knew it." Cat's voice. "*Damn*. That's what we were afraid of."

Why was it bad that she was cooler? Vaguely disturbed, she slipped into sleep.

Morning's silver light gave a misty patina to the cabin when she awoke. Devon, who needed a shave, sat on the bed close to her. He slipped an arm under her shoulders and lifted her to a sitting position. Slowly he fed her a cup of vegetable broth that was rich, flavorful, and full of shredded cabbage—where had that come from? After she had taken all of it, he set the cup down and then turned the pillow with his hand and plumped it before he laid her back down.

"Some people," he said calmly, "will do anything to attract attention."

A return to the temporary benevolence. *That's fine with me*, she thought, *since I'm weaker than a tin candy kettle*. She retained a hazy memory of making a spectacle of herself the day before on deck. She grinned weakly and said, "Hullo."

"Is that all you've got to say for yourself?" he said with feeling. So she sheepishly added, "Good soup."

He laughed, pressing the side of her neck with long, graceful fingers. It seemed to her that he was searching for fever, but he showed neither surprise nor relief when he found no evidence of it.

"How do you feel?" he said.

"Good. But like a stewed grouse." With a knit brow, "Am I not cured?"

"We'll see." His smile was carefully arranged to cheer and to instill confidence. It was so well done that it didn't occur to her to look under the surface. And there was another, more urgent issue that needed to be settled. Merry gathered her nerve.

"I don't doubt you're disappointed that I was too ill for a whipping."

"Heartsick. I've been up all night wringing my hands over it."

One thing was certainly true. He *had* been up all night. Sleeplessness, like every other state, loved his face. Nevertheless, she could see its fine bite.

He moved to take her hand, and it lay small and curving in his as he touched it gently to his lips. Tiny sparks grew under her skin where his mouth had touched.

"I suppose you think that falling ill was my just deserts for running away from you?" With her free hand she made a project of wrapping one red-gold curl around her finger and gazing studiously at it. "All things considered, it was easier on your dignity than on mine for you to find me in such a mess."

"A mess? Was that what it was?" He gave her a wide-eyed look that she realized was an imitation of her own. "My dear! And here I was thinking you were happily rusticating on a balmy island. It must have been refreshing to get away from all men after your months of patiently enduring the stag-and-drake atmosphere on the *Joke*."

He waited for her brief smile to bloom and fade away before glancing down at their entwined hands. She watched curiously as he stroked the tip of his forefinger over the pansy surface of her nail plates. His expression was soft. Had she actually surprised some real spark from him? The promise of that settled like a moody stranger in her heart.

"Poor Windflower. Did you really think I was going to beat you?"

Cat came into the room with her breakfast in time to hear the last, and he put in grimly, "Why shouldn't she? You ought to see yourself when you're angry."

Devon watched Merry slowly withdraw her hand and lay it in a slack fist on the pillow beside her cheek. "You're right. I should," he said as he stood up, making room for Cat to bring the tray to her.

Feeling awkward, light-headed, bashful for no good reason, Merry met Cat's gaze and said the first cheerful thing that occurred to her. "Look at me—healthy again, though Devon won't admit it. I want to dress."

"You can dress if you want to," Cat said, "but you'll have to rest on the bed today. You're better, not healthy."

"Why not? Don't worry so much." Merry was smiling. "What do you think is wrong with me? I hope it's the clap. Aren't you supposed to be good at curing that?"

Devon had suddenly discovered something of great interest outside the window and was regarding it steadily, a suppressed smile pulling at his lips.

Glancing at Devon, Cat said sourly, as though in explanation, "It's Saunders et al. They love to teach her blue language and listen to her innocently chirrup it back to them so they can laugh themselves to jelly. God knows what they'll think of the change in her when you decide to send her home."

This was new—someone talking about sending her home as though it were a thing that might happen soon. She thought of Aunt April as she waited a moment to see if Devon had anything to say about it, and when he didn't, she gave Cat a grin. "This whole experience may make my fortune someday if I become an authoress. Publishing companies are always on the lookout for women whose experience has brought them into contact with *peculiar* people." Congratulating herself for having slipped one in under his guard, she sat up and tucked the napkin under her chin. "Furthermore, just because the pitch of my voice happens to be soprano—"

"Of the upper register, particularly when excited."

"*Soprano*," she said emphatically, ignoring Cat's interruption and finishing her sentence. "I don't think it's fair to say that I chirrup. Why don't you and Devon want to tell me what was wrong with me?"

"Come now. Don't let your imagination tear downhill like a runaway wagon," Cat said. "It was a fever. What else is there to know? Save your energy for your breakfast. Do you have to use the—"

"No, and don't bring it up so casually. I'm not a heifer in a barnyard. If you don't mind? Cat, please don't hover."

But hover he did. She was not left alone, even while she slept, whether she liked it or not. Sails and Raven and Dennis the pig were with her the next morning when the chill started again.

The three of them with fingers and an opposable thumb had been making silhouette portraits of each other using nail scissors and paper pages torn from an old ledger of Morgan's. Merry was laughing at their amazement because, while they weren't bad at it, the profiles she made were mirror accurate. Dennis was shuffling around the room with Cat's paper profile sticking to the watery tip of his snout. Because she thought she had gotten well, she assumed, when she began to feel cool, that a northerly draft had stolen into the cabin, and wrapped herself in a wool jacket, and then, uselessly, in a blanket. In the end there was no hiding the terrible pattern she came to know in the days that followed: the disabling chills and throbbing head, the fever without mercy that followed for as long as eight hours afterward, and then the rapid cooling and torrent of sweat that left her stuporous with exhaustion.

The attacks came at regular intervals, as though some murderous clock in her body was calling them forth. On two days out of three she was ill, and in between she was well enough to sit up, to eat, to read, to talk, and to know that she was getting progressively weaker. Malaria, Cat admitted to her finally; it was treated with quinic and poisons like arsenic and strychnine. The trick was to kill the disease before you killed the patient.

These cures, recommended and accepted as they were, the best hope the age could offer, began to take their toll, and as the days went by it became harder for anyone to make her smile. Devon, gentle as none of them had seen him, helped to beguile her in the long weak hours between her paroxysms. He taught her every card trick he knew, every hand form in shadow play, every verse of his favorite love ballad. He filled the afternoons for her with riddles and fairy stories and led her in lazy conversations about comets and fallen kingdoms and the way hot roasted corn tastes on a fair day in autumn.

In both of them was a deep delight in the simple whimsies of life. The earth, with its endless subtle beauties of color and texture, was not wasted on Merry or Devon, for they both saw the clouds as pictures, the lichen against rough bark as scripture, and sometimes heard the wind as a canticle. Two other people might have discovered these things in each other and begun to celebrate, but Devon and Merry had too many distractions to notice. She only thought, when she had the strength for reverie, that the hours sped by when she was with him. His all-encompassing aim was to remind her of the many reasons she had to cling to the world and to keep her from guessing how close she was to leaving it.

Eventually even sleep became an effort for her, a time of dreams and discomfort and paralyzed half wakefulness. One night sand fleas from the island came to her in a nightmare, their wings shining with the moisture of her blood as they drove their venom repeatedly into her shrinking flesh. She awoke crying, rubbing her sullied face with the cotton sleeves of her nightshirt. Repugnance made her use too much force. The tiny bone buttons on her cuffs cut long raw scratches into her friction-heated skin.

She wasn't sure what sense told her that Devon was coming across the room to her.

"Merry, let me." He was separating the snarled ball that she was—the arms and hair and bedclothes. A damp cloth wiped neatly and thoroughly over her mouth, and then over her cheeks.

"Where else?" he asked. Gasping, she touched her forehead and closed her eyes as the cloth moved on her brow, over her eyebrows, to her hairline. After he finished, she heard the fresh splatter of water as he dipped the cloth and cleansed her again. Another woman might have been amazed at how accurately he had perceived her need and how quickly he had responded to it. Illness had eroded her interest in noting and being alarmed by his talents. She only knew she was glad that she was awake now, and that he was with her.

"Nightmare." She whispered the word automatically. He had guessed. From Morgan's desk the faint sheen of candle flame spread outward, dissolving in the distances and breathing like a lover on

Devon. She saw him like that when she opened her eyes, and saw
the nod he made to acknowledge her single word.

She was about to ask him how many bells had gone when she
heard a slow warbling call well up, as though from the keep of the
ship, to vibrate the humid air around her, and echo back into the
cradle of the sea. A second fluttering call blended in, growing with
the dying notes of the first, and then she heard a third tune,
spasmodically moaning; a primitive and lonely monster song from
the deep.

"Devon!" Her voice was trembling.

"It's only the whales," he said, remembering years ago, when
Sails had told him the same thing. "You can hear them talk on
clear, quiet nights like this. They sound melancholy in the beginning,
but after you've listened to them for a while, their voices are as
winsome as singing birds, though not as shrill." He stroked a rosy
curl from her forehead. "Can I give you anything to drink?"

Allowing him to support her in his arms, she gratefully took the
water he offered. He hadn't held her since the night of her escape
from the island. It felt so good she didn't want him to let her go; and
when he moved to lay her down, she clutched at his shirt.

"Don't you want to sleep?" he said.

"No," she whispered. And so, without speaking, he pulled the
bedding away and wrapped her in a flannel quilt and carried her to a
chair by the stern window, where he sat down, holding her against
him. A row of diamond panes frosted in starlight were open, and the
great aftercastle window showed a rippling moon dancing in the
wake. He tucked the quilt around her feet with care because, though
the night was warm, the effects of an external chill in her weakened
condition could be disastrous.

"If you're hungry—" he offered.

"No." The smooth, soft fragrance of his skin reached her through
his unbuttoned shirt, and she dragged at the shirt fabric that separated her cheek from his bare chest. When he saw what she was
trying to do, he helped her and brushed his mouth lightly over her
forehead once she was settled.

"I wonder what whales talk about," she said.

His arm tightened comfortably about her. "Hmm? The whales?
I'm afraid my Whale isn't as fluent as it should be." Tonight both

whale voices were genial and rich with haunting sensuality, and he could almost feel the tenderness in their love play, the underwater ballet of graceful massive bodies wreathed in moist oxygen. A sentimental thought for a man whose softer emotions were seldom about things like love and pairing. Devon became aware suddenly that he was tired. Contact with her body must have relaxed him, and it made him curious about what it would be like to sleep beside her, to weave in and out of dreams with her kitten's breath on his shoulder. And *that* was an entirely new thought for him, because though he liked to laugh and touch for a long time with his lovers, the idea of going to sleep beside them had always been vaguely unappealing. Morgan, naturally, had a number of theories about that, none of them flattering.

The girl was looking at him. "The whales," he extemporized. "They've heard that you're sick, down there, under the sea." A high moan. "Did you hear that? They're very sorry, so they've sent the patriarch of the humpback clan to the Arctic, where the north wind lives in an ice cave, to ask for cool breezes to make you comfortable while you're getting well. And when you've recovered, they'll take you riding whale-back."

She gave him half of a smile, and the skeptical glance of a child cynic whose faith in fantasy games had been lately shaken. He could feel the slight tug on his shirt fabric as she played with his buttons.

"Devon?"

"Yes?"

"This afternoon when I woke from my nap, I heard you talking and— Were you having an argument about me with Morgan? I know Cat thinks this room is better for me because the air circulates more freely, but if Morgan is annoyed about being put out of his cabin, I think—"

"Don't be so energetic. Just for a few days will you leave the thinking to us? It's by Morgan's order that you're in this cabin, and if there's a motive beyond simple charity in it, neither of us will be able to figure it out until he wants us to. And there's more to your being here than ventilation. Since Morgan's bed is mounted on gimbals, you'll feel the sea rolling less than in your bunk, which means you'll rest a little better. I don't know what you heard that sounded like an argument. Did Morgan sound angry?"

"Oh, no," she said. "Too pleasant, in that way he has. I heard my name mentioned, and he said something about—grapeshot?"

"Ah. That." Her hand arrived at his cheek, nervously questioning, a sign of some inner disquiet, and it made him wonder if it had become a torture for her to be as dependent as she was on men whose caprices had not always led them to treat her kindly. This time honesty was best. "I've been having trouble sleeping, and Morgan equates insomnia with melodrama. He said that I was sinking like grapeshot in liquid guilt."

Her head moved, and her disturbed hair made feather movements over his chest and belly that sent new blood tingling in surprise through his veins. As she spoke he was irritably cudgeling it back into its cool discipline.

"Do you mean," she said, "about me?"

"It would be nicer, right now, not to have to remember I was the one who frightened you so badly that you ran away." Turning his head lightly, he stroked her fingertips with his parted lips. Instead of the shy withdrawal he had expected, her fingers pressed his mouth, lightly exploring, as he brushed her softness with his tongue.

"I didn't know when I stole your letters that they belonged to Michael Granville," she whispered.

Against her fingers he said, "When did you know?"

"After. I began to guess in the boat when I saw your face." Then, desperately, she added, "Can't you believe me?" But before he was able to answer her, she moaned softly at a new stab of pain. The effort to consider the weighty yet delicate issue of Michael Granville had revived the submerged malaria headache, and it pounded raggedly in her skull, screaming for attention like a tattered beggar.

"Where does it hurt? Show me, dear" came Devon's voice, and she carried his proffered hand to her head, letting his clever fingers discover and soothe the shivery pain within her.

"Merry . . . I wouldn't care right now if you took every letter I own and boiled them for three weeks in a mustard foot bath." Holding her very close to him, he said quietly, "Love, I know there's no reason for you to think you can trust me, but this once, will you? I need to know who you are. It's going to take a long time for you to recover, and you could use someone of your own with you. You told me you had a family, and at the tavern there was a girl with you—Sally. Let me send for someone.''

She couldn't bear to have it all brought out again, and the temptation to have Sally with her might, with his nimble prodding, become too great for her to resist. Using every dram of her depleted strength, she put her arms around his neck, lifted her aching head, and laid her lips gently on his. Merry felt the light shock of his breath quickly indrawn, and the side of her breast, comfortably unbound inside her nightshirt, made tight contact with his tensed chest.

For a long time they held each other in that same floating touch. Without breaking the light bond of their lips he carried her to her bed and drew the bedclothes to her chin. When he finally did raise his head from her, it was to gather her flushing cheeks between his palms and stroke her there, staring down at her with a smile until he had watched her drift away from him, drowning like cherry blossoms in a pool into the depths of a peaceful sleep.

CHAPTER EIGHTEEN

The malaria paroxysm that came the next afternoon left Merry so severely weakened that she was alert for only a few minutes of the following twenty-four hours. Without consulting anyone Morgan changed course for St. Elise, the small island where he owned a modest indigo plantation. Even after she heard they had plotted a new heading, it didn't occur to her that she wasn't expected to recover. They had been too careful never to shake her confidence in that by placing steeled controls on their every nuance of inflection and expression.

Cat knew as much about the disease and how to treat it as anyone; no one could have done better, and there were many who would not have been able to keep her alive beyond the first days. The most dangerous form of the lethal malaria fever had entered the dearest of his patients.

He was grateful there was no need to tell Devon, whose clever golden eyes had correctly read the signs—her constant need to sleep, her failing appetite, her progressive apathy. Cat knew very well that when Devon had asked her again how he might find her family, it had not been to have them ease her recuperation, but because it was too cruel that she would have to die so far away from home and among strangers. But now, even if she had told him, it was no longer possible for any of her people to reach her in time.

Morgan had been in to see her, gazing at her while she slept. Cat didn't know which mask he had begun to dread more, Morgan's impassivity or Devon's cheerful efficiency. Uncapped emotion was worse. He found it unbearable to be in the same room with Raven.

Later that week they reached St. Elise, and the move into Morgan's villa was done with such care that Merry slept throughout. She woke in a wide airy room without a fireplace where arched windows showed the luxuriant greenery and crimson-tasseled blooms of a cashew tree. In the day's heat jalousy blinds dimmed the sun while they passed inside the breeze, and the immaculate cream-washed walls were restful and cool. The floor was an uncarpeted expanse of breadnut timber that shone like a tabletop and faintly perfumed the room with its orange polish.

During the hour she was awake, she had been able to drink some thin soup, to joke with Cat about whether or not she would take her medicine, and to meet Annie, the beautiful Indian girl who was married to Cook and whom Rand Morgan employed to manage his household staff in his absence. Often enough Merry had heard the others tease Cook about her, this heart-faced girl of twenty years whose father had worn a bone in his nose and for a Russian cutlass and a box of stale snuff had sold her outright to Cook. Or so the story went. Deaf and mute from birth, Annie communicated with hand signs, and she sat on the bed beside Cat, smiling and helping him teach some of them to Merry until they both saw Merry was too tired to continue, and then Annie had fetched a soft hairbrush and stroked it tenderly through the dying girl's golden curls, which ran like foam under her hands.

By the next morning Merry was in a coma. Devon had slept only a few hours in many days, and when he had passed out in a chair, they had put him in a bed in another room, so it was Cat who saw her slip under. Sails was with him, and Annie and Cook, and none of them was in any hurry to wake Devon up to see it. They had had to let Raven in to tell her good-bye, and that had drained all of them so badly that even Sails had felt his gnarled hands trembling by the time Saunders had pulled Raven from the room. No one had spoken since then.

Morgan stepped into the quiet with his eyes glowing like a fox's.

"Is this a wake, my little ones?" he asked, his smooth gaze finding and examining each of them. Crossing slowly to where the girl lay, helpless under the carved Spanish headboard of the big bed, he took her wretchedly white face between his hands.

"Oh, no, my girl," he said softly to her, "you are not going to die. Because I have plans for you. Because you're much smarter than your mother was. And because Cat knows better than to sit there like a dust box and let you die."

Even for Rand Morgan the cruelty was appalling. Sails felt a heavy rush of air in his lungs as he sucked in too sharply on a breath, and beside him he was aware that Cook was stiff as a wagon jack. And Annie was already on her feet and running toward Cat. She might not have been able to understand what Morgan had said, but she had seen what it did to Cat. The sharp change in that face, which rarely altered, struck the room's silence like a scream. Light o' God, to have placed that burden and that blame on a boy who was already raw with suffering and who had done everything for her short of cutting out his heart and feeding it to her, and Sails thought that Cat probably would have done that if it would have helped her. What could Morgan be thinking of?

Annie wrapped herself protectively around Cat's neck, her loose ebony hair sliding over his arms, her cheek tucked into his shoulder. And that in itself was a miracle. Six months ago Cat would have shoved her away, scarred as he was, and frigid, whatever anybody thought. The only contact he had allowed was Morgan's casual, infrequent touch, and deliberately rapid encounters with women of a certain order.

Forever etched in Sails's memory was a color portrait of Cat the
night they'd first brought him to the *Joke*. Come and see the boy I've
bought, Morgan had said, and there had been Cat, with face paint on
his cheekbones and smelling of violets, sitting on Morgan's bed, his
face about as friendly as a barracuda waiting under a rotting foot
bridge.

"It never does any good to ask," the boy had observed, dissecting them, chilly-eyed under curled lashes, "but I function better
when there's only one pair of sweaty hands on me at a time."

"You have very good diction for a twelve-year-old," Morgan had
said, blandly smiling.

"I've known men like you," the boy had said. "I know what you
want."

"I'm afraid you don't," Morgan had said, looking consideringly at
his exotic purchase. "You still have things to learn about men like
me, my child. And put your clothes on. It may take you a few days
to get used to the idea, but you don't have to wait anymore in
bedrooms wearing nothing but your gooseflesh."

Years it had taken to turn that savagely hostile brothel product
into the youth who could become a friend to little Merry, and when
she passed out of this world, she would carry a part of him with her.
Surely he needed to hear it was not his fault he couldn't save
her, and not the opposite. *What could Morgan be thinking of?*

Devon, awakened thirty minutes later, found Cat on the southern
slope near the house under the vast, horizontally spreading limbs of
a fig tree. Cat was seated in the deep shade near the trunk, his knees
drawn up, and on them, in his folded arms, he had buried his face.
His braid was wrapped like a collar around his neck, and one of his
thin hands clasped a large oval leaf that he must have plucked from
the waxy foliage above him.

Devon knew better than to offer sympathy. Instead he sat on the
grass and waited until Cat looked up. When the boy lifted his head,
Devon saw that he had not been crying. But it was the only time in
the years of their friendship that Devon had seen Cat look like the
teenager he was. Speaking calmly, as though this were any ordinary
day in their lives, Devon prodded forth the same discussion they had
repeated daily since she had fallen ill: about the medicines they were

giving her, the dosage, the frequency. Even in this moment of mutual panic their minds clicked into the accustomed pattern, and when they had exhausted the paces, Devon stretched out flat and stared up at the dark branches.

"Could we get her to swallow? Is it possible?"

"Probably," said Cat, "but by this afternoon I don't think so."

"What would happen if we double everything we're giving her?"

"I've told you. Convulsions. Death."

"If we increase it by a third?"

"Devon, we did that yesterday. I'm already killing her with the dosage that—" But Devon had uncoiled from the ground like a whip ricochet, dragging Cat with him, catching shirt front and braid in a crushing grip. For once, neither was acting as each glared into the extremity of the other's exhaustion.

In a voice he couldn't manage to keep under perfect control, Devon said, "All right, then. Now you know. I'm as close to the brink of some childlike useless frenzy as you are. Don't impel me to do anything I'll have to apologize for later. That girl is not going to die."

With helpless wrath Cat said, "Why not? Because Morgan told her not to? God and the Devil don't listen to Rand Morgan. Or do you think the celestial weight of our guilt is going to sift into her through the skin and keep her alive? Do you realize you're still calling her 'girl'? Does she have to be dead before you're willing to admit that from the beginning she was a woman to you? To me she's more than one more warm tup. *Get your goddamn hands off my shirt.*"

He was released with a speed that would have terrified someone less inured to violence, and found himself staring into Devon's cold fury.

"Don't examine too closely the chaste purity of your feelings for her, little monk," Devon said softly. "You might have a surprise."

"Yes! By all means, let's tally each other's hypocrisies. Is that mine? Then we'll do yours next. Why haven't you let her go?"

Devon allowed a frigid pause to develop. When he finally spoke, his voice was light and full of ice. "Every time I saw her, I reduced my demands so as to help her comply. It became almost comical."

"It shouldn't have, because the real comedy is that the relationship you were so sure she had with Granville was never more than a third of the reason you kept her." Cat stepped back, the sharp movement swinging his shoulders, and the braid fell from its loop around his neck. "You won't let her go because you want her. Even in that bloody tavern I saw it. It's a disease with you. You walk into a room with Merry, and you take in so much hydrogen that it's a miracle you don't float. But she's young and sensitive and well-bred, and that sets your chivalrous conceits flowing like springtime sap. You could have taken her; except that it was easier for your genteel conscience to deny yourself the cure of her body, even if that meant you weren't able to open the knot. An honest man would have raped her at once and let her go."

Devon had retreated a step, though Cat wasn't sure if it was in anger or to look at him from a fuller angle.

"Are you mad at me," Devon said slowly, "because I want to take her to bed, or because I haven't?"

"I'm mad at you because you've kept her a prisoner while you made up your mind whether your lust was more important to you than your bloody vanity. It would have been better to have ravished her and released her than to keep her living all those weeks in air turrets."

The shining oval leaf had dropped from Cat's fingers. Leaning forward gracefully from the waist, Devon swept it up and stood staring at the glossy cuticle, as though the bright color fascinated him, playing one slow finger along the vein paths. Looking again toward Cat, he said, "Why do you assume that I could have done either thing?" And then, "You don't know me as well as you think you do."

"Really?" The reply was heavily sarcastic. "Then you may have made yourself unnecessarily elaborate. What will become of your moral dilemmas when she's dead?"

Cat stopped, and though Devon couldn't feel the change in his own expression, he saw Cat shut his eyes tightly against it and cover his eyes and forehead with a long hand that was pitifully adolescent, thin and prominently boned.

Swiftly turning, Cat tried to walk away but discovered that his leg muscles weren't functioning properly. The first shock of the discovery was so intense he might almost have confused it with illness. Almost. Practical to the end, he decided to sink to his knees, catching himself on an outstretched hand as he fell. He knelt, fighting a blasting wave of nausea. It was minutes later, as it subsided, that he became aware of Devon's arm supporting his shoulders, the touch pressureless, infinite in its ability to warm and reassure.

Cat murmured, "I'm sorry. Honestly. I'm not sure how much of it I meant."

"It doesn't matter," Devon said.

When Cat turned toward him, he found that Devon was looking at him with an unpolished kindness strain left undimmed. It occurred to Cat that he had never seen Devon look so tired.

Exhaustion made Devon slightly misread Cat's expression. Devon said, "I apologize for dropping off sitting up. I should have been there with you when Morgan conducted his little drama."

"No. He picked a time when you weren't there. You know Morgan's methods. Divide and slaughter." Cat studied Devon's face. Through everything the man had asked nothing for himself, not sympathy, not tact, not even sleep. This was not the first time Cat had noticed how unselfish Devon was in his friendships, and if anyone thought differently, it was an illusion created by the strength of the impression Devon left on people. He felt Devon pat his shoulder and withdraw his arm. Wishing he was at ease enough with physical contact to have returned the light clasp, Cat gave him a glance that was as free from pain as he could make it and with the back of his fingers flipped the soft blond hair on Devon's forehead.

"You need a haircut," he said. It was an old joke between them. No one could remember the original context, but it seemed to have had something to do with Cat's hair being much longer. Then, loosing the last of his inhibitions about appearing pathetic, he said, "Please. Help me keep her alive."

Devon had settled cross-legged in the deep grass, twirling the leaf between two fingers. "You can depend upon it, child." He rubbed his eyes with the heels of his palms, as though he was clearing his brain, and as he lowered his hands he said, "You may not have any particular faith in the healing power of guilt, but I promise you that the heat of mine is going to keep Merry alive until she's at least three hundred. And she's more to me too than one more warm . . ." He lost interest in the sentence, searching in his pocket and then producing a piece of notepaper. He handed it to Cat.

"Tell me about this," he said.

Cat glanced at the paper. It was covered with his own handwriting, the neat slanting letters that had always seemed like they must come from a hand other than his own.

"Where did you get this?" Cat asked, as if he didn't know already.

"It was beside me when Annie woke me. Morgan left it, one assumes. I can't think of anyone else who would take the liberty of rifling your journal. What is it?"

Reluctantly Cat said, "An Indian remedy. I don't know how to use it."

"Have you tried?"

"Yesterday. Do you remember when Griffith kept Raven busy on the *Joke* making new rope handles for the fire buckets? Middle of the afternoon? I made up a dose, and Saunders fed it to one of the dogs." Cat was looking away from Devon, down the rolling meadow where a cotton tree sparrow trilled a scale that rose and fell sweetly. The boy felt the older man's scrutiny, and then a shallow relief as that scrutiny was withdrawn, an assessment complete.

"It died?" Devon said.

"I don't know if it would have died," Cat said. Inhibitions, irritation, and frustration were back in place, thank God, and he was able to keep the sticky misery out of his voice as he finished. "Saunders had to shoot it."

Devon made a murmur in his throat of muted sympathy as he tunneled his spread fingers thoughtfully through the grass before his knees.

"Too strong, then. It's a poison. We can dilute it."

"For God's sake, do you think I haven't thought of that?" Cat said. "Dilute it how much? And even then, how would I know if it's safe for Merry?"

On their trip through the fragrant shaded grass Devon's fingers encountered a young scorpion, and he let it walk onto his barely cupped palm. Cat's stomach muscles tightened involuntarily, even though he knew the small arachnid's sting was no worse than a severe wasp bite. He kept his lips stubbornly shut, and in a minute Devon gently released the scorpion and watched it slip away on its belly.

Devon smiled. "The Indians were right about quina."

"*Look*—"

"We'll work out a less potent formula, and give it to me first. Yes?"

"No!" The skin on Cat's cheekbones whitened and stretched like thin fabric. "Oh, no. Don't ask."

But Devon was already getting to his feet. "Assent with a civil leer, young'un. Do you think I'd let you kill me? It would be unspeakable to leave you alone to explain it to Morgan—"

"Not to mention packing you in a Malmsey butt and sending you home to Mother." Taking refuge in anger, Cat said, "Try not to posture, will you? I've got grief enough without having to depopulate half the island. I won't give it to you. You wouldn't be a fair test anyway. The body isn't a base metal vat that you can dump what have you into. Chemicals react against each other, and since you aren't full of arsenic like she is—"

"Give me that too."

"Wonderful! Instead of sending you home, maybe you'd like us to bury you beside the dog. What's the matter with you? I remember a time not long ago when you were sane. Will poisoning you help her?"

"That, my friend, is what we're going to find out."

In the end Devon won, probably because, as Cat would reflect later, when it came to relentless expertise in getting his own way, Devon was rarely outdistanced. Cat gave him the questionable medicinal concoction, and when Devon was alive an hour later—though not in what anyone would call a healthy condition—Cat diluted the mixture by another two thirds and fed it to Merry.

CHAPTER NINETEEN

The unicorn hadn't abandoned her after all, it seemed.

Merry found it in a dream of sharp colors that stretched at the edges like a projected globe from where she stood, a tiny figure clothed in pearly cotton under the sky-distant curve of an arched window. Her heart pounded gently with longing as she saw the dream creature canter across a shimmering horizon. There was a moment when it disappeared, and she was weak with fear, but it returned, circling and striking its hooves in the red dirt, and then rearing, its knotted ivory horn standing in the air as a glistening spiral. It paused and then galloped straight toward her growing larger, its nostrils softly dilated, its mane streaming. Great hooves, unclad in iron, threw a debris of grit and pebbles behind as it raced forward until it stopped ten feet from her and stood, quivering nervously. Shyness and an inexplicable dread made her approach it slowly, though the love and joy inside her was so strong that the earth melted like April snow under her bare feet; and the unicorn seemed to quiet as it watched her come closer.

It nickered softly to her, an invitation, though its muscles were taut in repose, as if being still were an effort, as if it were not easy to restrain its power, and this was a deference not to be long accorded. With trepidation and wonder she put her fingers into its mane and buried her face there also and learned with surprise that the hair wasn't coarse or odorous like the fibrous stuffing of Aunt April's drawing room wing chairs back in Fairfield, but was thick and soft like heavy silk, and fresh scented as a mown pasture.

The unicorn was tall, and her arms were imbued with unnatural strength as she pulled herself upward to its back, her breasts drifting over the rippling neck muscles, her legs lifting apart to receive the broad thrust of its body as she straddled it. The creature's life beat came to her, a caressing pulse below her cradling thighs, and then the great muscles stretched as it began to canter, and they moved together in long rocking strides. The sparkling green earth and the heavens caroled love hymns to them, and the sun dusted their united bodies with powdered light. Life fluids coursed through her surrendered body, and all parts of her had become healthy and distended with rich golden blood. Her fingers roamed under the unicorn's mane, embracing the warm hidden curves of its muscles. Rushing air burned her throat as she pressed herself deeply into its back, and her exhaled breaths came forth in many colors and blended with its own to bathe the sky in rainbow fluid.

On it went, the exquisite paradise that filled her until she was too exhausted to hold herself on the white back any longer, and sensing it, the great animal slowed to a trot, and then to a walk, and brought her to peace under the densely bunched head of a pear tree in blossom. She let herself slide to the ground, uncurling her heavy limbs slowly, and lay on a mossy bed beneath while white-touched pink petals rained over her in perfumed silence. Through eyes that could only open halfway, she gazed at the unicorn as it stood poised above her. But then, in one splendidly beating moment, the dove-whisper of the wind murmured to watch the unicorn because she was on the edge of a great discovery. . . . To watch . . .

The wind-command faded. Merry opened her eyes to Cat, bending over her with another of those eternal damp cloths he insisted on slopping on her skin every spare second he wasn't pouring his vile medicines down her. She observed fretfully that his braid, usually so perfect, had hair tendrils straggling out as if he'd slept on it; the cloth being applied tenderly to her brow made her feel sticky. And he had woken her from the unicorn. Merry lifted her hand and pushed at him.

"No!" she said crossly.

She saw him drop the cloth, which made a clammy water ring on the bedclothes, and look at her face with what seemed to her like totally unwarranted amazement. Before she had a chance to comment on that, he had snatched up her hand and was pressing it to his mouth with his eyes tightly shut. And then, to her chagrin, he was bending his head over her tightly clasped hand, and droplets of something wet were running into the center dip of her palm and from there down her wrist. Where was the water coming from?

"You're not coming down sick too, are you?" she asked him irritably.

He had turned his face away. "No. No, I'm hale. Merry . . ." His voice sounded strange. "Merry. You're going to get well."

"So you're always telling me. *I've* yet to see any evidence of it," she said with the natural peevishness of a convalescent invalid. "Where's Devon? Why is it so dark in here? I'm thirsty. And you made my hand wet."

In a state of bliss that was higher than anything he'd known in his life, Cat ran to satisfy her complaints; opening the jalousies, patting her hand dry, raising her head to give her water and nourishment. He had paused at a mirror to make a brief curious study of his eyes, which had unexpectedly produced tears for the first time since his infancy. Finally, when he was certain he had this surprising new ability under control, he went to tell the others that Merry would live.

Merry had never been told that she was close to death. In consequence she couldn't understand why her visitors were jubilant. And if anyone knew why it was three days before Devon came to visit her, they didn't see fit to reveal the reason to her. It would be a long time before she learned that Devon had spent those lost days fighting the heavy throes of arsenic intoxification.

St. Elise was a verdant saucer of land that belled upward in plump prosperity from the foaming tropical surf. Coffee and cocoa for export grew in a sheltered central valley, and here and there parcels of cleared earth held plantings of indigo that supported in plenty the nearly fifty families who made the island their home. Beyond the happy traces of civilization were magnificent unspoiled forests where butterflies flickered on blue iridescent wings and spring-fed brooks gurgled, tumbling bright pebbles beneath their warm crystal water.

Recuperation for Merry on St. Elise was a time of long afternoon naps and excellent meals from Morgan's chef, a young German who had apprenticed in Napoleon's kitchens at Malmaison. The villa itself was not a large one for its type, but it was beautifully made after the Spanish style and furnished with a discreet elegance that would have camouflaged to even a perceptive visitor that its owner was a pirate. Trying to find a clue from looking around here to Morgan's personality, or to Devon's, was more confusing than it was enlightening.

The only unpleasant surprise had been Merry's discovery that in her heart she had begun to hope Devon's tender care of her had been prompted by an emotion more profound than an active sense of guilt. Foolish beyond permission was the only way to describe that yearning, the more so because Devon had not tried to be alone with her since they had come to the island. If anything, it seemed he had made an effort to do the opposite. By now she must surely have learned how dangerous it was to care too much what Devon felt for her; how many times would she need to have that painful lesson repeated? What she must do was remake her feelings into a wary friendship and not agonize over things that were not likely to be. There was some comfort in knowing if it ever became more than she was able to control, she could discuss it with Cat—comfort, but not a cure.

The *Black Joke* had sailed, Tom Valentine in command. Rand Morgan had remained at the villa with a small number of the crew, including Raven, which meant there was a steady parade to her door of dripping buckets filled with sea creatures, of shells and starfish and snails as big as punch cups.

Quiet moments were spent with Annie, speaking in gestures and smiles. Not the least fascinating thing about Annie was that she was married to Cook, six years her junior, and if they shared a single trait, Merry was not able to discern what it was. In spite of that they appeared to love each other, which had a special interest for Merry because she had observed few such relationships in her life. It was not hard to understand how anyone, man or woman, could love Annie, with her easy dignity and intelligence; it was a little harder to imagine what Cook could offer her until Merry remembered that on the *Joke* the kitchens had been a retreat for her. There was an iron will and a kind of canny astringency about Annie's tough young husband that could be sustaining.

But he was from the fourth generation of a family of pirates, and

that affected his every attitude. The little Annie would reveal about
Cook's early treatment of her had produced in Merry an awed
respect for the Indian girl's courage, as well as a belated thankful-
ness that her own advent on the *Joke* had been under Devon's
protection. When Cook bought Annie, he was too young and had
been too roughly reared to make even primitive concessions toward
lightening her suffering and fear. He would never have beaten her,
and if he had been able to speak in her language, he might have tried
to reassure her, but as things had stood, it hadn't occurred to him
that it was wrong to use force on her as long as it was done without
excessive brutality; and because he had not grown up around men
who bothered to conduct their intimate relations with women in
privacy, he had not done that either. Raven had been appalled and
Sails gently chiding, but since the two of them, even together, had
been no match for Cook, in the end it had been Cat who, after three
days of listening to Annie's weeping, had taken her away from Cook
with the admonition that if he wanted his plaything back, he would
have to learn to take better care of her. So Cook had been forced to
listen to Raven's advice and to Sails, and if the kindnesses Cook had
shown Annie in order to appease Cat had been delivered sarcastically in the beginning, in time his own basic kindliness and Annie's
charm had begun to knit them, man to woman, in an alliance that
had more to it than fleshly unions. As Cook had said rather glumly
to Morgan a month later, "There's more to love than two pelvises in
a tussle."

It had become one of Morgan's favorite quotations. In fact, in the
weeks afterward Morgan had only to utter the words "As young
Cook says . . ." to wring groans from his auditors.

The air outside Merry's window was warm and genial, and as
soon as she was well enough to sit up, they carried her out to rest in
Morgan's terraced garden. The villa sprawled behind with its fret-
work decorations and wooden porches. Sunlight spilled upon the
bright shingled roof and bounced like a sprite through the fountain
spray and on the well-raked walks of crushed limestone. Scarlet lilies
startled the eye from shady corners, and iron frames dripped twining
branches heavy with lavender blossoms. Raven put it rather well.

"Neat," he had said to her on her first morning outside, "as the Pope's toothpick. Do you want sun or shade?"

He had been settling her on a Chinese Chippendale bench in the early sunlight when Morgan brought her the sketchbook. Her initial reaction was cold terror. How did he know she could draw? But if Rand Morgan's dark, thorough eyes had seen the color leave her cheeks, he hid it under a facile smile that was hard to interpret. Instinct warned her not to disclose her distinctive talent, but the pleasure of having a pencil in hand after so long had by midmorning made instinct seem akin to superstition. She received a tremendous and genuine response to the charcoal drawing she did that morning of Raven, and the charm of that made it impossible to stop. Much later she would remember that praise was the flat plane of a quick-edged sword.

Strong and healthy some weeks after that, Merry sat under one of a lovely avenue of shaddock trees, on a blanket in the grass. Beside her Raven was stretched out with a book propped open on his bare chest and his head on the pork belly of Dennis the pig. Cook and Saunders lounged nearby. Annie lay curled on her side, her arching toes against Raven's hip and her head pillowed on her husband's thigh, her sable hair coiled between his legs. He was lifting it and letting it fall as he frowned over the copybook in his hand, his short freckled nose wrinkled slightly in perplexed disgust.

Raven and Cook were studying, a routine that Morgan had insti-gated in their earliest days on the *Joke*, although no one was quite sure if the lessons were intended to promote their education or to test the patience of Will Saunders, who was supposed to be their teacher. Both Cook and Raven were quick learners, but that made them no easier to instruct. Raven's attention span for passive activity was notably abbreviated, and Cook had a tendency to dispute everything. If he was told that *i* followed *e*, save after *c*, it was woe betide Will Saunders if Cook found an exception later that Saunders had forgotten. Just now Cook was saying, "What kind of a problem is this, Saunders?" Glaring at the book, he read aloud: "The stagecoach is drawn by four pairs of horses. How many horses are two horses and two horses and two horses and two horses? How many horses are four times two horses?" He tossed down the book, spine upward on the grass. Then he said, "How in the name of Jesus should *I* know? I don't know a damn thing about horses."

Saunders was lying on the grass with his heels crossed and a wide-brimmed hat covering his face. From under the hat, "The question doesn't have a damn thing to do with horses, matey, and you know it."

"Well, Jeez." Cook began to warm to the subject. "Bloody thing's so easy that there must be a trick to it."

"What's the answer?" Saunders showed no disposition to emerge from under the hat.

"I refuse," Cook said, brightening at the incipient argument. "Damn, it's too easy. I'll be blast if it ain't an insult to my intelligence."

Moving with reluctance, Saunders pushed off the hat and sat up. "You've got tongue enough for two sets of teeth," he said irritably. Glancing at the book on the grass by Cook's knees, he said, "Well, for the love of Jesus, you've brought out the wrong book. Is that what you've been looking at for the last hour? You went through that book in three days nine months ago, as you are more than well aware."

To Merry, who had halted in her drawing of Cat and begun to giggle, Saunders delivered a reproachful glance, said, "Don't encourage him," and vanished again under the hat.

The shaddocks were hung with cannonballs of golden fruit, and ducking through them, Devon glimpsed Merry in an innocent moment, the residue of that earlier laughter still bright, her exquisite cheeks dappled with skipping sunlight that wove through the sheltering leaves. Her soft brushed curls haloed her smile and licked in airy tendrils against the fine-boned hollows under her ears and near the base of her jawline. Dainty, drifting shadows beaded the shell-pink fibers of her gown. Annie had made the dress for her from a simple pattern carefully cut of Flanders muslin that cupped Merry's sweetly rounded breasts and showed, in faint depressions, the honey-soft line of the hips and the curved surfaces between her tucked legs. Desire came to Devon in a light sting that brought with it the lucent memory of her flesh pliant against his fingers and the breathtaking arch of her breasts under his palm.

Cat was seated on a low stone wall stringing his mandolin and posing with not very good grace for Merry's dexterously wielded pencil. Spanish jasmine, growing to one side, suffused the air with its fragrance, and an inch from the toe of his high boots was a tiny hummingbird moving beelike in a vibration of gold and green feathers as its beak plunged repeatedly into the corolla of a nodding honeysuckle. There were, Devon noted, a lot of things to distract Cat, but the long-haired boy's fierce early years had given him an unerring sensitivity to human realities. From Cat's expression, focused with candid clarity on Devon's eyes, Devon knew that Cat had seen him looking at Merry, and Devon wondered idly what his own face had shown. Probably the inbreaths of hydrogen.

Devon stepped forward as Merry glanced skyward toward the wild golden-toned twitter of a bird which darted across the stretching band of a sunbeam. Pointing, asking what kind of bird it was, she upset her ivory pencil box, which had been unwisely balanced on the pig's rump. Trotters flailing, the pig scrambled to its feet, dunking Raven's head on the blanket to receive a haphazard shower of rolling pencils.

Merry was on her knees immediately, laughing in dismayed apology, pulling pencils out of Raven's loose waving curls, dusting graphite powder and cedar shavings from his bare skin. Retrieving an erasing rubber from under his ear, she said, "I'm dreadfully sorry. What a stupid thing!" Seeing that the pig had retreated in umbrage to Cat: "And poor Dennis. But does anyone happen to know what kind of a—" Suddenly Merry fell silent. Poised as she was, half leaning over Raven with her chest a handspan from his, the boy under her could not move unless he wanted to contact that wonderful feminine body, which was not a good idea with circumstances as they were. Tilting his neck to look up and backward, he was able to see, as he had guessed, that Devon had come, and that Merry was staring at him. It was amazing to Raven, as it was to the others, that Devon had begun to avoid Merry, especially when one thought of the risk he had taken with his own life to save her. For an unknown reason Devon had forbidden them to tell Merry about it. Was it that same enigmatic motive that had made the man behave toward her like a remote if friendly acquaintance since she had reawakened from the coma? The only certain thing about any of it was the hurt it was causing Merry. *Damn.* Why couldn't anyone seem to solve it?

Raven glanced up once at Merry and then tipped back to smile lazily into Devon's receptive gaze.

"See the fun you miss by spending half the morning closeted with Morgan in the study?" Raven said, stomping with unabashed verbiage through the embarrassing intimacy of the moment. "It's taking Merry forever to draw Cat's picture because all she wants to do is look at birds. Now she's overset her pencils over some weightless bit of feather and bone, and God knows what it is, mon. We keep telling her we're only good with pigs."

Merry had gratefully used the time Raven made to recover. Straight-shouldered, she settled sensibly on her heels, her smudged fingers laid flat on her lap, and strove for a natural expression of welcome.

"It was a swallow," Devon said, smiling at her. "Latin name: *Hirundo poeciloma*."

Eyeing Devon with disfavor, Cook said, "God's sake. Even the Latin. You'd think this was a bloody university."

"Don't worry," Cat said, tuning his e string. "He's a fake. He only learns the common ones. If it had been a puffin, you'd have seen him humbled."

"But you ought to hear me with vegetation," Devon said, grinning. "I can go on and on." He began to laugh at Cook's expression of alarm as he dropped easily to the blanket beside Merry. "But I won't." To Merry: "Will you show me your drawing, Merry mine?"

Merry was disappointed to find that his use of her name as a casual endearment had thrown her again into vivid disarray. She had a certain fear, irrational she hoped, that she might drop her gaze to his lips or to some other unsuitable portion of his anatomy. There must be a better way to manage. These waves of feeling were becoming more like a cruel prison every day. She handed him her sketchbook.

Devon studied her drawing of Cat, gave her an apt compliment on its quality which she took more pleasure from than she wanted to, and then he asked her in an amiable tone if she had ever done this for a living.

The question surprised a laugh out of her. "Certainly not," she said. "Do people buy pencil sketches?"

"That might depend on the subject," Devon said. It was a casual remark, made without thought or any intention other than idle discussion, but it went so neatly to the heart of Merry's one real offense against him that her laughter flattened into alarm. Devon was fishing out a pencil that had rolled under Annie's hem, and though no one would suspect the fate of a relationship could rest on the retrieval of an errant pencil, the act prevented Devon from seeing the apprehension in Merry's face and beginning from that to make the right sort of guesses. Like lost lovers that pass separately within minutes through the same door, Devon and Merry came as close as a glance to learning a crucial thing about each other. Of course, Rand Morgan would have probably made the point that a simple solution isn't always best when one deals with a complicated problem.

Raven, who *had* been looking at Merry, saw her apprehension, and although he had no way of knowing what it meant, it was logical for him to act protectively. When Devon looked up then, it was not toward Merry but toward Raven, who was demanding in an exuberant way to see the picture too. And so a moment that could have bred so much drama passed without solving or creating any new problems, as Raven began cheerfully to solicit critiques of the drawing on Merry's behalf.

From Will Saunders, supporting himself on an elbow: "Beautiful. But as it's Cat, Merry love, do you think you've developed enough of the sneer?"

Getting out of his studies had put Cook in a good mood. He said, "Sneer? By crow spit and wildfire, if that ain't an injustice to poor Cat. Hey, with all of us knowin' under that witchy tongue beats a heart warm as the tail fins on a dead sturgeon." Wiping a brown stringy curl out of his eyes, grinning at Cat, he said, "What we really need to do, see, is to take off your clothes and drape a sheet over your lap. And we'll give the picture to Morgan on St. Valentine's Day."

Raven was making a point of clearing his throat, and Cook caught the warning in it and turned to see that Morgan had joined them and was standing, with a bland smile on his face, by a flowering shrub. "Oh, bloody hell," Cook said and turned red.

"What a delight it is to discover my name on your lips," Morgan said in a tone that managed to convey the opposite without any visible energy. "Don't squirm, my lad, or you'll drop Annie's head off your knee. She's asleep, have you noticed?"

Heavily relieved by the turn of subject, Cook drew aside a mound of shiny jet hair to study Annie's face, the clear brown skin lax and glowing in sleep. "So she is! Bless her little soul. Well, Jeez. Did the same thing yesterday. Dropped right off to sleep in the middle of the day. I suppose I wake her up too many times at night," he said with self-reproach.

That drew sputters of outright laughter from his listeners.

"On one occasion in particular," Morgan said rather obscurely. The black gaze dipped cordially to Merry and then sprang to Devon. "Aren't you going fishing, my dear?"

"Yes," Devon said, starting to get up. He smiled fully at Merry. "Something distracted me. But I'm going now. Precious and fading are my idle days."

"Well," said Rand Morgan, "that's true. Why don't you take Merry?"

In the ensuing silence Merry heard Cat say tersely, "Why should he? He's already got bait."

Merry hardly caught the sense of Cat's words because her every feeling arrowed to Devon. He didn't want her to come with him. Rejection was there, clear as water, in Devon's face. She had not thought to spend the day with him, she had never been fishing and never particularly desired to go, and yet, seeing that he didn't want her with him cut her ill-protected heart like a steel spar. Against all force of will she must have been showing her hurt, because Devon's expression changed quickly. Fondness or something like it washed into his vivid eyes and flooded, hot and pulpy, into her veins.

"Would you come with me, Merry?" Devon said slowly to her. "Who knows what the pair of us will be able to catch?"

It took a little while to talk Merry into an assent because his invitation had been reluctant and because she was certain it did her no good to indulge her need to be with him, but in the end the temptation was beyond her power to resist.

When she had run into the villa to fetch a bonnet and Devon had gone to the front entrance to wait for her, Morgan walked to Cat, who had been silent after his one comment. Annie slept on, but Cook, Saunders, and Raven watched incredulously as Morgan caught

Cat's jaw in the bite of one wide hand. Black eyes burned into pale-blue frost.

"Keep it under control, babe," Morgan said softly. And left them.

A shocked silence ensued as the three tried to digest and interpret the extraordinary thing that had happened. Morgan, against all precedent of custom and courtesy, had disciplined Cat in public. Reviewing the preceding minutes in their minds, not one of them could understand why it had happened.

At last Raven hazarded, "Is it—is it Merry, Cat? Surely she's safe with Devon. He'd put his whole hand in boiling rice water before he'd hurt her."

Not answering, Cat stared at Raven as though he couldn't see him. He turned, walking and then running lightly, in the direction Morgan had taken. Behind him Saunders stared at the half-strung mandolin lying deserted on the gray stone wall.

"I wonder," he said, "if we'll ever know what *that* was about."

Running slowly, Cat caught up with Morgan much farther down the slope, beside the villa vegetable plots where Morgan's sable hair stood out against the brilliant light-green leaves of the young plantains. Cabbages and carrots bumped from the earth in squat lateral rows, and above them were small weedless tracts of parsley, sage, thyme, and the succulent jade shoots of ginger and arrowroot. Morgan, Cat saw, had stopped and was awaiting him beside a castor oil plant. So be it.

As Cat approached, Morgan gave him an extravagant smile and stretched an arm to the side, as though offering that space, that embrace, to Cat's shoulders.

"Come with me, my dear," he said. "I have an appointment in the village."

Cat froze where he was.

"If I'd known we were going to have theatricals," said the boy, "I would have brought my face paint."

Morgan dropped his arm in an easy movement and let his smile take on an edge. "What are you so worried about? I've kept her alive this far, haven't I?"

Livid with frustration, Cat snapped out, "You unseemly arrogant son of a whore—you've tried to kill her. *I've* kept her alive."

"Allow me to rephrase," said Morgan evenly. "I should have said, I've provided to keep her alive."

"Then why the devil won't you let me do that? She's too weak yet. If he puts his bastard in her—"

"Babe, you've already told him that. He knows."

"He'll forget. You've arranged things so he'll forget. Merry doesn't understand what she does to him."

Morgan's eyes glittered with laughter and shone, lusciously cloying like black cherries. "Doesn't she? Then you ought to have explained it to her."

"Am I her dry nurse?"

"Aren't you? I thought you volunteered long ago. And I thought Devon was supposed to cure himself on her body. Didn't you tell him that? Or does she fluctuate in and out of a state of being rapeable? Since none of you has the faintest idea what you want, then you are all going to get what I want you to have, which—"

"Is misery?"

"Which for *you* is the opportunity to discover how it feels when you can't protect something you love."

Cat recoiled like an animal from a flame thrust. He stood, digesting the words by slow degrees, the delicately toned eyes filled with startled distaste. "Rand . . ." For the first time he heard something akin to fear in his own voice. "Don't use her to teach me pain. Anyone. But not her."

"I can't stop it now for your sake, child. There are many more involved than you." The black cherry eyes had become much gentler. "You're one of the lives in my world; but you're not the center of it."

It had come—the careful loving rebuff Cat had known would come one day. For years, on Morgan's warning, Cat had been preparing himself for it, and now that it was here, Cat was surprised by his own readiness to receive it. He was well aware, in the long run, what Rand Morgan expected him to do.

"I've never asked," Cat said, "to be the center of anyone's life. I don't think I could stand it. This is bad enough already." And as Morgan cracked the tension with purling laughter Cat added, "Look, once she as good as told me that she *does* have some kind of secret that might make Devon harm her. Is that true? Do you know about it?"

"Of course I know about it. Do you think I'd grapple in blind space? Yes, she has a little secret, and she's hung on to it with extraordinary tenacity. I was sure she would break down and tell him, or you at least, a long time ago. Her overdeveloped sense of honor has made this more difficult than even *I* would have prescribed, but I have to admit I wouldn't have her be other than she is." A second time Morgan raised his arm in an offered embrace, and with a sigh Cat stepped into it and received the heavy weight of Morgan's arm across his shoulders. They walked side by side through the plantains. Cat watched the leaves tossing restlessly under the greedy wind-fingers that shredded the tender greens along their transverse veins.

Presently he remarked, "I suppose you have this so elaborately worked out that if I interfere, the chain of reaction would tip the continents and drown us—"

"—like all the dogs on Atlantis. Something like that. Remember it later, please." Morgan smiled at the sky. "My hens don't lay square eggs."

CHAPTER TWENTY

Merry ran ahead of Devon on the green pasture that dipped toward the beach. The scent of guinea grass filled her skirts. Tiny pink-winged moths fluttered before her in a giddy mist, and her uncovered hair billowed in sun-gilt clouds around her face. The borrowed bonnet hanging upon wide ribbons from the crook of her arm had become a flower basket overflowing with the colors of St. Elise. She—or Devon for her—had freely plucked from the island blossoms:

sprays of sapphire starflowers, regal scarlet trumpets, milky roselike buds, velvet blooms of cadmium yellow.

Things had been easier during her illness, when that septic lethargy had dulled her to his masculinity. Now, when he touched her, even in the innocent act of handing her a flower, Merry felt like she'd swallowed the whole flotilla of pink moths. She was aware of the pleasure-promise within the sensual curl of his lip. She remembered the lazy worship of his lovemaking, when he had held all of her in the caress of his mind and body. Few other men had charm that came as easily or ran as deep.

The meadow entered the tranquil shadows of an allspice grove. Merry slowed, letting her senses feast on the hauntingly aromatic perfumes issuing from leaves and bark. As Devon came to her side his nearness tickled the front length of her body even though he made no move to touch her. His expression was pleasant but abstracted. Probably he was thinking about fishing. It made sense. In her dreams she was writhing under the clever drift of his hands; in his dreams the writhing object was likely to be a trout. Romance was so complicated that it must take a genius to work it out. Aunt April should have told her. But then, Aunt April could never have predicted Devon. No one could have predicted Devon.

Drawing a red blossom from the hat, she began to lace its stem to another that was apple-flower white.

"Unless you were born on a moss bed fully formed like a pixie on the day I met you," Devon said, "you must have had some sort of a life."

Her head snapped around quickly under his amber gaze. So he hadn't been thinking about fish. Much she knew about men. It was somewhat lowering to reflect she couldn't tell from looking at him whether she was on his mind, or lines, hooks, and bait; but there was nothing she could do about that either.

"I suppose I did," she said, threading a plum-colored flower into her chain.

"What kind of a little girl were you?" he asked.

"Mousy. Always daydreaming. I wanted to please"—she said it lamely—"everyone."

It seemed as though her very soul was melting under the compassion in his eyes. His smile was an endearment. What did *this* mean?

"How did your hair look?" he said.

"Also mousy." She concentrated on her fingers, weaving another blossom to the first ones. "Little pieces slid out of the ribbons and fell on my face. And I had a skinny neck. People spelled when they talked about me."

"Spelled?"

"Yes. The wives of my father's friends used to say, 'Such a well-mannered child. What a pity she's so h-o-m-e-l-y.' " How aggravating it was that after so many years she couldn't tell the story without a slight constriction in her throat. "My aunt said that I must learn to say, 'I may be h-o-m-e-l-y, but at least I'm s-m-a-r-t.' "

She had thought to amuse him and was surprised, glancing sideways, to find that his sculptured lips had no smile. A hand on her shoulder stopped her, and she was turned gently toward him. They were separated by only a thin air cushion as his palms found and raised her chin.

"What you are and have always been," he murmured, "is lovely." His mouth came, a slow glowing pressure on hers, withdrawn before she could press back and show him the fevered urgency in her heart.

And so with much constriction of the throat, thousands of moths in the esophagus, and very wobbly ankles, she resumed her stroll with Devon toward the beach. They had gone about five steps when he said, "Do you know, there are times I find you so entrancing that I have to remind myself that you're a living woman and not the supernatural expression of my fantasies. We *have* ascertained, haven't we, that you aren't a pixie?"

Since it was the most unordinary thing anyone had ever said to her, Merry didn't immediately regain her voice. Her nerves were in numb shock, as if she'd hit her head on a cupboard. She swallowed convulsively and worked two red blossoms in a row into her chain of flowers. She had no idea whether he was sincere or whether this was merely an elaborate style of flirtation. It sounded sincere, but if that was so, why hadn't he wanted her to come with him today? Why hadn't he spent more time with her lately? She ought to have gulped down her pride and gleaned what she could from Cat. The only safe course now was a light response.

"Absolutely, I'm not a pixie," Merry said. "The sad truth of the matter is that I'm a jellyfish changed by a wicked witch into a girl, and that's why you can see through me on clear mornings.''

"I'm ready to see the inside of you," he said softly, smiling down at her, "time of day notwithstanding."

As beginnings went, it was promising. Devon invented fantastic cures to break the spell. Some of them were winsomely bawdy and sounded like things she'd like to try. (Heavens! She wouldn't admit it though.) Stirred and uncomfortable about it, she halfheartedly uttered a laughing protest and got back a smile from him that turned her bones to clotted cream.

Simulating innocence, he said, "I beg your pardon. But you could hardly expect me not to become intrigued by a fascinating project like finding new ways to turn you into a—"

"Jellyfish," she finished for him. "Don't worry. No one has more of an aptitude for that than you do." But the tone of her voice was faintly dejected.

Acute as he was, Devon caught her unspoken distress and neatly altered the subject. Because it happened so quickly, Merry didn't have time to decide whether his motive was boredom, pity, or something more complex.

Ebb tide had left a playful rubble on the white coral sand. Piles of seaweed dried under the sun-oven baked beside sponges and wave-torn chunks of fan coral. Dainty violet crabs ran to and fro among the fresh-hued tidal litter, making what meal they could of stranded codfish. Palms swayed to the sea's unending water carol.

Devon's canoe was secured among the leathery foliage of the seaside grape trees, and a good many of those crimson-veined leaves and red berries had dropped into the canoe's bilge along with yesterday afternoon's rain puddle. Together he and Merry cleaned it out.

On the water, once they were beyond the churning surf, the canoe rode like a chamois cloth over oiled glass. Clear sea quivered behind them into a whispering wake; beyond the short, easy strokes of Devon's paddle the bay was quiet. Heat blossomed in waving tails as the canoe passed light as a floating feather through a bobbing flock of man-o'-war birds. Feeding pelicans dropped on flagging wingbeats toward the disappearing diamonds that lit the placid water.

On the day before, Devon had set a fish pot. The light wood

marker made a dancing speck in the glossy distance, and they approached it slowly over a pristine underwater landscape of honeycombed limestone caverns that were carpeted in undulating marine grasses. Starfish clung by prehensile arms to hidden niches, and fantastically colored fish schooled and swirled in the deeply drifting sunbeams.

Morgan's German cook had packed them a small lunch, and Merry's rummage through that basket turned up a long piece of sugarcane shed already of its green outer layer. She settled back against the bow, abandoning herself to the lapping movement of the canoe beneath her body, and to the warm penetration of sunlight through the cloth over her breasts and legs. She had made the colorful chain of flowers into a wreath, settling it timidly upon her apricot curls, where it tipped seductively forward as she bent her head to the sugarcane. Bringing the thick stalk to her lips, she nibbled the cane fibers to release the sweetly flowing juices and sucked gently on the tip. Tepid sugar water dripped into her throat, and she drank in a softly rippling swallow. Escaping drops pearled her pink lips, and she caught them in an arcing sweep of her tongue.

Across from her and watching, Devon had drawn a single breath that was out of rhythm with the others and that focused her attention on him. His eyes were hooded fires, a forgotten smile lingering on the surface of his mouth. With no very accurate idea of what he had on his mind, Merry smiled back, sat forward with the flower wreath dropping endearingly over one eyebrow, and said genially, "Would you like to share?"

"Another time, lady bright," he said, not taking his gaze from her face.

The fish "pot" was a woven canework box with narrowing jaws, a trap for unwary sea creatures. Devon pulled it up by the attached rope, and as the trap broke from the sea shrimp flooded through the lattice with cascades of aerated saltwater. Inside the pot were four fish. Devon identified them for her—a white hind splashed with scarlet spots, a pink goatfish, and two snappers with golden bellies and yellow fins. Merry couldn't help noticing they didn't like being pulled from the water any more than she had ever liked being thrown into it.

"I suppose," she suggested carefully, "that now that you've

had the fun of catching those beautiful fish, you'll be letting them go?''

His grin assumed she was joking. Working the rope into a damp coil, he said, "They taste as good as they look."

Merry studied the effective movements of his well-formed hands as he untangled a small and disgruntled squid from the trap's interior and tossed it back into the sleeping bay.

"I don't think I could enjoy the taste of a fish I'd met face to face," she said reflectively, putting her hand outside the canoe and stirring the water with sticky fingertips.

Devon's eyes traveled to her wet fingers and followed the line of that graceful arm from her rounded shoulder to the deliciously pretty face under the lopsided flower crown, dusky lashes innocently lowered against the creamy cheekbones—and that ridiculous little nose. Her face was a delight in color and in form, but it was not the face of a woman he would ever have anticipated would wield this kind of power over him.

"Merry!" he said in mock reproach, remembering suddenly the scenes so similar to this one that had led him at the age of ten to stop letting his sister come fishing with him. The thought produced the smile he was trying to hide. "I can't believe you want me to let them go. Why, that snapper is more than two feet long!"

The too-small nose took on a mischievous tilt. "Pooh. It's only a foot and a half."

"Damn it, it's two feet if it's an inch."

"One foot nine inches," she said, "and that's my last offer."

Her manner was still oh, so playful, but some abstract sense told him that for her this was no game. She meant to test him. It was like her suddenly to see the fish as a symbol of her own captivity. He had never met anyone with her amazing sentimentality. More amazing still was how that delicacy of mind had survived those weeks on the *Joke* and contact with men like Eric Shay and Max Reade . . . and of course himself. He carried that thought to his fingers as he opened the box's latched back and sent the trap again into the calm waters. One by one the fish went their ways, tails twitching.

In the meantime Merry was resisting the urge to toss her arms around his neck and shower his blond hair with kisses. Among other deterrents she'd probably upset the canoe. From her brother, Carl, and her cousin, Jason, she knew it was usually useless to ask men and boys not to shoot squirrels or catch fish. Devon had understood her. She knew her uncontrolled smile was silly and a little tremulous.

Devon's grin had equal elements in it of affection and amused exasperation. Shaking his head slowly, he began to laugh, and she laughed with him until the floral wreath made its final slip and plopped down over her eyes.

The canoe moved idly for a long time near a hilly shoreline heavy with groves of coconut palm and straggling beds of prickly pear with their profuse baubles of flower and fruit. Staring in a happy daze at the scenery, Merry was recalled to her surroundings by Devon's voice with the prosaic reminder that even though the heat was unseasonably mild, she had better cover her arms and face because God only knew what Cat would do to the pair of them if Devon brought her home with a sunburn. Merry struggled into a straw bonnet and shawl as she watched Devon relax against the stern, trailing a line baited with enough sprat to sink the wire hook of its own weight.

"If something bites," he said, holding her in a lazy gaze, stretching his long, handsomely proportioned legs out before him, "can I keep it if it's u-g-l-y?"

To cover the soggy wash of love she was feeling for him, Merry answered his teasing with a face. "Man's work, isn't it—fishing?"

"You ought to go with Raven. He ties the line around his toe and falls asleep. Once he caught a turbot, and a shark ate that and dragged Raven through fifty feet of water." Then, "You realize, of course, if one of those fish had been served to you at dinner, you would have eaten it without a qualm."

She rested her chin on her fist. "I know I haven't always been philosophically consistent. I'm to work on it," she said, thinking about certain lectures from Cat. Shifting her body, she dug in the picnic basket and discovered her sketch pad. "Sometimes I think I should be eschewing animal flesh altogether."

"Doubtless, mine included. Good Lord, what are you doing? Are you going to draw a picture of me?" he said.

"Why, yes, but only as part of the scenery. Imagine yourself as being a rock or a tree."

"Stones have been known to move and trees to speak." Devon

spoke the quote with a half smile. "What would you like me to do? Must I not talk? Or shall I be amusing? Would you like to hear about this canoe?"

"Yes, indeed," said Merry, making a rough outline of his hair, which shone in the tropical sun like late-summer wheat.

"The canoe," he said, "was a silk-cotton tree, hollowed by axes and by burning. Cat and I made it a few years ago—a very wholesome project, mind you. Morgan was beside himself to see us so constructively engaged. Do you know—you have a unique ability to sit for a long time on your heels. Love, stretch your legs out."

Her eyes of horizon blue became very wide. Steadying herself on the sides of the canoe, Merry shyly unbent her knees until her feet alternated with his in the white sunlight that leached color from the canoe's bottom. She had taken off her shoes, as he had, and his clean, tanned skin heated hers. The sharp classical cut of his bones was evidenced even in his feet, which were as charming in their appearance as it was possible for that under-valued, ill-regarded body member to be. *It must be love*, Merry thought. *I adore his feet*.

"Tell me more about the silk-cotton tree," she said with a gulp.

"It has a sensitive soul, you know. It's widely believed that if you throw a stick at it, you'll be visited with misfortune."

"If the silk-cotton doesn't like sticks thrown at it, how on earth did it react to axes and fire?" she asked, working with her pencil on the humorously arrogant tilt of his upper lip.

"Very well, because we'd taken the precaution of pouring libations of rum at its roots. The best superstitions always have an antidote." Drawing back his leg, he used the top of his foot to gently rub the plush inner curve that stretched to her toes. As soon as she saw what he was going to do, she expected it to tickle. The surprise was that the ticklish feelings occurred neither in the manner she had anticipated nor in the places. A blush began, spreading in from her cheekbones toward her nose, and to cover it, Merry picked up her sketch pad, as though she had to study her drawing from a closer vantage. Safely hidden, she was able to say, "Devon, why does Morgan live here?"

"Instead of, perhaps, in a tent on the coast of Spanish Florida? Because he's a rich man, my dear."

"Don't the other island families mind that Morgan's a pirate?"
she asked, secretly fanning her blush.

"If they do, they don't say so to his face," Devon answered
good-humoredly. "St. Elise is so isolated that I don't think they
realize what the name Rand Morgan means in other places."

Willing the blood from her cheeks, Merry took the bold step of
lowering the sketchbook to her knees again. She could only hope
for the sake of her self-respect that he didn't know the full extent of
the things he did to her. Casually she said, "How did Morgan come
to own the island?"

There was a slight hesitation which made her look up at him, but
she could discover nothing unusual in his face.

He said, "Rand bought it from the St. Cyrs."

"As in the Duke of?" asked Merry, astonished by the eerie
coincidence of it, remembering that the Dowager Duchess of St. Cyr
had been the catalyst for the disastrous chain of events which had
brought her here. Merry reminded herself that she must not appear to
know more about the famous St. Cyr family than the average
well-read person might. Her ability to anticipate him was improving,
because the next question Devon asked was, "You know the family?"

There was a keen edge to the question that Devon took no trouble
to conceal, and that made her uneasy. Or perhaps it was his soft
exploration of the base of her toes that she found disturbing.

"Who doesn't know of the St. Cyrs?" she said. "The current
duke is highly regarded in the United States, you know, for his
opposition to the Orders in Council that permitted the British Navy
to blockade American ports." She waited to give him the opportunity to defend his country's hateful atrocities. Either he was in no
mood to argue, or he had no strong feelings on the subject, because
he made no comment.

The other item of note about the St. Cyr family was that the father
of the present duke had been the world-renowned botanical painter.
His wonderful volume of nature drawings was one of her favorite
possessions; it was in her trunk with Aunt April.

Shading the shapely hollows beneath his Attic cheekbones, she
ventured, "I can't imagine how the distinguished St. Cyrs could
have an association with Rand Morgan."

"Ah—the St. Cyrs are a loose family, my dear. Did you know

that the late duke married the daughter of his head gardener? The
dowager duchess wore mourning for a year after the wedding and
sent her son and new daughter-in-law a wagon of vegetable marrows
on their first anniversary.'' Fitting his sole to hers, he continued.
''The St. Cyrs had this island ceded to them by Charles II on the
condition that they pay 'unto his majesty yearly and every year one
fat sheep if demanded.' As Morgan says, there's quite a tale behind
the sheep. . . .''

It was a good day for talking. The kindly fates, after separating
Devon and Merry in experience and temperament, had looked back
with regretful sighs and cast camelia garlands of warm conversation
to the ill-omened pair. The young man who was a spy and the girl
who was a spy-of-sorts had earned this fate-given opportunity, he for
the sacrifice he had made for her, though that meant he must accept
her honesty on faith alone, which was not an easy thing for a man
who had never learned to trust his lovers. And if he was deserving
for his sacrifice, she won her laurels for its opposite, for the meager,
unheralded act of heroism of withholding from him the secret that
was not hers to reveal.

So, when anyone would think that they wouldn't have much to
talk about, neutral subjects arrived for them the way shells appear on
the newly strewn seashore with each flooding tide. Devon had the
kind of natural charisma that would have made a crowd of two
thousand listen with bated breath as he discussed the digging of a
drainage ditch. At age eighteen Merry Wilding was not so talented.
Most men would have been happy to stare at her by the hour; only
the kind ones would be equally content to listen to her talk; that
would come later in her life. And though not one of his myriad
discarded mistresses, however fond, would have called him *kind*,
Devon delighted even in the most naïve of Merry's minutiae. There
was little he had not seen on the battlefield or in the bedroom, but he
could still find drama in her story about the time she had seen
lightning strike a windmill and ignite the canvas covering on the
vanes to dancing flames. When little fish nibbled the bait from
Devon's line, he laughed and didn't put it out again.

Later he rowed them to a cove he knew where the beach skipped
inward between two dormant volcanic peaks. Primitive forests bright-

ened the twin cones and reflected with them in the shimmering film
of water that iced the ivory sands as the waves withdrew.

Together Devon and Merry beached the canoe beside a pile of
driftwood and wandered along the wave line. He casually held out
his hand, and she took it, letting the dangerously unresolved problems between them ride out with the tide.

The sand was heated gossamer, deep enough to cover their ankles.
He made her pause before a great conch shell that lay half-buried in
the glittering silt. A large butterfly perched atop the shell, its translucent yellow wings parting and closing in soft, gentle beats. He
picked up the shell and held it to her, and as she reached for it,
feeling its hardness and satiny texture beneath her fingertips, the
butterfly took wing. His hands spread under hers, supporting them,
taking the conch's weight as she gazed into its swelling folds. The
pure colors dazzled her, pearly white along the rim deepening first to
pink and then to a brighter scarlet hue, until in the inner mysteries
where the light could not reach, the shell became a lovely mixture of
dusky purple and hazy deep red. Their joined hands carried the shell
to her ear, and the silver-toned roar wept into her senses. Sunlight
stung her shoulders, sea moisture found her lips. The bright golden
hairs on his chest lifted at the casual affectionate touch of the
ocean breeze, and she longed to rub her cheek against their softness.
Smiling at him, she raised her head, and they walked again. He
carried the shell, with his fingers curled into its open lip, and
slipped his other arm around her waist. Her head rested on his
shoulder, and her hair, blown by the trade winds, streamed across
his chest and throat like fine gold dust.

Eden.

They found a brook that fed the aqua bay with spring water. Two
pelicans had landed among the black rocks there and preened their
feathers and tossed water over their wings as Merry and Devon
strolled by them, following the freshet inland. The foliage of the
giant mahoganies met overhead in a natural arbor that allowed
sunlight to seep through in pale-green bands. The freshet fed a
stream, and that a cascade of rapids widening at the base into a
secluded pool. An aged frame of limestone swept along the far side
of the pool. Masses of wall marigolds exploded between the broken
stones along with heavy blossom bundles in red and violet.

Mincing like a fawn over the sharp little rocks at the pool's edge, Merry walked into the shallows as Devon set down the shell and followed her with more assured steps. The pool was fed by a warm underground spring which she could feel rushing over her feet, and as they waded they found to their delight that it was quite deep, and she leaned back luxuriantly into his arms as the warm, relaxing fluid lapped about her thighs. A mound of swollen scarlet flowers dripped from the limestone outcropping overlooking the pool, and the musky scent tickled at her nostrils. She sighed with joy at the wash of sensations. The sunlight, falling down through the arch of trees above them, probed at her, awakening her, playing across the freckled cheeks, the tiny nose, the huge heavy-lidded eyes. Her thick hair tumbled over her breasts like the cascade that spilled down the rocks behind them, and he could feel her breathe beneath his wrists as he encircled her from behind; it was such a pleasing picture to him, one of lovely skin tugging at thin fabric, wet and diaphanous where the water had done its work—it seemed like she was a new creature, half human, half flower, her gown swirling about her like petals.

He turned her to him, and she leaned back against the soft fall of flowers, lifting her chin, letting the sun touch the most delicate and unreachable softness of her throat, her back arching gracefully, bending under the warmth of his hands on her sides. Their bodies touched, his hard and muscle-knit, hers soft and yielding, holding each other in a soul-spinning embrace, his desire and her response as innocent and as rich and as floral as the bud plumes lying splendidly against her cheek. Her lips parted slightly as she breathed the perfumed, nectarlike air.

He studied the young face, remembering the dark hours when death had laid its coldly beckoning hands on her, and his kiss, when it came to her, was chaste and urgent. But the free-flowing fire between them began to soften and shape their mouths, and the pressure of his lips increased. . . . He pulled back then, pleasuring in the sight of her, learning the full curve of her cheek with the caress of his finger.

She tilted her head under his touch, inadvertently brushing her own lips against his; and drew back, startled by the heat rising within her. Suspended in tenderness, she held the impression of his willing male flesh upon her mouth, the form of the alien lips, which were firm and winning. Her lashes danced open, and her eyes met his subtly tempting gaze.

He murmured, "Kiss me again." And then, softly, "Please."

Initiating their contact was awkward for her, perhaps partly because he was infinitely more skilled than she. "Please," he had said, and stood courteously silent. He touched her lower lip, gently rubbing back and forth there as it distended under his thumb. The water touched warmly at her thighs with innocent provocation; the sun was constant upon them, a halo. Finally she put up her chin, gazing into his eyes for a moment before she closed hers, and pressed her mouth to his in a full, open kiss. When she broke from him, she was trembling so that he had to support her with his hands, and her cheeks were hotly flushed.

As though she believed she were making a confession that would surprise him, she said, "I'm never sure if I'm doing it the right way."

Laughing huskily, he collected her body and dragged her close. "Then you'll be reassured when you see I'm too overcome to paddle us home."

"That wasn't really an answer," she said.

Stroking back her hair with his palm, he said, "Oh, my dear, I'm sorry." He smoothed his lips into her rosy curls. "I didn't know you wanted a real answer." His fingertips thrilled in light strokes over the quivering skin on her neckline. "There aren't ways that are right or wrong. Please yourself. That's all you need to do with me, Merry. Watching as you touch clouds takes me there with you."

With a graceful movement he plucked her from the water, nurturing her in his arms, and carried her with her legs dripping to the flat ocher shelf of a boulder. He set her on the rock, standing in front of her as she stretched back on her hands, losing herself in the sudden penetrating sensation of hot, hard stone beneath her thighs. But her gown was heavy with spring water and clung like gauze to her hips, and driplets melted from the fabric and explored the inside of her thighs in an oddly dulcet manner. She plucked at her wet skirts and began to wring them out, trying without success to avoid baring her legs.

"I should take you home," he said. "You're"—his gaze traveled the length of her, taking in her slim, shapely body, and below, the pale skin of her legs, the dainty swelling muscles of her calves, the way her legs were slightly parted on the rock—''wet.''

She dropped the tangled hem, lifting her shadowed, delicately veined lids to stare at him wide-eyed, and tried to say something intelligent about being taken home, but her voice faltered, and the words that came out were, ''Yes—take me . . .'' And suddenly she was inside his embrace, with his kiss dissolving her living will into his. Her mouth was a full pink bud, widespread to him, open to the heavy stroke of his tongue. An ancient, primitive force controlled her hands as she encircled him, one palm flat on his back, the other seeking his neck, twisting into his silken hair, fighting to heighten their contact. She swallowed his kisses like honeyed broth, each one both sating her and increasing her thirst until she was as helpless as a drifting poppy.

She lost pace with her breath. Her body became a foreign thing to her, her blood spinning through veins that seemed delighted to swell and pump; her nerves were shocked and burning under her hard-running desire. Scattering hot, open kisses, his lips coursed over hers, into her ear, into the softness of her throat beneath the sensitive curve of her jaw; and she pressed herself against him in an agony of erotic tenderness. His hands were a murmur against her body as he cupped a palm beneath her, catching her closer, spreading her legs with his other hand, sweeping her aching warmth into the narcotic hardness of his hips. She gasped at the bright flare of sensation, and he caught her head as it fell weakly back, cradling her, nibbling at the whiteness of her exposed throat, feeling her swallow beneath his lips, stroking the light tattoo of blood so close to her skin, feeling the vibration of the soft moan that escaped through her parted lips.

As their mouths searched for and found each other she gave herself deeply to him, twining closer, and his breath became quietly arhythmic.

''Merry—sweet Merry . . . I didn't bring you here for this.''

''Th-this?''

''To love you. I didn't bring you here to make love to you.''

''No? Devon?'' she said in a husky little voice. ''If you were going to make love to me, what would you do next?''

He kissed her, lovingly and long, with a caressing intensity that left her limp everywhere, and said, ''If I was going to make love to

you''—his hands moved in a slow pattern at the back of her gown—''I
would want to be closer to you . . .'' Laying his forehead softly
against hers, he brought one of his hands to her cheek and massaged
it with the back of his fingers. Then he separated himself from her
slightly and with his fingertip tugged at the line of fabric that hid her
collarbone, and the muslin fell an inch, revealing the milky fairness
of flesh never gilded by sunlight. He kissed its creamy softness, and
his heart caught at the beauty of her shyly blooming sensuality as
she closed her dusky eyelids and leaned into the curve of his arm.

It was time to stop, and he knew it, but before will and common
sense could coalesce, his palm slipped along her collar and curled
over her shoulder, and that gentle act freed her gown so that it
drifted by gravity into a sighing pillow around her hips. A startled
exclamation sprang from her lips, and against the heady sylvan hues
of the tropical pool her smooth skin and pink colors seemed sharply
human in nakedness. Unaffected embarrassment made her move
instinctively to cover her breasts, but he caught her wrists, one in
each of his hands, and murmured, ''No, love. Don't.''

His hands moved with her trapped fists, pressing her backward
into a crisply yielding mound of scarlet blossoms behind her on the
limestone wall. Ruby flowers nodded against her cheeks and trembled among her curls, and the flood of scented blooms fed over her
arms. The grip of his hand faded on her wrist, and his candied touch
spread slowly down her arm and became a feather stroke on her
breast. The unhurried glide of his fingertips was a banquet to her
senses, and yet the raking invasion of love fluids was excruciating to
her delicate tissues, and there was pain in the erotic ache of her
moan. His fingers abandoned her breast briefly and searched the
flowers for her childish wrist, and after he had discovered her white
hand, he carried it back to her breasts. Inserting his hand into the
cup of her much smaller, squarer palm, he whispered, smiling,
''Ah, love, you're as dainty as a toy. Show me, Merry. Show
me how you want me to touch your body.''

Her fingers pressed his hand urgently closer, and his fingers
spread, fanning over her breasts in deepening strokes, his thumbs
passing in scorching circles over her nipples. The breath quickened
in her throat and in his, and her skin quivered under the sweetness of

his hot respirations as his mouth wandered over the inner curve of her throat, his hair skimming her chin.

She felt his lashes touch her skin, and the sigh of a whispered endearment, and then his lips rolled softly back and forth over her nipple, and his tongue stroked her moistly, easing the heady action of his fingers until her heartbeat began to pound in the depths of her body, and all she knew was her need to give herself to the wonder of his mouth.

"How soft you are, Merry—soft as a catkin," he murmured. "And made in the colors of a wild rose. Angel. Oh, angel, love . . ." He dragged her into his arms. She felt the thud of his pulse as her naked breasts moved against his warm flesh and the hard pressure of his hips on her inner thighs. Her hands caught in his hair, pulling his head down to hers, and she opened herself to the stroke of his hard, coaxing kisses. The gauzy warmth of her wet gown clung in gently moving folds to her thighs and belly, teasing the feverish flesh there and the ache of her lower body where she was throbbing with a bell-like timbre, like a sweet promise, and she whispered his name as a plea and a moan, her pulsebeats coming thick and stinging.

She felt him lay her back against the rock with gently trembling purpose, and then the wash of filtered sunlight and warm air as his body left hers. At the shock of it her eyes flew open, and she saw that he was leaning with one palm against the rock and that the other covered his face. The skin exposed between his fingers had an enchanting flush to it, and his hair had tumbled forward in lovely and wanton disorder. And—shakily—he was laughing. When he dropped his hand from his face, she could see in his eyes the daze of frustrated longing. He said, "Merry. My sweet Merry. Ask a little question, get a great big answer. *If* I were going to make love to you, that was what I would have done next."

CHAPTER TWENTY-ONE

At sunset Merry found Cat alone on the veranda. He was sitting on the balustrade, one leg extended, the other bent, under the curve of a Moorish arch. Beyond him she saw the forests turning dark green, and a magenta sky, which suffused the young pirate with transparent orange-colored light that washed through his unbound hair and over the orchid resting above his ear. From the mandolin his fingers teased the minor chords of an erotic love song, and he accompanied the rich notes in a voice that was well trained, charmingly modulated, and emotionless. Merry stood within the ovoid of thrown light, watching the death of the wounded sun and listening to Cat sing, and when the last vibrating note faded, she could not speak because his songs always affected her in their sadness and beauty. Nor did she tell him it had moved her, because she knew he despised compliments.

At length he swung down his legs, laid the instrument carefully against the porch, and plucked the orchid from his ear, settling it with some tenderness in her curls.

From this close Merry could breathe in the roselike odor that clung to his hair and see the faintly opiated softness in his eyes. Annie had been right. Cat, for once, was not perfectly sober. There had been, Merry gathered, some kind of falling out with Morgan; and no one was willing to tell her anything about it beyond warning her not to question Cat unless she wanted to get her head snapped off.

She found the orchid with her fingers and smiled. "It's beautiful, isn't it?"

"No."

"No?"

He said, "Orchids remind me too much that flowers are the sex organs of the plant. I like my flowers to be more"—he touched the bloom and then, softly, her chin—"discreet."

"You're as bad as Cook," she said. This morning, when she had chanced to make a remark praising the sparkling seascape, Cook had said prosaically, "I can't see what you find to admire in the ocean. Jeez, what is it besides diluted fish piss? When you think of all those fish in all those centuries . . ." And then encountering severely critical looks from Cat and Raven, he had added, "Oh. Sorry, Merry. Fish *urine*."

"Mmm" was all the answer that Cat made to her. He climbed back on the balustrade, extending his hand to her. "Come here, sweeting," he said and pulled her gently between his knees, so that she was leaning heavily into him but facing away, and his hands began a hard, slow massage of her shoulders. "How does that feel?"

"Wonderful," she said, and in a minute he turned her over with her breasts against his thigh and her hair dripping in a dense spill down both sides of the balustrade. Baring her neck, he brought the flat of his palm down to knead her weary muscles.

"So Devon didn't take your maidenhead this afternoon," he said.

"How do you know? How would I know? He might have, for all I know about it. No one tells me anything." Then, curiously, "How do you always know when I want my neck rubbed?"

"You slump." His clever fingers were slowly pulling the tension from her muscles. "You may have noticed that I'm three sheets to the wind and the fourth shaking."

"Yes."

He felt the tightening of her cheek against his hip as she smiled.

"Didn't the others warn you to stay away from me?"

"Yes," she said again. "But I've never seen you intoxicated. I couldn't resist." For a joke she said, "Are you going to assault me?"

Fantastic coral lights shone like buried gems in the mass of her curls, and he pushed his fingers inside one of them and began to stroke her scalp. "It must have been quite an afternoon if you've come back wanting to be assaulted," he observed.

"It was. Cat, have you ever seen a white oak cheese? The painted kind that unscrupulous peddlers will sell instead of real cheese? I bought one on the first occasion that I went by myself to market because the peddler who sold it to me seemed like such a kindly man. When I brought it home, Henry—that was our indentured servant—"

"The one who put the ants in your luggage?"

"Yes! What a good memory you have! Well, Henry said, 'Missy, when you buy cheese from a man, you got to learn to look at the cheese, not the man.' "

"I'll be interested to see how you intend to apply that to Devon," he said.

"Nothing elaborate. I just thought I'd say, do you think Devon would sell me a white oak cheese?"

Six months ago Devon would have sold any woman not only white oak cheeses but wooden nutmegs and oak-leaf cigars as well. Now Cat was not so sure—but that didn't mean the man was no longer dangerous. Cat picked Merry up with a firm grip on her shoulders. Looking straight into her bluebell eyes, he said, "I think that whatever his intentions are, by the time Devon is finished with you, you're going to feel like someone's put your body through a cider press."

She blinked twice against the dying light that was dusting her lashes with pulverized gilt. Then she said simply, "I think so too."

When he let go her shoulders, she tried to sit up beside him, jumping and arching her body backward, and after her second failure Cat grabbed her under the arms and hauled her onto the porch rail by his side. She sat, kicking her legs into the blue ruffled folds of her skirt. "We could talk about *your* problems for a while," she suggested baldly.

"I don't have any problems. Morgan says I just skitter like a newt through everyone else's. . . . I won't be here later, so if we're going to skitter, we had better do it now."

Being ready to talk and being able to do it without crying are two separate things. Glancing sideways at his shadowed face, she wondered how she would be able to put her emotions into words without drenching him with a tear-burst. It was a subject that she could only approach indirectly.

"What . . . what would you think of a woman who fell in love with a man who made her his captive?" she said.

"I'd think she was trying to save her neck," he replied. "If that woman's a friend of yours, you ought to advise her that a love like that doesn't have much of a future."

"She knows that already," Merry said, putting her hands on her knees. "But . . . she's less and less able to do anything about her feelings. And now that it seems as though the man is going to let her go, she can't bear the thought of leaving him." From an orange tree beyond the shaddocks came mockingbird song that filled the pause like tuned bells. "Why do you think this man would be kind to my friend while she was ill and then avoid her afterward?"

The opium had irritated Cat's eyes, and he closed them, wondering briefly how addicts could stand the attendant discomforts of frequent drug use. As the soothing eye fluids did their work he realized that this time he would have to answer her questions. Devon obviously had chosen not to talk about it with her, and Cat was grudgingly forced to concede the wisdom of that. Devon had evidently decided to free her, because unless he had given her reason to so believe, she would not have thought it possible. And he knew Devon would not change his decision unless some terrible act of Providence should intervene that— Cat stopped the thought. Rand Morgan specialized in terrible acts of Providence, and Rand, for some fathomless reason, did not want to see Devon and Merry separated. Protective fear for her rinsed like camphor through Cat's veins, and as he opened his eyes he saw that her hands, clinging to her knees, were beginning to tremble. The boy had to think a moment to recall what her original question had been. Then he said, very carefully, "If the man has some attachment to your friend, it might be difficult for him to let her go. It would be best for both if that attachment wasn't nourished."

In an oddly unmetered voice she asked, "But what if she decided of her own will to stay with him?"

Within the warm envelope of evening air Cat's fingers had become quite cold. That was one offer she must not make to Devon. "And spend the rest of her life as his unprotected dependent?" Pity had roughened his soft tones. "Running after him, nibbling his crumbs, to climb or plummet at every swing of his pitching fancy

like all the others before her? She couldn't wish that for herself—
and if this man feels anything for her, he wouldn't wish that either.''
Suddenly addressing himself no longer to the hypothetical friend, he
said, "God knows, you don't have the temperament to be a whore
of Devon's.''

After an aching moment of silence she said, "Did he tell you
that?''

"Not in those words.''

"But something like that?''

"Something like that,'' he said.

"I suppose,'' she said in a small halting voice, "that marriage is
not in the question?''

Marriage. Cat's mind absorbed the word with a shock. She
wouldn't have bothered to ask if she'd known Devon's full name.
Oh, Christ, what an innocent she was. The Windflower. If there
weren't a thousand other obstacles, Devon's complicated sense of
honor would never permit him to solicit her hand while she was his
prisoner. Affection was only another trap. If he loved her enough to
ask, that love would prevent him from doing it. But all Cat said to
her was, "As things stand, marriage is not in the question.''

Sometime during the course of their talk she had covered her face
with one hand, and spiraling copper-bright tendrils fell from her hairline to invade her fingers and her thumb where they rested on her
brow. Brokenly she said, "If this is the way love feels . . . Is it
always this painful? How do people survive? You can't imagine
what it was like this afternoon—to have him hold me and whisper
love words and kiss me—and then to pull away, laughing and
shivering.''

But Cat could imagine it. The picture of it had haunted him until
he had fogged the images from his mind with opium: Merry, bitterly
hurt and confused, and Devon, worried for her, caught with such
brutality in the web of his own contradictions, and heartsick from it.
What had Morgan expected them to discover in this emotional morass?

"Devon was shivering. How were you?'' he asked.

"I wanted to retch. After, he was so kind and charming—which
only made it worse. If this is love, I hate it.'' She lifted her head,
and the dimming light showed a blue tear on the edge of her nose.
Blotting the tear with a freshly sunburned wrist, she said, "I prom-

ised myself I wasn't going to cry, so I insist you discount that tear." A second tear rolled down to replace its fellow. "That one too." She curled her upper lip into a rueful grin. "This won't happen to me every time I kiss a man, will it?"

"Are we planning to kiss a great many, then?"

"Go teach your granny to suck eggs," she retorted, imitating Raven's drawl, groping for any game that would help her escape the ready tears. She didn't want to cry. Tears, by their very triteness, were a sane and human balm to sorrow, and the wintry emptiness inside her seemed to have little to do with normal mortal processes. She didn't feel as though she'd lost someone dear, or had a severed limb; those things she could have grieved over. This was like having died unborn. The pain was outside and around her, pricking at her skin, her eyelashes, the membranes inside her nose—but within her was only the chilled reflection of a soul that will not acknowledge its own agony. Yet this dull, suspended agony was bad enough. She was in no hurry to feel its full brunt.

A small family of mastiff bats lived beneath the shingles of the roof, and Merry heard the scratch of their small claws on the eaves as one by one they launched themselves swiftly into the air. Oh, to be that free. Thank heaven for Cat, warm and trustworthy at her side, and ready to be teased. She said, "Maybe I will kiss a great many, if I can figure out a way to make them hold still for me."

"Rain comes when the wind calls," he said pleasantly "You won't have any trouble getting males to cooperate. Ask one. You'll be on your back faster than a bee stinging chain lightning.'

"Will *you* kiss me, Cat?" she said and almost could have laughed aloud at his expression. "Just one little tiny kiss?"

"*Christ.*" His eyes had widened slightly, and light speared the glowing filaments of his irises. "I don't give little tiny kisses."

"All right, then. Beggars can't afford to be particular. I'll take what you have. If you argue anymore, you know, I shall be quite cast down. You did tell me that males would cooperate."

"If you think I can kiss Devon off your mind . . ."

"I don't, I don't!" Her shy madonna face warmed into a picture of openhearted, impish mischief. "I just want to compare."

"Brat," he said in soft amusement, lowering himself in an unhurried way from the balustrade. "I'll tell you what. I'll kiss your friend—in the interest of clearing up her confusion."

Merry's heart was hammering as she jumped down with him, though she had begun to grin, and when he turned toward her, she dissolved in an irresistible fit of giggles. Trying to stop them was like trying to push froth into a bottle, and laughter quivered through her voice as she said, "Where do you want her to stand?"

"It would be fine if she stood just where you are," he said.

"And what do you want her to do?"

"Nothing," he said. "I'll do—what has to be done."

"Should she close her eyes?"

"Yes, and her mouth as well." He stepped closer, letting his gaze play lightly over the velvet of her eyebrows and lashes and her lips, with their delicately female satins. Dusk whispered through the shadowy porch, but the last streams of orange sunlight nuzzled her brow, embowed her cheekbones, and drifted in a heart-shaped patch upon her chest that led the eye pleasantly to the soft valley separating her breasts.

She had thought only that he would press a single sportive kiss upon her, so the brush of his hand against her cheek startled open her half-closed eyelids. Cat's head was slightly inclined, and she saw that his gaze had narrowed fractionally. The one upraised hand gently drew away her hair, and his eyes took on a drowsy look as he allowed her fingertip to trail suggestively over the most sensitive folds within her ear. With another man she would have been afraid, but this was Cat, and she knew that in some remote and cerebral way he loved her.

His fingers whispered over her face, seeking and slowly stroking nerve points, knowing where, how long, how much to caress. Her skin gained color under his touch; her eyes became enormous; her throat tightened. By her nose his little finger encountered a forgotten tear. Gathering the sparkling drop, he smeared it slowly over the curve of her lips and blew it gently dry. One hand came lightly to rest on her neck; the other supported her cheek as he sought her with his kiss.

"And now," he breathed, "she has to open her mouth." His thumb began a slow compelling rotation upon the frozen muscles of her jaw. "It's only Cat, Merry. Open for me." Soft kisses of languidly altering pressure wrung acquiescence from her lips, and they parted for his voluptuous pleasuring. Her mouth drank from his the scent of roses, the heady opium imaginings, the promise of sweet erotic riddles unveiled.

When he permitted her lips to leave their silken bondage, she gave him a round-eyed look that would live for months in his dreams. Then she turned to stare out across the fading landscape, and breathing unevenly, he laid careful hands on her waist and buried his face in the fragrant skin on the side of her neck, letting his hair pass in a sigh over her breast. He stood so for a moment, feeling the smooth caress of her pulse, and then he released her completely and went to lean against the porch with his heels crossed.

To Merry it was as though a portal had opened and she had briefly glimpsed his other life. It had been a courtesan's kiss—subtle, airy, tempting beyond reason, and spiced with urgent earthy pleasures. Given enough time, he could probably wring responses from a hearth plaque.

Whether he received any portion of the pleasure he gave was a question that could only have been answered by a person of much wider experience than she. Comparisons were irrelevant. For Devon the act of love had been always a feast of the senses; for Cat it had been, at best, a wearisome duty. In the ensuing silence his fingers discovered and began to caress the bare inner curve of her arm.

Merry slapped his hand away. "You've already made your point. Don't become obnoxious. I know when I've been taught a lesson."

"Including, one hopes, not to be so blithe in offering your lips to all comers?" he suggested sweetly. "But what did your friend think?"

"You know very well what she thought," Merry said firmly. "And don't try to pretend you don't. You nearly burned off her hair ribbons. Now I—no, I mean, she wants to know what comes next."

"Well, I'm not going to show you *that*. You must have formed an idea."

"Of course I have. But goodness, what if the full truth is a shock to me? What if I emerged half-crazed from my marriage bed?"

"That," he said in a dry tone, "would be highly unlikely." Then, with resignation, "Oh, all right. I don't suppose it will harm you any."

There are probably not many people who are introduced to the facts of life by a lecture beginning: "Now, look—and pay attention, will you—I don't want to go over this a dozen times. Furthermore, if you don't like what I tell you, don't squeak and fuss at me. I didn't design the world."

It should not be thought, either, that his vocabulary for such things was the same as hers, and after several shocking experiments she said, "Cat, please, do you have to use *those* words?" With opiated patience he asked her what words she preferred, and when she told him—hesitantly—he grimaced and said, "What the devil kind of words are those for a grown women to use about her body? Merry, infants give up that kind of talk with their third birthday." There followed a brisk exchange in which both parties dispelled the tension that had arisen between them by casting aspersions on the maturity, and indeed, good taste of the other. Merry had gotten much closer to being able to give tit for tat, but Cat could still get the best of her when he really chose to. Only the suspicion that she might not find him so forthcoming with this particular line of information in some future, more sober moment kept Merry from marching, in high dudgeon, from the porch. In the end they compromised on the clinical, and though Cat was wont to give a certain acid emphasis to words he considered unnecessarily euphemistic, his explanation was thorough, detailed, and dealt with variations. After he had dealt satisfactorily with all the points raised by her challenging questions, Merry was so much enlightened that Cat, holding his erstwhile pupil in a gently sardonic gaze, was perforce to say, "There now. With what you know, you'll be able to send your husband from your marriage bed—half-crazed."

Merry's spirits were hardly elevated by an evening spent alone in her bedroom reading *English Hermit; or the Unparalleled Sufferings and Surprising Adventures of Phillip Quaril, an Englishman, Who Was Discovered upon an Uninhabited Island in the South Sea, Where He Had Lived About Fifty Years Without Human Assistance.* The *Joke* had returned from a successful hunt; someone had brought a skiff-load of women from one of the other islands, and everyone, even Annie (with apologies), had gone to the beach to drink, to dance, to talk. It was by Devon's order that Merry was not permitted to attend, as she heard third hand from Raven (also with apologies). The party was likely to get rough, and besides, a British man-of-war had arrived, and there were two officers aboard who were to meet with Devon on the beach, and he didn't want them to see Merry. Something, Raven said, to do with safeguarding her reputation. . . .

Merry retired quite late. She was sitting on the bed braiding her hair by the light of one candle when she heard footsteps on the greenheart floor beyond her door. Only she and one middle-aged serving maid had remained at the villa, and after hours of listening to the hollow silence of the empty halls, the steadily approaching footfalls had an eerie resonance. Worse than eerie came a moment later, when the footsteps halted outside her door and then Rand Morgan entered without knocking. Under the best of circumstances he was a frightening man. At midnight in a nearly deserted house Morgan was the living embodiment of any maiden's worst fears. Deeply gasping, Merry dragged the bedclothes over her nightgown and exclaimed, "Oh, no!"

Her words hung awkwardly in the unsettled air, sounding—she realized sheepishly—a little foolish. Morgan's dark brow had ascended in amused incredulity, and he had fixed her in a humorous regard that was decidedly unflattering.

"My poor girl, can it be that you think I might be contemplating some impropriety?" he said, managing to convey neatly by his tone that she was overrating her adolescent attractions.

Cherry-spot blushes burned her cheekbones as she stammered a disclaimer. Taking no notice of her stumbling phrases, he said, "Put on your clothes. I'll wait for you in the main hall."

He closed the door and left her before the command had fully made its imprint on her will. Abstract visions of accident and illness rose before her. Annie? Raven? *Devon?* Morgan had not gone four steps down the hall when she appeared at the doorway, calling in an anxious voice, "What's happened?"

"What a runaway imagination you have, nestling. Nothing's happened."

"But then why—"

"I," said Rand Morgan, "do not enjoy having my orders questioned, and particularly not by vain and clumsily timorous children. I can see through your nightdress, and if you don't change it immediately, I shall be left with no choice but to believe that situation pleases you."

In a thrice she was behind her door again, remembering glumly that Saunders said of Rand Morgan: "You obey his first order, or he carves his second one on your liver."

All her clothing was borrowed from Annie, and Merry slipped quickly into the sky-dyed gown she had worn at sunset. The fabric was a fine crepe, but the color was too bold to be fashionable by European standards. Merry had a flitting recollection of telling Annie a few days ago that it was a great shame that the designers had lately been confining women to pastels when the more intense colors were so enlivening. However, it was a not much enlivened Merry Wilding who met Rand Morgan in the main hall. His black gaze flickered over her, and then he began to walk to the door, commanding her to follow with an economical hand gesture.

It might be pushing her luck, but as they were walking together down the porch steps Merry couldn't help saying, "I hardly think a person should be said to have a runaway imagination because they merely inquire why they are being commanded from their beds at midnight."

"Ah," said Morgan. "Did that rankle?" Subjecting her quickly combed hair to a critical survey, he added, "I take back the word *vain*."

He watched with a hidden smile as she tried surreptitiously to further order her wayward curls, and said nothing more until they came to the edge of the wooded path and she hung back uncertainly.

"I do hate to use unnecessary force on women," he murmured.

Merry was physically, mentally, and emotionally exhausted, and on top of that Morgan was frightening her. And he had the unmitigated gall to make her feel embarrassed about it. Losing her temper and her good sense along with it, she went stomping down the path with her hands raised sarcastically in the air like a prisoner of war. Large cruel hands closed over her shoulders, and Merry was dragged very nearly by the scruff of her neck back to face Morgan's great height. With her chin in the harsh pinch of his thumb and forefinger, he said in a level tone, "Before you were born, little chick, I had raped more women than there are teeth in your hair comb. I admire spirit and character in the young of both sexes, but that doesn't mean I'm willing to tolerate a lot of snubbed-nose impudence from a chit your age. Mind yourself."

It was surely his casual mention of his crimes against women that made Merry furious enough to ask hotly, "Or what? Will you mistreat me until you've driven me to opium the way you have Cat?"

There was a flashing second afterward when she thought, *Dear Lord, what have I said? He's likely to kill me!* His jet gaze ate the details of her face with an arrested curiosity, and then, to her bewilderment, he began to laugh softly.

"Now, that's how a lady should fight, nestling. With her tongue. Lose your temper with a man, little Merry, but not your dignity."

After giving her underlip a gentle tug he let her go, and she walked beside him on the path, although it was a good many yards before her wobbling knees recovered. Moonlight picked out scenic details with metallic brilliance: the feathery head of a palm tree, colossal stems of bamboo that nodded like reeds, and the glinting reflections as the night breeze turned over leaves on the tall mahoganies above their heads. Within the deep-blue cloak of the heavens the crescent moon lay on its back like a ghostly grin. Bats marred the lunar surface as tiny flecks; much lower came the dim, crooked flight of nightjars, and in the pastures here and there one could just make out the forms of slumbering beasts. Geckos whistled like penny trumpets, and the humid air buzzed with the song of numberless tree frogs. Rand Morgan's thoughts drifted to another time, another climate—far crisper than these balmy tropics—and another girl, younger than this one. . . .

With the sweetness of a dream the snowy clouds of English hawthorn had sobbed scent around them as they ran hand in thirteen-year-old hand down the hillside over a tender carpet of spring grass. The wind caught her thin hair ribbons and billowed her pink dimity skirt, and when he had stopped to gather her for his kiss, she had looked up at him and whispered, "*Pleasth*, Rand. Be gentle." And God, how gentle it had been. He was so enchanted with her that nearly two weeks had gone by before he told her in a moment's irritation because she'd restricted the free use of his hands that she might as well act like a baby if she was going to lisp like one. Innocent honest eyes of periwinkle blue had smiled at him as she said, "Don't you like it, then? Oh, Rand, I'm glad. My other beaux admire it so, and I grow weary of always having to lisp!"

Through that dying vision Morgan saw Merry Wilding walking with her delicate steps through a Caribbean night; Merry who was slimmer than that other girl and more fragile, with a fraction of the self-confidence. But that infusion of vigorous American blood had given Merry a nimble intellect, a gallantry lacking in the frivolous and delectable creature her mother had been. With that thought Morgan felt the playful chide of that ever-present spirit: *"Take care of my daughter, Rand."* I will, love. I will. . . .

"Did you really cut the emerald you wear from the stomach of a priest?" came Merry's voice, pulling Morgan back.

"A defrocked priest, my dear," Morgan answered. "He had stolen the jewel from a rectory in Barcelona. Being not an especially quick-witted gentleman, he pretended to swallow the stone when we took his ship. I slit the emerald from the front of his cossack." For Merry the question had been the equivalent of putting one toe in a hip bath to test the water. She hardly knew more about Morgan now than she had on the first day on the *Joke*. He was not a man who encouraged familiarity, and the loosest of his crew generally exercised discretion when they gossiped about him. The awe inspired by the legend of Rand Morgan had remained fresh in her mind. Until tonight he had never appeared to take much notice of her, for which she had been devoutly grateful, while recognizing that he seemed to know a great deal about things he appeared not to notice. "Are we going to the beach? Did Devon change his mind about wanting me to be there?" she asked.

"Yes. No."

"Do you mean that you're taking me to the beach even though Devon doesn't want me there?"

"Yes."

Merry swallowed a tight lump in her throat. "Would you take it as evidence of character and not of impudence if I were to ask you why you're doing this?"

Morgan's only answer was a humorless chuckle. Often when she was with him, she had to fight being overwhelmed by the sensation that she only was as high as his waist. The illusion of being dwarfed hung upon her persistently as she helplessly whispered, "Why?"

"Because, nestling, Devon is about to pierce one of your little mysteries—"

"W-what?"

"—and it would be best if you were there," Morgan said calmly. "It suits my plans better if Devon isn't aware that I troubled to bring you, so I'm going to tell him you were hiding and watching the party wistfully from the bushes and I—"

"*What!*"

"—merely invited you to join things. You are free to dispute it, of course, but I'm sure you recognize that, given the discrepancy in our experience, I can be more convincing in a lie than you can in the truth. As always, you have the option of carrying your troubles to Raven, but I'm convinced you will have the good judgment not to, because you must be as loath as I am to have that boy's infatuation for you lead him into any more problems than it has already."

Merry had stumbled to a halt. Morgan's hand, inexorable on the small of her back, began to push her forward again. From the beach she was beginning to hear the noises of adults at play—laughter, music, loud conversation mixed with the bass of the surf.

"You could also run from me," Morgan continued in a low tone. "If you do that, I shall catch you and do some exceedingly unpleasant things to your pretty body that don't leave any marks, so my advice is— I beg your pardon?"

"I said: Oh, help," Merry whispered.

"You," said Rand Morgan, "have gotten yourself into a uniquely complicated situation and you will have to get yourself out of it. What I'm providing is the opportunity. Has Devon told you why he hates Granville? I see not. Very well. It's time you know that Michael Granville murdered Devon's sister."

And with those words the pirate captain pushed her firmly with him onto the beach.

CHAPTER TWENTY-TWO

The boisterous gaiety on the beach detonated within Merry's senses, and shock waves arrived as tremors on the surface of her skin. Beyond, at the quay, the *Black Joke* was lying to within shouting distance of the British frigate, and the shore fires made the upper reaches of the masts appear and disappear like ghostly sentinels. On the shore a bonfire in a ditch spat smoke and cinders as juice from a spitted pork carcass sizzled down into hungry flames that leapt in blue fancies at the nourishment. Glaring firelight threw the relaxed, inebriated faces of the revelers into deep shadows, and they seemed to be wearing fantastic tragicomic masks as they raised rum bottles and a wineskin that heaved like a living thing from the stress of rapid depletion. Dark eyes gleamed in bearded faces; white teeth shone as they tore into hand-held chunks of roasted meat. The ship's orchestra labored near the fire in a welter of smoke haze and the spicy scents of liquor and roasted pig. Merry knew the men well—the giant Turk in a turban who played something that looked like an oboe, Max Reade on the harmonica, Terence Teaswell gleefully clanging a mismatched pair of cymbals, and coaxing lilting strains from the violin, the man they called One-eyed Jack, who wore no patch over his empty eye socket. An odd miscellany of talent, and yet they produced the sweetest ballads and the liveliest dance tunes on the Atlantic seaboard. The voices of the revelers were now lifted in shouting song, a wild pirate song that started low and ended high, with stops and starts in between, the orchestra clashing, whining, tooting, and whistling like some illegitimate mating of a Scottish pipe band and a harem orchestra.

The women were strangers to Merry. Most, like the men, had bared their chests. Twitching patterns from the flames shone on their wine-ripe, sweating flesh, and their gaily colored skirts swept up dry sand in time with the music. There was hardly a soul clothed enough for Merry to look upon without a mortified flush, and yet she found a naïve exuberance in the sea of warm, unclad bodies, as though they were spirited children who had tossed off their clothing to frolic in a summer shower.

Merry stood with Morgan among the fallen fronds at the base of a palm tree. She was dimly aware that the tall pirate was giving her this moment to assimilate the catastrophic thing he had made known to her. But she didn't seem able to do that. Her love for Devon had become the most earnest and immediate force in her life. Sensation, when it came directly from Devon, howled like a cyclone into her consciousness; but the tragedies attendant on that love arrived drop by drop, an endless caustic trickle. Merry tried to imagine a woman made of Devon's flesh, a sister, but she could not. Merry tried to remember Michael Granville's face; she could not do that either. They were like cloud pictures to her, distant specters; and yet she knew that hidden inside the opaque folds of time there was a murdered girl with light hair and golden eyes who deserved her pity. Morgan's warning was delivered with a purposeful intent that could never belong to a facile lie. And Merry had known from the day Cat carried her aboard the *Joke* that Devon's hatred of Michael Granville existed on a plane beyond reason. Grief for him and for his submerged pain burned her to the soul, and with it came a gripping fear.

As she might have seen stars blink one after another into a purple evening sky, Merry began unconsciously to identify her friends.

She heard Cook before she saw him. He was sitting on a canework mat with his freckled forehead pressed to Annie's. His fawn curls bobbed against Annie's black hair as he fed her pieces torn from a fragrant hunk of pork, stopping to kiss her lingeringly between each. The hand not employed in feeding Annie was fending off Dennis the pig, who was showing an unseemly interest in sharing their meal.

"Jeez, you disgusting porker," Cook was saying. "It's a bloody cannibal you are. This could be kin of yours, for all you know.

Jeez!" He grabbed up the rum bottle that Dennis had overturned and started to guzzle. "Someone ought to make you into a Christian."

Merry saw Devon on a firm grassy rise, reclining with the golden grace of a demigod, his perfectly cut shoulders against a log. A crystal goblet from Morgan's fine set, half-filled with wine, rested on the ground by his hip. With a softly creased smile he was talking to two British Marine officers. The scarlet military coats stood out like cardinals in a winter garden and drew Merry's attention to the men who wore them. One man, sprawled comfortably upon a dark boulder, had a wide clownish mouth set between waggling jowls. His tall crowned hat was askew, and he had unfastened his belt to give free rein to his girth. The other man appeared to be painfully ill at ease in this piratical company; he looked as though he would rather be anywhere else in the world as he sat ramrod straight on a rock, occasionally running a thin hand nervously through his sandy hair.

Higher on the shore a mammoth silk-cotton tree dripped lianas like many ropes from its wide branches. The boy beneath was three-quarters turned from Merry, but there was no disguising the long ivory braid or the gleam of a gold hoop on his hollowed cheek. A young woman straddled the thigh he had braced against the tree behind her, and with her eyes closed and her brunette hair streaming over her naked shoulders, she rode him with her hips, straining into the palm that was skillfully handling her breast, tilting her head to permit his slow caress of her throat.

Some of the men had begun to notice Merry. Eric Shay saw her and followed the direction of her shamed gaze. Cursing under his breath, he stomped over to Cat, and as Merry watched, Shay cuffed Cat on the shoulder, speaking gruffly in a distant pantomime. Cat swung immediately. Briefly he met the urgent appeal in her eyes and then transferred his gaze to Morgan, and the boy's expression deepened to pure anger.

But Dennis had spotted Merry and with porcine enthusiasm began trying to scrabble up her legs and into her arms, depositing gritty hock prints on her borrowed gown. Others began to turn, to salute Morgan with huzzahs and raised bottles, to call bleary affectionate greetings to Merry. Many had not seen her since her illness, and she was quickly drawn into a loose circle to be teased and petted and admired. She began automatically to respond; trying to find comfort in a fondness that she knew would never lead them to protect her from Rand Morgan or from Devon.

Annie, who had taken less to drink than the others, saw the trouble in Merry's face and tried with friendly anxiety to find out what the matter was. Realizing that Merry's sign language was too limited for a clear explanation and frustrated by her inability to communicate with Merry, Annie tugged on Cook's sleeve and signed to him that Merry was not happy. Inebriated and amorous, the last thing that Cook wanted was to be presented with one of Merry's insoluble problems. Annie had to pick his hands out of her bodice three times before, with an irritable groan, Cook asked Will Saunders to find Raven and see if he couldn't bring up a smile on Merry. Saunders, in a kindly mood, left off his drinking to fetch Raven, who was trying to bury himself in the sand with a young woman wearing four strands of pearls around her waist. Saunders dragged the protesting boy over, knocking the sand off him as he came. When Raven saw who he had been summoned to entertain, he enveloped her in a hug and made her the focus of his sweet besotted attentions until the young woman with the pearls removed one of the strands and tossed it over Raven's shoulders before she ran off toward the sea, laughing, calling Raven's name in soft invitation, flinging away her clothes as her bare feet flew over the damp sand.

With an amiable grin Raven ran after her, making the parting comment that with as much rum as that girl had in her, he had better go along and see that something didn't happen to her.

"You mean," Saunders called to him, "to make sure something *does* happen to her." Shifting his gaze back to Merry, Will Saunders bent slightly at the knees, laid his hands flat on his long muscled thighs, and leaned forward to look into her face. "Tell me about it, Merry lamb. What's made you so cast down? Has Devon been blowing hot and cold on you again?"

"Will, Morgan told me that something—"

"Hey!" Cook said, wiping his mouth on the wad of his discarded shirt. "Devon's right up there talking to that Captain Airmouth—"

"Eremuth. Captain Eremuth," Saunders corrected.

"Aye, well, and isn't that what I said? Christsake. Why don't you play cupid, Will?"

Will Saunders caught Merry before she had time to understand what he intended, and as he hefted her over his shoulder he said laughingly, "Up with you, sweetheart. And struggle a little, because we don't want him thinking you're too eager for him. We'll put you where you want to be."

"Will! Are you taking me to Devon? Will, no! No!"

"Why, darlin', you're almost an actress," Saunders said. And in a moment he murmured something to Devon, dropped her at his side, and quickly left.

Merry felt Devon enfold her in his arms, the clasp light, protective, calming. He must have been able to feel the coldness of her limbs, the trembling tension in her muscles. She sought his eyes, and in their wine-hazed golden depths she sensed the inquiring frown that wasn't showing on his face. *Why have you come, Merry? Why are you afraid?*

Nothing had changed. Whatever Morgan thought was going to happen had not occurred yet, or she would surely have been able to feel the difference in Devon. She couldn't even tell that he was angry, though he must be, for all that he was disguising it. Morgan, with an urbane mask covering his saturnine features, was sitting on the other side of Devon and by now would have had ample time to imply to Devon that she had come here of her free will in defiance of Devon's express orders. So Devon must have been angry, though his gaze was only plowing her steadily, as though to unearth the roots of her distrust. Behind her the fat British officer began to chuckle.

"Ah, Devon, Devon," said the man. "Never without the amenities. By Jove, what a queenly creature! No wonder you missed your meeting last month in Bermuda. Couldn't pull yourself off the saddle, eh? She's a highflier. I never have seen such hair."

On the *Joke* being Devon's supposed mistress gave her an elevated status. With men from Devon's own class the case was otherwise. Clearly this was what Devon had wished to spare her when he had forbidden her presence. Of course she should have known that her association, even involuntary, with the *Black Joke* would bring her virtue into disrepute among men and women of convention, and yet in the disordered course of things she had not quite realized until this moment how lowly that would be or what feelings of anguish and humiliation it would cause her. To deny that she was what these arrogant Britons thought would, of course, be stupid. Only danger could come from prompting these men to look into her past.

Merry saw Cat appear from the shadows to join Eric Shay and Joe Griffith, who were dicing just within earshot. Looking clean and pale in the firelight, Cat dropped lightly to his knees beside Shay, speaking to him in a quiet voice that did not carry beyond, and in a moment began to dice with them. The light-blue eyes never turned toward Merry where she sat huddled wretchedly by Devon, feeling branded and debased, the greater part of her awareness tied to Devon's hands, their slow movement dispensing compassion and understanding at her back.

"I believe, Prufrock," said Morgan, addressing himself to the fat officer, "that before the interruption we were about to delve into this great invasion fleet that England is sending to trounce her rebellious former colonies in the United States?"

The shock that passed through her body was severe. She knew that Devon, close as he was to her, must have felt it before she was able to control it.

Prufrock took a noisy swallow of wine. "And about time too! We've a mind to teach those American rapscallions that war is not to be declared against Great Britain with impunity. They're going to get the drubbing they've been asking for since June of 1812. Now that we've got Bonaparte out of the way, we can afford to put more of our eggs in the American basket. By the time the fleet arrives from Bordeaux to join the Marines and the naval units we have based in Bermuda, we'll have twenty thousand troops ready to launch an attack on New York."

"New York, is it now?" said Devon. "The last I heard, you had your hopes pinned on beginning in the Chesapeake Bay. Who told you there would be twenty thousand troops? Our enshrined commander Vice Admiral Cochrane? He'll never get twenty thousand, and you can tell him I said so. They'll need most of the Army in France to keep order and men in Flanders besides; and Prevost has been begging London to reinforce his position in Canada. They won't be able to put him off any longer. You'll be lucky if you see four thousand men from Europe."

"Pessimist!" Prufrock said good-naturedly. "Do you forget the light artillery?"

"No," Devon said, "but you should. Wellington will never let it leave Europe."

Eremuth, who had taken no part in the conversation, leaned suddenly forward and addressed himself earnestly to Devon. "If you would only come back with us to Bermuda. I know you won't take a commission, but if you would stay there and organize the intelligence as Cochrane wants you to . . . instead of merely reporting to him. Devon, Cochrane listens to you."

"Not well enough," Devon said, casually pressing his wineglass to Merry's frigid, trembling lips. He waited until she had choked down the swallow of amber fluid, watching her intently before he looked back toward Eremuth and said, "Now that General Ross has been appointed to head the troops, Cochrane can listen to Ross. Together they can march the Invincibles through the trackless wastes of America dropping from heat and disease until someone at Whitehall has the mettle to sign a peace treaty."

"My boy, you don't know the mood back home," said Prufrock. "Chastise the savages! says the *Times*. . . ."

Merry, staring fixedly at the longboat approaching the shore from the British frigate, was finally able to block out the voices around her. *Invasion! Invasion* . . . The word roared again and again in her mind with the force of exploding rock. This might have been a scene from the fantasy heroics of her childhood: *Merry Patricia Wilding Overhears a Most Dangerous Plot to Attack Her Nation and Swiftly Warns Washington!* How fertilely her imagination would have overcome all obstacles, contriving the message in a bottle that would float to the Potomac and be washed up miraculously at President Madison's feet, or her black-of-the-night escape from St. Elise, desperately paddling in Devon's canoe. Anger about these British plans would have been mixed with bold excitement if life had not already taught the hard lesson that it was nearly impossible to escape from a ruthless and experienced man when one was eighteen years old, with few survival skills, no money, and an open ocean to cross. Devon had planned to let her go. Could he with what she knew now?

A sympathetic finger gently tilted her chin. Again she met Devon's

questing gaze. Inches separated their faces; his head was slightly to
one side, so that only a bare movement from either would have
brought their lips together. Foolishly she felt a hollow, aching need
for him rise within her, as though her femininity were a painfully
opening bud thirsting for his flowing sunlight. Cat had not been so
poetic. When you love a man, he had said, you'll want him to be
inside you, Merry. Naturally she had denied it hotly, but later, alone
in her bedroom, staring without seeing at the calfskin cover of
English Hermit, she had said aloud, "It's true, it's true." To see
Devon's long-boned hand curved upon the goblet, his thumb rubbing
unthinkingly over the smooth glass, was to long for that light caress
to be transferred to the taut skin of her neck. Studying the firm
sensual curl of his mouth made her burn to thread her fingers into his
golden hair and pull his head slowly to her breasts, to lie under him
until his lips and tongue drove her to red, writhing madness. Desire,
Merry had discovered, was a strange spirit; compelling, apt to
appear at inconvenient moments, and not particularly responsive to
common sense. And though she was warmed by Devon's obvious
support of a peace between the United States and Great Britain,
there was no doubt he played an important role in the British
military, for all that it was difficult to tell exactly what that might
be: as spy, writer of reports, or advisor to that man so hated in her
country, Vice Admiral Sir Alexander Cochrane. *That* was power.
How could he possibly release her after the things she had just
heard?

Prufrock spoke. Devon turned to answer. On the shoreline Merry
could see the British longboat land and put out a boy who carried a
leather document pouch. The gilt buttons and excessive gold lace on
his red coat marked him as a rich man's son; straight-shouldered and
immaculate in his carefully pressed uniform, the boy sighted the
British officers beside Devon on the rise and began to make his way
toward them through the drunken pirates, with a certain terrified
bravado that was mixed with large parts of awe and envy. When he
had come close enough, Merry saw him stare with the worship due a
hero at Devon before he saluted and handed the leather pouch to
Eremuth and then stood at a respectful distance with his eyes forward,
his hands behind his back.

"I mentioned earlier that I had something I needed to show you," Eremuth commented, opening the pouch's thong bindings.

"Bills advertising for my capture, didn't you say?" Morgan asked blandly.

In front of Merry's eyes the world froze, remained that way for a silent moment, and then leaped into a wild somersault. Morgan's black gaze whipped her face and then returned with an interested smile to Eremuth, who was speaking.

". . . we decided that it would be best if you saw them yourself, Devon. What makes these bills different is not only that they are illustrated, but that they are done so with enormous skill. Furthermore, there are likenesses of others on the *Black Joke* as well as of Rand Morgan. And of three of our most effective agents in the Washington area. Yes! You may well look surprised. In fact, we were astonished. But, frankly, what disturbed us most was to find your portrait in the group, Devon. I can hardly convey the degree of alarm we felt when we realized that you were operating in the United States with such a risk of exposure! If you had been seen by anyone familiar with the poster, they would have hanged you and asked questions later. Well, that's neither here nor there," he said, handing the sheaf of papers to Morgan. "It was only good fortune that we were able to put our hands on them. A loyalist assistant in the printer's office notified our people, and the bills were ultimately smuggled into Canada. . . . Well, Captain Morgan, what do you think?"

"But they're charming," Morgan said. "Here's one I find particularly taking." He read, "Pirate known as Cat. Wanted for piracy, brigandage, kidnapping, rapine, and mayhem. Fifty dollars reward."

Merry's insides were a house of cards, falling, falling as Cat got up and strolled toward Morgan.

Malevolently grinning, Morgan read on, "Age seventeen, eighteen, or thereabouts. Tall. Slender build. Very pale. Well-favored." Morgan handed the sheet to Cat. "They certainly want a lot for fifty dollars."

It was impossible to guess what Cat was thinking as he studied the paper, gave it back to Morgan, and said, "It's nice to be wanted."

"Have you noted the style of the artist? Highly distinctive, wouldn't you say? One would know it immediately if one ever saw it on another occasion.'' Eremuth transferred the pages to Devon, saying, "What do you think?"

Perhaps there had been some clue for Devon in Morgan's grin or in Cat's expressionless assessment. Perhaps as Devon withdrew his hands from her and slowly sat up he knew already. The long shapely hands received the drawings. Golden eyes skimmed over the pictures as he quickly studied one after another, taking no greater interest in his own portrait than in the others. They were distinctive, as the British officer had said. Trapped between Devon's fingers as alike and yet as individual as a row of apples were face after face from Merry's unmistakable hand. There, minimally altered by the careful printing process, Merry saw her own firm varied pencil strokes, her distinctive cross-hatching, her reed pen detailing. They might well have carried her signature. The only surprise for Merry, seeing the pictures after so long an interval, was how childish and inaccurate had been her insights. She had made Morgan humorlessly satanic, devoid of the more suave menaces. Cat's sketch was of a youthful Norse raider who was incapable of conceding to his softer impulses. And Devon—she couldn't then, nor could she now capture that natural wealth of perfect male contours and radiant flesh hues that hid a unique and complex character.

Merry's heart had begun a double-headed beat, an intense *ba-bang, ba-bang* that reverberated through her lungs. Though her skin surfaces were numb, she knew that she must have lost color. She felt Cat's gaze as a firm and sustaining grip as she heard Prufrock say, "Our artist is obviously an older man. Extensive training, I should guess, probably in Italy. Talented fellow. Pity. We've orders to short-cut his career.''

"Kill him, do we mean?" questioned Morgan in an emotionless tone.

"Regrettably," Eremuth assented unhappily. "If the artist was less talented, if the subjects were chosen with less discretion, then we could afford to be merciful." Addressing himself to Devon, he said, "As you've pointed out so aptly in your reports, our intelligence network is poor. You, I believe, used a stronger word. Since so many on the *Black Joke* were subjects, we had hopes that you would have some idea who might have done them. Could you put your hands on the artist?"

A warm wind sucked the cold sweat beads on her palms and licked at her bodice, cupping the fabric into her breasts and midriff. Wisps of hair irritated her temples. Acid fluids ate the surface of her eyes. Time moved heavily, the seconds rising to collapse awkwardly, like a warped cartwheel. Her self-control was stretched to its ultimate limit before Devon stood in an even flood of motion.

"I'll take care of it," he said.

" 'Pon my word, lad," insisted Prufrock. "Your orders to return to England come directly from Whitehall. No one intends you to trouble yourself in the matter. If you'll but give us a name—"

Devon slapped the papers into Eremuth's open hand. "Have I indicated that I'd relish an extended debate? Leave this to me."

Heaving himself to his feet, clapping speckles of sand from his clothing, Prufrock said good-humoredly, "If that's how you'll have it, then. As far as debating goes, you're the last soul alive I'd have one with. Likely I'd end up with my brain bent in more knots than a Chinese puzzle. You were always too clever for me by half, and well you know it."

The pulse in Merry's ears had become so loud that she could hardly follow their final exchanges and the round of amiable pleasantries and expressions of good will that passed between the men. Prufrock began to amble toward the longboat, the brightly uniformed British boy at his side. Eremuth would have followed, but Devon halted him with a gesture. When Prufrock was too far down the beach to hear him, Devon said, "Were you able to find out for me if Granville sponsored a girl to travel with him on the *Guinevere*?"

"Yes." Eremuth's hand raked his sandy hair and settled on his hat. "I'm afraid I have precious little information about her, however. It was difficult to discover anything without drawing attention to the inquiry, and you had specifically requested that I exercise extreme discretion."

"I appreciate that, Richard," Devon said. "Thank you. What did you learn?"

"You were correct. Granville did sponsor a girl named Merry to sail on the *Guinevere*. I couldn't find out her family name, but one of the clerks recollected that her New York address was given to be the same as Granville's. It seems that— Devon! I can see this is not welcome news to you. I'm sorry."

"It's of no moment. Please go on. It seems that?"

"It seems that the young woman was a *chère amie* of Granville's," Captain Eremuth said frankly.

"How do you know?"

Eremuth's dark-red flush became evident even in the sparse light. "There was some comment among the dockhands on the evening the young woman boarded the *Guinevere*. A rare piece of goods, I believe, was the assessment quoted me, though apparently her countenance bespoke the innocent. Anyway, Granville was quite friendly with a few of these dockmen, so that later when he came to board, they were able to induce him to confide his connection with the girl."

"Richard. Be blunt."

"Bluntly then." Eremuth's blush spread to his hairline. "Granville told them that appearing the innocent was the girl's most highly developed accomplishment save for—for—" He glanced at Merry. "Devon, there's a jest involved that I would be loath to repeat in front of any young female, regardless of her status."

Slipping an affectionate arm around Eremuth's stiff shoulders, Devon began to walk with him toward the beach. During the whole course of their conversation he had not once looked at Merry. The strains of his voice, detached and cheerful, streamed back to her on the night breeze: "Heavenly days then, let's get out of mixed company so you can tell me about it. . . ."

Everything she saw dissolved before Merry like a melting waxwork. For some time she felt and saw nothing. When her senses awoke again, it was to the tough security of Cat's arms. His words were a soft streak of sound to her ears.

"Merry, listen! Don't fight me, Merry. I want you to come with me. Quickly! Merry, can you hear me?"

"Yes. I— Cat!" Long bleeding scratches were dark runners on his forearms. Staring at them confusedly, she asked, "Did I do that?"

"My fault. I put my hands on you too quickly," he said, dragging her to her feet. "Come now."

Her body seemed unable to obey his dictates. She hung back, trying to sharpen the hazy images in her brain. "How long have I— How long has Devon been gone?"

"A few minutes. Christ. Your skin is as cold as a hatchet. Merry, you've got to let me get you away from here before—''

"Before Devon comes back?"

Moving silently, Devon stepped from blank shadow into the smoky edges of the firelight. His strikingly perfect features were relaxed, his stance as easy as his voice had been. He was even smiling, a faintly sugared curve of the lips that made his eyes shine like warm, glittering crystals. Merry had almost forgotten that smile. She had not seen it since the morning after she had accidentally destroyed Michael Granville's letters in her first attempt to escape. His face might as well have been a beautiful mask, with the soul stripped from it. There was no limit to the price Merry would have paid in this world or the next to be able to obliterate the sleeping damnation from his gaze.

Cat said, "She's tired. I want to take her—''

"If you have that inclination," Devon said, his tone serene, "then you're welcome to take her after I have."

In the loaded silence Merry felt her slamming heart labor, shuddering like a dry bellows. Her fingers found and tightened on Cat's arm. Devon still had not looked directly at her.

"*Look.*" Cat's voice had studied hues of cool derision. "If the question is whether or not you're going to dismember her, it seems to me that—''

Devon interrupted. "The question *isn't* whether or not I'm going to dismember her. The question is merely into how many pieces."

"Would you let me finish a blasted sentence?" Cat asked. "For the world's greatest disciple of eternal moderation you're making quite a display. I realize you've known more and cleverer hypocrites than I have, but on the slight chance that, God forbid, you might be wrong, why don't you think about this overnight? There's time enough in the morning if you want to be a bastard."

Finally Merry felt the brutal attack of Devon's brilliant eyes as they found and held hers. Slowly he walked forward until they were so close that she absorbed the heat from his body. His gaze held her numbly silent as he brought a hand to her throat, closing with elaborate gentleness upon the fragile cords, the frightened, pulsing fibers. Experienced fingers discovered and lay, barely pressing, against the nerves and arteries that carried her life.

Cat knocked Devon's hand away from her with a fist. "Oh, stop it, will you, you bloody viper?" Cat said with grinding anger. "What will that prove?"

"I thought you wanted me to demonstrate moderation," Devon said softly. "Why do you worry? She's got more defenses than a wolf bitch."

"How pleased you must be," Cat said. "What a bloody relief. Just when you were running out of room to move, you've found a reason not to admit you love her."

Close as she was to Devon, Merry saw the spare widening of his eyes, the snapped breath, the startled tightening of his lips as the shaft went home. Emotion sprang like a sea wave in his eyes and then vanished entirely.

"Oh, my . . ." Laughter stirred in Devon's eyes above the fury. "Drag out the siege engine. We're getting lethal. Is it love that makes me want her? Have I been in love with all the others, then?"

"Bless my soul," Cat said scathingly. "What's changed? Only a while ago you told me she was more."

"More irritation. More trouble. And bloody less satisfaction. I want to talk to her. After that you can do what you like with the remains." Devon glanced to the side, where Morgan reclined non-committally on a boulder. "Call him off, Rand."

Obediently Morgan said, "Cat." Then, after the single word engendered no response, "That's enough, babe. Come here."

Cat turned to Morgan with a lazy grace that was almost feline, his braid twitching as though it had life. In a voice that prickled Merry's nape hair, Cat said, "You're part of my universe, Rand. Not the center of it."

Amusement minced lightly through the occult blackness of Morgan's eyes. "There's a trick to this, my pretty ones. One must learn to court sentiment delicately. The pair of you fuck it to death." The small German pistol cupped in his hand seemed to have appeared there by some deadly sorcery. The barrel was aimed at Merry. "I'll make this much easier. If one of you doesn't back away quickly from that girl, I'm going to put a bullet in her." Morgan cocked the pistol. To Merry he said very gently, "Stand still, my dear. We'll try not to make this fatal."

Both men knew Morgan would pull the trigger if one of them

didn't concede, but it was Cat who moved swiftly backward, putting ten feet between himself and Merry before Morgan finished speaking. There Cat stopped, breathing deeply to keep his voice under control.

"If we're going to play Wisdom of Solomon," he snapped, "someone ought to remind the potentate that according to the biblical corollary, I should win."

"We have a new version," Morgan said. "The winner is the one who wants the girl even with a bullet in her."

She heard the rustle of blood on its vein-passage through her ears as Devon's abrupt hand gesture directed her to precede him to the path. On the whole of the walk to the villa he neither spoke nor touched her. The island filled her senses with unnatural intensity. From the black flirting vegetation she almost felt the scrape of crowded stems. It hurt her eyes to watch the fireflies as they drifted in upward curves and disappeared again like twinkling fairies. The night song of the forest was a symphony in crescendo. She could hear the ruin of each withered leaf crushed under her feet, the clatter of displaced gravel, the sharp sigh of the fabric of her gown as it rubbed into her thighs. Noises, sights, and smells were a battering intrusion upon her raw nerves.

Inside the villa he led her through the empty, echoing halls to her bedroom. He motioned her to enter and came in after, shoving the door shut behind him.

Only the wan oblongs of moonlight that washed through her open windows saved her room from total darkness. Fear and the quick, strenuous uphill climb had taxed her strength. The heavy arhythmia of her breathing mixed with the low sounds of his sure motions as he lit the candle beside her bed and then lit the wall sconces with their brilliant mirror backing. Clear topaz light flickered over her bed sheets where a hairbrush and the crumpled bedgown lay as she had hastily discarded them. Her book lay open on a small table nearby. A slow gust ruffled the pages, making a nervous, papery murmur. Devon snapped the book closed and turned to face her.

"Uncover yourself for me," he said.

She stood, not moving, staring down into the loose cup of her knit fingers, aware of the slight expansion of her chest that came with each irregular inhalation.

"Didn't you hear me, daffodil? Undress. There's no need to be embarrassed. Just do the same things for me that you would for Michael.''

Rather vaguely she said, "Michael?"

His hands shot out and jerked her to his body, so she could feel each rise and shallow, each plane of his ribs, and his tight stomach, and hips. He smelled sweet and sandy, his breath was faintly aromatized with wine. The smile had vanished.

"Michael *Granville,* you glib slut," he said. "Granville. Do you forget the name so quickly? Why should you forget when you know him so well—every last unholy inch? The games are over between us, queen of the angels. How you've held yourself back. This time I want you to show me. I want fireworks, sweet virtue . . . Roman candles, skyrockets, Catherine wheels. . . ."

The steady pressure of his body against her chest was as acute as a blow, and her restricted breathing came fast and without depth, searing the moisture from her throat and chattering teeth. Under his savage fingers her arms felt as though white-hot lead had been driven into her flesh.

Once she whispered his name as he lowered her to the bed, pressing her lightly into the down mattress. His hands had moved to her shoulders, his thumbs playing back and forth over her naked collarbone. His knees held one of her upper legs in a warm cradle, and as he leaned forward to take her lips her softness and hidden nerves experienced the nuzzle of his hard thigh, and she strained to escape it, turning her head into the glistening rose-gold web of her curls.

Devon's fingers, searching within the soft filaments of her hair, were able to find and capture her chin, dragging her face to him until he could cover her lips in a moist kiss that sent flame ripping through her body. His soft motions grew longer, deeper, more lavishly beguiling, until she was damp and helpless, no longer struggling against the demands of his lower body, but needing to dissolve into him.

Her love-desire for him carried to the moment when he shifted his weight and began to smooth her skirt up. Shame grew in the void of his withdrawn kindness; the floral scented night air felt like lye on her exposed thighs. Covering her blood-suffused cheeks with trembling and suddenly rigid fingers, she whispered, "Devon, the candles . . . please, can you put them out first. . . ."

There was a shocking quiet in the room as he stopped moving. He seemed almost to have stopped breathing. With her hips pinned to the bed between his knees, he took her wrists in his hands and dragged them away from her face. One of his hands was large enough to hold both her wrists; with the other he began to stir back the dewed hair tangles that clung to her lips and eyelashes and cheeks.

"Open your eyes, Merry."

Her sluggishly functioning brain was slow to obey him.

"Look at me! *Now*, angel. I can reconcile myself to the queasy certainty of having spent three months coaching a whore in the more trifling preliminaries of lovemaking, but I warn you, don't continue these piteous displays of virtuous hand wringing."

He dropped her hands, limp and half-bloodless from the violence of his grip, her palms creamy white as they nested in the ruby tones of her swirling curls. Slowly, beginning at the inner curve of her elbow, he trailed his finger along the buried blue path of her vein. Reaching her wrist, he curved his fingers around it and carried the small freckled hand to his mouth, pressing a lightly sensual kiss to each swelling surface of her palm, and then, spreading her thumb and forefinger, on the tender, unveiled flesh. As he loosed her hand he said, "Merry . . . What a foolish mistake for you. All I needed was your honesty." His hands curved into her palms, separating and linking their fingers, pushing her hands deeply into the billowing mattress. "Transform for me, Windflower. Show me what you really are." He lifted their mated hands, brushing her cheekbones with the side of his finger. Softly he said, "What's this? I hope these aren't tears, sapphire eyes?"

"No. I've given that up." Her voice quivered like a guttering lamp. Then, rather limply, "Would it interrupt your agenda of torture if I were to blow my nose?"

"Not at all. I can adjust to anything." He released her hands and tossed her a corner of the sheet. "Think of the bedclothes as one big hankie." Hostile shell-gold eyes watched as she snuffled dolefully into the bed linen. "You haven't done much talking up to now," he observed.

The urge was overwhelming to throw herself against his chest, to weep, to tell him everything, to beg him to believe her. But to do so in his present mood would be to invite a death sentence for Carl and Jason. Perhaps. Always perhaps. Only one thing was obvious. His clemency was less to be hoped for at this moment than at any time in the past.

"I'm sorry," she said gruffly, sensing within herself the crumbling ruin of her unnatural passivity. Her voice was disappointingly the same as it was always; not the richly beatific voice of a martyr, but young and rather soggy and typically ineloquent. She couldn't keep herself from chattering out, "But being ravished and called bad names doesn't bring out my talkative side. All I have to say is that I'm innocent but since denials are only likely to incite you to greater violence, I hardly think it would behoove me to—"

"My, my," he said in a satiny voice. "We did have something to say, didn't we? So you didn't draw those pictures, then?"

A pause. Then she said, "Oh, why don't you toss me off a cliff and have done with it?"

"In this part of the world," he said, "we only sacrifice virgins. Tell me about the drawings. Who paid you for them?"

A longer pause.

"There are men on the *Joke* who'd garrote you if they knew about this little indiscretion of yours, my pet. Tell me about the pictures."

"There's nothing to tell. I did them after I saw you in the tavern. Morgan was cutting off fingers. Cat said he wanted to slit my throat. And you—you—"

"Yes?"

"You unnerved me. You still unnerve me. I can't tell you more than that. You wouldn't listen if I did. No matter what I do, you'll think it's a defense: if I talk, if I don't talk. If I cry, if I don't cry. Whatever I say will be a lie to you." Her voice had degenerated to a tear-choked whisper and then finally to damp gasps as she said, "I don't think I deserve to be raped."

He stared at her, all emotion concealed behind his wide-set, opaque eyes. Abruptly he released her. She watched him face toward the wall, his hands braced against the freshly painted plaster. He was standing quite still, with one knee slightly flexed, and there was a barely visible tension across his shoulders, as though there were some powerful thing inside him that he was trying to bring under control.

From that position he said, "I'll never let you go back to him. Never."

Tears of angry frustration dribbled into the front of her dress as she sat up. "I don't want to go back to Michael Granville. So what," she said desperately, "*are* you going to do with me?"

He turned slowly toward her, his eyes as severely bright as fire embers. "Why, what else can I do, Merry flower? I'm going to take you to England as a prisoner of war."

CHAPTER TWENTY-THREE

Falmouth, Cornwall, September 1814.

To Merry, standing beside Cat on a Falmouth jetty, England was a rain-drenched waterfront. Tall row houses shimmered in a haze upon a terraced hillside; whitewash and dun stone among the choppy shag of shrubs and grasses. From a victualer's shop abutting the dock area came the smoky tang of frying sprat and the laughter of young apprentices as they teased each other over breakfast. Early as it was, the town was wide awake. Wet flagstones rang under the stout wheels of lumbering carrier's wagons and the lighter carts that drew produce to the market gardeners, the butchers, the hotels. Undaunted by the drizzle, women were outside sweeping the slick sand from their doorsteps and taking a shovel to the offal that had gathered from yesterday's traffic on the shining cobbles before their houses.

More than three hundred great ships bobbed like floating gulls in the vast bay, while sturdy punts streamed busily between them and the wharf on a hundred separate errands. An oyster-catcher caught Merry's attention, a black and white dart in a silver heaven. She followed its flight until it passed over a mail packet making a slow departure under sticky sails, passing within hailing distance of where the *Black Joke* rode at anchor.

From where Merry stood, the *Joke* appeared to be one more innocuous vessel, nodding under the stern gaze of Pendennis Castle. Passing in a skiff under the *Joke*'s bowsprit not half an hour ago, she had seen the bright flare of the colors of Great Britain flapping proudly over the ship, and the fresh painted name on the prow. The *Eagle*, it had said. There was no clue to the casual onlooker that this was a pirate ship turned privateer with a rich load of spoils lashed in her hold awaiting division with the crown, and a dark-eyed boy wearing chains in the fo'c'sle.

It had not been a particularly pleasant voyage. Raven had been incarcerated about a week ago, following an incident with Devon that no one would talk to her about beyond admitting that yes, it had been something to do with her, but she'd better keep her oar out of it anyway. Late that night she had heard Morgan's quiet voice in the passageway outside her door.

"Yes, Tom, I'm aware of that, but this way at least he can't get into trouble. Much as he's made a nuisance of himself lately, I don't want to whip the child a second time. I know Raven is frightened for the girl, but I doubt Devon's temper could support another one of Raven's fits of weeping."

"And Cat?" The voice belonged to Thomas Valentine.

"Cat, thank God, is not a fool. He'll do as he's told."

Valentine said something in a low tone that made Morgan laugh.

"Not you also, Tom?" said the pirate captain. "I thought you were immune! No, Devon hasn't confided in me what he plans to do with her. I would tend to think. . . ." The closing door of Morgan's cabin shut from her the trend of Morgan's thoughts, which was probably just as well. They were not likely to afford her much comfort.

She remembered well the only two sentences Devon had said to her in the course of the journey, and even those had not been in the strictest sense spoken *to* her. She had fallen from the rigging where she had been climbing with Raven, and though it was not a long fall, she had landed awkwardly and dislocated her thumb. It had been one of those days when one just doesn't feel like being mature about an injury. Light-headed with pain, she had fled, yelping, from Cat before he could undertake the excruciating process of setting the thumb. In the end it had been Sails who caught and held her in a gently steeled grip, clucking soothingly as Cat did what he must. Surrounded as she was by anxious sympathizers, she had no idea Devon had come on deck in time to witness her treatment until it was over. Then, with his expression sealed, he had walked forward through the suddenly silent pirate crew and looked for perhaps a minute into Merry's face, though it had actually been to Raven that he had said, "I don't want her up there again. Is that clear?"

Otherwise, he had said nothing to or about her. When she met him on deck or in a passageway, his glance was indifferent and did not linger. Watching his face in those moments, she found it hard to believe that she had ever seen tenderness there. It might be that she had been deceived by her own willingness to find it. If she lived for one thing now, it was the day when she could cut him as cleanly from her heart as he had swept her from his.

The broken feeling between her and Devon haunted her days and nights, along with the endless frightening questions about what he would do with her in England. And, especially in the first days at sea, there had been the barren and bestripped feeling that came from missing Annie, whom she had come to depend on for friendship and support more than she'd realized. Cook had stayed behind as well, because Annie was to have a child. They had even solemnized their common-law marriage before a priest at Sails's urging on the day before the *Joke* sailed, and it was the riotous and unusual preparations Raven and Will Saunders had made for the wedding that had provided distraction during those terrible days following her estrangement from Devon.

She'd had a birthday on the *Joke*. Strange things, birthdays. You wake up in the morning to find you've aged a year. Of course, that morning she had not thought of it at all. It had not occurred to her until midafternoon when Cat was about to write in his journal—fascinating reading, Morgan said—and had casually mentioned the day and the month. The date had hovered for a while in her mind, as though there were something familiar about it, and then she had remembered: today she could claim another year.

But the woman who stood beside Cat on the Falmouth jetty seemed much more than a year older than the one who had mounted the New York pier beside Aunt April. There was a certain irony, if one had the stamina left to note it, in the observation that she had finally arrived at her intended destination.

This morning Cat had awakened her from an uneasy sleep at dawn with a light touch on the cheek.

"Merry? I have your breakfast. Devon wants me to bring you to him on shore."

Since then there had been silence between them. What was there to say? Morgan was right. Cat would do as he was told.

Ahead she could see the traveling carriage waiting on the narrow quayside street, the horses thrashing the pasty moisture from their haunches with short-cropped tails and rolling their massive shoulders against their collars as a postilion in a tall hat adjusted the far trace. She turned quickly to Cat.

"He's taking me away?"

The young pirate hesitated. Then, "The carriage's hire is paid to London. Merry—"

Her face tilted upward to search his eyes for some sign of hope or comfort. Rain bedewed her eyelashes in tiny clear pearls and shone on the curve of her cheekbone until he covered her face with his own, just touching her brow with his lips. In that moment the clatter of hoofbeats brought a rider around the vehicle.

"How bloody touching." The lightly arid voice above them was Devon's. "Is this going to be an extended farewell, or is it possible that— Thank you, Cat. You can put her bag on the seat beside her."

It was hard not to feel lost forever as she rode alone in the jolting carriage staring through the leaded window glass at the melancholy grandeur of the Cornish hills.

The sweeping lonely valleys, the high jagged tumble of cleft boulders, the stark villages with their wet windblown trees and cob walls seemed bleak in the half light, though an occasional distant shaft of sunlight falling through an open seam in the clouds would lend the rough terrain a quality that was eerily peaceful. How foreign this place was to her. Even the churches, ancient chapels under moorstone slate roofs in shades of tawny yellow and green and russet, seemed gaunt and forbidding. She slid her hand into her valise and drew out the cloth bag that held her collection of shells, putting them one after another onto the dark drape of the cloak that covered her lap so she could touch the beguiling tropical contours. As always, she saved until last the great conch she had discovered on the St. Elise sands that day with Devon. Riding outside, he must be wretchedly wet by now. Merry tried to let that thought console her.

It was very late when they stopped at an inn. She was so tired and travel-battered, she barely glimpsed Devon in the scattered flashes of impression she received in the short walk through the yard where wood, horses, and men were dissonantly pitched drums for the deluge from the skies. There was a chambermaid, hot food, and a feather bed with a warming pan in a private room. Before first light the chambermaid was back and the order was reversed: bed to food to cold yard to carriage, while she was still stunned with sleepiness.

Exhaustion dulled her to the landscape, and she had missed much in the darkness. The rain had stopped, though a glance out the window might show her a ferny stand of oak rising from a coiling base of blue mist.

By midmorning, when the carriage stopped at a pretty inn of dressed stone, Merry's legs were stiff, her behind felt like it had been beaten with a grain shovel, and she was awake enough to be frightened and desperate. A meal of tea and toast, lamb chops and eggs was brought to her in a small parlor, deserted except for two middle-aged ladies in silk pelisses and their apricot poodle, who jumped from lap to lap eating potatoes from their plates.

It had been months, and seemed years, since Merry had been among gentlewomen. They seemed like creatures from another life; and though it didn't occur to her to ask them to help her, because the lady facing her reminded Merry of Aunt April, if only in her air of refinement, Merry couldn't stop herself from smiling wistfully at her. She had forgotten how she herself must appear—disheveled, oddly dressed, seemingly alone. The look Merry received back was repelling in the extreme, and Merry dropped her eyes to her plate, aching with hurt, and wondering how low it was possible to sink.

Somewhere in this unfriendly land there was, perhaps, one friend. Aunt April might be here. If the *Guinevere* had sailed before it was discovered that Merry had disappeared, Aunt April might have sailed on to England. In wartime surely it would not have been possible to return promptly to the United States to search for her missing niece however much that might be her wish. It was another point for the list of ironies that in a sense Devon was right about her. If there was a way to do it, she was going to escape from him and find Michael Granville. She had many reasons to be wary of that man, given the lies he had been spreading about her, even factoring out Morgan's horrifying claim that some action of Granville's had led to the death of Devon's sister, but Granville was the only man who would be able to tell Merry where she could find her aunt. As a knight of the realm, Granville must be relatively easy to locate. She supposed she was obliged to Devon for giving her the idea.

After weeks of hardtack, toast with fresh-churned butter was a delight, even cold and under these uncongenial circumstances. She was eating the last bites as the ladies left the parlor to walk their little dog. Immediately after their departure Devon came in, his unbuttoned greatcoat open over the long line of his leather breeches. From the energy in his step no one would have been able to guess that he had spent the better part of the last two days in the saddle. She tried to banish her feeling of utter defeat as he looked straight into her eyes, picked up her cloak from the back of her chair, and held it open.

"Come" was all he said. She didn't move. "Are you finished?" he asked.

"Yes."

"Well? Then, let's go." She stood but made no move for the door.

"What's the matter?" he said.

She could hear the exhaustion in her own voice as she said, "You've set too fast a pace. A moment ago I drifted off and almost woke with my nose in a lamb chop. If you could only let me have the afternoon to rest—"

"No."

"Then only an hour."

"An hour," he said, "is not going to do you any good. If we stop for an hour, that's an extra hour we'll have to travel after night-fall. The sooner this is over, the better for you."

Infusing her soggy backbone with some stiffness, she resettled her spine into a more noble posture. "If you don't mind, I'd like to know where we're going."

He took a step forward and settled the cloak around her shoulders, and she conquered an impulse to step away.

"I'll let you know"—he fastened her cloak—"when I'm in the mood."

"That's much too good of you," she answered with sarcasm that tried hard to be withering. "Would it spoil some international tactical arrangement and plunge the empire into chaos if I could have five minutes to comb my hair?"

"Comb it in the coach" was his laconic answer as he took her arm, propelling her toward the door. She pulled out of his grip.

"Hang it, Devon, I want five minutes to use the convenience." She felt her cheeks turn crimson.

"Well, for God's sake, why didn't you say so? I don't know your code," he said.

At his worst the man had an inherent decency that even he couldn't escape. When it turned out the outdoor privy was unusable after flooding from the recent heavy rains, Devon rented her a bedchamber and told her with a sudden almost reluctant kindness that if she really thought an hour's rest would help her, she could have it, but no longer. Her face must be looking more weary than she realized.

The bedchamber was clean and old-fashioned, smelling faintly of the home-brewed ale used to gloss the fine oak wainscot. It more than made up for its deficiency of not being on the ground floor by possessing a window that faced toward the back of the inn, with a wide tiled porch directly beneath supported by stout poles that appeared to have been designed with shinnying down them in mind. And she might have gotten away too if the landlord had been as conscientious about keeping his roof in repair as he was about preserving the finishing on his wainscoting. And if it hadn't been his practice to keep his geese flocked in a pen directly beneath.

It was a sorry spectacle of an escape attempt; in fact it ranked as her worst. The flustered geese trumpeted their fury at her and ran

about her in circles loosing feathers while she sat winded in the ooze
under the new gash in the porch roof, with splinters of lathing and
bits of plaster falling on her head and a broken window pot of
geraniums between her legs. The gander spread his ruffled wings
ominously and stood before her like Gabriel reprimanding a sinner.
Through a forest of arching scrawny necks Merry saw the people
come running; the ostlers, the stableboys, the hired postilion, the
kitchen maids, the two ladies with their yipping poodle, the landlord
and landlady, and finally Devon, who dragged her out of the mud
and feathers and across the fence. But this was a different Devon
from the cold-eyed stranger who had put her in his coach this
morning. This was a smiling, urbane Devon who dripped tact like
warm molasses, apologizing to the landlord even as he slipped him a
note for the damages. When it became clear that the landlord's
curiosity as well as his temper was aroused about what purpose a
young woman might have in hopping around on his porch roof,
Devon's smile increased in power and became at once rueful and
convincing. The hand he laid on her shoulder seemed a kindly
gesture; only Merry felt the threat in the pressure of his strong
fingers. Her jaw clenched with humiliated rage as she listened to
Devon tell the titillated mob that she was the runaway youngest
daughter of a Frensham barrister (the tone of voice managing to
convey neatly that she had been much indulged) and then continue to
describe himself as her older cousin, who had barely rescued her
from a disastrous elopement with a penniless foot soldier (a gambler
and unprincipled wastrel if only she could be brought to see it!).

"Why, of all the unctuous, deceitful— How dare you!" Merry
cried, unbearably mortified by the severely critical expressions directed toward her. Too tired to quite know or care what she was
saying, Merry turned pleadingly to the landlady, who had at least
shown more concern for Merry's possible injuries than for the
broken porch. "It's not true! I beg you to believe me. This man is a
pirate. He's kidnapped me and held me for months on his pirate ship
and refuses to release me in spite of my pleading."

She might as well have saved her breath. Truth is so often no
more impressive than its herald—and she made a thoroughly unim-
pressive herald. It was with despair but not surprise that she saw
compassionate condescension alight convincingly on Devon's features.

"Oh, Nan," he said to her, laughing. "How could you? Very well, then. As you say, I'm a pirate, and I've kidnapped you."

"But you have! He has! He's telling the truth!"

It was no use. None at all. The landlady began to tut-tut, the kitchen maids to giggle, and the ladies with the poodle to talk about the want of conduct prevalent among young females of this generation. The landlord clapped Devon heartily on the back and proclaimed him the scourge of the Seven Seas, adding with a sly wink that he supposed the shot was to be paid for in pieces of eight! There was a good deal more of that kind of badinage, which Devon allowed to continue until, apparently, he felt that he was well revenged.

A mile from the inn he stopped the carriage beside an arched stone bridge above a brook where cows rustled, half-concealed in the rushes. She shrank from him but had no strength to fight when he entered the carriage with a length of rope and bound her wrists.

"I'll say this for you," he conceded grimly. "You try."

Evening came, a smoky mauve lip on a black horizon. They had stopped often to change horses. Twice he had brought food to the carriage, and she'd had to eat it with her hands tied. She'd had to ask him to make a third stop with choked-back pride. This time the "convenience" was a beech copse where wasps zigzagged among tiny hawkweed flowers, and convenient it was not, because he refused to untie her wrists. If his acute golden eyes noticed the trail on her cheek left by tears hastily knuckled dry with bound hands when she came back to the carriage, he gave no sign of it. Mentally retracting everything she'd thought earlier about his basic decency, she was so wretched, she almost had the relief of being able to convince herself she hated him.

She slept, or it seemed so. A gray veil settled over her vision; a soft roar muffled all other sound; her mind carried meandering dream images. Awareness came occasionally in swiftly vanishing stabs. Some fragment of her stuporous brain registered the choked turnpikes, the change in sounds and odors, the brilliant flash of bright-lit shop windows glancing off her eyelashes. She slid into wakefulness in a still carriage, her body crumpled over her valise. Her spine felt like a stiff iron pipe, her eyes burned from lack of rest, and her throat was sandy. Devon, gathering her upright, was shrouded in rotating star points. Blinking rapidly against the altering intensity of light and the fresher air as he drew her outside, she pulled out of the steadying arms, her pattens clicking against a pavement.

"Don't," she snapped. "I can walk."

"As you wish," he answered impassively, not taking his hand from her elbow. Her strained eyes focused on his unreceptive features and then turned wildly over her shoulder toward the street alive with the chime of bridle and harness as elegant town coaches passed upon its great breadth. Buildings of immense proportion lined the even pavement, their Corinthian pilasters and dazzling Venetian windows dwarfing a frontage of darkened shrubs.

"Where am I?" she whispered.

"In London. Portland Place," he said, taking her valise in one hand and escorting her through an openwork iron gate toward a portico that housed the fan-vaulted door of a tall Palladian mansion.

Disoriented by fatigue, she said, "This isn't a prison?"

"I suppose that would depend on one's philosophical bent," he said, but then seeing she was much too tired to make anything of that remark, he added, "No, it's not generally considered to be a prison. Frightened out of your wits, are you?"

Letting her anger show, she ground out, "Would that please you?"

"It might. Everyone likes to be taken seriously. To which I add the homily—"

"People must lie in the beds of their own making," she finished. A weary tear tickled down her nose, and she removed it quickly with the hunch of one shoulder.

"Precisely. How nearly in concert are our minds."

Her back, which she had been able to keep straight in front of him for most of the day, began to slump. "I'm too worn out to be particular. Show me *any* bed, and I'll sleep in it."

He laughed. It was the first time she had heard him laugh naturally in weeks, and she had forgotten how appealing and tender his face could become, the corners of his eyes relaxing into an engaging crinkle of smile lines, the ashen-blond hair purling in the night air.

"All in good time," he said. "There's someone I have to talk to first."

Her bound hands lifted, palms upward, toward the doorframe, and she said wonderingly, "You know someone who lives *here*?"

"Yes. Come along, Merry pet."

Exhaustion and terror clenching at her throat, she watched Devon raise his hand to the paneled mahogany door and beat an imperative summons on the heavy brass knocker.

The door was opened almost immediately by an imposing personage with spaniel jaws who was unmistakably a butler. His chilly "How may I serve you?" dissolved into astonishment as he stepped back, staring at Devon, his sparse gray eyebrows mounting his forehead.

"Your Grace!" he exclaimed.

"Good evening, Harris," Devon said in a tranquil voice, drawing Merry ruthlessly into a deep entrance hall. He glanced toward the graceful upward curl of a marble staircase. "Is Cathcart in?"

The butler seemed to have recovered himself, like an old but sturdy chair taken to the upholsterer's. "Indeed he is, Your Grace. His lordship has just this minute arrived home and repaired to his dressing chamber." Walking to a doorway with a handsomely carved architrave, he continued, "Permit me to offer Your Grace the use of the library. There's a fire made up within, and I think you will find it quite comfortable. And if I may be so bold, Your Grace, as to say how happy an occasion your safe return is and will be to your family and acquaintances—a happy occasion indeed. Lord Cathcart will want to be informed of your arrival without delay."

"Thank you." Devon's hand on her arm forced forward Merry's balking footsteps.

She was perhaps not able to control her emotions as well as she might have wished in times of duress, but recent bitter experience had trained her to keep thinking. Pulled despite her shallow resistance into a large well-ordered library, she closed her mind to the Chinese rug, the aged monastic manuscript supported in an open position on a library table. Devon stood by the door inquiring genially about the butler's gout and rejecting an offer to surrender their outer garments. She was just wondering whether that last might be interpreted to mean they would not stay here long when the phrase *Your Grace* seemed to unclot slowly from the rest. Badly shaken to learn that Devon was on saunter-in-at-midnight terms with an English lord, and shamed by being handled brusquely in front of such an obviously reputable gentleman as Mr. Harris, she had failed to register the title. If *Your Lordship* was the form of address for a marquis or an earl, then *Your Grace* must be the proper mode for a— For a *what*? Who was this man? The soft closing of the door behind her generated a hiss of fear in the nerves that surfaced her skin. She turned to find Devon standing alone by the doorframe, regarding her steadily, the closed expression opening in the marigold firelight to a steely courtesy that encouraged her to voice her thoughts. She heard her own voice whisper, "*Hirundo poeciloma*. You knew the swallow. And the gull—you trained it to come to you. Because you are the son of a naturalist, aren't you? And an artist. No one has ever understood my drawings as clearly. And that—that night on the beach I heard you speak almost with sympathy about the American cause." His expression was lightly interested; as though she was revealing no more than the solution to some childish riddle. *A house full; a hole full; you cannot gather a bowlful. What is it? Smoke.* His casual fingers had begun to uncatch the buttons of his greatcoat. At sea, in Rand Morgan's world, this man wielded great power. Her only chance had been that his danger would fade without Morgan's legions behind him, but she saw now with bitter frustration that instead it would grow, blossoming like herb of grace, into something more omnipotent than she ever had imagined. Staring fully into the intense mosaic gold of his eyes, she said, "Now I understand. You are Devon Crandall. And the Duke of St. Cyr, aren't you?"

CHAPTER TWENTY-FOUR

Brian Farquhar, Lord Cathcart, stared distractedly at the hurried flash of his carefully polished Hessian boots as they descended his black marble stair. Potbellied water drops were scattered like buttons on the bottommost step. Little Lyn must have had another accident with his shaving water; when she was away from under his housekeeper's firm hand, nothing could induce the girl to use the servant's stair. "T'other is so much grander-like," she was wont to pipe, and if Harris noted the spill, Lyn was sure to receive another sharp scold. With an exasperated sigh Cathcart bent to soak it up in his handkerchief.

The library door, he saw, was closed, and behind was Devon, back intact after more than a year of wandering in hell's own company to places God only knew. America? Canada? The Caribbean? Rumor had placed him in all three, often at the same time. And now he was here, his return as cavalier and careless as his departure. His family didn't know of his homecoming, that much was certain. Not two hours ago Cathcart had been sitting with Devon's mother, Aline, helplessly watching her wilt under Countess Lieven's subtly malicious quizzing about the absent duke. Cathcart remembered how he had cursed Devon silently for the agony of worry he so readily inflicted on his loving family. Perhaps it would be more judicial, Cathcart reflected, to curse instead the circumstances that had made Devon as he was.

Still fresh in his mind were the time-framed pictures of Devon as the beautiful, too perfect child demigod, creating remarkable machines generating electrical current that no one could understand but the boy himself, and running through the silvery beards of a barley field beneath the dark golden-tinged wingbeats of his eagle. Aline used to whiten when the majestic predator landed, deadly talons slashing the air, on her son's slight forearm, but Devon's father would only put back his great mane of tawny hair and laugh. Jasper Crandall had been that kind of man.

Jasper's death was one of those abstruse tragedies that leave one feeling flawed and unrelentingly mortal. A healthy, interested father sitting with his gifted son studying leaf sections under a microscope, Jasper Crandall had lifted his head, set down the small tweezers in his hand, and slumped forward in death, his brain massively hemorrhaged.

Much later that same night, retiring to the black solace of his own bedchamber, Cathcart had heard a light, clear-voiced command coming out of the darkness that had said, "Put out the candle, Brian."

Cathcart's uncomfortably dilating pupils had found Devon sitting dry-lashed on the bed, his bright head flossed in reedy moonlight. "Why did my father die?" There was a shattered soul in the thoughtful childish voice, and Cathcart, numb from the loss of the man he had respected above all others, had heard himself blundering foolishly through empty phrases about divine will and submission to fate. He had spoken at length, the words coming haltingly. It was not until the clock of French porcelain on the mantel chimed the hour of midnight that he realized Devon had left quietly and he was alone. From that hour on Devon had found his own answers.

Uncrouching from the step, Cathcart glanced with rueful distaste at the water-heavy handkerchief in his hand and dispossessed himself of it underneath the hall porter's chair.

Devon stood by the walnut sideboard, helping himself to brandy. Cathcart was vaguely aware of a girl in a muddy Pilgrim's cloak standing beside the fire. A young female, Harris had dryly termed her. After asking Harris several times if he was quite certain the young person was indeed a *female* and receiving Harris's patient, pitying reassurances that yes, surely it was a girl and not Cathcart's absent son, Cathcart had lost interest in her beyond his inevitable irritation and awe that Devon had the temerity to bring one of his haphazard trollops to the town residence of his godfather. The lateness of the hour hardly made it any better. But as Devon turned, setting down glass and bottle, Cathcart found himself forgetting everything beyond the brainstorming warmth of Devon's subtly delighted smile. Devon crossed the room in clean, quick strides to take him in a charmingly exuberant embrace.

Held at arm's length by his godson's strong bronzed fingers, conquering his filling throat, Cathcart said awkwardly, "So you're back."

Devon separated his hands and shrugged, a continental gesture. "As you see." The boy looked good—brown and self-possessed and superbly physically conditioned; the rich heavy hair had been eating sunlight. He had grown into the engagingly fashioned looks that had been almost overpowering when he was younger; maturity had revealed outwardly the extent of the inner depth.

"You haven't been home?" Cathcart asked, knowing the answer, testing the water.

"No. I'm counting on you to advise me where the batteries are placed before I approach the citadel. Are they well—Mother, Grandmother?"

"Yes. Yes, of course. But I don't have to tell you that you've been sorely missed." The one comment, and no more. Lord Cathcart had learned with Devon it was best not to lecture. "Tonight I was with your mother."

Devon eyed Cathcart's knee breeches with an appreciative grin. "Carlton House?"

Cathcart felt his face soften into an answering smile. "Carlton House," he agreed. A small movement from the silent figure by the hearth drew Cathcart's attention to her. Reluctant as he was to permit or acknowledge her presence, he said politely, "Have you eaten, either of you?"

"Yes. Recently." As though he had observed Cathcart's unwilling interest, Devon looked in the girl's direction and said, "Come here, Windflower. The good marquis would like to see what you are."

Her back, encased in cloak and hood, was toward Cathcart. He watched the slim shoulders square. The weightily resettling fabric of her cloak snagged the dark hood at its base, spilling it backward to release a thrilling dance of cherried honey curls. She turned where she stood, her gaze flying defiantly to Devon's.

Lord Cathcart was not a man who gaped at women. He had spent the better portion of his adult life in a deep if chaste love for Devon's mother, Aline; for ten years he had enjoyed a more intimate and discreet liaison with a lovely and sophisticated woman whom he supported generously. Nor was he a lad in first flush who felt his body stir to every lure, but wish it or not, Lord Cathcart knew he had begun to stare at this young girl. Half his reaction certainly was admiration, but the other half was pure fascination with her incredible similarity to the Italianate oval-faced ideal. She might have stepped from a sea-flecked shell. Beneath deep, fantastic eyelids, her gentian eyes were bright as a wren's, their vision outwardly directed and unself-aware. The chin was small and solid, made as though to fit in a man's hand. Only the nose was not meticulously proportioned to its setting, though the very delicacy of the fragile teardrop nostrils added to rather than detracted from the charm of her features, lessening the classic severity. She carried herself with more dignity than her years warranted, though the face was a study in sensitivity. You wanted to smell the fragrance of her hair. What in the world was this solemn fairy princess doing with a man of Devon's reputation?

"Good evening, Miss—?" Cathcart tried kindly.

"Her name is Merry," Devon said, his tone matter-of-fact. "It may not suit your notions of politesse, but you'll have to call her that; I don't know her last name."

The young girl's show of spirit was dying into wan bewilderment as she looked from Devon to Cathcart, and it appeared to the marquis as though the cautious blue eyes were having trouble assessing him. It came to him then that she was tired, very tired. The radiant skin had disguised that at first. Gratefully Cathcart experienced the dissolution of his instinctive male reaction into something reassuringly paternal. She was, after all, hardly more than a child, and from the glances that had passed between her and Devon, it was evident he had used her like a vandal. Admitting wryly to himself that only a moment ago he had been planning not to acknowledge her, Cathcart approached the girl, gentling his expression because she seemed ready to cringe from him. Good Lord, what had

Devon been doing to her? He had never seen a woman look upon him with fright before, and it distressed him. At something of a loss and growing increasingly angry with Devon for placing him in this situation, he said, "Welcome to my home, Merry. It must be hot for you in front of the fire in your traveling garments. If you'll allow me . . . ?" She stared at him in a stunned way, though she made no protest as he loosened the clasp underneath her chin and drew the cloak from her shoulders.

Her hands, small even for a woman of her refined bone structure, were folded neatly into the lap of her skirts. In a second's horror Cathcart saw that she was bound.

"What the devil!" He took her wrists together and examined the deft bindings. The flesh beneath the rope was scraped and cold. Intense anger strained his words as he rapped out at his extraordinary godson. "Have you taken leave of your senses?" To his annoyance Devon showed no shame; in fact, he appeared to be a little amused.

"I'm sorry. I knew you'd be shocked. But she keeps trying to run away from me."

"I should think so, if this is a testament to the style of your conduct with her." It had hardly been Cathcart's intention to make the young duke laugh, and when Devon did so, the ruthlessly insouciant attitude outraged the older man. "This is abominable! Even for you!" he continued. "How long—" He glanced at the girl, who was beginning to blush. "How long has she been under your protection?"

"Oh, my protection, is it? A vastly ill-suited euphemism." Devon twirled the brandy in his glass and took a long sip. His eyes went to the girl's face. "She's been with me on the *Joke*."

"Devon, no! Surely you haven't allowed those devils of Rand Morgan's to have access to her?"

"Rand Morgan's 'devils' would eat soot if she fed it to them with her baby fingers. She was ill once, and they spent so much time weeping into their shirtsleeves that there wasn't a dry bicep in the fo'c'sle. I couldn't have talked them into forcing her if I'd wanted to. Don't let your imaginings run into the morbid, Brian. And I don't know why you profess to be so shocked. I've had the distinct impression from certain past lectures that you thought I was capable of anything," Devon said dryly, coming closer to take the dark woolen cloak from Lord Cathcart's arm, throwing it over a library chair. "She's not the pippin she looks. I took her out of Michael Granville's bed."

Understanding struck Lord Cathcart like a leaded glove. Ominously calm with one eyebrow sharply lifted he asked, "And a man of your breeding would use a woman for revenge?"

For the first time since his arrival Cathcart saw his godson's eyes gleam with unclouded temper. "Why not? It's precious little I've had of *that,* thanks to you and Rand. Anyway, I have other reasons for keeping her. She has a certain gift that some irresponsible idiot—Granville, one supposes—encouraged her to put to the wrong use, and now Cochrane would like her disposed of. She's fortunate that she's too fetching a little monkey to butcher." The final words were spoken more gently. "There's nothing you can do about it, Brian. She's not your burden."

But Cathcart faced back toward the lovely haggard girl, taking her hands, strapped together as they were, and holding them sustainingly in his own. Letting his sincerity show fully in his features, he said, "I'm very sorry, and I intend to do what I can to ease your situation. For the moment all I can do is make you comfortable. Please tell me how I can best serve you."

Rather than comforting her, the sympathy seemed to confuse her, and Cathcart began to wonder if she had become so accustomed to having her wishes unregarded that she'd forgotten it could be otherwise. The gaze she turned on Devon was one of heartrending doubt.

Devon managed to look perfectly composed, even entertained, under her pathetic scrutiny. He said, "If you want to do something for her, Brian, perhaps you could have a cover brought so she could lie on a couch? I've brought her in two days from our landing in Cornwall, and she's half-unconscious for want of rest."

"For goodness' sake, then, let me give her to the housekeeper," Cathcart snapped. "The guest room is prepared. At least let her sleep in a bed."

"Absolutely not," Devon said. "I don't trust her. She's already nearly drowned, contracted malaria, and fallen through a roof into a goose trough trying to get away from me. There's no telling what new way she'll find to kill herself in London."

From that position Devon was not to be moved. Cathcart himself brought a woven cover of dyed lamb's wool and a dish of the herring salad that had lately formed a part of his own supper as well as a compote of nectarines, some biscuits, and milk. It was better for the servants to see him rummaging distractedly in the kitchen than to come into the library and find Devon had tied up a young girl. Aline, at least, would be spared being regaled with that tale over tea.

The girl herself said nothing through it all, nodding or shaking her head when asked a direct question, the determined set of her shoulders disclaiming his pity even while exciting it. It did not seem to occur to her that Cathcart might really be able to help her. She made no appeal to him, and it became increasingly obvious to Cathcart that she had come to accept as the natural state of affairs that any man she met would collude in her internment. It said much about the impropriety of the conditions under which she had been living that she was able to accept with aplomb the indignity of having to lie down on a couch before two men, one a stranger, and try to sleep fully clothed. But when the time came, and the couch had been prepared for her, she stood by it uncertainly, seeming unable to do it after all.

Devon came to her and physically laid her back against the cushions, removing her pattens, handling her as if she were a doll.

"Have no qualms," he said to her. "Lord Cathcart is a gentleman." As if he was answering a mute appeal in her eyes, Devon drew a thin dagger from his boot. Quite unsurprised by this unorthodox and alarming action, she accepted unflinchingly the passage of the shining blade between her wrists as Devon sliced open her bonds. He tossed a blanket over her and said, "Go to sleep, brat."

The fluid ease with which Devon handled the dagger ought to have been enough to throw most young ladies into hysterics, but the amazing creature on the couch merely blinked twice, said thank you to Devon in a soft, cultured voice, and went immediately to sleep.

Scarves of blue and violet flame twisted on the black hearth logs as Devon delivered to Lord Cathcart the letter that came, disappointingly, from Rand Morgan and not the disinterested son Cathcart longed for. The first part of Cathcart's conversation centered on that boy, the young pirate, scarred and braided, whose image resided like a burr in Lord Cathcart's heart. And when he reached the point

where, as always, the pain in his voice grew too great to expose
even to Devon's articulate sympathy, the talk became general, reviewing systematically the events of the last year, the affairs, both
public and private, that had taken place in Devon's absence. An
interested, always intelligent listener, Devon drew from Cathcart
a comprehensive account of English life during the past ten months,
save one important development that Cathcart was steeling himself
to reveal. As so often happened with Devon, Cathcart found himself
expressing thoughts that had existed before only as experiments in
the quiet of his own mind. Considerations of time became secondary.
The hour was past two when the conversation turned to the Bourbon
government in France, to Devon's lack of confidence in the peace
with that country as long as Whitehall refused to blockade Elba, and
to the soon-to-be-convened Congress of Vienna.

Lord Cathcart made silent note of the frequency with which
Devon's gaze strayed to the sleeping girl. Several times the Duke of
St. Cyr walked to the couch and stood looking down at her, seemingly unaware that he was doing so, though once, when the girl's
petal lips fell apart and she began to snore lightly in breathy,
feminine gasps of utter exhaustion, Devon had leaned over the back
of the couch smiling at her with an absorbed tenderness. The cover
had fallen from her shoulder, and he gently pulled it up with hardly
a break in thought, while Cathcart, watching them, was hard put to
remember what in the world they'd been talking about. Clearly this
relationship was not simple.

The conversation moved logically from Napoleon to Devon's
grandmother. Rather suddenly Devon said, "Twice I've asked you
what mischief Grandmother has been about. Twice you've altered
the subject. If it's going to be that bad, shall I pour myself another
brandy?"

Cathcart smiled reluctantly. "I don't mean to be overdramatic.
But I'm afraid she's been plotting again on your behalf."

The narrow green bottle in Devon's hand paused halfway to the
glass. In the ensuing silence Cathcart saw the girl open her eyes and
lie quietly, staring without focus at the bust of Homer in a wall
niche.

The brandy bottle clattered briefly against the rim of Devon's
glass. Setting the bottle down, Devon said mildly, "Well?"

"She's back to her worries over the succession."

"That's hardly a surprise." Laughter softened the golden eyes that were fixed upon Lord Cathcart. "God forbid we shouldn't pass on the dynasty. Someone ought to let her know I can breed without her help. She must have presented me with two hundred hapless prospects. I didn't know there was another eligible woman in England left unsurveyed."

Sharply aware of the young girl knuckling her eyes on the couch, Cathcart said, "Precisely. As far as I can follow her train of thought this time, she seems to have the added notion that a wife and heir would keep you in England. She's old and lonely and—" Cathcart broke off, watching Devon walk restlessly to the mantel. This clearly was a poor moment to mend fences. More loath than ever to reveal the whole of the fruitless debacle, he forced himself to begin again. "Anyway, she's taken a new tack in finding you a bride."

"Useless," Devon said. "The slot stands to be filled shortly."

Staggered as much by the flat dispassion of the announcement as by its content, Cathcart waited for his godson to say more. When nothing was forthcoming, he disciplined his composure and said, "Not being privileged with that information, she's attempted to produce for you a girl. One can't be sure what she has in mind. A notion, perhaps, that through it she might somehow win back your esteem."

"Damn," Devon said succinctly. "What girl?"

"To wit, a well-bred American maiden."

Devon eased one lean shoulder against the mantel. "I wasn't aware she knew any."

Cathcart wasted no time trying to figure out whether Devon was referring to Americans or virtuous girls. "She doesn't. The young girl in question is one Rand Morgan has an interest in."

"I can assure you," Devon said, giving his godfather a hard look, "that Rand Morgan isn't interested in young girls."

A man of profoundly conservative instincts, Lord Cathcart had worked hard, particularly in the last several years, to keep himself from becoming a prig. Still, there were certain things he would never be able to hear with equanimity, and among them were references to Morgan's broad-based decadence. Morgan's morals were no matter of indifference to Cathcart, and could never become so as long as his son remained one of the pirate captain's most famous disciples. Cathcart flushed, glancing at Merry, who was beginning to look disorientedly around the room. To Devon he said, "Does the name Wilding mean anything to you?"

The younger man thought a moment before he said, "James Wilding—Assistant Secretary of the United States Treasury. His son is a young firebrand of some renown; the only brain, they say, on Armstrong's staff. He gives British Intelligence fits. But, then, they're stupid. I recall the name coming up once in conversation with Morgan. He never told me he had a connection with them."

"The connection was with the firebrand's mother, from the days before she married Mr. Wilding. The lady was British and has evidently been dead for some time. How Morgan knew her, or when, I don't know, but he had formed enough of an attachment to have placed someone in the household staff to watch over the motherless Wilding daughter, a tar from the original crew of the *Black Joke* named Cork; a rascal, so Morgan told your grandmother, but reliable in his way."

Merry, on the couch, had grown deathly white, her eyes wilting gentians. Thin, waving strands of her hair were glinting captives on her damp brow. This was too cruel. Lord Cathcart made himself the promise that as soon as he was done telling Devon about this particularly unpleasant business, he was going to insist that she be sent to bed. Or at least try to insist. If there was one thing Devon was *not*, it was malleable. Cathcart went on, "Your grandmother corresponded with the Wilding girl's aunt in America at Morgan's request. Morgan seems not to have ever told your grandmother in so many words he intended one day to bring Miss Wilding to England, and yet that was somehow the impression she was left with. In consequence, she got it into her head to bring the girl to visit her—"

"The devil she did! In the midst of a *war*?"

"I'm afraid so. She seems to have been taken with the idea of having a disposable bride awaiting you who was of such little social consequence that she might be rejected if you didn't find her to be . . ." He seemed not to be able to find a way to express it.

"Sufficiently nubile?" Devon offered in a silky tone. "Poor Miss Wilding."

"Poor Miss Wilding indeed," Cathcart agreed grimly. "Your

grandmother had few choices as to how to bring the young lady to
England. She penned a letter to Miss Wilding's aunt that included a
half promise to arrange an advantageous marriage for the young girl
and gave the letter into Michael Granville's keeping with the instructions to deliver it himself and bring the two women back with him
on the neutral ship.''

"And you let that happen? With Granville behind me in succession to the title?'' There was icy incredulity in Devon's eyes.

"You know I would not have,'' Cathcart shot back angrily. "But
Letitia made sure I heard nothing of it until after Granville sailed.
Wires were pulled at the highest levels. Your grandmother stands as
close to the Queen as ever she did; I don't need to remind you how
the royal family feels on the subject of your marriage.''

"No,'' agreed Devon, pushing himself away from the mantel and
setting down his untouched brandy on the side table with a loud
clack. "You don't. From your expression I take it that Granville
killed the girl?''

"So I fear,'' Cathcart said, regret searing his voice. "There's no
proof of anything, but the girl disappeared from the *Guinevere*
perhaps even before she was out of port. The girl's aunt is here
now—staying with your mother—and it was the aunt's belief at first
that the girl ran away to be with her father; since then we've learned
that the girl did *not* arrive at her father's home, and the father claims
the aunt had no authority to remove her from the country and
demands that she be restored to him immediately. It's become an
issue at the peace talks, because the Americans are understandably
skeptical about Whitehall's claim that we don't know where she
is. . . .''

Devon was no longer listening. He had turned to stare at Merry.
She was looking back at him, handfuls of the blanket clenched like
knots beneath her fingers. Her sleepy lips were parted, and in her
wide-open eyes was an expression of utter wonderment. Slower than
they to understand what had happened, Cathcart found Devon's
features difficult to read, though Merry, apparently, was having no
trouble. She murmured something, an inarticulate flutter in her
throat; and bolted toward the door.

CHAPTER TWENTY-FIVE

Devon caught her before she could run out of the room, slamming the door shut. She desperately tried to kick him. He deflected it expertly, but she had spent a lot of time with Cat in the last weeks learning to defend herself, and it was a small, tired triumph to see that though Devon could hold her, it was not easy for him.

"I demand to be taken to my aunt!" she panted, struggling against his grip, her wrists twisting and turning under his palms, despairing that the resolute facial expression Cat recommended she adopt in all struggles with Devon must be losing most of its effectiveness with her hair flying over her face.

"All in good time, daffodil. Oh, no, don't try that again or you're going to arrive in front of her in little tiny pieces. How much do you think— Ouch!" He slid a bent finger between the small sharp teeth that had just clamped down on his forearm, trying to loosen her bite, watching sardonically as the feminine jaws opened only to close again ruthlessly on the new target of his finger. "Do you want to speak," he asked, "or gnaw?"

The finger tasted like leather reins and horse sweat. Expelling it from her mouth, she was brought up short by his long hard hand, which caught the length of her jawline and forced her face to look upward into his. "Enough, you little tiger. Tell me just how far this conspiracy has gone."

"What conspiracy?" she shouted back. "I've told you the truth from the beginning. Part of it, anyway. I was dragged from my bed by those monsters Cat hired to search Granville's cabin. I was there because of the ants. I *told* you that! I even told you"—her voice had begun to shake—"about Henry Cork."

"So you did," he said with false civility. "Coming to England, you were. To marry a duke?"

"I didn't know anything about that, and if I had, you can rest assured they would have had to pin me down like bobbin lace to get me on that ship. All I knew was my aunt was homesick and she wanted to visit England." She broke, exasperated past bearing by the contemptuous rake of the hard gold eyes. "But there's never any use talking to you!"

"There would have been a great deal of use talking to me—if you had told the truth. In the tavern; that was your brother. That's why you kept those rosy lips sealed all this time—to protect him? That's rich. Do you understand what I might have done to you if I'd been a shade more convinced you were Granville's light-skirt? And Morgan . . ." The taut grip on her jaw tightened unknowingly. "Did Morgan arrange to have you brought aboard the *Black Joke*?"

"I don't know. No. I don't think so," she said, "or else Cat would have had to know; he brought me aboard. And I'm almost sure he didn't know."

"What makes you so sure?"

"I don't know." She was trembling; her thoughts capered like leaves in a wind eddy. "Devon, please; that hurts." The grip moderated at once. "I'm so tired. You know it all now. Everything. At least about me, and as for the rest of it, and about Morgan knowing my mother . . . I don't know. I can't believe it. I want to see my aunt. I want to go to her! I can't think anymore. Take me to my aunt."

"Not yet, Merry pet. There's something we have to do first." Devon glanced over his shoulder at Lord Cathcart. "Produce us a special license, Brian. Poor Miss Wilding is going to become a duchess."

Merry Wilding had borne up as best she could under forced confinement on a pirate ship and malaria. She had seen the man who held her fate transformed bewilderingly from pirate to duke, weaving with terrifying speed from protector to persecutor and back again. Now, at two o'clock in the morning, and for motives unabashedly hazy, that same man had the arrogance to announce offhandedly over his shoulder that he intended to make her his wife. It was one peach too many in the fruit bowl. Every last gram of her strength went into the circular upsweep of her arm, every bitter degree of temper tightened her fist as she planted a bruising punch on his chin. The force of the contact ripped through her muscles, wrenching her every tendon from wrist to shoulder, and her knuckles crackled like wren bones, but there was no question who was hurt worst. Two inches higher and she might have broken his nose. In the fireplace even the flames cowered.

At least half a minute passed before he could speak. Then, weakly at first, he began to laugh, though he had no breath to spend, and because he couldn't seem to stop the laughter, he collapsed into a chair, in a graceful descent of long-shafted limbs and tumbling blond hair. His shoulders shook like an isinglass jelly. It occurred to her suddenly that he was as tired as she was. The difference was that he had the discipline to disguise it more thoroughly.

"No, beloved," he finally managed to gasp, "we have our clichés reversed. You strike a man when his proposal is *in*decent. When a man asks you to marry him, you simper, blush behind your hand, and say, 'Sir, you do me too much honor—' "

"I wouldn't marry you—" she started, her eyes flashing.

"I know," he said, gasping softly. "If I were the last man in Europe. For all the flax in Flanders. If I paid you."

"If my life depended on it!" she snapped.

"Be reasonable." Below eyes dewed winsomely by the side issue of his laughter, Devon was laying careful fingers on his jaw. "There's only so much mortal danger I can arrange on your behalf." He turned, smiling, at Lord Cathcart, who had been sitting in his chair as though someone had riveted him there. "Don't feel you have to stay to protect me. I'll try not to incite her to violence a second time."

Cathcart bore the look of a man hovering unsteadily between outrage and the strong desire to laugh in spite of himself. "A more well-deserved punch I have yet to see laid. I can't in conscience walk from the room and let you bully a distraught girl into an enforced marriage for reasons of expediency."

"If there's one word that *doesn't* apply to this entire venture," Devon said with real feeling, "that word is *expediency*. You wouldn't use words like *expediency* to me if you'd been responsible for an eighteen-year-old girl left to wander at will on a Caribbean privateer. Please go, Brian. We're beyond chaperonage."

Merry saw that something in Devon's tone must have convinced the older man, for he rose, though reluctantly. Halting before Merry, he studied her eyes calmly and touched her cheek lightly with his forefinger. "If you shout for me, I'll come," he said and went from the room, closing the door behind him without force.

Into the ensuing silence Merry found herself saying, "He's *much* too nice to be a friend of yours."

"I suppose he is," Devon said equitably. "You know—or don't you?—that after the months you've spent on the *Black Joke* that marriage is the only thing that can keep you from social ruin."

The distant couch was looking very good to Merry, but her legs were saying, Don't even try. She sank where she stood, her knees on one of the lion-dogs that leered from the blue Chinese carpet beneath her. "Social ruin means nothing to me. I grew up in a farming village in Virginia where my aunt and I were as ostracized as was Christianly possible. I walked in the country, sketched, practiced on the pianoforte, and did embroidery on linen. Aunt April kept a list in the back of our everyday book, and I'll have you know that in my lifetime I've made two small shawls in white work; a raised work panel of David and Bathsheba; a set of eight needlepoint chair covers in flame stitch; four full-sized bed covers—one in candlewick embroidery, one in looped wool, two in crewel; three cross-stitch hand screens with birds; *and* six pincushions in red furnishing silk embroidered with clear and gold beads—of honeysuckle among ripe corn."

"God in heaven! And I took you away from all that?"

Resolutely ignoring the interruption, staring at the wandering hair strands that had crept forward over her shoulders, she said, "I promise you, Devon, I'll adapt perfectly to an isolated spinsterhood."

"I'm not so certain," he said. "My dear, with a rearing like yours it surprises me that you didn't bend to Mother Earth and kiss the feet of the first pirate who offered to abduct you."

She brought her fingers up to her temples, as if trying to hold together her afflicted headworks. Desperately she said, sotto voce, "I'll kiss any portion—within reason—of the first person of *any* persuasion who hands me to a nightgown and a real bed." Through coma-edged nausea she saw Devon stand, walk toward her, and lower his body cross-legged to the carpet before her. His palm gently lifted her drooping chin; his head had to tilt a little to gather her attention.

"Merry Wilding, I'm going to give you everything in this world you'll ever want," he said in a very soft tone. "Along with maybe a thing or two you don't want. And first, love, that means my name."

And in the end she had said yes. Well, perhaps not yes precisely. What she had really said was (irritably), "Oh, do what you want. You will anyway. When have you ever shown the faintest consideration for my opinion?" It was not a blush and simper behind her hand, but, then, this was not an ordinary marriage. And even as things stood between them, there was a part of her that wanted as much as he did to marry quickly before one or the other of them had time to change his mind.

They were wed in the pink-washed country villa of Lord Cathcart's older brother, an Anglican bishop, strong-boned and gentle with narrow pale eyes. Devon allowed Merry to sit down for the ceremony, which was a mistake, because she fell asleep immediately.

Devon's lips roused her in a lightly teasing passage over the soft flesh below her ear.

"Darling," he murmured beguilingly, "wake just for a moment. You must say 'I will.' That's all. Come, love. Two words only."

But in another minute there were more words to repeat, and she mumbled them in a state of semiconsciousness. She cried like an infant when he woke her one more time to sign a paper, and through a maze of tears she heard Lord Cathcart's brother say grimly that for this night's work unfrocking was no more than he deserved.

Morning was a bright obscenity when she was brought yet again from the carriage. She had a quick impression of a playfully gabled roof line and warm, stone-embellished brick before she was carried inside and transferred to the custody of cooing, excited strangers— thankfully female—in fine linen aprons who called her "Your Grace" in loving tones and led her up a creaking oak staircase to a comfortable and elegant bedchamber hung in mint-green satin damask. Here she was helped to bathe by Mrs. Bea, an elderly lady in gray-blue silk who had an immensely soothing way about her. She had been, so one of the younger maidservants whispered to Merry, a nursery

helper in the days of the duke's own father, and head nurse to the
duke himself. Master Devon he was then (though he was born a
marquess, his father didn't hold with calling little children by high-
sounding titles). It was Mrs. Bea who had heard his first words—only
nine months he'd been, fancy that! Looked right at the lace cap Mrs.
Bea was about to set upon his little head and said, "Silly hat!"
Pulled it right off his head too, he did!

The soft night-robe with blue satin ties and diamond-shapes
quilted into the sleeves was Merry's own, a stranger since the night
she had been dragged unconscious from the *Guinevere*. Reeling
from the magic of that, she asked Mrs. Bea with some bemusement
where Aunt April could be found and learned that she was spending
this week in the London house with Devon's mother, but without a
doubt they would rush back to the country when they heard! Giddy,
competing imaginings attacked her mind, demanding attention and
interpretation as her head nested at last on her pillow. But the sweet
scent of vanilla grass rose from the bed linen, and her senses
flowed into one another slowly until no sensation was separate or
comprehensible. And then, gratefully, she slept.

Merry woke to strong afternoon sunlight that made a bright, bold
outline of the mullioned window upon the Hollie point curtains. The
bed was still dressed in light summer hangings. Beyond the satin-
wood bedposts her drifting gaze picked out velvet flowers—blue,
salmon, white, and pink—in a porcelain jug; muted sunbeams were
glowing wetly in its underglaze-blue decoration. The furnishings
were graceful of line and prettily inlaid with stained tulipwood,
ivory, and ebony to form floral patterns as lustrous as lantern glass
under the many coats of polished lacquer.

A serving maid appeared soon, her manner friendly, perhaps a little
awed, but practical rather than servile as she showed Merry to the
adjoining dressing room, where Merry's own clothing from the
Guinevere was clean and waiting. She ate rice soup on a tray, and a
delicious *turbot à la crème*, with dressed cucumbers, stewed chestnuts,
and a poor author's pudding, which the maid told her laughingly was
"a much lighter version of the publisher's pudding—which could
scarcely be made *too* rich!"

Merry dressed in a cameo-pink satin dress, never worn, that Aunt

April had bought for her in New York. Crystal beads glimmered in
the slashes of the Spanish sleeves. The full-length glass showed her
that the reeded back of the gown swayed interestingly over her hips
as she moved, though it seemed like the sort of thing there was
hardly any point of making note of on a day like today. Watching
her hair being dressed in pink ribbands, the vacant shock of the last
two days began to recede like mist fading from a water meadow.
The first real emotion she could isolate and label was guilt. It
seemed grossly negligent not to be having hysterics. There were a
thousand reasons to be furious with Devon; probability contended
that he had married her only to further another scheme against
Michael Granville—whose name she had come to hate like poison.
She was an American patriot. What was she doing married to a
British duke who spent the better part of his time on a pirate ship?
Logic rebelled. But then logic had been rebelling since the moment
Michael Granville had told her in New York that she was to sail to
England. Obviously her logic could rebel until two Sundays came
together for all anyone seemed to care.

All that seemed sure was that the trapped feeling that came from
loving Devon had vanished. She felt a change in her body, a
weightlessness; an almost chirrupy frivolity that belied her uncertain
situation. The buoyant joy of her body belonged to an enchanted
bride on her wedding morning; all it wanted was to go into Devon's
arms. What a poor helpless thing was her heart, captured in spite of
all her effort to the contrary by this one man. She felt a jittery
shyness about facing him. At the same time each moment that
delayed her going to him was excruciatingly long.

By the time the last satin ribband was plaited into her curls, the
back of her nose ached from the clustering pressure of suppressed
tears, but her eyes looked splendidly stern and rather purposeful. No
doubt that illusion owed itself to the expensive New York modiste
and the maid's clever hands. The mind behind the firm gaze was
remarkable for nothing so much as its total *want* of purpose. Determined to face Devon with the brave mask intact, she asked direc-
tions of the maid, who was touchingly misguided enough to smile
thrillingly, as though there were some magical element of romance
in a newlywed wife's searching out her handsome, noble husband.

The corridors were long and twisted like the arteries in a badger's lair. Golden-brown floors hummed an old wood melody under her feet, and their subtly warped surfaces didn't seem to belong in a duke's palace. There was nothing of a palace here, beyond what was certainly a priceless collection of European masterpieces grouped with uncalculated abandon on walls hung in buffed-yellow tabby. This was an old and well-loved home; the owner had spent lavishly and cleverly on charming decoration and informal comfort and not a halfpenny on pomp. If the house were not Devon's, she would have been entranced. Exquisite ornaments begged for her study, faces gazed warmly at her from their gilt frames, and passing windows revealed a waltz of flashing color from the gardens. Happiness, Merry decided, could dwell here. It was a melancholy thought.

Rearming her nerves, she stepped into a wide, sunny apartment to find Devon alone, seated at a rosewood writing table, dumping blotting grit from a fresh letter back into an ornate silver sandbox. Rested, combed, and clean, his complexion fresh as this morning's biscuit, wearing the intricate white cravat and meticulously tailored trousers that were the costume of men of his class, he still looked to her like a pirate, and it amazed her that his cheerfully doting servants could see him only as a tot in a cap, though older.

"I don't know why I married you," she said aloud, from the doorway. "It's been nothing but ho-hum since."

His glowing gaze swung quickly to her. After a pause in which he seemed to examine her face, and then the skillful allurements of her gown and elaborate hair arrangement, he said pleasantly, "I don't know why you married me either. Why did you?"

Because I love you. "Because there didn't seem to be any other way to get some sleep." Merry stepped into the room. Her new perspective softened the flare of backlight from the windows, and she could see his face in better detail. Rested he was, but not relaxed and not manufacturing any defenses to hide it either.

He set down the paper; his fingers formed a long curve beside the sheet. "If the reason you married me was to protect your brother, I want you to know that it wasn't necessary. I wouldn't have hurt him."

"Heavens, I realized that last night the moment I learned you were a gentleman." The emphasis on the last word was soft and bitter, more bitter, perhaps, than she intended. He sat as he was, not moving, and she was not sure how she knew—though perhaps it was by some change in his expression perceptible only to a sense keener than eyesight—but she realized her words had stung him. Such a thing had never happened before. Or at least if it had, he had never allowed her to detect it. The other possibility was that it was not her words that had hurt, but her tone. How much remorse did he bear (if any) for abuses past? Plenty, she hoped, and that was the bitterness speaking again. There were two ways of handling this. The first was for her to figure out in some rational, organized fashion just what it was that she wished from him. The second was for her to stop thinking and obey each passing emotion until she had openly displayed every feeling to him.

She wandered farther into the room, trying to overcome the silence by seeming to study her surroundings, which made it particularly fortunate that this was an interesting room to study. Otherwise she might have looked a little foolish.

The apartment had an air about it of a hundred projects left uncompleted. A dissecting puzzle that was a map of England lay on a center table with the southern counties missing. Upon a canvas cloth on the window bench someone had begun transplanting pink and crimson geraniums from individual terra cotta pots to three glazed earthenware tubs; only one lovely arrangement was finished, and on the heap of rich earth tiny weeds were beginning to sprout like trees on some miniature hillock. Unclipped threads dangled from a stand of tambourwork. Periodicals were jumbled with books on a side table, and a scattering of handwritten recipes sat atop a commonplace book with a paste pot.

Without really deciding to she seemed to have stopped evolving plans. Plan A, Plan B, Subplan B in case Plan B went out the window, Alternate Plan C if Plans A and B failed . . . *Why had she married him?* Her first refusal had been so resolute; it was hard to understand why her resolution had wilted miserably. At the very least she wished she'd held out for a day or two.

Her back was to him as she uncorked the paste pot, opened the commonplace book to the oval of painted fabric that was a page marker, and began to daub paste on the back of a recipe with her ring finger. The recipe was for common Flemish tarts, and that made her smile. Close acquaintance with Raven and Will Saunders had permanently altered the tone of her mind.

"Will my aunt come today?" she asked, flipping the recipe on its back and pressing it onto an empty page.

"Tomorrow."

"And your mother also?"

"Also."

Merry drew from the basket a small scissors with brass blades shaped like a stork's bill and began to trim the ragged edge of another recipe. "What sort of a person is she?"

"My mother? A grubby urchin. She spends most of her time pulling roots and earth from one pot and squashing them into another. When I was a child and wanted to find her, I went through the house following the trail of humus."

Surprised by the image, she pasted in that recipe and had started to trim a third when his voice came to her again.

"Merry . . . I love you."

One of the scissor blades sliced into her finger. She released the finger grips in a sudden movement, and the scissors fell, clanging and open-spread on the table. Dark scarlet drops from her bleeding finger spattered the white pages like red petals strewn on virgin snow.

"Fiddlesticks!" Her heartbeat was heady, the rhythm of a folk drum. "You didn't love me yesterday, when you thought I was connected to—you know who. *Then* you tied me up."

There was a faintly apologetic pause. Then he said, "Being angry at someone isn't the same thing as not loving them."

The wounded finger curled tightly into her fist. "You're trivializing what you did to me. People in love don't mistreat each other."

His voice, coming to her over her shoulder, was webbed with strain. "You have a few things to learn about love if that's what you believe. It's a saber with two edges, Merry. I could have borne your being Granville's mistress. What I couldn't stand was the thought that while you were in my arms you might have been acting."

In a way, albeit unwillingly, that was something she could understand. Cat's kiss, with its careful ambiguities, had taught her that much. "Why would you rather trust in dockside gossip than me?"

"*Damnation*, Merry, can't you see you were the last person I had any motivation to believe in? I *wanted* to believe you were guilty, so I'd have an excuse not to let you go. Though there was part of me that always knew you were the person you seemed." Then, quietly, "I was almost able to let you go once, after you were sick on St. Elise, because I had so much saved-over guilt."

"By then I wanted to stay," she said, staring down at her fists.

"I know. But why? You were isolated, dependent, stripped of everything familiar . . ." The brittle voice stopped, as though dissatisfied with its own urgency. When he began to speak again, his voice was calmer. "You knew I wanted you. How much of your response to me was because you were afraid of what might become of you if you refused to indulge me?"

She would have spoken then, but he intercepted the words by saying gently, "No, love, you don't know, and neither do I. There isn't any way to be sure. For that, at the very least, I had to set you free. As restitution it wasn't too impressive, I know—I was trying to listen to some remnant sense of justice."

"Some remnant sense of justice," she repeated, as though it were worthy of being mulled over. "That phrase has a certain something. And it's particularly eloquent when applied to you." She turned and found he was standing beside the desk, his expression open as she had never seen it before in the soft interior shadows. "A remnant sense of justice. It lies there withered like a Montgolfier balloon. If only we could inflate it or something, so you could have a real conscience instead of a useless scrap to toy with when it suits you."

Just outside the window a breeze tossed the crown leaves of a walnut tree, and their shadows drifted over his face. "You don't have to retreat into symbolism; I'm not Rand Morgan. You want me to understand that you find my apologies vacuous and self-serving."

"I find your apologies thinner than skimmed whey!" she said hotly. "That night in my bedroom you *attacked* me."

He wondered how many years would pass before he could call up that memory without being sick at heart from it. Very gently he said, "I can only hope that with time I'll be able to fill you so totally with my love that you will be able to shed the sting of my abuses."

"*And?*"

"And I'd see my hands cut off before I'd hurt you again. Ever."

The corners of his eyes began to play with a smile. "Love, have a care. You're coming close to listening to an apology."

If a hundred men were to smile at her, not one could affect her as deeply as the barest glimmer of suppressed mirth-light in Devon's eyes. The muscles around her mouth begged her to respond. Thank heavens her wrists remembered the rope he had put around them yesterday.

"Listening to isn't the same as accepting." Once the words were out, they sounded childish, which was a disappointment. One always kept hoping one would be able to outgrow the occasional clumsy remark. Especially at moments like these. Gathering back her retreating dignity, she said, "You seem to be thinking far ahead of me, so I have a question. Just what is it you want?"

Leaves rippled beyond the muting window glass; as gentle was his gaze, holding her as he said, "I want to wake each morning with your breath on my shoulder. I want to sit talking to you before the fire on rainy days." Softly, "I want to sleep with your back curled into me, and your breasts under my palm."

His warmly animate glance strayed to her firm lower lip, to the faint vibration of the pulse on the incline of her throat, and then to the swell and fall of her breasts. The golden eyes were strained as they returned to hers. "Merry, if I can't be with you now, I don't know how I can stay intact for one more day. Whatever was there that helped me not to take you before has gone. It seemed to vanish on the *Joke* on the way to England. When I heard your laugh across the deck, when I turned to look at you, I wasn't sure each time that I could keep myself from going to you. . . . Love, I need you. Will you come to bed with me?"

His naked urgency shocked her as much as his readiness to show it to her. From Devon the last thing she would have expected was this blunt, almost shaken plea. Her blood flamed in answer—her breasts ached for the offered caress.

"I don't think so," she said, trying to maintain an expression of cool reserve. "I've just come from bed, and I can't think of a single reason why I'd like to go back." Reserve fled as he combed her with a curious smile and went to shut the door. She scampered like a hare behind a chair-backed settee near the window bench.

She had surprised him. That much was evident. He folded himself into the nearest chair and studied her impassively. Finally he said, "You could put down the flowerpot, Merry pet. I can see this won't be a simple adjustment for you, but you're not on the *Joke* anymore. One shout from you would bring the entire household and half the garden staff at a run."

"You're the Duke of St. Cyr. Your servants would gainsay you nothing!" she said and then immediately felt rather embarrassed. Even for her current state of burning sensitivity it sounded a little theatrical.

"You'll find out," he predicted. A dry smile hovered on his lips. "They'd gainsay me in a second if I tried to force myself on a woman. Whatever you might think of me, these are very respectable people. They've known me all my life—I was concerned they'd keep you awake for hours telling my baby stories."

She stared at him. Then, "As the matter of fact, they did tell me one or two."

"I hope it wasn't the one about the time I ingested my name in alphabet tiles?"

"No. The baby cap."

"The alphabet tiles will come." He sighed. "Anyway, there you are. Safety." He gave her a fresh smile that went straight to her heart. "I have an idea."

She watched him lever himself upright, trying to concentrate on anything but the sensual promise of his limber body as he crossed the room and began to dig in a lower drawer of the desk. From a tangle of pottery marbles and ivory spillikins he collected playing cards into a deck and came to her, shuffling them.

"My mother hasn't straightened a drawer in twenty-five years," he said. "Don't run. Watch." He set the deck on a small tripod table beside the settee. "Cut them."

He was calm suddenly, and there was a playful curve to his erotic mouth. Warily she looked at the cards, and then at his face. "Why?"

"I'll tell you in a minute. Go on."

She bent forward and divided the deck with an exasperated snap. "Now what?" she asked, gazing suspiciously at the back of the cards, which carried a picture of a dog balancing on a ball, jauntily tipping a striped top hat.

"Now," he said, fanning out the cards, "we draw. One card each and the winner has his or her choice about our conjugal arrangements."

"That's the most preposterous thing I've ever—"

"Be practical, Windflower," he interrupted with what seemed to Merry like heartless good nature. "We have to find some way to settle things. Do you have a better idea?"

"You *might* agree to leave me alone."

His smile this time was new to her, breathtakingly soft and lush with whimsy. He lifted a hand to the warmth of her throat, his fingers moving in gentle inquiry over the delicate curves of her flesh. "Love, it's the only chance I'm likely to give you. You'd better draw."

Her heartbeat was tolling furiously. "How do I know you'd abide by the draw if I won?"

"Because I wouldn't have proposed it if I didn't intend to carry through." His palm came down on the back of her hand. His fingers spread hers, lacing through them, to cup into her palm and carry her hand to the cards. In a soft imperative: "Do it."

Pink mist rose in her cheeks as she shook off his hand. Her fingers wavered over the cards and then quickly flipped one over. Nine of clubs.

He looked at the card as though in thought before he reached out to draw his own.

"W-wait!" She herded the cards into a pile, picked them up, and studied them. They seemed to be a regular deck; but she shuffled them thoroughly and spread them out once again.

Devon's eyes had suddenly filled with laughter. He turned over a knave of hearts.

"It's a trick. I know it!" she said, grabbing up the cards and carrying them distractedly to the window, examining them under the dappled sunlight. One at a time she stared at them. She laid four in a row and stared at them. The same. The dog pictures appeared to be all exactly the same. The cards fell from her fingers, and she dropped her face into the open cup of her hands.

"Shall I undress," she choked out, "or would it suffice if I lean my back to the wall and draw up my skirts?"

He moved behind her. His hands came to rest on her shoulders, sloping carefully inward to the bare skin at the base of her neck. His thumbs sought her nape, caressing her with steady ease. She could feel the soft displacement of her hair as his lips touched at random among her curls.

"What I'd like," he said softly, "is to walk with you out-of-doors. Will you come?"

Out-of-doors was not the manicured and slightly aloof formality of Grecian summer houses, velvet lawns, and sternly perametered flower beds edged in topiary. Devon's home was a working farm and one of the loveliest spots on earth. The house itself, a cottage orné in pink brick peeping between strawberry trees and a weeping ash, was called Teasel Hill, for the teasel his mother grew to invite goldfinches. Yellow roses climbed busy outbuildings around a courtyard of rosy sandstone gravel where harness brasses jingled on returning teams. The scent of the forge, of buttermilk, applesauce, and clean straw mingled warmly, and through the open door of the barn Merry heard the hiss of the thresher's flail. Colored ribbons untied and caps atumble, a group of little girls were playing trey-trip by the dairy while across the yard beneath an ironwork hoop heavy with deep-violet clematis their elders were admiring the much cross-grained block of elm resting on a farm sled that had been chosen for this year's Yule hearth. Men stripped off their hats, and white aprons began to bob in curtsies as they saw Merry with Devon, their smiles ebullient and welcoming. Merry was discomposed by the gleam of moisture in the eyes of many of the older people as Devon introduced her to them.

Suddenly a group of five women, young wives and girls Merry's own age broke, laughing, from the rest, and crying, "Quickly, Your Grace! This way!" they seized Merry and pulled her at a run around the delicate gray-blue spire of a juniper and through a maze of buildings to a kitchen garden. A chinked stone well crouched in a burst of azure-blue and fluffy white asters, and drawing water forth swiftly from the well, they bade Merry to drink it at once. Nervous, because teasing pranks of this sort on the Black Joke sometimes had rough endings, Merry drank and was applauded gaily.

"Look! The gentlemen are coming, and too late now!" said one young woman, whose lilac-pink dotted skirts swelled prettily with the evidence of her advancing pregnancy. " 'Tis the marriage well, Your Grace, and it's said that whichever spouse drinks here the soonest after they wed will rule the marriage. When I wed my Robin, he ran here straight away from St. Andrew's Church.''

"He was the first to drink then?" Merry asked.

"Nay," said the girl with a sparkling glance, "for I'd carried a bottle with me to the church!''

Devon received a good deal of keenly witty commiseration on his defeat from the men, as well as laughing self-reproaches that they had forgotten to remind him about the marriage well. In the end Devon had taken Merry's hand in his and said laughingly that all he wanted out of life was to be ruled by this small hand. Probably, Merry thought cynically, it was all for show, though the kiss he pressed into her palm tingled sparklike in her breasts.

An irresistible lad in skirts with blackberry stains on his lips was tugging on Devon's coattails, and Merry watched Devon lift the child into his arms, telling him with a smile that he'd grown two feet at least. As though it were an old joke between them, the boy answered that he'd *always* had two feet, and did His Grace know that he was to have his first real trousers on Michaelmas and that Hannah More had had kittens? In a whisper: Did His Grace think the new duchess would care to see them?

The toddler's sharp-eared grandmother was quick to say sternly that the duchess would not want to be crawling around in hay barns looking for kittens. The blackberry stains began to droop at the corners, and Merry protested impulsively that she would love to look for kittens, particularly when they belonged to such an illustrious mother.

Beaming smiles rewarded Merry's words. Both intimidated and warmed by the delighted affection in the faces around her, only beginning to understand the intense emotion the people on Devon's estate would feel for his wife, Merry tried to listen with an air of intelligence to a lively discussion on the genealogy of Devon's cats while one of the young women fetched a quilt of blue plate printed textile to protect Merry's gown for the expedition.

Hannah More lived in a distant meadow inside the thatched barn that housed feed for the cattle pastured there in the winter. Country folk were busy on the driveway near the farm; the sunburnt hedger worked among hedgerows daintily scattered with red hips of the wild rose; the milkmaid in her yoke balanced on the stepping stones of a stream whose banks were overhung with herbs and flowery shoots. A plowboy's whistle lilted through green boughs weighted down with ruddy-cheeked apples.

The sky was a rich oiled blue, and sunny breezes licked the harvest stubble and Merry's skirt as Devon led her through a field. Alone with him amidst the melody of thrush and blackbird, passing under plump hazelnuts on high branches, she was becoming increasingly aware of a restlessness in her body and of the closeness of his.

The barn was in a vale beside a small chestnut wood. Primroses and harebells grew near the door, and inside Devon found the kittens in the loft. Merry pulled off her pink-dyed kid shoes and silk stockings to climb the ladder and sit with him on the wide quilt.

Kittens, she discovered, loved Devon. A tiny calico ball bravely climbed his chest with unfurled claws. Shiny black paws batted at his hair, and peachy small tongues tasted his cheeks. Hannah herself slipped through the great hills of fragrant hay to sit at Devon's hip. Black except for an immaculate white spot on her nose, she groomed the fur on her chest until apparently she felt the visit had been long enough and then carried the kittens off one by one, her tail waving proudly in the air, the end bent like a banner.

Devon had stretched out on his side, his head resting on the lazy prop of a long-fingered hand. He didn't speak, and neither could she, but she felt the flesh on her cheeks and chest burn. The wind had tousled his hair like a lover's hand, and in his sculptured face his eyes had an intent, sleepy glow. Through the outline of fabric she could see the long elegant muscles of his body, pressing in places against the cloth. Light poured from a high, narrow window to form a veil of woven silver touching the symmetry of his cheekbones, his shoulders, his upper thighs. Twice her eyes strayed down the line of his body and then lowered in a shaken way.

His voice, though quiet, was startling in the silence.

"Why do you look away?"

Sitting on her heels, caught in the throes of an embarrassment that was, for once, strangely pleasant, she said, "I don't know." As she inspected the quilt it occurred to her suddenly that his stillness was deliberate. He must be wondering whether another approach would provoke another retreat. There had been a very real curiosity in his question, and the need to search out the delicate shift of her mood.

For a moment she was exasperated with her own complexity and rather ashamed that he was forced to cater to it; then she forgave herself because when it came right down to it, he wasn't exactly simple himself. But here they were at last, married, and warily together, and in spite of everything, wanting each other. Or at least she wanted him, and he *said* he wanted her. Grateful, and frustrated that he had chosen this, of all times, to be patient, she plucked at a blue pucker in the quilt and said, "Devon? What does it make you feel when I look at you?"

The half smile was warm, a little rueful, and very human, his features no longer those of a beautiful and soulless idol but of a man, with his own sensitivities.

"Pleasure," he said.

She stretched a hesitant finger and lightly stroked a fold of his white lawn shirt. "And if I touch you?" she whispered.

His eyes widened in response. In a low tone that had a faintly breathless quality to it, he said, "Touch me. I'll try to describe it for you."

Desire long denied was rioting in her veins as he moved invitingly closer. Her trembling fingers loosened one by one the mother-of-pearl buttons of his shirt as she watched the soft tumbling fabric open over his taut sun-gilt skin. Shy inside, and numbly aware that not much more than an hour ago she had denied hypocritically any desire to be with him, she stood up, her feet apart, her toes curling for balance on the thick quilt with its undependable foundation of hay. Devon's gaze was passing over her in light inquiry; she saw his lips part and catch a hard breath as she put her hands behind her and began to open her gown. In a love daze she slid to her knees by him, clad only in the slippery silk and white lace of her chemise, its openwork hem teasing her thighs. Her fingers caught his shirt, spreading it slowly over the rise of his chest and the tight-knit modeling of his stomach. Beautiful, the fresh expanse of naked flesh looked beautiful to her, though she wasn't quite sure what to do with it. But the wind-dusted fragrance of his skin was so sweet to her senses that it was making her head reel. Like one of the kittens might have done, she lay at his side, nuzzling her face into his firm belly just below his lowest ribs. Underneath the velvet luxury of his skin his chest muscles contracted harshly. He said her name once, a ragged inhalation as she showered exuberant, inexpert kisses between each rib and over the delicately fleeced curves of his chest.

"Describe it," she whispered with husky cheerfulness, trailing the pink tip of her tongue upward, and then descending in earthy, lacing patterns.

"The word that—" His rough murmur failed. Her body pressed close to him, her breasts a soft, unconsciously thrusting caress against his hips. "Merry—" he whispered thickly. He sought her cheek with an unsteady hand, the fingers penetrating her hair, the little finger wandering lower to find and stroke the elaborate inner surfaces of her ear. "My love, the word that comes to mind"—his breathing sharpened again as her hands slid over his thighs—"is torment."

Putting her head back with a slight laugh, she looked up into his face with its satiny eyelashes and love-flush. "You needn't think I'm completely ignorant about what happens between men and women," she said. With slumberous satisfaction she added, "I've talked to Cat."

"Have you?" He was gently massaging her earlobe, his smile a luxuriant haze. "A masterful source. You probably know more than me. What approach did he take—skyrockets and roses, or gears and pulleys?"

His little finger wandered across the lift of her cheek to her nose, circling the petallike nostrils with his fingertip, then dropping downward to her upper lip. Her lips parted under his gentle probing and her eyes drifted closed as his fingertip barely entered her mouth, exploring the wet silk interior, carrying the moisture outward to dew her breath-dried lips.

Against his fingers she said, "Neither. We used Latin words." Suddenly she rolled a single revolution away, her eyes brilliant with laughter. "I'd better run back to my valise for my notes." Stumbling upright, she swung on her heel. She stood poised as though for flight, her foot sunk within the quilt into a furrow in the surface beneath. As she shifted her feet slightly apart to catch her balance she felt Devon's hand encircle her ankle from behind. His grip was ever so soft, a caress.

His lips touched her ankle, his breath feathering over her skin. Expert fingers began to massage her calf. The other hand stroked higher; she drew a soft, shuddering gasp as palm and fingers spanned the back of her thigh, his finger grazing the swell of her buttock. Touching his mouth to the hollow behind her knee, he pressed lightly nipping kisses there, his hair brushing with flossy softness of her thigh. Any desire she'd had to play and be silly faded into an intense need that grew dizzily under the pressure of his exploration.

"Every part of you is so dear to me," he whispered. Kneeling behind her on the quilt, he slid a steadying arm around her waist, over the slick fabric of her chemise, its hem riding up to fan daintily at her hips. "Lovely . . . lovely Merry . . . your legs are beautiful" —the sensitive male fingers followed the silken line of her thigh upward—"so straight and strong. You can't know how long I've wanted them to hold me."

Agonized by the pressure of his arm so close to her breasts, she caught his wrist in shaking fingers and dragged his hand to her aching flesh, gasping as his fingers cupped her. Through the glossy cloth his thumb sought her nipple, prodding it to erection. The other hand slipped between her legs, caressing the heavy satin of her inner thighs.

Her eyes had drifted closed, her hands clasping his arm and wrist for support, absorbing its gentle motion as it shaped and lifted her breast and then wandered to the creamy plane above. His hand cradled her throat, soothing her thundering pulsebeat when his other hand slid under her chemise up the trembling flesh of her leg to the silky curls there. Very gently he let his fingers enter her, though not deeply, and felt the hard shivers rack her slender body and the clench of her fingers on his arm.

Murmuring his desire, he let his hands glide over her rippling undergarment to her hips, turning her to him, his fingers spreading on her bottom. He pulled her close, enchanted by the provocative form of her bare legs against his skin. Need for her ran like flame-licked brandy through his body. With searing tenderness he nestled his face into the warm cloud of her kitteny softness. The gossamer texture of her curls on his lips intoxicated him; and her fragrance, the sweet-brier tang of her bath soap tinged in nectarous awakening, possessed his rocketing senses.

But he felt her straining to escape him, whimpering, "No . . . oh, Devon, please . . ." Looking up into the blue eyes darkened with arousal and heated distress, noticing the blush staining her cheek-bones with twin rose-hued crescents, he saw he had shocked her. New to this as she was, she needed his moderation, but smothered as he was in desire that had been deferred until he was almost crazy from it, there was a panicked moment when he was afraid he might not be able to give it to her. He tried to remember a time when he had been as she was now, tender and untried, though he seemed not to be able to think of anything except her heat and colors and firm cherub's flesh. Fighting to conquer the mindless demands of his appetite, he tightened his arms on her hips, drawing her down, rolling her onto her back, forcing himself to gaze down into the unguarded blue of her eyes.

Stroking her cheek with the backs of fingers that were shaking badly, he said, "Forgive me, little flower . . . You're so fair, every petal . . . Help me, Merry, please. Please, love, tell me to be gentle with you. . . ."

The blue eyes snapped shut, the earnest lips twisting daintily in a martyr's frustration. Painfully she whispered, "Don't be gentle, Devon. Be *quick*."

He had begun to laugh then, and he was laughing yet when he came down to her again after shedding his clothes and slowly drawing off her chemise. His lips descended to her throat in a hungry caress before his mouth covered hers, glorying in the way she rose to meet his kiss, opening herself to his searching fingers. In a moment she murmured, "I g-guess marriage isn't so ho-hum after all."

He smiled against the soft underside of her breast. "Under all circumstances," he murmured, "a humorist." Taking her nipple deeply into his mouth, he gentled his knee into the quilt between her thighs, his hands beginning the ravishing, unsteady journey upward to her face, tracing the intricate weave of bone and muscle beneath the thin fabric of her fevered skin. The movements of her body were hard and restless under his, her face, wreathed in damp curls, turning from side to side on the quilt. Dusty filtered light brightened the sheen of moisture on her eyelashes and on her swollen coral-colored lips.

Catching her chin, he held her still to receive his kiss, gently swaying her face with his hand to vary the shape of their contact, penetrating her thoroughly with his tongue. Distraught whimpers fluttered from her throat, and her small hands twined around him as his lips formed the words "I love you, I love you" in a rough convulsive whisper against her burning mouth and he parted her thighs with gentle caresses. And then, gathering her slight body into the safe harbor of his arms, he eased himself into her melting warmth.

An act of love, done in love. He had never experienced it, and its miracle cascaded through him as though it were the unseen resonance of some great carillon. Little thrilling arias sang in undiscovered nerves. For him, for this moment, all senses slept except the sense of exquisite wonder at the joy she was to him. He wasn't aware that his eyes were closed until a small sound came to him from some brilliantly colored void beneath him.

Opening his eyes, he looked down through many layers of iridescent love-gauze into hot bluebell eyes, pearly skin, and a panting, slightly open mouth that held an expression that he could only call—oh, dear God, he could only call it disgruntled. Love, pity, and—regrettably—amusement came to him in a roseate flood. Flaying the threatening laughter brutally into submission, he thought, *No, Lord, no—don't let me laugh at her. She's so proud.* In this as in all moments she had that absurdly guileless dignity that had managed to touch his heart from the very beginning. He wanted to say something to comfort her, but with body and mind free-floating in a honey bath of sensation, it was not easy to be promptly coherent. A sweat-tipped tendril danced at her temple under the erratic flow of his breath, and he brought a hand to her face to touch it back with his fingers, wondering how much of the aching tenderness that was twisting his heart was showing in his smile.

"Why are you still?" she said, as though her anxiety had forced her to speak.

He connected in a softly unfocused way with the frown in her eyes. "To help you, little one. I won't"—he stopped, to consume a gasping breath—"move until you've had time. Are you— Dearest love, have I hurt you?"

"Well—yes." The voice was small and glum. "I liked your hand better."

This time he had no choice but to bury his silent laughter against her shoulder. When he could trust himself to speak, he said, "Don't despair, sapphire eyes. I hope"—a long, uncontrollable shiver of passion passed through him—"presently to be able to make things better for you."

"*Hope?*"

Irresistible laughter swallowed him again. "I only have instinct, dear one. I've never been anyone's first lover before." As soon as the words were out, he could hardly believe he'd said them. The appalling reference to experiences past, and at such a moment—the utter confusion of his bliss was the only thing he could think of to account for such tactlessness; but studying her in dismayed concern, he discovered that his words seemed to have pleased her.

The dazzling color of her cheeks enclosed a lopsided smile that was just sardonic enough to fascinate him. Pushing her soft nose into the nerve center of his palm, stroking him with her open lips, she said softly, "Instinct?"

His fingers stroked her nose and lips while with his free hand he resettled her body beneath him, keeping himself deeply in her. Bringing her mouth to meet his, letting his hand drift to her throat and lower, he whispered, "Love, together we can find where the clouds are born."

CHAPTER TWENTY-SIX

One of the kittens had come during the night, waking Devon when it climbed his hair with struggling clawholds, padding across his shoulder to his chest. He lifted his hand absently to stroke its plump, furry body, and the kitten turned once, in a circle, batting his cheek with its tail, and then settled in a lump under his chin. In the absolute silence its purr seemed loud. Below, with her head nested in the hollow below his shoulder, Merry slept on.

She had fallen asleep soon after their lovemaking, while their bodies were still tangled together like bright ribbands on May Day, and he was murmuring love words to her, trying to find some way to tell her that she had entered his soul like sunlight.

The soft-dying day had crept under the thatch eaves to glaze the shadows in thin jewellike colors. Swallows twittered in the skies overhead, and hedge crickets bantered with the dusk; and as he had drawn his young wife's sleeping body under the folds of the quilt he had wondered why men asked more of life than this. Gazing down into the helpless oblivion on her face, he had seen her again as she had been at the crest of her rapture. The fierce sweetness of it had possessed him so totally that he couldn't remember when or even whether he had reached his own fulfillment. He savored the jubilant emotions for a long time before he slept.

Now it was too black to see anything, but Devon could feel the kitten stand, stretch, resettle. And atuned as he was to her faintest movement, he knew the second Merry woke. He could even feel her moment's bewilderment as she found she was pressed intimately to a man's body. Then she tensed, and he felt her breath, drawn quickly in shock, as it flooded against his nipple. Before she could start to withdraw from him, he said softly, "We have a visitor."

His fingers followed the line of her arm until he reached her hand, and carried it to the kitten. He could feel her expression change against his skin—perhaps to surprise—and the contraction of her arm muscles against his chest as she began to stroke the kitten. Her fragrant hair tickled his face as he strayed slow kisses there and caressed the lovesome geography of her, the flat, solid muscles in her back, the flesh of her nape under its warming hair-cover.

"Do I seem different to you now?" she asked in a hushed voice.

His wrist arched comfortably over her ear; the side of his thumb rode the potent softness of her cheekbone. "No. I seem different to myself."

"How?"

"Wiser. And younger. Nearer to myself . . ." He put a finger on the tip of her nose and wiggled it gently. "I meant all the words I said to you, Merry."

"I didn't." Sudden tears scratched her voice. "I'm sorry about what I said—you know, *during*—about not liking things. It turned out not to be true."

In the quiet he could hear her swallow the pooling moisture in her throat. Finding the underside of her chin with one finger, he tilted her face upward toward his. In this total absence of light he could see nothing more than the faint shine of her eyes, but their exhalations swirled together like cloudscapes under a sable moon. "Do you know what, Windflower? It's appalling that women are made so their first love is painful. Whose idea was that, do you think?" Her watery chuckle quavered against his chest. "If it had been up to me, things would be much different."

Comforted, she snuggled against him, her fawn-soft breasts moving in an unknowing massage on the high shallows of his rib cage. She seemed content to lie in the peace of his arms, lulled toward sleep by the knowledgeable persuasion of his loving hands. A minute passed. Her voice came to him, a low melody.

"Could it be true? Were Morgan and my mother—" She broke off, as though the relationship defied description.

"I don't know. I haven't started thinking about it yet. I think it's something I'll have to prepare myself for by three days of fasting and meditation. Did you have any inkling?"

"I'm not sure." The kitten yawned, a tiny sigh. "On the night the British officers came to St. Elise, Morgan made me come with him to the beach. He *knew* that I had drawn those pictures before he saw them, and afterward I thought, *How did he know?* Is he clairvoyant?"

"Morgan is many things, but a clairvoyant is definitely not among them." Devon stretched his hand backward above his head to free a reed from the matted hay. He put it between his teeth, tasting the sharp wild grass flavor on his tongue. "Could your servant—"

"Henry Cork?"

"Yes. Henry Cork. Could he have heard you talking with your brother about the drawings and somehow passed that information to Morgan?"

"It's possible. He often hid in strange places, but we thought that

was to keep Aunt April from putting him to his chores." Her sleepy
voice intoned the words slowly, as though she found the whole thing
a hopeless bewilderment. "If Morgan knew from the beginning,
why didn't he tell you?"

"I wouldn't have kept you then." Folding her into the warmth of
his body, he felt a thrill of protective fear for her pass like
metal fibers through his nerves. "God help us both, love, but I'm
afraid those months of turmoil were my half brother's notion of
matchmaking."

Cat could have thought of another name for it. Alone in Lord
Cathcart's library, waiting, waiting . . . He had conducted several
useless cursory examinations of the room; but there had been nothing to distract him except perhaps the book on probate law that lay
open on Cathcart's desk. Except for the book the room was bleakly
tidy. Even the marble bust of Homer had not so much as a dust mote
on its eyelids.

Plucking an abridged history of Rome from the shelf, he had
carried the calfskin volume with him to the couch. The Roman
Empire. It was, in a convoluted way, his favorite period of history.
One couldn't find a more acute allegory of human civilization than
the Roman coliseum, wherein the selfish, complacent multitudes
gazed from their smug tiers at the sad struggles below. Rand Morgan
would have done very well in Rome.

Three days ago in Falmouth Cat had watched the traveling carriage bear Merry off, and then he had gone directly back to the *Joke*,
where Morgan was poring over a sheet of figures, a candle assisting
the pale dayshine. He was a striking figure, his ruffled shirt opened
over the iron chest muscles, his hair darkly glossy, the color of apple
seeds. Smiling, he had looked up at Cat, his eyes black mocking
embers.

"So—did she weep down your shirt buttons?"

Ignoring the taunt, Cat had walked to the desk and picked up the
sheet of figures. "Have you figured out yet how much of a bribe
we'll have to give Customs?"

"Yes. That being done, I'm going to shore, where I want two
things: to have a meal and to have a woman, and that means if

you're going to be emotional at me about Merry, do it while I pull on my boots, or you'll have to scold my empty nightcap.''

Cat set down the page. ''I wish we could come to some kind of uniform agreement on whether I'm supposed to have emotions, or not have them.''

''Very well,'' Morgan said agreeably, picking up a boot. ''You can have emotions. Abracadabra. Wasn't that easy? Now, look around inside your skull for your common sense. You see? It remains in residence. No one makes you surrender your logic in order to feel. Hand me my other boot.''

With temper chills biting like teeth in the lining of his stomach, Cat wrenched up the boot, strode with it to the window, pushed open the casing, and flung Morgan's boot into the harbor, where it drowned in a crown-shaped splash. Its halo of disturbed water had expanded and vanished before Morgan spoke.

''That might have caught my attention, but think of the poor fisherman who pulls it up on a line instead of a sea bass. . . . I don't know what you're worried about. The chit can handle Devon.''

''Rand, she doesn't know that. She's frightened. And she has good reason to be too.''

''She has *no* reason to be. Why do you think I let him drag her off on St. Elise? They've both had a chance to see that you can pour anger into him until it steams from his ears like hot sulfur, and even then he can't harm her. What else would you like to know?''

Cat took a long silent breath of the moist air that cascaded through the open window. ''About her mother.''

Behind him Cat heard silence. A low laugh. A voice. ''Here.''

Turning, he caught Morgan's other boot, lightly tossed.

''Why do things by halves? Send down a pair.''

So Cat threw the second boot after the first and sat down on the window bench, watching Morgan stretch out in a chair, cross his stockings at the ankle, and rest his hands on the naked flesh of his abdomen. For a long time Morgan stared at but not into Cat's eyes. Elbows braced on the chair arms, the pirate raised his hands, knotted absently in prayer fashion, touching his own lips with the steeple of his fingers.

''When I was thirteen,'' he said suddenly, softly, ''I went to England to see my father. Literally to see. As one *sees* the pyramids.

It was five years before the war of 1793, and I'd been smuggling with a crew of Corsicans all winter. When spring came, I landed in Margate with a pocket full of coins and made my way to Teasel Hill. On Sunday morning I sat on the churchyard wall and saw them all—my father's exquisite child-bride, and Devon, squalling his bloody head off under a hundred ells of lace, and Jasper himself, beaming down at them as though they were all the angels in heaven. They disappeared into the church without looking around.''

The gnawing in Cat's stomach had grown more intense. ''That was all?''

''That was all.''

''Did you want more?''

Morgan grinned. ''From my father, no. But I wanted to unwrap his smothering infant and swive his wife. Neither thing being possible, I thought, *Well, I've seen them* and set out across the meadows with my thumbs tucked in the waist of my ragged knee breeches.'' The hands relaxed, conjoined still, against his chest. ''That afternoon I saw her. Her. The girl who became Merry's mother. She was my age, but in most ways a child, and I first saw her walking in a dry ditch with strawberry clover all in flower. Her silk skirts were spread out all around her like willow boughs, and her ringlets were filled with wild apple blossoms and falling down on one side; and she had put her bonnet on a lamb that she was trying to lead on a red ribbon, as though it were a puppy, but the lamb kept balking and chewing the ribbon. Her eyes were light blue, the color of robin's eggs, and they opened round when she saw me standing in the lane above her. Then she grabbed my hand and drew me into the ditch beside her, putting two fingers on my lips and saying ''Ssh!'' when I would have spoken. She whispered to me that I had to be very quiet because Indians were coming. And when I told her that I didn't know there were Indians in England, she touched my lips and said ''Ssh!'' again. England was full of Indians, she said, only they had to stay mostly out of sight because people made such a fuss when they saw them. Sometimes, she said, she let the Indians scalp her, and sometimes she hid. And the next time she opened pink-bud lips to speak, I put my fingers on her mouth and said ''Ssh. . . .''''

The dark gaze was blind, the smooth jet irises catching quills of light like the seed globe of a thistle. ''I stayed until late May, working for a chandler in Leatherhead, seeing her when she could slip away. On the last day it rained, and we met under a beech tree, with celandine growing in a mat beneath, the flowers closed in the poor light, and she said it seemed as though the sun had drawn closed its shutters." A long pause. Morgan's eyes returned to Cat's. Mildly the pirate said, "I had to leave her, you know. Her family would never have allowed me to court her openly. Too gently reared for friendship; too wellborn to marry; too young to bed. The temptations were too great, which was why I tried not to learn what became of her, but I imagined her cherished, and happy, and in time . . . married. Years later I discovered by chance that her family had left England in a state of poverty. I had the *Joke* and money, and I searched for her, but by then she had died. There were two children, Merry and an older brother; and a widowed husband—James Wilding."

Cat released an aging breath from his lungs. "Wilding. The famous ones?"

"The famous ones. The fanatical ones. James and Carl Wilding . . ." A terse smile touched Morgan's firm lips. "He was probably better to her than I would have been. My only consolation. I left someone with the children—"

"I know. Merry's Henry Cork."

Morgan's brow skipped upward in mocking admiration. "How long have you known?"

"When she was ill," Cat said, "she told me all about Henry Cork, and the man bore a certain resemblance to old Hezekiah, the gunner's mate that Sails used to tell stories about. Big practical joker. I found his name on a copy of your old manifest on St. Elise. Hezekiah Cork."

"My, my. You have been rowing with both oars, haven't you? Hezekiah Cork. He wasn't much, but at least I knew I could trust him not to seduce the girl the day she reached puberty. What I haven't quite figured out yet is what she was doing on a ship bound for Britain in Michael Granville's company, and why he would go to so much trouble to besmirch her reputation. Although I suspect Letitia's fingers in this somewhere."

"Devon's grandmother?"

"Yes." Morgan uncrossed his ankles. "She reposes immense

confidence in Granville's integrity. And you see, I'd been toying with the idea of bringing Merry to England if the political situation in America continued to deteriorate. I had Letitia maintain a correspondence with Merry's aunt so that if I had to move her, it could be done through an intermediary. At that point there seemed to be nothing to be gained by terrifying the girl with the knowledge that I had an interest in her. In the end I decided she'd be safer where she was." He studied his toes, flexing them. "It turns out, of course, that I was wrong. It was fortunate you brought her to me."

" 'All the while he by his side her bore. She was as safe as in a Sanctuary,' " Cat quoted sarcastically. "And you decided she'd do for Devon. Please, if you happen to pick someone out you want me to marry, just say 'Marry her!' and I will. Don't drag me through all the cellars in hell by the seat of my inexpressibles first."

"Nonsense." Morgan's smile was disquieting. "I only provided proximity. They did the rest. I wouldn't have encouraged it if I hadn't seen in the beginning that they were in love. You're worried about Merry; then go after her."

Morgan's words had taken Cat off guard. He said quickly, "Do you mean it?"

"Certainly. You might begin looking for her at Cathcart's. I gave Devon a letter to deliver to him."

There it was. The trap, neatly closing. He might have known. Through hell by the seat of his breeches. Why had he ever expected anything else?

"Why do you always have to be so bloody thorough?" Cat's eyes grew colder than the icy fluids that had suddenly filled up his veins. "Was the letter about me?"

"My dear, what else do I have in common with the saintly Cathcart? Certainly it was about you. Run along to London and find out what's becoming of our little nestling. But first," he said with a malicious grin, "find me something to put on my feet. I don't intend to brave the wet cobbles of Falmouth in my stockings."

Sitting in Lord Cathcart's library three days later with the history of Rome on his lap, Cat thought angrily that what Morgan deserved was to walk over live coals in his bare feet. He flipped open the expensively bound volume. It was printed on wave paper. Good

God, who could read it? A gift, obviously, from one of the illiterati. Most of Cathcart's friends were men of letters, weren't they? He looked on the front leaf. *For dear Brian. From your sincere, loving, and affectionate friend Aline. On Christmas Day 1813*. Aline. Devon's mother. That was interesting. After years of benign devotion here was Devon's mother giving Cathcart books with love sandwiched pathetically between sincerity and affection. As an approach it was probably too subtle for Cathcart. She would have done better with *Dear Brian. Aching and damp for you in my lonely bed. Pension off your mistress and I'm yours. Aline*. It must be difficult for her. Rumor had it that she was a woman of unassailable virtue. Enough men, certainly, had tried to assail it, including the royal scion himself. Poor woman, and here she was, chaste as unsunn'd snow and reduced to trying to send blurred signals at her late husband's best friend. Cat closed the book cover. Maybe he was reading too much into a simple inscription.

Outside, a carriage stopped in clanging rhythmics of iron upon rounded stone. With unwelcome emotion writhing in his stomach Cat heard the muted sounds of Cathcart's entrance, the indecipherable rustle of his conversation with the butler. The door opened. Lord Cathcart entered.

They stood in the quiet and looked at each other. Father and son. The man and the only living creation of his body.

The boy had his looks from his mother—the sturdy bones, the square hips and shoulders, the relaxed elegance of the carriage, and the odd tintless hair that had enchanted Cathcart nineteen years ago. Cathcart had met her on his Grand Tour, and though she had blossomed from the purest flower of Swedish gentility, and was only twenty, she was tainted already by disgrace, and there had been plenty of people to warn Cathcart not to marry her. But Cathcart had been young and naïve, and his insight was colored by the generosity of spirit that later made him a beloved and enlightened philanthropist; he had believed in her completely, ignoring or forgiving every sign that she might not fully return his regard, and attributing her heavy use of oral opiates to the stresses of her unquiet nature. When she deserted him after five months of marriage, it had stricken him to the marrow of his soul, and it was five years before he had recovered enough to allow Devon's father to gently prod him into hiring a young lawyer to find out what had become of her so that they could gather the evidence for a divorcement. The lawyer was a conscientious man; it was not his fault that when he traced the woman to the Caribbean brothel where opium overuse had finally stopped her heart, no one there had thought to tell him she had left a child. Probably none of them took any interest in the parentage of the filthy and abused scraps of humanity that slept in the hen yard, the malnourished survivors of the abortionist's sporadic competence. They became better kept and better fed as they grew older, and a source of labor or profit.

It had been Rand Morgan, with his myriad sources, and his curiosities, and his own much less overt philanthropy, who had heard the old scandal from Devon and decided, because the frail underside of the seemingly pious had always interested him, that Cathcart's investigations had been criminally lax and if it were ever convenient, he might look into the matter himself. And Morgan's looking into the matter had produced Cat, and the documentation that the boy had been born in a month that placed his conception during the only period in Cathcart's marriage when it would have been impossible for his wife to be unfaithful.

Four years ago Lord Cathcart had been introduced to the existence of his child by Devon, who had met him in an inn fronting the Thames. "Brian, you have a son," Devon had said gently and began the careful, compassionate explanation of Cat's life in a narrative that avoided judgments but could do nothing to buffer the horror of the full truth.

The horror had been crushing. Morgan had brought the boy in, and Cathcart, searching beneath the surface for a child, could see only a braid, and an earring, and the eyes, old eyes, and an existence he could barely imagine. Trying to reach through those things, he had found in Cat (dear heaven, that name—he couldn't bring himself to use it) a hard-willed and intelligent adolescent who was bored, impatient, saw no significance in their relationship, and who, it was clear, was here only because Morgan had commanded it and it was his habit to obey Morgan. No, there was more than habit in his obedience to Morgan; there was something deeper. How intimate had their relationship become? Discipline and the need to preserve his own sanity had kept Cathcart from following that thought to its conclusion.

Twice, at Cathcart's insistence and with Morgan's bland consent, there had been experiments in which Cat came to stay with him in London. Both occasions had been failures. What would a third failure do to them both?

Lord Cathcart watched the boy put down the book and stand, candle-glow irradiating like a phasm from the smooth coils of his braid.

"I'm here," the boy said, his expression remote, his tone polite. "I hope you don't mind."

"No. I'm pleased." Cathcart had learned to keep his phrases simple. In the past anything more had sounded surprisingly insincere, even when it was meant from the heart. It was harder for him than it was for the boy; because love for a son was ingrained in Cathcart while Cat had no need for a father. And on the *Joke* he'd had a whole shipload of potential fathers, if he'd wanted one, and all of them less alien than an English marquis. "I appreciated your letters."

There had been two, delivered at odd times of the night by disreputable-looking scoundrels four months after they were dated. The first, eighteen months ago, had said, "Alive. On the Atlantic. Cat." The second, in March, had said, "Devon gave me your letter. I don't understand why you say you need to see me. I've never noticed that my presence does anything beyond distress you. If you call my relationship with Morgan 'an infatuation' once more, it's unlikely that you'll hear from me again. Cat." The words may not have been friendly, but they were the closest Cathcart had ever come to an exchange of substance with his son.

Cat acknowledged his father's appreciation with a slight wary nod. Then, coming right to the point, he said, "Has Devon been here?"

"Yes. Last night."

Urgently, "Was there a girl with him?"

"Yes. Merry Wilding. He married her this morning."

"Jesus! He married her?"

Recoiling inside, unfamiliar as he was with the workings of his son's mind, Lord Cathcart misinterpreted his wonder. The surprise in Cat's gently sardonic inflection sounded like callous incredulity, as though he could hardly imagine why Devon would marry her, when women were to be used and discarded.

It took so much of Cat's concentration to absorb that change in Merry's situation that it was a moment before he realized Cathcart was watching him in rigid silence. *I've said something wrong,* Cat thought. *Already. Was it the "Jesus"?* He was trying to figure out whether it would make things better or worse if he apologized when Cathcart said, "You knew her on the *Joke*?"

That tone. Accustomed as Cat was to thinking of himself as Merry's . . . almost her foster parent, it required some abrupt mental gymnastics to recognize that this stranger whose only claim on him was that they had both spent a minute or two between the thighs of the same woman—under entirely different circumstances—this self-righteous stranger saw him as one of her captors. And of course, in a way, he had been. Before, all of this had been only irritation. Having to spend time with this gentle, balding scholar at Morgan's insistence—irritation; having the man's gawky, gossiping servants stare at him as though he were about to run off with the silver—irritation; being introduced to Cathcart's noble friends with their slack-jawed fascination—well, all right, that had been a little more than irritating. But this—prior to now only Rand Morgan had been able to make Cat feel this kind of vivid hot and cold anger. The feeling he usually had with Cathcart, the feeling that he wanted to retreat and retreat, switched with shattering speed to attack.

"Did I know her in the biblical sense, do you mean?" he snapped, his eyes wide and brighter than he knew.

The last thing Cathcart desired was to strike his son on an open nerve. Truthfully he had never thought the boy had one. Could Merry Wilding have touched him as she had Devon?

"No," Cathcart said. *God help me to say the right thing,* he thought. "Devon assured me that she was protected from that. We don't have to discuss it."

"Why not? Because you can't stand to hear the truth about the way I live? Because you don't want to know that I brought her on the *Joke* against her will, that I held her down so Morgan could feed her opium, that I left her in Devon's bed, knowing that he might—" Cat broke off, hardly recognizing his own voice. Odd quick catches separated words and syllables. The vowels had soft slurs. His throat ached. What was this? Guilt. Guilt for every time she had needed him and he had turned away. Guilt for the rough words he had spoken to her on those first days when he could have been comforting and kind. Now she was married. And safe. And as he had done once before, when he had realized she was going to survive the nearly fatal attack of malaria, he was crying. Of all times, of all places for this to happen—he thrust his face into one callused palm with a sound somewhere between a gasp and a groan. In a moment he felt himself being drawn into the warm oval of his father's arms. He would have cast off the hug because he usually hated being touched, but this clasp was startling in its strength and tenderness; and the darkness around him began to recede though the sobs came harder, painfully racking contractions in his esophagus. He murmured, "This is so bloody embarrassing."

Cathcart remembered asking Devon once if Cat ever smiled. Devon had said, "He has a sense of humor, but no, he doesn't smile. When you know him better, it won't matter." Devon was right. It didn't matter. As warm as a smile was this disarming ability the boy had to express with such candor that his tears embarrassed him. Absorbing the precious weight of his son's body, gazing down at the neat pale hair, Cathcart saw that it was not tintless, as his mother's had been, but held the delicate sunny ivory shades of a pear blossom.

"Did you come to care for her a great deal?" Cathcart said thoughtfully.

"Someone had to. At first she was so helpless—" Cat heard Cathcart chuckle, not as Morgan would have done. This sound was sympathetic, gently interested.

"She's not helpless anymore. Last night she landed a wallop on the underside of Devon's jaw that almost knocked him out of his waistcoat," Cathcart said, watching his son lift his head, the pale lashes webbed with blue glittering tears.

"Did she? Poor midget, his jaw's the only part of him she can reach, unless he leans over," Cat said shakily, blinking. "He's been acting like an ass lately. I hope she knocked some sense into him."

"I think she did," Cathcart smiled. "He seemed more reasonable afterward." He felt the slight gather of tension in his son's well-muscled shoulders, and he stepped back, gently releasing the boy, not with regret but with grateful wonder that he had had this brief first chance to hold his unchildlike child. "Can you stay? We should give them a few days alone, and then, if you like, we could visit them."

Cat nodded. As he took the comfortable chair Cathcart offered and settled into its velvet upholstery, it occurred to him that there was one thing Cathcart offered the people around him that Morgan never gave to anyone. Peace.

CHAPTER TWENTY-SEVEN

Dawn frosted the loft with sun-shot colors that spangled the fragrant rolling surfaces with prisms and sipped night broth from the magenta shadows. Awakening to a gush of hot, voluptuous sensations, Merry felt Devon's warmth beside her, his palm a deep pressure on her breast, kneading, flexing, shaping the full mound that was softly burning under his touch. He had uncovered her to the muted sunlight and to his gaze, and her first memory was of her own flowery wantonness under his hands last night. She whimpered, curling away from him, and sat up with her back to him, the bruised hay snapping under her. Her arms crossed over the blood-hot flesh on her breasts, her hair falling like a crepe lisse curtain between her parted knees.

"What is it, Windflower?" His voice, behind her, was a gentle whisper.

There were any number of things, including the unfamiliar delicacy of her body, holding yet the sweet flavors of his lovemaking; and her diffuse uncertainties about the strength of his love; and her fears about the wisdom of this hurried marriage and . . . and . . .

She felt his hands spreading the curls on her neck, uncovering the highest point of her spine. His open mouth slowly brushed her there; his tongue followed in a rough caress, a liquid, tingling circle that sent stinging pricks of pleasure in an aching trail to the base of her spine. She moaned, a deep sigh, and she felt his breath halt and come more quickly on her skin as he heard it.

"I love your pleasure sounds, Merry. I love your voice. I love to hear you, husky with wanting me," he whispered.

His fingers were moving on her back, sending cascades of shivers through her, a reminder of the quivering heights he had carried her to. . . . One of his hands smoothed over the yearning swell of her hip, while the other courted the vulnerable flesh on her nape, moving under her hair to cup and caress her throat before lazily stroking her mouth with his fingers.

"Open your lips, little one," he murmured into her foaming curls. "Let me . . . yes . . ." His thumb dragged across the rise of her lower lip, curving gently inward to the warm and moist interior, his fingers supporting her chin. Then the hand left her face, wandering downward through the lush garden of her hair until his fingers were just below her breast, lifting its softly swelling weight in his curling palm, his thumb pressing upward on her nipple, dewing the hardening, aching flesh with glossy moisture, the wetness easing and deepening the dizzying contact.

"Yes . . . oh, yes, love," he whispered, "*oh, yes,*" as she arched herself against his hand. A slow delicious sweep of movement brought his other hand to her belly, massaging her taut resisting flesh to pliancy. She felt the teasing rise and fall of his breathing on her cheek, the prickling, shifting pressure of his lips tasting the side of her neck, the damp fire of his tongue-stroke on the tip of her ear.

"Come back, my love. Turn back to me." His need for her flamed in the beguiling voice. "You've drawn my image with your clever fingers. Now let me print it on your heart." His breath, a soft exhalation, stirred the curls that hung as a nodding bouquet over her earlobe, sending vivid shock runners to the peaks of her breasts. Cupping the pink crest of her shoulders in his palms, he pressed her backward into the nest of the quilt.

"Lie with me and watch the morning brighten. Lie with me . . ."

His whisper, a heated flush upon her nostrils, carried the fragrance of kitten, of the spicy hay with its complement of wild meadowsweet, of the warm innocent scents of sleep. "Lie still, love. I only want to touch you." His hands moved to her body, a heady, eager exploration of her—her fingers, the structure of her wrists, the highly sensitive skin on the inner bend of her arm, the sturdy muscles of her upper arm, and then outward, over the refinements of her body, turning, stroking, caressing her charming parts, and with as much love, the small imperfections of flesh or form that made her a woman and not a statue or goddess created from mixed colors on a palette. His palms and fingers and lips painted what she was, real and appealing and breathless from the sensual quest of his fingers.

Gasping softly, she whispered, "How s-still do you want me to lie?"

His husky laughter caressed her nipple as his lips came downward to capture it, massaging it in shuddering waves with his tongue, his hair stroking back and forth on the throbbing surface of her breast. Sensitive, experienced fingers coaxed her to fever, contouring the fretting muscles of her thighs, and then shifting, so that his hand lightly cupped the rise of her silky curls, molding her, kneading her to a lavish fiery ecstasy with the flat of his palm. Wet dancing kisses covered her breasts and then found her open, swollen lips, nuzzling them hungrily, roughly, sinking his tongue into the delicious richness of her mouth. Little cries, weak moans wept from her throat. She sought his warmth, her feet burrowing like lithe mice into the quilt to arc herself in heightened closeness to the hands and mouth that were bringing passion to her in spearlike thrusts.

Whispering, "Your breasts are so beautiful. I love to feel the weight of them in my hand . . . all down you . . . the softness under my tongue . . . here . . . here," he tucked her body beneath him, and the joy of having all his flesh against hers tickled through the eroticized pathwork of her nerves.

"Devon . . ." Her voice was almost silence, a dawn-lit breeze upon the leaf of a sweet violet.

Their gazes found each other, the meeting infinitely sweet, yet defocused, a slow unlocking of self to prepare to become one with another, greater self, as though they were twin bright beings melding within the golden streamers of a comet. His mouth hovered barely

above hers, absorbing her dreamy breaths, and feeling one catch
against his lips at his first light touch inside her softness. With
heart-expanding slowness he brought himself fully into her, the entry
as deep as he could make it. The pattern of her breath changed
against his skin as her swollen lips tightened into a smile that
gemmed her eyes with blinding radiance, and it was not the shape
and color of her eyes that moved him—those he could hardly
see—but their expression. And then even that was lost as the fierce
need of his body to have her engulfed every part of his spirit, and it
was no longer necessary to look at her expression because they were
so wrapped in each other that he could feel every thought, every
feeling that sprang from her in colorful word-pictures. The night
before, when he had loved her, the experience had been so close to
worship that he had hardly seemed to feel his own pleasure, but now
his skin and hers were flushed with erotic warmth, and the exquisite
fit of their bodies was moistly feverish, and each was learning the
serrated cadence of the other's pulse. Under the shower of sprinkling
light they moved in primal rhythms, each sensuous flow of motion
tender, uniquely human, and loving, until the voluntary matched
rhythms of their bodies escaped control, and with rapt blindness, eyes
closed, they saw each other only through their senses.

Swan's-wing clouds dappled a turquoise heaven. The autumnal
sun smiled on midmorning, and Devon and Merry, preparing to
stroll back to Teasel Hill, found that such a simple walk posed all
kinds of logistical problems. No matter how lovingly he finger-
combed her hair, or with what housewifely briskness she brushed
dried hay leaves from his shirt, they were both tousled and untidy,
and while they had never looked more beautiful to each other, they
bore every obvious evidence of two people in their honey-month
who had spent a night of love in a hayloft. The idea of walking
through a busy farmyard in her present condition caused Merry a
certain anguish, and so the Duke of St. Cyr and his duchess decided
there was no choice but to sneak into their own house. They crept
along walls fragrant with plump nectarines and peaches, musical
with bees. To avoid being seen was everything, and they hid behind
oak trees, where acorns fell on them in a pattering shower; and
collapsed with silent laughter behind a cider press. Through an open

window in the breakfast parlor they made their stealthy entrance to
the house and were flying up the staircase together under the quilt,
winded and helpless with laughter, when a young parlormaid happened to come into the entrance hall to dust and was so startled to
see a lumpy blanket running up the stairs that she shrieked in alarm.
Foiled at the eleventh hour, they had to return downstairs to explain
and comfort, and Merry learned that yesterday Devon had spoken no
less than the truth. At Teasel Hill two shouts brought the household
and half the garden staff on the instant.

Merry's aunt and Devon's mother, Aline, arrived at midday in a
black and silver phaeton driven by Devon's mother. Was it really
Aunt April with her soft hair dressed in fleecy Parisian curls, the
carefree bite of autumn in her cheeks, her lilac-colored pelisse
giving a lilylike delicacy to her spare frame rather than bluntly
exposing it? Merry met her at a run halfway up the fine stone steps
of the front porch. They kissed, hugged, smeared each other's
cheeks with clear gelatin tears, and buried their running noses, so
alike, in linen handkerchiefs. And Devon's mother, a petite figure
with golden tendrils falling from her Bibi bonnet over the standing
collar of her full blue percale coat, was doing some crying of her
own.

The afternoon was for renewing bonds, and for smiling. By
bedtime Merry was hoarse, April was hoarse, Aline was hoarse, and
Devon said teasingly that his ears were hoarse. April and Devon's
mother had heard a carefully sketchy version of Merry's story from
Lord Cathcart in London. Merry and Devon embroidered it upon
request with details to support its basic fallacious premise: that
Devon had rescued Merry from a pair of knaves who had stolen her
off the *Guinevere* intending to hold her for ransom. The falsehood
was the same one that would be let out to society at large, and it was
designed, strangely enough, to protect Merry from the kind of
tasteless speculation that the insensitive are likely to inflict on
female captives. In protecting Merry the story also couldn't avoid
protecting Devon, and for that Lord Cathcart and Devon both had
apologized so profusely that Merry had been secretly amused. She
might have told her aunt the truth; Devon had left the choice to her,
but what would it serve beyond her aunt's suffering? Aunt April had
already suffered enough worry. There might be a small part of

Merry that was afraid she had not forgiven Devon everything, but
she couldn't use her aunt to exact revenge. And when Devon drew
her into his bedchamber that night, undressing her in a crystalline
fog of moonlight, kissing each revealed part of her and whispering
his love, her exalting body had no thoughts of vengeance.

He left her at dawn because, as he had told her the day before,
they would be expecting him at Whitehall to explain his copious
bundles of reports and the raft of conclusions he'd drawn, which
were not likely to be very popular with anyone except General
Wellington, who was coming to oppose the American war himself,
according to Cathcart. And though Devon did not tell her so, he was
seized by a desperation more fierce than any feeling he'd ever
known to find Michael Granville and make certain Merry's safety,
although he too had lost all thoughts of vengeance. There was a dark
sucking spot in his conscience in the place where his hatred for
Michael Granville had been, and in it lived the fear that he might
lose Merry. On St. Elise when she was ill, he had never believed
she would die, no matter what the surface of his logic had told
him. He had taken Cat's concoctions to offer his own life for hers,
and he had been so clothed in the mantle of self-certainty that
afflicted so many of his blood—his father, his grandmother, his half
brother—that he had been convinced, truly convinced, that the focus
of his will must preserve her life. That blind arrogance stunned him
now. What had ever made him think he was more than any other
man?

Last night as she slept he had moved downward in the bed to
enfold her waist in his arms, catching the downy softness of her
thighs against his tightening belly, and to lay his cheek carefully on
the undercurve of her breast. Drowsiness had begun to drift through
the churning excitement of the past few days, but he had kept
himself awake, listening to her working heart. Moments had passed
in utter peacefulness. Then a nameless dark feeling had crept from
the blank folds of night, and the muffled thrum within her chest had
taken on a frightening fragileness. His arms had tightened around
her, his lips pressing into the musky warmth beneath her breasts,
over her heart. He was not a man given to surrender to the morbid
fancies of his imagination, and yet a steely coldness crept into his
stomach as the macabre idea came to him that she would be taken

from him to pay for his brutalities to her. Sleepless, he had sent a barrage of humble prayers spiraling toward heaven, probably to a stern God who was thinking with a twisted smile that it was a long time since he'd heard much from *this* quarter. In the silence of his mind Devon promised, and begged, and pleaded, until the blankness of slumber had overwhelmed him, and he had awoken before sunrise with the vague idea that an exasperated God had heard enough nonsense and put him to sleep.

Waking Merry with gentle kisses on her eyelids, he had made love to her sleepy, hot body, and to her winsome mind, and then left her after another aching kiss. He had stopped once in the airy bedchamber where his mother slept, to touch her cheek and smile, seeing that she was chewing on the lace cuff of her nightshirt, remembering his father teasing her about the quaint habit. Thank goodness Cathcart had been here to look after her while he'd been gone. Thinking that never again would he allow another human being to suffer for his own obsessions, Devon left the house, praying that when he returned he would have cured himself of the most dangerous one.

And Merry sat up alone in Devon's wide bed, hugging her knees with naked arms, and began to worry.

CHAPTER TWENTY-EIGHT

Crimson berries nodded gaily among the feathery leaves of the mountain ash tree above Merry's head as she sat with her aunt and Devon's mother three days later. Ducklings paddled on the garden's glimmering pond and wandered, quacking, among the sunlit asters.

388   LAURA LONDON

From the unshorn yews robins whistled, their darting shadows sweeping fleetingly over trailing fuschias, the mellow roll of freshly scythed grass, and ornamental stones with their gilded lichen crusts. Aline had directed her long-suffering steward and a footman to bring the pianoforte into the garden. Wouldn't it be charming on such a nice day to have music among the leaves? Puffing and grunting as they bumped the instrument down the porch steps, the male servants gave no particular appearance that they agreed. Aunt April teased that Aline only wanted it outside anyway, as a stand for her gardening tools, and the rapidly growing collection of trowels and work gloves and plant snips that landed on the pianoforte's back did nothing to belie that accusation.

Merry sat at the pianoforte trying to pick out the notes of a popular melody while her aunt stitched on a tambour and Aline began to massacre the weeds in a spearmint bed beneath her sundial. Grubby, Devon had said of his mother, and when a footman came bearing an envelope on a silver tray, Aline left little soily fingerprints on the paper as she picked it up.

Small, impetuous in her movements, quick to smile, Aline Crandall was difficult to dislike. She was by turns playful and enchantingly dour, and she seemed to regard the world outside her garden as a strange, startling place to be approached with caution. She was shy with acquaintances, and with all except her closest friends, warm and wary at the same time. Of the generosity of her nature there could be no doubt. Aunt April had revealed to Merry that on April's arrival in England, frightened, dejected, fearful for her lost niece, Michael Granville (a most attentive man for all the frigidity of his nature, April asserted) had delivered her unto Devon's grandmother, a dreadful female, who had demanded to know in a powerful shout what had she *done* with her niece. All had been a nightmare until Aline arrived with Lord Cathcart to bear off Aunt April to the safety of Teasel Hill, where she had been made to feel welcome as a friend and companion, though she had no claim on them for all that Aline said that any victim of Devon's grandmother's conniving became a sister of *hers* on the instant. In the long months of separation, being helpless and able to search for Merry only through the tortuous channels of diplomacy, April had drawn strength from Devon's mother. It was nice to think that one thing, at least, had gone well. Nice. But again—ironic.

A frown gathered on Aline's face as she read the note. She looked up from the page and said, "We have to go to a ball." She added with mournful satisfaction, "I knew it." She stuck the letter between her teeth, chomping downward in a comical gesture of derision, and Merry found herself thinking as she had many times in the three days before how Devon's mother bent one's preconceived notions of duchesses. Her appearance illustrated the point that it was possible to be an alluring beauty at age forty-two, even though her hair was usually collapsing like a stack of acrobats, her fingernails were chewed to the quick and, more often than not, grimy, and she had a gap the width of two straws between her front teeth that she poked at nervously with the tip of her tongue when, as now, she was taken with some serious thought. She dropped to the pianoforte's bench beside Merry, thrusting her forefinger meaningfully at the crest on the embossed envelope.

"This always means trouble," she sighed. "The mark of the Crandalls."

It was a unicorn rampant, the archetype of Merry's dreams. She must first have seen it, then, on letters Devon's grandmother had written to April so many years before—the mythical animal which had taken life and grown in Merry's dreamy heart. The unicorn. Devon's heraldic device. An unaccountable smile narrowed the corners of her lips.

"Devon's . . ." She took the envelope from Aline, moving like one in a daze.

Aline's fingers went to the keyboard, picking out a bright melody, depositing smears of topsoil on the ivory keys. "Well, it might be Devon's, but you've probably seen by now that he doesn't care a bean about the trappings of his rank. His armorial emblazonments might bear a wheat sheaf and two teacups for all the interest he's ever displayed in them. Mind you, we have a great bronze statue of one—a unicorn, that is—in the linden grove that Devon's grandmother had shipped all the way from Italy for him on his christening. *Such* an inappropriate present for an infant. And Lord Cathcart says the unicorn isn't native to British legend in any case."

"I'm not so certain." Aunt April, glancing up from her tambour frame, looked not so ready to dismiss the graceful creature. "What about the bicorne and the chichevache? They are like the unicorn in appearance, are they not?"

"Alike, but different." Aline finished the short melody with a sloppy trill and folded her hands in her lap. "Do you know about them, Merry?"

"No." Merry didn't look up.

"The bicorne," Aline said, "happy creature that he is, roams the countryside feeding on henpecked husbands. When you see drawings of him, he appears always as very plump and satisfied, his prey being so abundant. The chichevache, who only eats dutiful wives, has all its ribs showing from starvation." Wickedly grinning, "From what I know of your spirit and Devon's, I don't think we'll have to worry about the pair of you becoming a meal for either beast. What we have to worry more about is becoming a meal for your grandmama-in-law. She wants us to visit her."

With startled dismay Aunt April said, "Oh, no!"

"How bad could she be?" Merry, used to pirates, began to smile.

"She bellows," said Aline firmly. "She belittles. She throws her snuffbox. Not with men, though. I don't go next or nigh her unless I have Devon or Cathcart with me. Not that I'm a coward," she added hastily, misinterpreting Merry's expression. "But when I see her alone, what she wants is to chastise me for things Devon does, which are *not* my fault. He's a man now, and I don't mean to hang on his coattails." The wide-set hazel eyes grew rueful. "I couldn't control him if I wished. Even as a child he didn't need me. He was always—just himself. He's changed, though." A smile flashed. "*Love.* Oh, please, don't look embarrassed. I don't believe I've been happier in years. Finally Devon says he's come home to live, and he's hardly spent more than four consecutive nights here since his fifteenth birthday. It was hard for him, having no one of his very own, and he doesn't like a thing that men of his class are supposed to enjoy. Cards bore him, and so do prizefights and horseracing and driving in Hyde Park and gossip and talking about sorts of snuff; and he *will* not have a valet—so there you are."

Trimming a thread, Aunt April ventured, "And yet, Aline, even the *flower* of the ton speak highly of him."

"So they do. Hypocrites! It's impossible not to please them."

Devon's mother rubbed her nose emphatically, leaving a smudge on the tip. "It's all due to his rank, and his—well, his etcetera. They followed Jasper the same way. Whatever he did became the fashion. When he married me, two of his most slavish admirers actually wed their gardeners' daughters also, though one was twenty-five years older than the groom. And after we bought Teasel Hill, farmers could hardly find feed for their stock that season because the aristocracy was so busy thatching cottages for themselves with it. That makes me think! Merry, can you dance?"

"I—well, perhaps a bit."

"A bit won't be good enough. The old duchess is giving a ball to introduce you into society, and you have no idea how *they'll* sneer if you don't appear to advantage on the dance floor. You'll be such an object of envy that the least little thing you do will be dissected." She broke off, laughing delightedly, pulling Merry to her feet with both hands. "You have the drollest face! So expressive! First let's see what you know of the waltz. Say that I were a man and were to put my hands—so—on your waist. What would you do?"

"Retreat to the other side of the piano," Merry said promptly.

"And pert also," Devon's mother observed with a grin and a lowering brow. She lifted her skirts calf-high. "Watch my feet. Can you imitate the steps? Slowly at first . . . Oh, that's good. Very good. Then turn. Yes. Oh, April, are you going to play for us? What a wonderful idea!"

Watching Devon's mother lift her arms to the shoulders of some imagined beau to gaze dreamily into his eyes, Merry grinned as she saw from the corner of her eye that Aunt April was surreptitiously wiping soil from the keys with her handkerchief. Swaying to her aunt's first experimental notes, Merry waltzed dutifully if stiffly over the grass, her skirts belling as she circled a bed of blue asters, feeling a little ridiculous but not caring, and thinking of Devon's hands—so—on her waist. Her waist. Her hips. Her thighs . . . Rarely had three days seemed so long. For all her doubts, this was a lovely place, and her days were almost idyllic; but there was no ease from the ache of missing him, of picturing him in London surrounded by fawning companions. Friends, peers, old lovers . . . A thousand uncertainties roiled through her mind like spanking wingbeats, and she had ten questions for each of those. Through cautious inquiry she had learned that Aline had borne another child, Leonie, an engaging tomboy who had fenced and swam and played captain on the estate cricket team; Aline mentioned her from time to time with sad eyes. She had died eight years ago, Aunt April said, on a voyage to renew a friendship with a schoolmate in Jamaica. If Michael Granville was connected with her death, no one here seemed to know that. Aline spoke of him casually as her late husband's cousin, a favorite of the dowager duchess, and that was enough probably to account for the vague distrust Aline seemed to have for him.

Aline's animosity toward Rand Morgan went much deeper. She couldn't speak his name without her eyes becoming opaque with anger, and her most profound bitterness toward Devon's grandmother sprang from her conviction that it was Letitia who, Aline said, had engineered Devon's acquaintance with Morgan. Fond as Merry was coming to be of Devon's mother, she had to admit to herself that the accusation seemed a little extreme; unless Devon's grandmother was a madwoman, she wasn't likely to have wanted to expose Devon, on whom she clearly doted, to the influence of a man like Morgan.

Having a famous pirate as part of one's family seemed to be an interesting if explosive circumstance. Interested, sympathetic, Merry wondered if Aline knew that Morgan was her late husband's son, and if she didn't know, how she accounted for Devon's affection for the man. The espionage link, perhaps. It was no wonder the Crandalls intrigued people on both sides of the Atlantic; as a family they were fascinating, with their secrets, their abilities. And now, for better or for worse, Merry was one of them. A queasy stomach inevitably accompanied that thought.

Glancing down suddenly, Merry saw she was surrounded by ducklings, attracted by her swinging skirts. She stepped left to avoid one tiny yellow ball; then quickly right to miss another; then she toppled backward. Ducklings scattered in a golden star burst. Aline swooped laughingly down to pull her upright.

"Aren't they a nuisance?" Devon's mother said. "*Most* ducal residences have the good fortune to have swans. These are Devon's ducks, or their descendants, anyway. Did he tell you? No. I don't suppose it's the sort of thing young men are given to confessing to their brides." She swept a duckling up and handed it to Merry, demonstrating how it liked to be petted. "When he was seven, a whole brood of ducklings followed him home from the river one afternoon—orphans, they must have been—and they seemed utterly convinced Devon was their mother, and they followed him everywhere. It was the funniest thing. *Such* a mess at suppertime. They slept in his bedroom at night, and when I came to wake him in the morning, I'd find his head and shoulders all wreathed in little bits of fluff, hopping up and down on him, trying to wake him to take them to feed. Poor little things, they got so used to him that they wouldn't learn to swim; they just struggled and floundered and coughed when he put them in water. Do you know how he taught them? By taking them to the river and sailing off in his sailboat. At first they stayed on the bank, crying so pitifully, but soon enough they hopped into the water to swim after him furiously. And my husband said—he said—" She stopped, nonplussed. "I don't recall quite what it was he said, though I suppose it will bother me all afternoon until I think of it. . . . Well, never mind. Anyway, it was something clever. He was a hideously clever man, you know."

Merry smiled, stroking the duckling. "Was part of the reason you chose to live here instead of at the historic residence of the St. Cyr family that you wanted your children to have a more normal childhood?"

"Yes." Aline flopped down cross-legged on the grass, collecting ducklings on the stained pink dimity over her lap. "Aside from the fact that the St. Cyr manor has ninety bedrooms and two great wings, I still could not live in the same building with Devon's grandmama. She's absolutely ruled there for fifty years, and it always seemed cruel to me for the eldest son to bring home a young wife to outrank his mother." Suddenly impish, she rested back on her elbows. "I hope you won't have the bother of me living here for too long." Ignoring Merry's protest, she continued, "Tell me, what did you think of Lord Cathcart?"

It was more than a casual question. Merry was glad she was able to answer with sincerity. "I thought he was charming and kind."

"And chivalrous," Devon's mother amended glumly. She folded her arms as a pillow under her head. "I can't tell you how much he

respects me. All these years he's been the best of friends to me."
Still more glumly, "He has a mistress."

Taken aback, having no idea what to say, Merry finally asked,
"Is she beautiful?"

Aunt April spoke from the pianoforte. "If you like tall, mannish
females who stride and brighten their hair with chemicals."

"Don't be so loyal." Aline grinned. "She's beautiful. I've seen
her at the opera. They aren't in love, people say, but it's an
oh-so-convenient relationship." She grimaced. "How I'd like to
cause them both a little inconvenience. I've known since June that I
love him, but nothing's worked. If I sway toward him in the garden,
he turns all concern and takes me inside to rest from the heat! And
when we had to take shelter in an abandoned cottage after being
caught in the rain, what should he do but make me a long speech
about how I mustn't be afraid, because he placed my honor above all
things. I could have *wept*. I'm convinced that things would have
been much easier if I'd fallen in love with a libertine. Why, April,
are you giggling at me?" Aline propelled herself to a sitting posture.
"How dare you? When I know you've a beau-ideal of your own—
the way you dream off sometimes."

"Humdudgeon," Aunt April maintained stoutly, though to Merry's
amazement her aunt's cheeks were reddening.

Smiling with creamy satisfaction, Devon's lovely, grubby mother
flopped backward in the grass. "Humdudgeon nothing. We're all
three of us infected with the same disease. *Love*."

The London season had ended some months earlier, but when the
senior Dowager Duchess of St. Cyr gave a ball, the upper ranks of
the British aristocracy sighed and sent their best jewels to be cleaned.
Postilions brought their full-dress livery out of camphor and prinked
their carriage horses, blacking hooves, currying, oiling tack. Mo-
distes and milliners and hairdressers smiled over their profits.

Walking on Devon's arm among pillars and statues and grand
strangers, Merry had time between the smiles and murmured pleasantries to take stock of her impressive surroundings. *I will not be
afraid, I will not be afraid*, she had said over and over to herself on
the carriage ride to the ball, and now, to her amazement, she
discovered that she was not. Over the months she had become

accustomed to the hard talk and tempers of rough men; compared to them these genteel pale ladies and their smooth-tongued escorts were startlingly tame. She was too much an American to turn meek under the stare of an exalted title; she was too much a product of Morgan's careful if inconspicuous tutoring to let down her guard in this unexplored environment.

It fascinated her how little Devon seemed to care for all this. She had thought his mother must be exaggerating his lack of interest in the ton. Merry found Aline had hardly told her the half of it. This—the light, superficial interchanges, the flattery, the cunning invitations from painted pouting lips—bored him. Only when they met his grandmother had Merry felt his interest stir.

She was a grand dame indeed, Devon's grandmother. It was small wonder people were afraid of her. Her piercing dark eyes were filled with a mocking scorn that reminded Merry of no one as much as Rand Morgan. She was not tall, she was not attractive; but she gave the impression of being both. Her first words to Devon were "It's been three years since I've seen your face. And now, by God, I give a ball to countenance your mewling bride, and what thanks do I have for it? If it had been left to that rabbity mother of yours, your wife would be my age before she made her curtsy. You're still angry at me, I suppose, for having you transferred out of the European war last year. You might have given me a chance to explain instead of running off to Morgan! By God's teeth, you and your damned heroics! Do you think I wanted to see the last of the Crandall blood enrich some European cabbage patch?"

"Not only do I dislike your interference, I dislike your methods," Devon said, the voice soft, the eyes hard. "You've been too busy forcing favors from your old lovers. The night I left England, the street pamphlets carried a ballad about the great St. Cyr family tradition of patriotism—how both you and I served under Wellington."

One thin ash-gray eyebrow tilted. The fan in one kid-gloved hand snapped open, snapped shut. "I can hardly be blamed that the canaille will carry tales about their betters. What do the penny ballads say about your hole-in-the-corner marriage? Yes, look savage, if you like! How did I feel, not to see my only grandson wed in a church? It was all vengeance, I suppose—that nattering fool Cathcart and his talebearing. You know all, I suppose. Have you told Morgan yet that you've married his filly?''

Merry felt Devon's hand tighten on her arm as he said grimly, ''Rand is aware. He should be delighted after the months he's spent throwing Merry at my head. Between the pair of you everything's been done but leaving her stripped in my bed. It seems to have escaped both of you that Merry is human—she thinks, she breathes, she feels, and whether anyone believes it or not, so do I, and I won't tolerate another attempt to toy with us like a pair of trapped ferrets. I love her.''

From her vantage point of near objectivity, ignored like a gnat, Merry had watched the fight move from Crandall to Crandall, seeing in the clash of strong spirits all the good will they were missing in each other. Or they might have seen it, but the years of suspicion and conflict had left a history between them that would not be rewritten overnight. It was clear they were not people who thrived on family harmony. They simply seemed to believe it would be impossible to maintain their independence without struggle—not that either of them was likely to have analyzed the other's motives. There were too many other things on their minds for that. Even so, the Crandalls' family problems seemed to her to be far from hopeless. What they needed was a sensible, interested neutral party to escort them diplomatically through the channels of threatened pride. But though she had that thought, it would have amazed her to learn Rand Morgan knew that in time she would become that person.

Though her surroundings might be foreign and worrisome, Devon's hand on her arm was a warm, enlivening pressure through the soft white satin of her glove. With a sideways glance she made a lover's inventory of him: the angel's face with those bright demon eyes, the fluent body that managed to look just slightly overdecorated in tight breeches and a king's blue frock coat. No neckcloth in the vast room was tied more simply—a knot and a twist—but on Devon it appeared raffishly suggestive, as though it meant to come off as easily as it had gone on, and Aline had said with a grin that Merry need only wait till the *next* ball to see half the young cubs there with their neckcloths worn in the same lax fashion.

As though he felt her study, Devon turned to smile back into her eyes, and Merry's blood quickened its course when he bent to touch his lips to her ear.

"Look at me like that again," he whispered languorously, "and I swear I'm going to take you to the first unoccupied room and make love to you. As it is, come dance with me. I want to take you in my arms."

The silvery essence of twenty perfectly tuned violins flooded from the hidden musicians' gallery, tingling through her limbs. His hands took and held her lightly. His touch carried her like fairy dust on a summer wind. His gaze was a caress.

She suddenly spoke. "It was a trick, wasn't it?"

"Love?"

"The cards with the . . . the card deck you made me draw from. You knew how to draw a higher card."

He started to smile. "You'll remember the dogs wearing little pointed hats? On the face cards the hats have an extra stripe. It's very hard to see." He held her in a hot, lazy gaze that teased. "Don't spare my feelings. Confess. You never would have come willingly to my arms if you hadn't lost the draw. It was a debt of honor." He drew a quick breath. "Love, don't smile like that. You're tempting me beyond all reason."

The intimacy of the embrace, the tremor of her skirts as his legs moved against them, seemed to turn her blood to coursing sherry. The air she breathed was the same, a honeyed golden fluid, transformed by alchemy from equal parts of the rustle of silk, the warmth of many bodies, laughter, the singing strings, and the exotic mingle of perfumes. Vivid candlelight bathed the sweeping dancers in a benevolent amber gilt, unflawed and splendid, and Merry felt like a bird flying through bright fields of cirrus clouds, her bones weightless, her muscles light bands of taut and graceful strength. This was the first time she had danced in a man's arms. The first time. And with Devon.

There were other dances, other partners. Men, some young and eager, some older, with poise and contagious humor, held her in the weightless movements of dance. By every dictate of her nature she ought to have turned shyly from their glowing compliments instead of laughing them away; she ought to have blushed when they teased her instead of issuing rejoinders and rebuffs that made their eyes

shine with smiles. She had become so accustomed to the company of
men that it didn't occur to her to be bashful. Some eyes followed her
with fascinated envy, but to most she seemed dazzling, self-possessed
beyond her years, refreshingly natural.

Only one man, watching her, understood fully how much of that
"natural" ease of manner she owed to the ironclad ethics of a pirate
captain who wasn't likely to get much thanks for it. Cat stood with a
shoulder propped against a black marble pillar, assessing Merry's
success, following the elegant swirl of her skirts. The ivory Berlin
silk draped like a spill of crystal moonlight over her figure, the
bodice tantalizingly deep to expose the St. Cyr rubies that rose and
fell so fetchingly on her lovely chest. Jesus, they became her.

Cat looked away because it wouldn't do her any good to be
pointed out as the object of his interest. The glances he was drawing
were not so benevolent as those she received. He was far too
experienced to miss the interest that focused on himself, the upraised
quizzing glass, the giggle stifled hastily behind a fan, the timid
peeks from little blue-blooded virgins, and often the frankly sexual
interest that gleamed under lush feminine lashes and, once in a
while, male ones also. On the *Joke* the relationship Morgan allowed
the world to believe existed between them had been Cat's protection;
the looks he was getting now were what one might call the afterglow
of Morgan's patronage. Morgan's legend was too widespread for it
to be possible to hide the fact that the stainless Cathcart had a son
who was Rand Morgan's companion, and a pirate. Choosing not to
infect Merry with that taint, he did not allow her to approach him
until supper, when under the distracting cover of clinking glass
and porcelain he let her see him slip through one of the tall glass
doors into the garden.

It took Merry ten minutes to rid herself of the many escorts who
seemed, for some mysterious reason, intent on attaching themselves
to her. Finally in desperation she sent them off on disparate missions,
to fetch her punch, a syllabub laced with wine, pink champagne, and
made a silent escape.

The gardens of the Dowager Duchess of St. Cyr were large by
city standards, with acre upon wooded acre holding off the encroach-
ments of urban development behind high stone walls frilled in a
tangle of whispering ivy. Hugging herself for warmth in the

damp coolness of the night air, she ran down the veranda steps into the vast chaotic haze of the deserted garden with its softly leaping shadows and peastone paths blackened by twining branches that met overhead in rambling arbors. The gravel was painfully cold and cutting under her thin dancing slippers as she slowed, lifting her rustling skirts, and peered down an alley between the glossily blackened foliage of twin dark hedges. She began to walk again, stepping quickly, catching the cool waxy scent of holly.

"Cat?" she called softly, entering a small clearing that echoed with the tinkling of an unseen fountain. The moon's dead light destroyed color and showed objects only in musty, distorted forms. She thought she heard a sound behind her, and her heart began to thump unevenly in her chest. *"Cat!"*

"Merry? I'm here." Firm, strong hands came from the blackness to grip her shoulders. His fingertips brushed against the bare upper swell of her breast as he found her hand, carrying it to his body so she could find his braid. He felt her tremble, relax, stir.

"Devon told me," she said softly. "I could hardly believe it. Who would have imagined that half the British aristocracy would be floating around the Atlantic on a pirate ship?"

"Two isn't half," he said dryly. "And in my case the link to the upper elect was a matter of pure chance. For all I know, Morgan had the papers with my birth date forged."

"Don't!" There was a kind of frantic anger in her voice. "Don't put new images in my head of Rand Morgan and his conspiracies. I can't live with another one. For months I've felt like someone's tied me cross-shaped to a cartwheel and made me go around and around, head up, head down." She laid her cheek on his chest, feeling the embroidery pattern of his waistcoat on her skin, inhaling the faint aroma of cognac on his breath. "Why did you keep running away from me tonight? Devon told me that you probably would but—I don't understand."

"I know. I know you don't. But it's one of the few ways I can help you, sweetheart. Don't take it away from me." Her fingers trembled slightly in his clasp; he tightened his grip gently and slid an arm around her. "Back there"—a movement of his head indicated the direction of the house—"do they frighten you?"

"Not so far," she said. "But they may eventually. Devon's

mother, Aline, seems to be terrified of them. Actually I met a soul or two I might like to become friends with.'' The point of her nose was cold. She warmed it in his braid. With deliberate mildness: "What do *they* think of your earring?''

"They think it's''—again the dry tone, although this time tinged with amusement—''very French. I know you've had too many surprises already. Could you abide another? It will please you, I think.''

Her curiosity aroused, she let him lead her through a pergola thick with the perfume of roses, content to let him guide her steps, since he seemed to be able to make his way through the darkness with confidence. They spoke in low voices as they walked, the questions they asked each other careful, so careful, their answers careful also, because the subjects dealt with were sensitive ones. He told her in a superficial way about his short time with his father, and she saw from the things he didn't say how difficult it had been. She told him, with humorously chosen details, about her short marriage to Devon; and he saw from the things she didn't say that she was filled with doubts about her wisdom in beginning this life as a British duchess when another nation had her heart, and she still seemed hardly to believe that Devon really loved her. Silent understanding, unspoken reassurances flowed between them as they strolled through the night, his head slightly bent to catch her whispers, his arm around her shoulders, hers lightly encircling his slim waist. A few minutes brought them to a terrace of flagstones set in sand, floating in patches of light from a Japanese temple lantern. The sharp etherlike scent of peppermint wandered from the darkness beneath the trees surrounding the reaching branches of an aged apple tree with a wooden garden seat on wheels beneath. She could see Cat's face well as he turned to her.

"If I could produce one man for you, from the *Joke,* who would it be?''

Astonished, she stared at him for a moment. Then, hardly daring to hope, she said, "Raven?''

A distinct rustle came from the apple tree. Twigs bobbed.

"And what would you have done,'' said a bright, euphonic drawl muffled by apple leaves, "if she'd said Sails?''

She looked up, laughing delightedly. Raven was lowering himself

from the branches, flexing his loose limbs sinuously, like a snake
with an inky curl falling from his red bandanna over one eye. He
offered her an apple and a lovingly mischievous smile. "Taste it,
m'love. 'Tis the fruit of knowledge," he said, delivering the apple
to one of her hands and the smile to her lips.

"Behave," Cat said, "or we're going to enact a new version of
the story, and the serpent will be expelled from the garden."

"Heavens, then, I'm tame!" Raven protested, releasing his laughing captive.

"You're not," Cat corrected him. "You're more than half-sprung,
but if I stay, someone's bound to remark my absence, and I want to
tell Devon where she is before he gets nervous, so—"

"So go back. I shall return her intact. Unless"—Raven swept
Merry with a flattering inspection—"I decide to run off with her
instead." Over his shoulder: "Go on. I'll keep her safe, you know."

Casting an exasperated eye over Raven's raffishly piratical
appearance—the leather breeches and vest, the top boots, the knife
belt with its bronze dagger—Cat said, "*Try* not to let anyone see
you then, or God knows how we'll explain it."

Cat's quiet footsteps disappeared swiftly, and Merry couldn't
resist throwing herself into Raven's arms a second time, exclaiming,
"How on earth did you know to come?"

Raven conquered the venal temptation to prolong the embrace and
gently disentangled himself from it as he said, "Cat told me. The
Joke docked in London three days ago, and after Morgan told us
about how Cat had gone to stay with his fine gent of a father, Will
and I decided to pay him a visit. What a mistake! For one thing, we
should have thought not to wear our bandoliers—scared the deuce
out of his servants. And then, when we were walking with Cat to a
sitting room on the upper floor, a little chambermaid with her arms
full of bed linen stepped from one of the doors. No sooner does she
set her brown eyes on us than she drops her armload at her feet and
shrinks back to the wall squeaking out '*No, no*' like she was in a
play. Well, you know how it is with Will. He wouldn't have paid
the least heed to her, but *that* was like issuing him an invitation.
Tossed her down on Cat's bed and kissed the wits out of her—or so
you'd think, the way she squawked about it after, poor chit. Lord
Cathcart was there in a flash and his manservants, speakin' bandog and

bedlam. I wanted to hide under the bedclothes, I was so embarrassed. Damn that Will. Mind you, we've all of us been a little off our stride since you've been gone. Miss you, y'know. D'y'know what I did until you took supper? Watched you through one of the upper windows.''

"No! Did you?" she asked, starting to laugh again. "I wish I'd known. But I don't know why you think you have to sneak a visit with me when you'll see Cat openly."

"You funny little thing, what would you've had me do? Come in and ask you for a dance? It wasn't my kind of an affair, I promise you! Was that your aunt that came in with you? Pretty, slim lady? I didn't have a bit of trouble picking out Devon's mother—saw her dancing a *boulangère* with Lord Cathcart. Handsome female, for all that she had a red wine mustache. She has hair just like Devon's; looks as though it were spun from sunlight. And there was Cat, prinked up like he came out of a bandbox with his braid in a velvet ribbon." His liquid gaze dropped to her throat, making, with a smile, a professional assessment of the jewels nestled there. "How does it feel to be holding up a king's ransom in stones?"

"They're uncomfortably heavy! Devon's grandmother sent them, and though Aline said I didn't have to wear them if I didn't choose, there didn't seem to be any compelling reason to offend the dowager by refusing. It's such a large necklace, the dressmaker had to cut the gown especially to accommodate it." He gave her a grin which told her he'd noticed, and she said, in a retort to the grin, "How are you finding London then?"

"What this city needs," said the young pirate with strong conviction, "is a good sewer. And I don't just mean the Thames neither! Dirty brothels too. You're hard put to see a thing you want to sit down on, much less lie on. At sea all a soul wants to do is sight land, but once we dock, it don't take long to get bored with the wenching and the boozing. It's a disciplined life, the sea, and the truth of it is, I don't adjust so readily to leisure, especially when it's in a port where I have to watch the riot and rumpus I can kick up. But I'm not sorry we'll be fixed here for a while—because it's plain as a pulpit you can use your friends. Here I thought to find you every bit aglow, but that hardly seems to be the case. You've got more on your chest than sparkling rocks, no matter what Devon says about how certain he is that he's going to make you happy, even if he has to pull stars from heaven and lay them in your hands to do it."

"Raven! Have you talked with him, then? He's been in London these six days and only returned to Teasel Hill late this afternoon. Could he have visited the *Joke*?"

"You could say so. He came last night to the *Joke* and had a turnup with Morgan that they could hear halfway to Guernsey. Nor was Devon too pleased with Sails, neither, being as he was in Morgan's confidence the whole time, though he didn't like the scheme above half. What I didn't learn then about how it was with you, Cat told me this afternoon."

Blushing a little in the fluttering light, Merry said, "You must have been astonished to learn that he . . . about the marriage!"

Raven gave her a gentle look and stroked the underside of her chin slowly with a curved finger. "No. Before we were in sight of Land's End, I knew what Devon meant for you." Her expression of utter incredulity and puzzlement brought a light smile to his lips. "He came to me after they had me clapped in iron bracelets, y'know, because he couldn't much bear the thought of me weeping myself sick over you. Soft at heart, he is; I told you. He said he meant to have you as soon as he could once find out who the devil you were. What he wanted was the truth first, and then he was going to make you his own, even if you were a doxy from the back streets. And when I asked him if he meant marriage or a house on Green Street and maintenance, he said he'd be damned if he'd leave you to your own devices in a hired house; he meant marriage. So y'see, sweetheart, that's wh—" The break in his words was abrupt. His palm closed delicately, insistently over her mouth, and when she startled and tried to pull away, he tightened his fingers. He shook his head sharply, holding her eyes in an intent gaze, and then released her quickly and disappeared into the flat blackness between two honeysuckle bushes, his movement a smooth flow that hardly disturbed the shrubs' heavy crop of ornamental berries.

Surprise was the only thing that kept Merry from demanding to know whether he'd taken leave of his senses. She stood in the sudden quiet, looking around herself at the haphazard patterns of the lantern's silty light. Not a sigh of air touched the slumbering foliage.

Raven's last words were ringing softly in her ears, and she was
frowning bewilderedly over his unexplained retreat when suddenly
an oddly metallic thrill slithered like cold mercury along her nerves.
Fear. The feeling came from another plane, a long buried instinct
that erupted without logic like the fret of a dog lifting its half-
napping head to growl at some faint, ominous echo of a sound.

Then she heard it. A rustle. A hiss of displaced vegetation.
Footsteps printing stealthily on moist soil. Her first shamed impulse
was to dive headlong into the honeysuckle bushes behind Raven, but
as quickly she soothed her overwrought imagination; because what
could happen to her here, of all places, and with Raven so close?
And for goodness' sakes, it must only be Cat returning already, or
some chance guest rambling in the garden's inviting coolness. Only
her heart grinding uncomfortably against her ribs refused to be
soothed.

A dark shadow plunged in the blackness of a far thicket. And then
a man stepped into the clearing, the light slowly showing her the
contours of his face. His eyes were dark hollows shaped like peach
pits. The doughy glow of the light's cornmeal rays suffused his
cheeks, catching brightly in his eyebrows and profuse side-whiskers,
limning the severe sculpting of his nose and his sharp-cut nostrils.
She knew him. Before she saw the green-silver glint of his eyes, she
had remembered that face. His name left her lips in a whimper.

"Granville." Fast-rising, involuntary terror surged through her.
This man above all others had come to be the nightmare nemesis
who had been the distant author of her most wrenching unhappiness.
Her fear was anguished, riveting. It was only when her eyes flew to
the glimmer in his hand and she saw the light dancing off the silver
furniture of a small double-barrel pistol that her limbs thawed to
allow motion. She retreated from him, little tumbling half steps
halted by the wooden bench pressing into the backs of her thighs.

"Yes," he said in a soft tone. "*Run.* Run away, you idiotic scrap
of skin and blood. You have no notion how much it would please
me to be provoked into burying a bullet in your hair. Unless what
you have under it is empty, you'll stay where you are. And don't
bother looking around so hopefully. I know you're alone. I saw the
boy leave you."

"H-how—"

"For a week I've been trying to get close to you, my pretty, and bloody hard it's been, as well as Devon has you guarded. I never quite expected this little piece of good fortune. A helpful juvenile, Cat. I had him once when he was a child. Did he tell you?''

Three thoughts hit Merry in such rapid succession that she had to force her mind to capture and hold each one. The first was that on the instant whatever doubts she had entertained about who might be right or wrong in Devon's apocryphal and confusing battle with Granville had been totally resolved in Devon's favor, and that thought was surprisingly potent in its power to give her comfort. The second was that the "boy" he had seen leave her was Cat, and not Raven, and she was not as alone as Granville thought, which was a comfort also. Her third thought was not so much a rational concept as a flash of blinding rage that this man would use such a hideous weapon to attack her. Like a seed fallen upon fertile earth, even that last impression nurtured her, turning her feelings away from her own fear and channeling them into a tidal wave of protectiveness toward Cat. This creature was not a phantom. He was here, and human, and she must face the repugnant necessity of dealing with him. Her icy anger made it easier to pretend that she had regained her composure and her courage.

"What do you want?" she asked in a voice carefully shed of color.

He laughed suddenly, standing where he was, the sharp sound curling like acid in her senses. "What do I want? You puling trollop, your pretty husband has been chasing me the width and breadth of the country since three days after he set foot in Falmouth. Now that he has the proof he needs to convince himself—if not a court of law—that one of my raiders brought down a ship with his sister on it, my life isn't worth a stone penny. Don't show me that face of bovine innocence! I know he had my letters stolen from the *Guinevere*. Before he had proof, Cathcart and Morgan kept him off me, tender souls. They didn't want him to trade his life for mine. But there's enough in those letters to implicate me in feeding information about British shipping to American privateers, if he's broken the code. And—clever youth that he is—don't try to tell me that he hasn't.''

She had no intention of telling him anything of the sort. Nor did she mean to reveal that those papers were no longer a threat to him, through a soaking she'd given them in her attempt to escape Devon.

He seemed to take a queer satisfaction in her silence. "Interesting of them to take you as well. By the time it occurred to me that the papers must have vanished through Devon's busywork, I regretted I'd been so gentle in my methods of disqualifying you as the future Duchess of St. Cyr. Obviously he didn't believe the charming tales I spread about your easy virtue in New York."

Merry could have enlightened him about that as well. Again she kept her mouth resolutely shut. Was he trying to see what information he could shock out of her?

Granville's narrow lips stretched into a soft crescent. "My consolation was thinking of the things Devon surely must have done to you before Rand Morgan bothered himself to notice who you were. And with Devon's repressed sensitivity it must have been quite a moment for him when he realized what an innocent you really were. Come here, poppet. Why are you hesitating? Come." He was drawing a round golden object from his pocket, displaying it to her by a dangling chain. "Study it, Merry. Is it familiar?"

Moving stiffly, without grace, she crossed the clearing to take the offered object in her hand, trying not to touch his skin, though she wore gloves. Her heartbeat slowed almost to a standstill as she studied the thing she held. It was a Swiss watch, gold, with a fine enameled back and rose diamonds on the face, and Merry knew the inscription before she read the elaborately engraved words. *To Carl, on the occasion of his eighteenth birthday. With fondest regards. James Wilding.* It had never, to her knowledge, left her brother's possession. So rarely did their father make a gesture of affection, Carl cherished this one.

In an aching voice Merry whispered, "How did you come by this?"

"He gave it to me. No. Let me be more accurate. I took it." The smile, a cruel one, extended this time to his eyes. "He's here in London with me, did you—"

"That's a *lie*!" Anxiety had sharpened her voice.

His brow rose over the smoky green glitter of his eyes. "Is it? If you think so, my fair delight, you and I have nothing more to say to each other. Farewell." Smiling sardonically, he flicked her cheek with a careless finger. "Have the watch as a keepsake. Your brother surely won't have any further use for it." He turned as though he would have left her, but she stopped him with a terrified protest.

"Please! No! I don't understand . . ."

"Pay attention, then, because I've wasted enough time here already. Your brother followed you to England—or at least he thought he was following you, having no idea your route would be so circuitous. Not, I'm afraid, that his advent to the country was aboveboard. He came in by way of a smuggler's punt. What a singularly rough and ready pair you are, to be sure! It's no wonder you do so well for Devon." Granville's smile twisted into a sneer. "He came to me because I had been your escort to England and he wanted to know my version of the events surrounding your disappearance. The poor lad thought I would be sympathetic because he knew I had passed information to the Americans. I wish he hadn't let me know he knew that. It presented me with a very grave problem. I could hardly let him run around England with that sort of information. For one thing, he's a little impetuous. He might be caught and questioned, and tough-minded as he is, he's very young, and I have small confidence in his ability to hold out against an experienced inquisition. Son of a gentleman or not, they'll certainly torture him if he's discovered; before they hang him, that is. I'd have disposed of him quietly at once if he hadn't been your brother."

Doggedly forcing herself to contain her rising panic, breathing in the untidy rhythm of desperation, she backed to the garden seat and sat down on it, holding the watch in her two hands, as though it were a delicate thing made of glass instead of gold. "What do you want me to do?"

"At five of the clock tomorrow evening there will be a black coach with the wheels picked out in red waiting at the southeastern corner of Finsbury Square. How you manage to get there is your own affair, but I imagine a chit of your ingenuity will think of something; but if you aren't in that coach by one minute past the hour, it will leave without you, and I promise you, my pretty, you won't have a second chance. Be there if you want to see your brother. Otherwise, he will cease abruptly to be of any use to me, and I'll let him die. You might, of course, choose to carry this story to one of your masculine protectors, which would also end his usefulness to me. It would be something of a relief to be able to dispose of him.''

"And of me," she said, her gaze resting bleakly on her hands, where the watch lay softly gleaming like a golden egg.

Granville's boot leather made a faint crinkling sound on the sandy flagstones as he joined her on the bench. The back of his hand rested on her cheek, turning her face toward him, though she flinched from his touch. Some of the fierce animosity had fled from the gray-green eyes, and in their depths was the dim mirage of an emotion that might once have been compassion.

"Why do you think I told you in New York that your aunt planned to take you to England? I had hopes you'd run home to your patriotic father and stay out of my net. Much as I regret it, poppet, I can't afford to care about your hurt. I'm not sure whether this will comfort you, but it wouldn't suit me to end your life. What I need now is to negotiate some sort of peace with Devon, and without having you whole and hale and in my power, I'd find myself very thin of bargaining capital." He stood. "Tomorrow evening at five. Finsbury Square," he said and strode quickly away, vanishing like a ghoul into the night's black serum.

In another moment Raven's hands closed on her wrists, holding them in a sustaining grip. She was standing, though she couldn't remember having moved.

"You heard?" she murmured tensely.

"Every word. M'love, I want to stay with you now, but I can't. I have to follow him."

"Why? What purpose will it serve if—" Interpreting the grim set of his mouth, she cried, "Raven, you can't *kill* him!"

"No? All right, lambkin. Don't fret. I'll only kill him a little."

"Raven, you can't! Didn't you understand? He has my brother!"

Raven was a gentle man, both by nature and by disposition, but he had been reared in a hard school, and his affection did not transfer readily from Merry to her brother. Nor did he have much faith in either the authenticity of the watch or the likelihood that Merry's brother would still be alive if he had put himself in Granville's orbit. And even if the whole unlikely story were true, Raven would have unhesitatingly sacrificed the unknown brother for Merry. But he was not proof against her sterling, honest gaze.

"As you wish it, m'dear, but I can't stand here argufying about it, or I'll lose him." He cast an impatient glance over his shoulder. "I'll just discover where he goes and then take the matter to Morgan—"

"*No!*"

"Well, then," he said, releasing her hands, starting to move across the clearing, "Devon."

"No! Raven, I don't think so. You have to allow me time to think."

"Hell and the devil, there's no time for thinking! I have to go."

She ran after him, dragging up her heavy, bouncing skirts. "Promise me that you won't tell anyone. *Promise*. We'll meet tomorrow morning and decide what to do."

"Fine! Good-bye!"

The impenetrable vegetation stopped her, and she had to call after him, *"Where?"*

He returned swiftly. "Hush! Noon at St. Mary Abchurch. It's near the Royal Exchange. And I hope to God that by then you'll have decided to see sense."

CHAPTER TWENTY-NINE

Outside Merry's window the sky had the dark luster of a ripe brambleberry. She had surrendered to a yawning abigail the formidable pile of arraignment she had worn to the ball: the heavy silk gown, the long gloves, the petticoats, the light stays, the silk stockings; and then sent the weary girl to bed. She had meant to remove her jewels and change the sheer chemisette for a nightgown, but exhaustion had overwhelmed her suddenly, and the burdens she had disguised under a smile and a slightly nervous vivacity came slipping back with a battering strength.

Devon had retired to his own dressing room, and she was grateful that for this moment at least she didn't have to pretend. Part of her wanted to crawl beneath the bed linen and give her mind to the nothingness of sleep, except that the hairpins that supported her classical hair design had been placed for effect, not comfort, and they were likely to keep her awake all night if she didn't remove them now. She dropped tiredly onto the stool before her dressing table and sat with her head drooping before she lifted her hands to her hair. Searching through her curls, she began to discover and withdraw hairpins, making each a *might be* for things that could come to pass if she told Devon about Granville's visit. *Devon might kill Granville and be charged with his murder. Granville might kill Devon. Granville might kill her brother. Devon might rescue her brother and yet feel obliged to deliver him to the British authorities. Devon might rescue her brother, try to protect him from the authorities, and then be charged himself with treason. . . .*

So deeply did she enter the world of her own thoughts that she didn't hear Devon come into the room, though he had made no particular effort to do it quietly. He came to the threshold, meaning to make some casual remark to her. The words never left his mouth. Instead he put one hand on the bedpost, watching her reflection in the mirror.

Weariness and, it seemed to him, some sort of soul-deep dejection had robbed her face of animation and hence a certain amount of its beauty, and he was reminded of the days when she was at the peak of her illness, when the ravages of disease had made her so plain that Cat had quietly removed all mirrors from her presence. It had been in those days that Devon had begun in some unconscious way to face the fact that he loved her, when the "fondness" he felt toward her had shone on undimmed, strengthening, and he had been forced to acknowledge that her physical self had little to do with the power she exerted over his heart. An errant memory came to him of holding her cold and shaking fingers under his as he dragged a rope around her wrists. Fear whispered through him like a white flame, and then its attendants, which he had recently learned to expect—

nausea, remorse, self-hatred. Was it some past base act of his that brought this sad look to her face? Meeting her aunt had made him comprehend wholly what kind of life Merry had lived before his own advent into it, and he understood almost more than he could bear about how frightened she must have been by what she had experienced on the *Black Joke*. A lingering haunted quality dwelt in her remote gaze, and while her sadnesses had always touched him, since their first full coming together, her emotions affected him even more potently. It was as though the membrane of some strange fruit had ruptured within him, spilling and spreading its seed through every chamber of his body. Seeing her thus, his impulse was to drop to his knees at her side and weep into her palms.

Her head moved slightly, lightening the shadows on her face. A cluster of candles on the dressing stand cast mock suns into the deep coils of her hair. Her eyes were very blue against the gold of her skin and the lush coral of her cheeks. The St. Cyr rubies winked in solemn splendor on her breast and on the delicate rise of her shoulders. There was an exotic quality to the famous jewels. The droop of the necklet seemed to describe the swell of her breasts; a gold-and-ruby cuff rested three inches above her right elbow; each of her lovely ankles—one stretched in a firm line before her, the other tucked up and under the ivory curve of her buttocks, barely revealed beneath her sheer undergarment—carried a dainty ankle bracelet of glinting gold links and small rubies. He had glimpsed them earlier, when some turn of the dance or other movement of hers had carried up her skirts enough to reveal the radiant gems and flesh.

A flicker of distress seemed to pass over her features. Her eyes focused, and she gazed into the looking glass and saw him. Her smile was brilliant, unthinkingly arousing; but it came too quickly, too defensively, and he felt a painful, swift stab of desire.

Long-standing habit had made it second nature to him to control his features. His face revealed the nuances of his feelings only when he made a conscious attempt to express them or when his emotions were beyond thought. And so to Merry his eyes seemed only thoughtful and alarmingly probing. As he had guessed, her smile had been a defense, but seeing him suddenly brought back the terror-subdued recollection that even on the *Joke,* when he believed the worst of her character, he had still loved her, and had told Raven so. Her smile dwindled; her throat grew tight; her pulse began softly pounding. Nor could she forbear to notice the picture he made, leaning with rakish ease on an upraised arm that rested against the bedpost. His other hand lay relaxed at his thigh, the long fingers negligently clasping a forgotten glass of white wine, and his unbuttoned shirt fell apart enough to give her a glimpse of the tough, inviting musculature of his chest and his stomach. Slippery candlelight smoothed like ointment over his hips where they shaped his breeches. She caught a breath as he spoke.

"What troubles you, my dear love?"

Their eyes met through the chill medium of the mirror. She said nothing. The faint shake of her head, which displaced the thick curls on her shoulders, was perhaps a denial of her mood.

He came to her at an unhurried pace, standing behind her, holding her gaze. His hand, slowly lifted, came to her cheek to chart its structure with the careful tracing of a finger.

"Dear heart, can't you tell me what it is?" he asked quietly. She answered him with silence, her eyes drenched with startlingly bright color and apprehension, and he recalled that she had spent time in the garden talking with Cat and, according to Cat, with Raven also. Probably she had shared what was in her mind with them, and the idea that they might be more in her confidence than he was hurt him. But he was perversely grateful for the wound. Suffering seemed the only way he had of paying for the unearned joy that loving her brought him. He had said as much yesterday to Morgan, who had merely opened his dark eyes rather wide and murmured, "What an interesting fancy, child. I hardly know whether to mix you a physic or congratulate myself on how much the year's done to improve your character."

Touching his fingertips along the rise of her cheek, he felt her flesh heat under his skin.

"If I could give you anything, what would it be, Merry?"

She sat curiously still, staring back at his reflection. Then a wry little smile curved her lips. "A moment or two without having to think."

Softly he said, "Love, I can give you that."

His face had taken on an intent drowsy look she could feel in the lower part of her body. Her pulse skipped a pair of beats, and the tightness of her throat spread to her breasts. She swallowed uncomfortably as the experienced fingers slipped downward, stroking lightly the taut sinews of her throat. The heat of his body came to her from behind, his hips pressing into her back just beneath her shoulders. His knee slid up to the cushioned seat, bracing his leg, the motion cradling her against his thighs.

"Drink," he whispered, bringing the wineglass around her shoulder, touching the rim to her lower lip. His other hand, cupping her throat, felt the rippling convulsions as she drank. A delicate massage of the soft underside of her chin tilted her head, and he bent, bringing his mouth down on hers. He drank the wine from her lips, tasting her flesh with his open mouth. Gently supporting her chin on his wrist, he slanted the wineglass to take some of the pale liquid on his finger and trailed it in a lazy path along the inner surface of her lips, following it with the tip of his tongue. The wine left a faint erotic glow where his light caresses applied it to the dove's-wing softness of her lower lip, the moisture aiding his mouth's exploration. Her eyelids fell shut, her lips swollen and slightly parted, her breath deliciously uneasy.

She abandoned herself to his touch, to the growing pressure within her body, losing herself in the melody of his murmured love words. His fingers were warm, slightly heating the sparkling wine before bringing it to the ripe nerves behind her ear, to her temples, to the thickly beating pulse in her throat. The heady fluid played beguiling tricks as the air cooled and dried it, leaving a hot, penetrating residue that saturated deeply into her fluttery senses. She turned her head weakly to the side, skimming her lips along his forearm, and then, as he offered it, his wrist, the rise of his palm, its warm hollow. And as his hands sank downward to lift and caress her breasts she heard a softly pleading sound escape her throat, and she said his name in anguished desire.

His quiet laughter flickered against her shoulder. "No, little flower. Softly, love. I need you too, but we have to give your body more time to be ready for love." His mouth, covering hers, caught her pleasure cry as his thumbs found her nipples, stroking them through fabric. Gliding over the moist surfaces of her lips, he whispered, "Tonight I want to pull the soul out of your body, Merry, and bring it together with my own."

She said something—a husky little utterance that sounded like "Yipes"—and he was laughing again as he slid his fingers under the narrow ribbons of her chemisette and drew it over her shoulders and down the smooth trembling flesh of her arms. Letting the fabric spill in a shimmer like new snow around her hips, he brought his hands back to stroke tenderly over the length of her hair, lifting it in a mass to his face, inhaling its hypnotic fragrance.

Peeking shakily upward, she watched the reflected image of her hair, a reddish tumbling cascade, as it mingled with his wild honey fairness. Her eyes had a liquid radiance, her mouth shone wetly, passion-flushes tinged her cheeks and neck. She stared at the puzzle of herself for a quick-breathing moment, until his hands found their way back to her breasts and she closed her eyes, gasping against the sweetness of his flesh pressing into hers. Her body pushed backward into the coaxing warmth of his thighs and bare stomach. Blindly searching, she brought an arm up to touch his face and to rub the back of his neck. And it was his turn to gasp as the motion arched her breasts into his fingers. Burying himself in the splendor of her curls, his palms pressed her overtender flesh, gently distorting the soft shape of her breast with their pressure. His thumbs, dewed in wine, slightly lifted her aching nipples. For a long time he held her thus against his body while his hands played luxuriantly over her bewildered flesh until she was hot and sweat-damped and shivering, and as he drew her to the bed she pulled at his clothing, undressing him with clumsy, shaking fingers as he laid her crosswise on the bed.

"Devon—I love you . . . love you," she whispered thickly. "Love me . . . love me . . ."

"I will, little flower." But instead he brought his mouth down to rock gently over her panting lips. His hand began a light kneading motion on the skin below her navel that traveled slowly to her lean thigh muscle and then, more slowly yet, to her inner thigh. She was in a restless delirium of pleasure and need before he dipped his fingertips in the wine and slipped them into her. The fluid lubricated her to the love-nuzzle of his fingers, and his gently careful touch had brought her almost to rapture when he withdrew them.

Her bliss-numbed eyes flew open, and he kissed away the gathering tears of confusion. His own eyes were warm and blurred as he murmured, "It can be even stronger . . . higher, Merry. Trust me . . ." And this time when he brought his mouth to hers, she met him with an open burning passion that exploded through his blood.

Holding her face in wet, unsteady fingers, he whispered, "Shall I— Yes, sweet flower, touch me . . . yes, again. Love, shall I make you fly? I'll show you."

He kissed every part of her. The lingering wine smears, heated and incensed by her flesh, were severely intoxicating. He could taste her from his throat to his loins. Her supple moist skin was like an expensive and subtle spirit: the fermented sepals of orchids, powdered silk, flecked gold and myrrh. He picked up the soft weight of her hair and rubbed it over her and himself, over her cheeks, her breasts, her mouth, his mouth. And his clever tongue, more articulate than it was even in speech, dragged her spirit to some high drifting heaven where her body shimmered like mist, in separate shining cells. She knew nothing beyond wet hot ecstasy, could not divide sensation into its parts; she could hardly follow the path of his hair brushing a rhythm on her skin or recognize that the shoulders and heels pressing so urgently into the bedclothes were her own. And then she saw him smiling lovingly, dreamily down at her as he entered her, spreading a smooth, exquisite voluptuousness through her, catching her writhing hips in a gentle grip and saying, "Slowly, love . . . slowly."

She had an unearthly beauty to her, her eyes with a ravished angel luster, her body answering his motions, quivering with exalted anticipation and then releasing a deep-rooted shudder each time he thrust himself slowly into her. As from a distance, he heard himself repeating her name, asking her in a shivering whisper to hold him, helping her to wrap her beautiful legs in their ankle bracelets around his body; and taking her face in his palms, he gazed into her feverish eyes and murmured, "I love you, I love you, I love you" until at last, under the worship of his body, she touched the heights he had brought her toward, in love, and his adoring hands caressed the tremors of her surrender.

Her fluctuating senses, battered by the potency of her release, led her to weep afterward, and he held and cherished her, curving her body to his in the way two bodies will curve together after love.

When he could, which was not soon, he rose and brought another glass of wine, and sitting up, he pulled her body, limp as a heavy sheepskin, onto his lap and into his arms. He fed her a little wine, and when he saw she could hardly swallow, he kissed the excess from her lips. To his delight she said in a cross little voice, "If *that* was the glass you've been sticking your fingers into . . ."

"Oh, no," he said, stretching an arm back to the bedstand to lift the other glass. "This is." With a wickedly teasing glint in his eyes he put the glass to his lips, and she watched with fascination and a little awe as he swallowed the remaining wine, savoring it. He gave her a smile of breathtaking charm, laid his fingers, barely touching, on her lips, and said, "Nectar of Merry."

CHAPTER THIRTY

However well placed Michael Granville's faith in her ingenuity may have been, it took none at all for Merry to escape Teasel Hill well before the hour she had appointed to meet Raven. Devon had been closeted since midmorning with his long-suffering man of business, who had been waiting with breathless impatience since Devon's homecoming to pounce on his elusive master and begin the formidable task of bringing the young duke up-to-date on the many details of his vast estates that required his attention. Aunt April and Devon's mother had remained late in their beds, recruiting their energies after the late hours of last night's ball. With some inner trepidation Merry asked Mr. Stanmore, Devon's steward, if he might order the carriage prepared for her, because she had some business to attend to in London. Without even waiting to hear her carefully rehearsed amplification he had excused himself with a smile and a promise that it would be done directly. Heady stuff that, for a girl whose servants in Virginia had known her from the cradle and were more likely to kindly direct *her* activities than the opposite. Merry's success with Mr. Stanmore almost emboldened her to ask for the key to the gun room because, though the weapons there were mostly of the sporting variety, Aline had mentioned once that it held also a small collection of pistols that Devon's father had acquired on his travels. But though there was nothing pleasant about the possibility of going unarmed to a confrontation with Granville, she was afraid that a sudden desire to examine the guns must occasion some notice. Someone might even mention it to Devon as soon as he emerged from his meeting, which under the circumstances would be disastrous. So, a little feebly, and not without a blush, she slid a knife from her breakfast tray into her garter, mindful of how Morgan's men often produced weapons from unlikely parts of their raiment.

A careful perusal of the London map in the library had led Merry to pick out an address at random that seemed in convenient circumstances to her destination, since this was hardly the sort of adventure it would be possible to undertake under the patronage of Devon's solicitous if obedient servants. She was somewhat daunted when the carriage drew to a polite halt on the cobbles in front of the appointed address, which bore a wooden sign with painted letters that read Dealer in Foreign Spiritous Liquors. The groom in blue ducal livery who let down the steps for her was too well trained to look at her askance, but she could see he looked doubtful, and as she swept onto the pavement she could only be grateful that she hadn't chosen the building next door, whose brass sign read Drain Pipe Lay Down Undertaken Here.

She remained inside for a few minutes, pretending an interest in the port wines and unsuccessfully trying to fend off the attempts of the obsequious proprietor to make her sample his merchandise. She narrowly avoided inebriation by ordering a round dozen bottles of the port to be delivered to Teasel Hill and took her leave of the beaming proprietor. Standing a little dizzily on the flagged pavement outside, Merry told the coachman that she had chanced to meet one of her particular friends inside who would escort her on the remainder of her errands and see her home afterward. The one virtue (in

Merry's mind at least) of the shop had been its very dirty front
window, as a result of which Mr. Bibbins, the coachman, could not
see within; he proved that British and American family retainers
weren't so different by asking respectfully who he might tell His
Grace was escorting her, should he happen to inquire. Pushed into a
corner, Merry named Lord Cathcart and had the felicity of watching
Mr. Bibbins's look of mild concern relax into approval. She could
only hope Mr. Bibbins wouldn't by accident encounter that much
respected peer on his way back out of the city.

Having rid herself of her kindly escort, Merry set off to meet
Raven. Her spirits were low enough to give the bustling, impersonal
cacophony of street noise a certain poignance. The high, white sun
was dissolving at the edges into a gray-blue heaven flecked with
huge clouds moving quickly in the wind. The air had more than a
nip in it and was filled with city scents and the clatter of traffic.
Shoppers jostled one another on the pavement of broad stones;
apprentices with ink on their trousers wended through a maze of
spruce clerks and assistants. The smoke-blackened dome of St.
Paul's loomed like a mountain over the three- and four-story edifices
below, and she gazed at it as she walked before dropping her eyes to
the scenes around her, capturing passing images in vignettes: bright-
cheeked schoolboys with their satchels, gazing at pastry in a baker's
window; a crossing sweep whistling a lively air as he took a broom
to the street, where wheels had worn it down; and before a
bookseller's, with windows displaying many volumes laid open for
inspection, a small dog hooked by his lead to a hitching post was
worrying a black felt hat, blown, no doubt, from the head of some
passerby.

The changing complexion of the surrounding facades told her that
she had entered the city's high financial district, and by the time
Merry reached St. Mary Abchurch, a pleasantly venerable red brick
edifice in a yard of patterned cobbles, she began to understand why
Raven had made this his choice. This was an area given over to
commerce, the staunch bastion of the middle class, and none of the
haughty nobility who had made her acquaintance at the dowager's
ball was likely to meet her here. At the same time this was no slum,
and though Merry had encountered her share of stares, it was an area
where an unattended lady could walk without molestation.

The church interior was dim and intimate. Toneless light sprinkled from oval windows in the somberly frescoed domed ceiling, glooming on the dark wood surfaces, leaving the corners in shadow. Only two persons inhabited the room: a gray-haired lady in a black bonnet hesitantly trying to coax a hymn of the forty-seventh Psalm out of the organ; and a woman swaddled in shawls who was grimly applying beeswax to the Communion table.

Merry was taking a seat in a paneled pew near the door when Raven entered, and the shawled woman took one look at his charmingly formed but obviously disreputable countenance and dropped her tin of beeswax. Raven, stopped mid-stride under the heat of her gaze, made some exclamation under his breath that was better left unheard in a church, walked lithely backward to the alms box, and then, in an expression of startling piety, deposited a guinea within. The woman seemed to content herself with being partially mollified; she returned to her waxing, though tightening the voluminous shawls virtuously around her plump bosom and casting periodic suspicious glares at Raven.

Sliding into the seat beside Merry, Raven said, "You're late, m'darling. I've been watching for you this quarter hour in the chophouse down the block." He tucked a shining jet-black curl back into his bandanna and cast a quick, dispassionate glance toward the Communion table. "Devilish place, ain't it? It's more than a body can imagine, why people think they're doing God such a service by building him a parcel of dismal houses. I shouldn't wonder if He makes the architects sit on hard wood benches for all eternity."

Merry returned him a smile, though a wan one, and he pinched her chin and said kindly, "There you go! That's better. Where've you left your carriage? Let me escort you there, and you can go home and be comfortable."

"If you think I can be comfortable until I've heard everything you discovered last night, you're mistaken!" she retorted in a whisper. "Besides, I don't have my carriage. I was set down some distance from here and sent the coachman home, so don't think I'm to be fobbed off so readily."

"You *walked*?" The words were uttered in the same tone he might have used if she'd announced that she'd ridden into the sacristy on a goat. He gazed from her pelisse of crimson velvet

bordered in sable to the matching close hat with its wealth of short
nodding plumes, to her soft kid gloves, her copious sable muff and
her velvet half boots in the same shade as the pelisse. With something near to a groan he said, "Merry, you *innocent*."

"Innocent!"

"Aye. And there's no use to be looking daggers at me, lass.
There's a lot worse things a body can be than innocent. The fact is,
females of your station don't go about on their own in London
unless they've a desire to be taken for the game pullet of some
highborn rakehell. You might at least have brought your maid."

There were some, probably, who would object to lectures on
propriety from a member of a notorious pirate crew, but Merry
merely said, "I'd like to know what I'd do with a maid on a chase
after Michael Granville?"

"Nothing. Because there ain't going to be any chase after Michael
Granville. Leastwise, not for you, lovey."

"You haven't told anyone about last night!" Quiet as it was, her
voice betrayed her alarm.

"No. I wouldn't squeak beef without letting you know first, but
y'know, sweetheart, I'm giving you notice now that I'm going to
Devon with the whole of it. For one thing, I put some enquires to
Morgan last night about Granville, and the fellow's a damned ugly
customer. Granville makes it his business to own a fleet of merchant
ships that he sets to sail heavily insured; then he turns over their
course to pirate raiders who steal the cargo, and Granville collects
twice, from the insurance and from the contraband. Some of the
fleet captains are in Granville's pay and play willingly, but when
they have an honest crew, if there's a chance they're suspicious,
Granville has the lot of them put to death. Sails says Devon's little
sister was killed in a munitions blast whilst she was traveling aboard
a frigate that tried to fight back, poor lass, so don't you see, Merry,
Granville's just the sort of cur that *would* make an end to you if he
had the least reason. And besides that, since I traced that jackal to
his lair last night, I've been followed myself, though I don't know
who the devil by. Some curst rum touch, by the looks of him and—
Oh, *damn*."

Following the direction of his eyes with some surprise, Merry saw
that the shawled woman was making her way down the aisle,

swiping her dustrag at the pews and giving Raven a baleful stare. Promptly Raven shed his intensity and beheld Merry with limpid eyes.

"You have the right of it, ma'am. *Abchurch* is a corrupt of the word *upchurch,* being that this church is set upon high ground, you know," he said, with the air of one well advanced in a gently instructive discourse. "As for your notion that the steeple is of a decidedly inferior quality, I can only say that, for myself, I find it very pretty. And I can't think what makes you doubt the authenticity of the altarpiece. For my part, I don't think Grinling Gibbons has ever done a finer work."

In an immediate change of front, the beshawled woman gave Raven a glance of warm approval and, frowning at Merry, shuffled off muttering under her breath about impertinent hussies who were no better than they should be.

Her lips quivering with nervous laughter, Merry turned back toward Raven and gasped, "Oh, you—you *devil*. How dare you make that horrid woman think I don't like her church! I never heard anything like it."

He grinned. "It was a little in Morgan's manner, wasn't it? I do it a bit from time to time to amuse Will, though I suppose I'll have the captain's boot in my seat if he catches me at it. As for the nonsense I talked about the church, it comes out of a pocket guide, which was the worst two shillings I ever spent in my life, because all it does is to describe a lot of places that no one in his right mind would want to see, like museums and government offices and lunatic asylums."

Perceiving that the woman was making her way up the opposite aisle, he broke off to say, in the voice of an earnest student of architecture, "You've noted, perhaps, that the cupola is supported by groined pendentives?" but rather spoiled this impressive utterance as soon as the shawls had passed out of earshot by adding, "Whatever the devil that means. Not that it's here nor there. Come on, then, I'm taking you home."

"In a pig's ear!" she returned inelegantly. "Either you tell me where you found Michael Granville, or I've a coach to catch at five o'clock on Finsbury Square."

"Now, see here—"

"I won't see here! All Devon needs to hear is that Granville made a threat to me to drive him to do—some desperate thing. He's not himself on the subject of Michael Granville. For all I know, if Devon discovered Granville had made threats on my life, Devon would gun him down like a dog. I won't let that happen, Raven. Do you think I'll stand by and see my husband hanged for killing a man like Granville? And I don't mean to let my brother die!''

''Damnation!'' he said in a low tone. ''Do you have to be so hot in the spur?''

''When it comes to protecting the people I love,'' she said fiercely, ''*yes*.''

The determined set of her small chin was beginning to give Raven a sinking feeling. ''What you've got no business doing, lovey, is protecting two grown men.'' Then, on a sudden note of inspiration: ''I'll tell you what. What d'you say we take things to Morgan? You can depend on him for a cool-headed judgment.''

''When pear trees bear peaches, I'll go to Morgan!'' she said bitterly. ''If he found my brother, Morgan would probably turn him over to the Army and, if they hanged him, say that it was character-building. And don't suggest we tell Will or Cat either. Telling them would be the same as telling Morgan because that's just what they'd do.''

From that position she was not to be moved. Tears trembled on her eyelids; she was plainly terrified, but she was no less stubborn for all that. When Raven threatened to carry her by force to Morgan, all she would do was give an angry laugh and invite him to try it. And while he was admitting to himself that the citizens of this civilized metropolis were hardly likely to allow him to waltz through the streets bearing off a struggling woman of her obvious beauty and youth, Merry told him, in a voice no less firm for its being overset by tears, that if he didn't take her to the place he had followed Granville to, she would approach a constable and tell him Raven had tried to steal her purse, thus keeping him in gaol until she arrived for her five o'clock appointment at Finsbury Square. The queer thing about it was, Raven could see she meant it. Which was why half an hour later he found himself in a hackney carriage with Merry on the way to the dockside address where he had seen Granville disappear.

Raven was furiously angry with her—an emotion rare for him—and scared half-witless that some harm would come to her, and it seemed that with all that emotion on his side he ought to have won the battle of wills. After he'd given the driver the correct address, he realized what he should have done was deliver her to a disreputable inn (how would she have known Granville wasn't there?), locked her in a room, and gone to fetch Morgan. He knew Morgan, or even Cat, would have said that even now it was his duty to knock her unconscious and carry her to one of them. But looking down at the proud blue eyes and harmless little nose, he couldn't find in himself the resolution to harm her. Once, when she turned her head to catch her first glimpse of the Thames, he did raise his hand, but it faltered. In his mind he felt the impact of the blow and heard her soft cry of pain and saw her body crumble; and he knew no fist of his could cause that to happen. Raven lowered his hand and with a heavy sigh began to load his pistol.

Merry's face and figure would have made her conspicuous even if she hadn't been dressed at the height of modishness. When an attempt to talk her into stopping at the inn where he was lodged to change into men's clothing failed, he had to direct the hack to a corner he considered to be dangerously close to their destination to avoid too long a tramp with her along the waterfront.

The door where he had seen Granville disappear and then, much later, reappear was located in a courtyard of muddy pink brick inside a quadrant of tall warehouses with granite portals. Yawning black entrances emitted the scent of molasses in quantity enough to grab Merry's throat as she slid stealthily behind a row of cerecloth bales beside Raven. A handful of burly watermen were rattling barrels aboard a tilted carrier's dray under the shouted direction of a warehouseman in a bent top hat.

She didn't need Raven's whispered admonition, "Have a care! They might be in Granville's hire," to make her dive obediently to his side and sit quietly trembling. Spilled sugar carpeted the yard so thickly in places that she saw men sink to the ankle in it, and the wind pranced off the river in damp gusts to throw the dirty grit in glittering patterns against the buildings. Beyond, the Thames was green, smelly, and busily absorbing greasy reflections. A mass of sails in different sizes made the river as crowded as the streets.

She felt Raven's tension beside her and was sorry for it, though there wasn't anything she could do about it. Her entreaties in the

hackney carriage that he leave her (with the pistol) to take care of
matters on her own had made up in nobility what they lacked in
sincerity, and she was ashamed of the ignoble relief she had
experienced at his shocked refusal. The remainder of the trip he had
spent alternately glancing out the window trying without success to
decide whether they were being followed and endeavoring with
austere gentleness to convince her that the only existence her brother
had in England was in Granville's evil mind, and if Granville in fact
did have her brother, and if he did know anything to Granville's
detriment, the lad would be long dead. It never occurred to her to
guess that Raven was doing his best to talk himself into hitting her
over the head, but if anyone had told her this, she wouldn't have
been surprised. She could see he was mad as fire. All she could say
in her own defense was that she had a feeling, as real and keen as
any truth, that her brother was alive and hidden nearby, and she was
the best person to preserve his life, and not any of the men who
cared much for her and nothing for him.

Or perhaps she was losing her mind. She was almost convinced of
it in another moment. The men loading the dray had begun a
good-naturedly bantering exchange of insulting jests about each
other's mothers. As she stole a glance around the must-scented edge
of her bale her eyes for some reason swept toward a far group of
barrels, and while she watched, Henry Cork rose to the shoulders
from one with a barrel lid on his head.

Merry sat back with her eyes tight shut, taking deep breaths.

"My mind's snapping," she breathed.

"Tell me something I don't know," Raven grated under the
covering thunder of barrels. "Keep your head down, or we're dead,
lovey. If those rascals catch an eye of those feathers of yours, it's all
the world to a handsaw that they'll know they've got either a female
back here or an ostrich. And let me tell you, it's more than probable
they'll want to explore out which."

Pushing down her offending plumes, Merry peered again at the
far barrels, saw nothing, blinked, and when a time passed with no
further appearance, decided that the shadow of a soaring gull must
have combined with some errant fancy of her imagination to serve her
eyes such a trick.

It took a further half hour for the yard to clear. The heavily loaded dray rattled off into an alley; the warehouseman and his helpers disappeared into a near door speaking eagerly about sharing a flagon or two of porter.

Another opportunity might not come soon, and another wagon might arrive at any moment to gather cargo or discharge it, so there was nothing for Merry and Raven to do but dart across the yard, dodging heaps of discarded packaging fabric, frayed twine, and broken cooper's hoops. The immense oak double door was locked, but it would have taken a gem of the locksmith's art to resist the insistent mangling of Raven's dagger. He dragged open one dark, dust-grouted panel of the door, glanced inside, thrust Merry within, and followed quickly. She had time for only a glimpse of a wide room lined in pitted stone, and a plunging staircase beyond before Raven drew shut the doorway. The closed portal blocked out daylight with eerie efficiency. A bitter chill pervaded the atmosphere, its bite sharper than even the unheated stone and the autumnal briskness outside. She shivered, digging her hands deeper into her muff as she listened to Raven locate by touch the lantern and tinder on a small bench against the nether wall that he had marked on his first glance inside.

"Why is it so cold?" she whispered.

"I don't know. It would seem to be coming from down the stairs." His voice was muffled as he bent over the tinder. He added hopefully, "If you're beginning to take fright, we can leave. No telling what's down there, I'm sorry to say. Ghoulies, belike, and werefolk and devilkins that chew the flesh of ladies. I shouldn't wonder if we'll run in upon all manner of spookish things. We'd better give it up."

"That's not going to work!" she retorted with dignity, though her knees were no longer offering her firm support. The frigid air was crawling over her skin like the expelled breath of a winter cloud; her eyelashes were soft cold threads against her cheeks. As a thimble of flame grew inside the tin lantern her spirit for this adventure plummeted like the dipping shadows around her. But she said, "If you're frightened, then I'll go to the front."

Pale light fell on Raven's suddenly laughing eyes. "Are you all in a rush, then, to be et? Well, all right, paladin. To the stair! But side

by side, if you please, and catch hold of my hand. *You* may be a
lion, but I'm every bit aquiver.''

The steps led down a short tunnel that opened dramatically into a
monstrous abysm. Raven's tiny light left most of its great size
undiscovered, but the giant stone walls dwarfed Merry and Raven.
Immense sheer cliffs burgeoned from the floor. Their lamplight
caught in thousands of glittering facets in these colossal structures of
ice, giving them a fantastical grandeur. The motionless air was dry
and arctic.

''An icehouse! Isn't that what it is, Raven? A vault where they
store commercial ice?''

''It looks like,'' Raven said, tilting the lantern in a way that sent
light spraying deeper into the pit. ''I'd heard these places were
big, but I didn't realize the half of it. Cold enough to freeze two dry
rags together, ain't it? One thing's sure—Michael Granville couldn't've
been making this his safe house from Devon, or the chill would
have—Stay! Did you hear that? It sounded as if a man cried out.
Merry! Lovey, no!''

But fear had clamped without mercy on her senses, and she had
grabbed up her skirts in a rude arrangement, her running footsteps
pattering on the shallow steps. Her blood was as cold as the air
without. She arrived fighting for breath at the stair foot, with Raven
just behind. He tried to catch her arm, but his care to keep the
lantern intact hampered him, and she wrenched free, running forward around the thick retaining wall, the sand floor sucking at her
boots.

Behind the wall a solitary figure lay in a frost-riven clearing. The
stretching oval of light fell on red-gold hair, a dusty and torn buff
coat. Sinking to her knees beside the shining head, Merry turned the
still figure with hands that quavered. The face was young and
marred by premature lining and a ragged growth of beard. Damp
sand clung in a paste over the closed lids and parched, gasping lips.
She could feel the man's blazing fever through her gloves. Behind
her shoulder she heard Raven speak.

''Is it your brother?''

''Yes,'' she answered numbly. ''It's Carl.'' Tears came to her
eyes in a sudden rush. ''Help me. Raven, I can't think.''

His hand rested briefly on her arm and gave it a gentle squeeze.

"Steady, then, Merry. He's alive, and that's the prime thing." He had set the lantern into the sand and was beginning to strip off his greatcoat. "The thing to do is to see what kind of hurt he's taken and then get him out of here."

The words, sympathetic and practical, stayed with her as she helped Raven carefully move and lift her brother, looking for wounds and shattered bones. They released the rope around his knees and wrists and discovered the bruise on his temple that accounted for the hazed state of his brain. It was hard to tell how long he'd been thus, but cold had descended to his lungs. His breath had a rattling sound.

Yanking the satin loop of the muff impatiently off her wrist, she laid it under his head as Raven wrapped him in his own greatcoat, and she was gently brushing the sand from his face with her bare fingers when she saw Carl's eyelids move. He moaned.

"Carl? It's Merry. Can you see? Here I am," she said softly.

"Mer—ry?" The word was no more than a rasp.

"Yes, dear. I'm here."

"Where? Yes, icehouse . . . few weeks, he's kept me upstairs. Upstairs . . . there's a small room . . . contraband. Merry—" The disjointed murmur dissolved in a harsh fit of coughing. She held him until it subsided. "Came for you when we heard the *Guinevere* had docked in England without you. . . . Father sick with worry . . . affection . . . never showed it enough, e-either of us."

Again and again she had to lift her hands from his face to strike the running tears from her cheeks with the back of her wrist. "Carl, you shouldn't try to talk. You'll need your strength. This is my friend Raven, and he's going to help me take you away from this terrible place—"

As though she hadn't spoken, he murmured, "Were afraid Granville might have harmed you. Dishonorable . . . Father says. Granville told me you've married St. Cyr. H-he's good man. Opposed Orders in Council." With the shadow of a grin, "Too bad . . . British." The amusement faded into confusion. Then, "Have to leave . . . quickly."

"So we will, matey," Raven said in a low, soothing voice. "You can nod right off again, old fellow, and leave the matter to us." The assurance in the persuasive drawl, combined perhaps with Carl's exhaustion, made the eyes that were so like Merry's drift slowly shut. For Merry's ears alone Raven said in hushed tones, "Can you take the lantern? I'll have to carry him. There's not a chance he'll be able to walk in this con—" A noise from the staircase brought him urgently to his feet, dragging his pistol from his belt. With Merry a rigid gold statue at his feet, he leveled his pistol at the edge of the retaining wall and snarled, "Come forward. But throw your weapon out first or be prepared to be fired on."

A pleasant voice emanated from the stair, its tone chiding. "If this is an example of the kind of hospitality you offer, don't be surprised if I make this my last visit." Devon stepped from the shadows, his cool gaze assessing the clearing and then moving beyond to the mammoth structures of ice. To Raven, "Uncock your pistol. You really don't want to fire it here. Look at the slant of the central stack where the tiers lean into the drain path. Moisture must be seeping up from the floor, melting the base along one edge. I don't know how stable it is, especially if there's a fault in the mass."

Obeying the polite command, Raven started joyously forward, relief brightening his eyes, but another voice, behind him, behind them all, brought his stride to a halt.

"Desolated as I am to contradict you, my dear, the pleasure of the host is mine. And let me assure you, I don't share your qualms about firing in these circumstances. In fact, I see a charming set of nodding plumes that make a delightful target."

Frozen in a protective posture over her brother, Merry found her voice enough to breathe the word "*Granville*." Holding a pistol, he stood twenty feet above them on a heavy shelf of ice that led backward into a black void. The ice around him took the lamplight in an arc of carnelian glimmers; wolfish shadows danced with subtle violence across his mien. A Corinthian's unfitted driving coat with many capes gave him the illusion of being overpoweringly tall.

Merry heard Raven's pistol thud into the sand. A slight twist of her head showed her that Raven was looking apologetically at Devon.

"I ought to have hit her over the head," he said regretfully. "Sorry."

Devon had lounged back against the retaining wall. "Take my word on it, it wouldn't have served. No good ever came from hitting her on the head. Myself, I've eschewed the practice. Merry pet, is the gentleman at your knee someone we ought to be interested in?''

"It's my brother, Carl." She turned fully to him, finding something infinitely sustaining in the pensive golden gaze. Whatever fears she had nourished that his hatred for Granville would lead him to act rashly were quieted. Whatever his thoughts, his surface was relaxed to the tips of his fingers. Anxiously she said, "You'll say, I suppose, that I should have trusted you."

The warmth of his smile brought flutters to her heart. He said, "No, I won't scold, sweetheart. But maybe you could explain what we're all doing here?"

"Enjoying a respite from the heat," Granville murmured. "The handsome youth on the floor fell into my hands some little time ago. As for the other two, at last night's ball I came to your oh-so-charming bride—"

"Spouting melodrama," Merry finished for him with a mocking glare worthy of Rand Morgan himself. And she held that glare without a flinch, even while Granville brought his hand higher and made his aim on her heart exact. She felt no trace of fear for herself; Granville would have had to be a madman to squeeze that trigger and destroy his insurance.

Raven, who was watching, however, felt as if the frigid air had penetrated to his bones. He was glad Merry couldn't see Devon's face. If she had, it would certainly have shattered her faith in Devon's objective calm.

Granville's heavy shoulders seemed to relax. "A solid departure from what she was in New York. Rand Morgan, I suppose, deserves the honors. One wishes he'd alter his curriculum with females. Do you know, when I left her last night in the garden, there was never any question in my mind that I'd be followed. All that remained to be seen was just which of Morgan's pretty-boy pirates she sent after me. My only task was to move neither so quickly nor so slowly that anyone would suspect I knew. In the general run of things, of course, I come and go through a more private entrance. Mind you, I hadn't planned on having the honor of your companionship also, St. Cyr. It changes my ideas, I think."

"If your new idea includes killing us all"—Devon's tone was unrevealing—"it has a hitch that I should probably explain. I followed Merry into London when I heard she'd left, and met her carriage on its way home. The coachman said she was with Cathcart. She was not. The next step was obviously to question Cat, who was visiting Morgan, but on the way to the inn we chanced into one of Morgan's men coming for Morgan at a gallop. Last night after Raven—as you say, one of Rand's boy pirates—began asking some pointed questions about you, Morgan felt it would be safer to have him watched also." A groan from Raven. "The point, *my dear,* is that I came ahead while Cathcart and Rand's hireling have gone to fetch Morgan to this spot. If you think Morgan will let you live after you kill me, I'd strongly advise you to do it."

Granville had absorbed a hiss of air. His exhalation made a swirling mist of breath vapor play over the flesh of his mouth and nose. "Run back to Morgan, then. You chose him years ago, when you might have had me. My feelings for you—"

"Have always been anathema to me, even before your men killed Leonie. Don't force these children to listen to you profess them." Devon's tone was no longer mild. "Stay awake and you'll see how far I'd go to protect them."

"Oh, no, let's have no heroics," Granville said. He was beginning to respire quickly. "Leave me and take the boy with you. I'll keep the girl and her brother. Collateral, shall we say? And if you make me a settlement I like the looks of, I may let you have them back intact. You know I mean my words. Get out."

In a stream of motion that began as a blur, Merry saw Devon's hand fly for his pocket as though to extract a weapon. The barrel of Granville's pistol took a rapid mark and roared, the report shatteringly loud. Blue flame and a wisp of spent smoke trembled in the raw air as a staccato of ear-splitting cracks rent the enormous vault from floor to ceiling. The icy plain under Granville seemed to bubble, and he fell and began to slide as the packing of straw and sawdust began to shower from the ledge. A shifting chasm yawned under him, swallowing him. Harsh fingers grabbed Merry, and she was half running, half being dragged across the sand. At the wall she hesitated, crying out, until she saw that Raven had her brother on his shoulder, and then they were scrambling up the stairs, Devon yanking her with him much faster than she would have ever believed it was possible to move. Like the crash of a hundred thunderclaps the shattering avalanche of hurtling ice wrenched the great warehouse with earthquakelike shocks. Only an arm's length behind them the retaining wall bulged as though it were only matting and then burst, ton on ton of ice exploding over its collapsing fabric. Rocketing chips and icy zephyrs foamed at their heels, and the stair swayed like a half liquid. They were met and pulled up the last quarter of the way by Morgan's men. It wasn't until Merry was standing outside in the startling daylight of the dockyard that she realized Granville's final bullet had struck home. With blood saturating his immaculate shirtfront Devon gave her a smile of friendly whimsy and said, "You bring the fresh strawberries, love, and I'll get the sugar. We'll make ice cream to last till Easter." He seemed surprised when Morgan gently took his shoulders and said, "Easy, lad" because he really had no idea how unsteady he looked. He might have spoken again, in protest perhaps, but instead he closed his lips and fainted into his half brother's arms.

CHAPTER THIRTY-ONE

The rain came at dusk in lively drops that gave a mossy scent to the ivy outside the inn window. Inside, sea coal glowed in the grate. A moist warmth crept through the light chintz hangings to the bed where Devon was sleeping and where Merry sat barefoot and crosslegged waiting for him to wake up.

It would have been reasonable to suppose that any young man as popular as Devon was with Morgan's crew would receive a great deal of sympathy for a bullet wound instead of having it treated as a very good joke. One would further have thought that his gently

reared and loving spouse would take exception to such heartless
revelry. Instead Merry was reassured because it told her more powerfully than condolences would have done that Devon's condition
wasn't serious, though she was far from agreeing that a wound
requiring the extraction of a bullet from one's shoulder deserved to
be pretty generally referred to as "just a scratch, by all that's holy."
It seemed like half of Morgan's crew had managed to stuff itself into
the cozy bedroom as Devon was put to bed, brought by the jocular
intelligence that Devon had put himself in front of someone's pistol,
and then damned if he hadn't fainted like a girl. Merry's indignant
protest that having suffered such a series of mental and physical
shocks was enough to make *anyone* faint drew fresh guffaws.

Devon had been conscious during Cat's minor surgery and fully
able to bandy words with his grinning audience. Eric Shay had
drawn roars of merriment by demonstrating Devon's faint in a
manner of greatly exaggerated daintiness. Joe Griffith spoke with
unctuous sympathy about procuring supporting broths and burnt
feathers to wave under Devon's nose in case he popped off again.
And Will Saunders composed a wickedly clever and bawdy verse to
this new delicacy of Devon's constitution (attributable, he contended,
to Devon's newly married state).

Finally Cat had ejected everyone but Merry from the room, saying
dryly that he'd be damned if he'd let Devon chortle himself into a
fever. Then he had fed Devon a mildly sedative draught and bore
Merry off to a private parlor for some refreshment, and after he had
eaten with her and escorted her back to Devon, who had fallen
asleep, Cat had left to look in on her brother.

With the adroitness for which he was famous, Rand Morgan had
acquired a covered cart to take Carl to the *Black Joke*, where he
could be cared for in secrecy and later returned to the United States.
To avoid suspicion on the part of the watchful (but fortunately
frequently persuadable) port authorities, Carl would be one of Morgan's
crew, who, having imbibed more blue ruin than he could hold, had
taken a chill after spending a night in the kennel.

Earlier, watching the cart with her brother rumble through the
excited confusion of the warehouse yard, Merry had turned to the
sound of Rand Morgan's voice. He said, "Sails and Tom Valentine
will take care of him, and you can visit him in the morning. Once

they've warmed him up, he'll throw off the chill fast enough." His hand touched and released one of her curls. "You know, nestling, you might have come to me. I wouldn't have let Devon do anything foolish. And I wouldn't do less for your brother than I would for you."

The too casual admission of Morgan's strange involvement in her life made her gaze up frankly into the snapping black eyes. "That's what had me worried."

He answered her with an enigmatic smile.

Merry stretched out her feet in front of her and spread and studied her toes, and then her husband. He was beautiful in the slight dishevelment of sleep, with a soft flush pinking the skin below his lashes; but it was not his striking male beauty so much as his undefended posture that moved her. Scene by scene she reviewed their relationship, and scene by scene forgave him or herself for every act of temper or quick judgment, and when she had done with those, her memory began to drift to warmer moments between them. After about ten minutes of this her cheeks were as warm as her thoughts, and she began to wish earnestly that he would wake up, although her conscience warned her against doing anything to achieve that end. For heaven's sake, the man had just had a bullet dug out of him.

There is a school of thought that holds that if one stares with enough intensity at a sleeper, the sleeper will waken, but after practicing this patiently for what seemed like forever Merry decided there wasn't a word of truth in it. Beginning at his ankle, she walked her fingers gently up his leg, hopping over the kneecap, trodding a little heavily on his thigh and his ribs, and collapsing her fingers on his good shoulder. Nothing. She leaned from the waist to exhale lightly on his hand. She might as well have saved her breath.

"All right, then," she whispered, lifting his hand to her lips. Peeling back his shirt cuff, she worked little nipping kisses down his thumb and then slow ones over his inner wrist. He didn't move. Cat must have given him a stronger dose of laudanum than she had at first suspected. Sighing, she held his relaxed fingers to her cheek and then let them slip to her lap, where they created an interesting sensation against her thigh.

"How can I wake you up, you ridiculous man?" she asked softly and almost jumped out of her silk gauze day dress when he answered,

"Not by playing with my unconscious body. That's more likely to make me pretend sleep indefinitely."

She began to laugh. "How dare you, sir!"

He gazed back at her from under sweetly drowsy lids. "I'm wicked past redemption, I suppose."

"Not *past* redemption, I think." Delighted to have him wake at last, she rested her chin on her fists and held him in a calm study. "I've put my mind to considering things, and I've decided that you're not much of a rake after all. All those months of opportunity and not a thing came of it until we had benefit of clergy."

His smile was slight. "The last thing I would have taken pleasure in forcing on you would be an act of love." He caught a strand of her hair and began to wind it around his forefinger. "Poor Windflower, have you been sitting here watching me snore?"

"I have, but you don't snore. Everyone else has gone off to some horrible place—the One-eyed Dog. I suppose it's a brothel."

He grinned. "No. A gaming hell."

"Oh! Are you a frequenter, then?" Her cheek was close to his wrist, and she rubbed herself against him there. "Can you hear how quiet it is? Raven said that was because when the crew of the *Joke* signed into the inn, the other patrons signed out. If you feel well enough to talk for a bit, I have something very exciting I'd like to tell you about."

He was caressing the wound curl with his thumb. "Every minute I see you, I feel better. Tell me about your something exciting."

"Well, with everything that happened today, I completely forgot to send a message to Teasel Hill, and so Aunt April arrived here with your mother! What do you think of that!" She had to laugh at his grimace. "You don't have to worry about your mother, because Lord Cathcart was outside and was able to reassure her about our safety, so she wouldn't have to come in and run a gauntlet of pirates, but Aunt April *forced* her way inside. Game as a pebble, Saunders said, and came straight into the parlor where I was dining with Raven—and half the crew almost. She swept me up in an embrace and said, 'My dear, you can't know! Aline and I have been in the greatest affliction. To leave without a word—and His Grace having ridden off after you, hell for leather, as the stableboy would say, though of course he shouldn't have, at least not in front of us.

Every feeling of trepidation from those terrible months returned! We went first to Lord Cathcart's, which I only hope may not have damaged Aline's reputation, because for myself I don't care, but we were in an open carriage, so Aline says perhaps it will be all right.' '' She paused to resettle her knees. "Raven was so funny about it afterward, because he misunderstood her completely, and he said it seemed like a devilish lot of trouble to go to to complain about a little cursing from a stable lad. You'll never guess what happened then!"

"Your aunt glanced around at the company and fell into a swoon?" he suggested innocently.

"A swoon! As though Aunt April would do anything so paltry! Oh! Oh, I beg your pardon. I didn't mean—'' Laughter over-whelmed her, and she could see the smile lurking in his bright eyes as he pulled her close with his good arm and played her laughter against his mouth, swallowing the thrills of sound, feeling the vibrations in her chest and lips. His kiss became more thorough, the trace of his tongue inside her mouth much deeper. But then the hand that had brought her to his kiss gently released her.

"Before I stop thinking about it," he said, "you'd better tell me what happened to your aunt."

Merry had been inclined to linger over the kiss, but she sat up anyway and was able with some enthusiasm to say, "Henry Cork! And he turned out to be Raven's 'curst rum touch'. Morgan had him follow us, you see, because Raven wouldn't have known who Henry was, because he's only just got to London, though he's been in Ireland visiting his sister and her husband. He was traveling with false papers, which shows that the world is in a sad state with more dishonest officials than anyone would suspect, though Morgan may call them 'flexible.' ''

"He would. Does your aunt still hold Cork to blame for the ants in your luggage?"

"You know, I have no idea because when he arrived at the doorway beside Morgan and looking so nice—almost natty, in fact, in a mulberry coat and stone-colored trousers—all she could do was stare at him. And then when he came striding across the room to pull her into his arms and kiss her, my only thought was, *Poor Aunt April—it must be like a nightmare for her to find Henry Cork suddenly in England hugging her in front of a room filled with pirates.* I would have gone to her and tried to push him off, let me tell you, but Morgan put his hands on my shoulders and pushed me into a chair—don't frown; he did it very gently, I promise—and it turned out Morgan was right, because Aunt April didn't seem to mind the kiss at all, although she looked rather bemused. And then Henry Cork made her the prettiest speech about how he hadn't had her off his mind a day since they parted in New York, and though he knew he wasn't her quality and never would be, Morgan had settled a nice size of property on him, as he'd promised for watching me all those years, and if Aunt April would consent, he'd like to court her, and didn't she know the reason he'd plagued her with all those tricks was to get a moment of her attention when he could. He led her out to the carriage so gentlemanly-like and kicked Max Reade in the shin because he hadn't doffed his hat. Cat says it might serve, because with a duchess for a niece and Henry Cork's money, she might not be shunned by the ton, or at least all but the highest sticklers, if we could think up some story to make his background sound more respectable. And you know, I think Aunt April wouldn't care so much if she was shunned just a little, because although in Virginia she pined for England and society, now that I see her here, she's just as content to putter in the garden and coze with her close friends as she is to go to ton parties. I think the"—she had to think about the best way to say it—"the pleasant quiet of our life in Fairfield changed her more than she knew. What are you thinking?"

"That I don't want our children to have Henry Cork for an uncle." But Devon was smiling.

The offhand mention of their children brought new color to her cheeks. "They may as well have him, since they'll have Rand Morgan also. Poor little things, we'll probably find them sailing the Jolly Roger from their cradle slats. But you had better go back to sleep. What am I doing, keeping you awake chattering? Go on. Close your eyes. *Close them.* There. And I can sing you a lullaby." But her singing voice was not as good as her drawing, and the song she chose was an American one which made reference not only to the villainy of England's ruling prince but to his girth as well.

Devon opened an eyelid and in a mild tone said, "If you will sing just a little louder, my heart, you'll insure our place in the history books, because by morning our heads will be adorning Traitor's Gate."

"Then never mind that. I'll rub liniment into your poor bruised body. *That* will relax you." She heard his indrawn breath as she laid a hand lightly on him.

Both his eyes were open now and shining. "You don't have any liniment . . . and I don't have any bruises."

"Quibbler!" Then, as though willing to concede a point, she said, "Well, perhaps not bruises." Her hands slid lower, and her voice was ingenuous and husky as she said, "Swellings."

A laugh, a breath, taken quickly. "My love, my own sweet love . . . my lily petal. I'm too damned weak."

"As though I care for that," she scoffed cheerfully. "I mean to ravish you. You'll find I don't share your scruples. It should be a good lesson to you."

As she carefully removed the pillow from under his head and laid him back, eddying her parted lips over his mouth, he said, in fervent agreement, "God, yes." Then when her hand began to coast down over his body: "I'm beginning to think you should have no mercy." He took another hard breath as her fingers wandered over the rise of his thigh. She could feel his flesh heat under her cheek and the crooked curve of his smile. "I don't know how it comes to be, but I'm feeling stronger by the minute."

She sighed, trailing the tip of her tongue over his lips. "Men are so easy."

Meeting her tongue, moving his lips against hers, he said, "*Flammable* is the word. Please, if you intend to assert your conjugal rights, carry on. Although—and I'm sorry about this—the way Cat's bound my arm, I don't think my shirt will come off."

But this morning she had tucked a small knife from her breakfast tray into her garter, and her shifting skirts twisted it against her stockings, reminding her of its presence. A gleam of humor lit her eyes. "What I have under my skirt may change your mind."

He watched appreciatively as she sat back on her heels and began to draw up her hem. "It may." His gaze widened lazily as he saw a small knife with a mother-of-pearl handle under the gold Brussels lace garter that circled her slim thigh.

"I come equipped with the necessities." Her breathless voice tried to sound informative.

There was an oddly disquieting smile in his eyes. "Every last one. And now?"

"You're such an unsuccessful ravisher, I'm going to show you how it ought to be done." A series of jabbing slashes opened his remaining buttons, laying his midriff bare.

Laughing, flinching as the inexpertly wielded blade skimmed his flesh, he said, "I suppose I'll have to make my way mother-naked back to Teasel Hill?"

"We pirates never trouble ourselves about whether our victims have a change of clothing. Revenge is *sweet*. How do you like this?"

"If I told you, love, it might ruin your revenge," he said huskily, lifting a knee to kick off the bedclothes. "Now what? Trouble?"

"Yes." She was sawing at the seam over his shoulder. "It's hard work being a swashbuckler. How do you ravishers always make this look so easy?"

He had brought up a hand to brush the back of his forefinger over her nipple, feeling a nerve-shiver run through him as it hardened against his skin. Sympathetically he said, "For one thing, we don't use dining utensils."

She had to gasp a little as his hand curved up and into her low-cut bodice, pressing under the warm thrust of her breast, caressing the nipple with his thumb. Feebly she murmured, "When one dines, one uses the proper utensils."

He slid her closer, freeing her breast from its aching confinement, and applied his lips and tongue to the tip. "Then I think I may come by my just deserts."

Her laughter was a sensual stroke on his brow. "I think, love, that your desserts have just begun."

When Cat returned much later to check on his patient, he found Devon asleep in a bed littered with the scattered tatters of his clothing and Merry's nose peeking out of the bedclothes, her eyes deliciously alight with amusement. And seeing the answering humor in his pale-blue gaze and questioningly upraised brow, she whispered, "Give me your hand," and slapped the knife into it. "There wasn't a bit of fight in the lad."

CHAPTER THIRTY-TWO

October brought the return migration of winter birds to England. Though they were often unseen, Merry could hear the shrill, undulating calls of geese as they passed overhead at night. Nutters rustled in the woods under turning leaves. The elms were a bright umber, and the Spanish chestnuts reared great golden boughs among glowing brown beeches and the russet flutter of oak leaves. Hedgerows sparkled with holly berries and the deep shimmer of luxuriant blackberries. Children sailed kites in the open fields.

Rand Morgan broke his overland journey to meet the *Black Joke*, again docked in Falmouth harbor, by spending a day with his grandmother at St. Cyr. In the late afternoon he returned to the Gentle Shepherd, bending his head to avoid the low hang of an alder branch as he came from a lane into the side yard of the coaching inn where the cider mill, the apple baskets, the vats, and the horsehair cloths were out and ready for an evening's apple cidering. He dismounted, tossed the reins to a groom, made his way upstairs to the comfortable parlor adjoining his bedchamber, and by the time he was joined by Sails, had settled into a chair, a handsomely proportioned leg in a dusty riding boot slung casually over one arm. He had a hookah at one elbow and a pitcher of beer at the other.

Lifting his glass to the sailmaker in a negligent salute, he quoted the sign exhibited in the alehouse below: " 'Drink here. The best beare.' Shall I give you a glass?"

"Aye," said the old man, smiling slightly, and took it from Morgan's hand, making himself comfortable in a woolen upholstered chair by the fire. While the captain was busy at St. Cyr, Sails had hired a gig to drive over for a look at Stonehenge, though little enough pleasure he'd been able to take in the place, because almost on arrival he'd fallen in with an elderly widower from Swindon who held sternly to the position that Avebury was by far the superior ancient monument, and went on at such length about the injustice of a fate that made Stonehenge better known, and spent such energy in detailing what he saw to be the many shortcomings of Stonehenge that Sails felt almost as though he'd been guilty of an act of ignominy by going there to begin with.

When Morgan asked Sails how he'd found Stonehenge, Sails answered rather forlornly that it wasn't the equal of Avebury. Considerably intrigued, because Sails had set out that morning in the best of spirits, Morgan soon had the story out of him, and before long Sails began to see the absurdity of the situation and was laughing and slapping his thigh over Morgan's pungent comments.

Plying his handkerchief against the moist amusement in his eyes, chuckling faintly, Sails allowed the pirate captain to refill his glass before he said, "How did ye find the duchess, your grandmama?"

Morgan inhaled a rose of blue smoke, stretching his arm along the chair back. "Brimming with sentiment. At luncheon she wept over having destroyed the letter Grandfather Morgan wrote to Jasper informing him of my upcoming birth. Do you know, she went so far as to say I would have been a— What was her word? *Magnificent*, I believe. I would have been a magnificent duke."

With a grin in his eyes Sails studied the huge shapely body, the broad shoulders, the strong molding of the jaw. "She had the right of it, I'm thinkin'." He took a slow swallow of beer and said thoughtfully, "It's something, how you never did resent young Devon. I remember the first letter ye had from yer grandmama about that laddie."

"Do you? Where was I? Algiers, I think."

"Aye, that you were, and in the very bed of a prime article of virtue and her sprinkling ye with rose petals. D'ye recall reading the letter aloud to me? A pathetic thing it was, all about how here was the young duke, fourteen years old and falling to ruin with a man's vices and all for want of a father. She feared he'd kill himself before he reached eighteen unless someone could take him in hand, and with what she'd heard of ye, ye were the only man to do it. Diamond cuts diamond, she said."

"Thus demonstrating a remarkable command of the language." A mocking smile curled the pirate's lip.

"And ye were so much better? It was daft, she was, or desperate, to persist until ye would finally take an interest and agree to kidnap him. 'Let's have look at my brother who's a lord,' ye said. 'And we'll teach him a whole new set of dissipations.' "

"So I did. It's amazing that she trusted me, isn't it? She would have done better to help Aline out of her depression over Jasper's death so she could be the mother Devon needed, instead of telling the poor girl at Jasper's funeral that he'd left a sideslip in the Caribbean who was a pirate."

Sails clucked and shook his head in a gently excusing way. " 'Twas the stress of the moment belike. Ah, well, it's all come right in the end, because here's Cat telling us that Aline means to have Cathcart." He set down his glass and gazed into the hearth. A note that was partly curious, partly apologetic came into his voice. "There's been a time or two, lad, when I wondered why ye never tried to make Merry fall in love with ye." He heard Morgan rise and the whisper of long muscles pulling against fabric as he stretched.

Then, "Do you imagine I'm pining over my little brother's wife?" Morgan's tone was quizzical.

"Well, now. Are ye?" Sails asked, continuing to stare placidly at the melting flames.

A pause. "They began to love as soon as they saw each other. How could I have interrupted that?" Morgan smiled carefully. "And what the devil would I have done with an eighteen-year-old girl?"

"Aye, there is that, of course," the old sailmaker admitted. "But it does seem hard that ye'll be losing all the little ones at one time. I know ye can't but feel that Cat belongs to his father, and I won't be arguing with ye, but it's my belief the boy will pine. And now he's to go to Oxford, by all that's holy.''

Raven's reaction to that announcement had become one of Morgan's more cherished recent memories. He could still hear the horror in the soft drawl when Raven said, ''*Oxford*! You mean Cat's to be forced to a university? Captain, I never thought to see the day you'd do a thing so coldhearted!''

Morgan came to lean against the table edge by the fire, his hands thrust relaxedly in his pockets, though his voice had the trace curtness of withheld emotion. ''It won't be easy for Cat. I don't know if he'll ever adjust completely to his position, but he has Merry and Devon as well as Cathcart. And if he doesn't learn to know his father now, he may never do it, and that would be a pity, because there's no other way for him to learn to understand the gentle side of his own nature. Have no fear. I won't let him languish.''

''I know ye too well to think that'' was the calm answer.

There was a companionable silence that had stretched for some few minutes before Morgan recalled the small oval locket his grandmother had given him, and he withdrew it from his pocket and flipped open the golden cover to study the miniature portrait within.

''And what might that be?'' Sails asked.

''Hmm? Have a look.'' Morgan handed him the locket.

The locket carried the likeness of a boy of about thirteen years, with dark silky curls, wary blue eyes, and a determined chin.

Morgan said, ''That unfortunate youth has recently inherited an earldom covering half of Worcester, and if the old duchess is to be believed, he's doing his best to leave it on the gaming tables. I take it he's some sort of a grandnephew to her. In any case, he was left in her guardianship and doesn't appear to have benefited much by it. He has a woman living with him that Letitia calls 'that French hussy.' '' Morgan leaned back against the table with his hair flowing in magnificent black waves from his temples, and a peculiar smile came to his wide lips. "It only seems—" she had said. "Well, what's the good in having a pirate ship if you can't send wild youngsters there for a year or two and turn them into something worth inviting to dinner?"

Sails was still looking at the portrait. "An orphan, is he?"

"He is," Morgan agreed.

"Shall we go have a look at him, then?"

Morgan shook his head, standing abruptly, a fathomless boredom settling into the depths of his heavy-lidded eyes. "Worcester is too far out of the way. I've got other things to do with my life than reordering other people's misreckoned adolescents."

The morning air had a snap to it, and the hills rolled with brilliant color when Morgan and Sails walked their horses through the village toward the post road. A grain mill stood on the village edge, its sails turning slowly, and within a pretty cottage garden nearby a tiny girl with a lamb stood behind a whitewashed picket fence. She stared at Morgan as he passed, in that bold, curious way children sometimes have. When he dismounted and came to her, she showed him solemnly she had new shoes, and when he asked her how old she was, she carefully displayed three dimpled fingers and told him the lamb's name was 'Tawberry. Smiling, he admired Strawberry, and her shoes, and the age of three and then touched her cheek with a gentle finger. Innocence—how does one preserve it? How does one give it back when it's lost? And then he thought of Devon and Merry, and how he had seen them in the garden at Teasel Hill, clinging to each other as though they were one person, laughing like children about some silliness only they understood.

The horses were fresh, and above the horizon Rand Morgan could see the slow rise of a bright sun. Worcester suddenly did not seem so far away.

The kiss of frost had turned the great lindens into clouds of rich sunny yellow. Translucent leaves fell in a sun-sprinkled mist over Devon and Merry beneath. He sat drawing on a sketch pad, one knee drawn up and his back against a tree. She sat on the high bronze back of the unicorn statue. Her hair was loosely flowing except for a single braided coronet plaited with violet mallow flowers. Her feet, softly shod in white slippers, swung slowly together against the unicorn's massive belly as she worked on a sketch of her own, and her white skirts waltzed and lifted in the breeze.

When she had completed her drawing, she smiled up at Devon and said gaily, "Are you finished? I am!"

"I finished a long time ago." He stood and came toward her, and as he did she turned her sketch pad to show him a cleverly detailed picture of himself riding the unicorn.

He stared at it with a laugh and a grimace and said, "Dear God, am I really that pretty?"

So she hit him playfully over the head with her sketchbook. "Let's see yours, then! You told me you'd inherited your skill with the pencil, and since you're the son of Jasper Crandall, who was one of the world's greatest painters of natural subjects—" She broke off with a light exclamation as he turned his drawing and she could see his work. After staring at it a moment she let out a peal of sparkling laughter because his pen had made her a stick figure with corkscrew curls, and the unicorn appeared very like a mastiff with a tusk. With laughing reproach she said, "I fear you've been sadly deceptive, sir."

"No, I haven't. I told you I inherited my skill at drawing, and I did—from my mother. And there you see the extent of it." He removed the sketchbook from her hand and set it beside hers on the grass and then came to stand before her, smiling in a way that made her heart fill up with love that was like nectar. With softened eyes they held each other's gaze until her hands came gently to rest on his shoulders, and she bent forward to find his lips. Their touch was light, the searching breath of morning upon spring's first blossom. Her hair draped over one shoulder and moved in a sweet-scented caress all over the side of his face and his hair and upper arm.

She lifted her head, just a little, to look into his eyes and saw the wealth of love and gentleness there, and he lifted his hands to her palms, entwining their fingers.

"Each day seems to make our love stronger," he said softly.

She answered, "How lovely our years will be. I give you my life and all the moments in it."

"And I give you mine, in peace, and if it comes, in hardship," he murmured. "I give you my soul."

And the leaves were gliding in floating, downward circles around them, to wink and glisten as she laid her cheek on his hair and made him the promise, "My love, I will have it with me always, and keep it safe."

Rebels and outcasts, they fled halfway across
the earth to settle the harsh Australian
wastelands. Decades later—ennobled by love
and strengthened by tragedy—they had
transformed a wilderness into fertile land. And
themselves into

WILLIAM STUART LONG

THE EXILES, #1	12374-7-12	$3.95
THE SETTLERS, #2	17929-7-45	$3.95
THE TRAITORS, #3	18131-3-21	$3.95
THE EXPLORERS, #4	12391-7-11	$3.50
THE ADVENTURERS, #5	10330-4-40	$3.95

Journey across 19th century Europe with lovers whose deepest passions are ignited, whose loftiest destinies are fulfilled.

The Heiress Series

Roberta Gellis

☐ THE ENGLISH HEIRESS, #1 $2.50
☐ THE CORNISH HEIRESS, #2 $3.50
☐ THE KENT HEIRESS, #3 $3.50